CONTENTS

PREVIOUSLY ON SOULBOUND 2   2

CHAPTER 1 – Peacock Without Feathers   5

CHAPTER 2 – Belief   17

CHAPTER 3 – Spreading The Faith   29

CHAPTER 4 – Maps   41

CHAPTER 5 – Guild Dungeons   52

CHAPTER 6 – Interrogation Gone Wrong   64

CHAPTER 7 – Building A Temple   77

CHAPTER 8 – Mokra Clan   88

CHAPTER 9 – Wendigo   100

CHAPTER 10 – Pestilence Lord   113

CHAPTER 11 – Scabs   124

CHAPTER 12 – New Powers   133

CHAPTER 13 – Testing The Waters   148

CHAPTER 14 – Arbiter Pelis   158

CHAPTER 15 – Split Decisions   170

CHAPTER 16 –Truth For A Truth   180

CHAPTER 17 – Arbiter VS Pestilence Lord   190

CHAPTER 18 – Smack My Bitch Up!   201

CHAPTER 19 – Family Problems   215

CHAPTER 20 – The Message   225

CHAPTER 21 – Dawn   236

CHAPTER 22 – Visitors   248

CHAPTER 23 – Angry Birds   260

CHAPTER 24 – Downtime   270

CHAPTER 25 – Ceremony I   280

CHAPTER 26 – Ceremony II   290

CHAPTER 27 – Monster of the Deep   299

CHAPTER 28 – Three Little Killers   310

CHAPTER 29 – Alarm Bell   319

CHAPTER 30 – Teleportation   328

CHAPTER 31 – Battle By The Bridge   338

CHAPTER 32 – Bitchslapper   347

EPILOGUE   356

SOULBOUND

BOOK 3

COPYRIGHT © 2023 BY

CASSIUS LANGE

PUBLISHER NOTE:

ISBN:

9798872498629

CASSIUS LANGE

PREVIOUSLY ON SOULBOUND 2

They breached our walls and entered the city, unleashing a storm of swords and magic upon Greystone. And yet there was a threat even greater than the Imperial Fist's endless legions besieging the city, the dark powers of Tan'Malas which spread their corrupted tendrils throughout the streets.

We did the best we could, fighting off both the Valtorian soldiers and the Dark God's animus forces which increased with every fallen soldier.

Slowly but surely the city would fall and there was little me and the Blood Moon Guild could do about it.

I was thrown into the midst of it all together with many other members of the Assassin's Guild. What should have been a simple scouting mission, turned to a massive battle in which I almost lost it all. The only good thing about it? I gained a loyal friend, Elvina, the granddaughter of the Shadow Sage. A great power struggle erupted as nobles and ordinary citizens died by the thousands.

My powers had grown significantly, but I wasn't the only one. Benny and his pet creature Legs evolved yet again into mighty War Beasts that were virtually indestructible. And despite all this, it seemed as though our new home, Brahma's Rest, wouldn't survive the chaos that ensued as Valtorians and animus littered the streets.

There was only one option, leave the city or face certain annihilation.

I managed to gather Grom's family for which the elgar was more than thankful. I got my trusty shopkeeper Mortimer and his family together with the entire dwarven Blackforge clan on my side.

I saved Selene from a vicious wound and she and Merek joined us as well. Our guild was steadily growing in strength and number as the city burned.

Before the Shadow Sage left for his very last mission, killing the king himself, he gave me a map fragment and in returned asked that I take care of his granddaughter Elvina for him. A promise was made and Elvina too joined us.

We managed to get our hands on a ship, barely escaping certain capture and death, got our people together with a full hull of supplies and took to the sea.

It wasn't easy to leave Greystone behind. As the ship entered the ocean I took one last look at the smoking city that made me who I am today. Would I ever see it again? I wondered as I activated the scroll the Shadow Sage left me with.

A teleportation sequence began transporting us into unknown waters. As the arcane powers subsided we found new land under a new sky.

A goblin met us after landfall, a curious creature who descended from the sky in a unique contraption we had never seen before, an airplane he called it.

He told us of his god, Tan'Malas. It was the only god these people prayed to. We didn't just teleport away from Greystone, no, it seemed that we teleported through time into a place that worshipped the very horrors we hoped to leave behind.

Determined to survive, we began establishing a colony on this strange new land. Tan'Malas or not, we wouldn't flee again.

CHAPTER 1 – PEACOCK WITHOUT FEATHERS

"So you are him? The newcomer that wouldn't show Duke Adan the courtesy and visit the castle?"

The man's hideous face was set into a sneer and his hunched back coupled with the colorful, flamboyant clothes that gave him the appearance of a court jester, didn't help much with lending him any authority.

I just sat there on my 'throne' as the girls called it. Grom had made it for me after we had several run-ins with the dukedom's troops. He figured I'd need to talk down on people from a seat of power. What better way to do that than to make a throne from God Beast bones?

The dukedom's soldiers were nothing to scoff at and were probably around the level of professional soldiers back in Greystone, but these guys weren't trained to fight people, especially not someone like us. No wars had been fought here for who knew how long. There were no arenas to hone their skills, while the woods and dungeons were the only enemies left. They were good at it, no doubt but killing monsters was one thing, fighting someone more skilled and dangerous was another beast entirely.

"Where's Banxi? I thought I made it clear that I won't entertain any peacocks like yourself."

"P—peacock? You dare—"

I cleared my throat and placed my right hand on the skull of the War Beast Benny had killed during our escape from Greystone. They called his kind God Beasts, though from what I gathered, both were the exact same thing.

The creature our pangolin killed had been a two-headed wolf-like beast with red and purple fur. The two heads had elongated necks with spiked ridges protruding from the top that gathered at the spine and ran down its back. It had six legs ending in long, sharp claws that had managed to dig deep into Benny's chest. A long, spiked tail ended in a blade-like 2-foot-long growth.

Grom had managed to incorporate all of the War Beast's body into the throne-like chair, with the upper two of its six legs forming a headrest above which the tail sat, pointing right toward the peacock messenger. The middle set of legs formed an armrest, and the lower two legs propped the middle ones up. Both heads hovered to either side of the armrests and had their fanged mouths open. Four empty eye sockets were focused toward the front of the bone throne.

I tapped the right head with my index finger and the emissary's eyes shifted toward the skull and then to the girls standing behind me. He gulped and licked his lips.

"Can't we talk in private?"

"No, we can't. My wives will hear of anything you have to say, so you can just save us the time. How is this going to end?"

"End? You can either submit or—"

"Go. Tell Duke Volarna that we do not give in to threats. We've marked our claimed land, so the next time he sends any soldiers our way, we won't just beat them, no, we'll kill them. It's been two months and he's been testing me, jester." My patience with these people was at an end. I had tried to play diplomat at the start, but the duke and his lackeys had no taste for it.

"J—jester? This is outrageous! I'm no jester!"

"Then why dress like a pimp, yo?" Benny shot his way. He was seated on a smaller throne sitting next to mine while in his pangolin form.

"Yes, what he said. Pimp."

"Pimp? What even is a pimp?" the man demanded. "I am Ventilo Volarna, third cousin to the duke and you will show

6

some respect!"

"Benny?"

"On it."

The pangolin climbed off the throne and slowly walked over to the messenger. I knew we couldn't kill him, or rather, we *shouldn't* kill him, but he was annoying, using someone else's name to throw his weight around. Well that, and to be honest, I didn't like the purple, yellow, bright red, and orange colors. He did look like a peacock in a way.

"What are...you doing?" Ventilo asked, taking a step back. "Don't come closer! Guards! Don't let him—ahh!"

Benny transformed into his Blood Beast form, towering over the small, balding man, and bellowed right into his face. Ventilo fainted.

"Not again," Jeanette grumbled. "Benny, look what you've done! He pissed himself!"

"Boss's fault, not mine. Have him clean it."

"Alright, alright. I'll do it," Sonya mumbled and used a water spell to wash away the piss and the unconscious man.

He had ten guards with him, but not a single one had even dared to move and several of them were visibly shaking.

"Take him back to Duke Adan Volarna," I said, waving them off. "No one will hurt you, but tell the good duke that if he wants to talk terms, he will have to come himself, and not before a moon has passed. I have more important matters to address."

Four of the guards grabbed Ventilo and carried him off as the other six fell in line behind them, looking about nervously. They got the message, so there was no need for me to sit in the throne chair anymore. It was uncomfortable and made me feel like an asshole.

"So, what now?" Emma asked as she threw herself at me. "Do we go for a round?"

"Maybe tonight. We need to go to the village. Food and supplies are running low."

"What? Do you think they'll want to sell us some after

we sent them...Vent-something packing?" Jeanette snorted.

"Why not? They need monster corpses and equipment. We've got an abundance of that, but they don't," I said, throwing her a wink. "Besides, Mortimer's charisma is even higher than mine, which is almost impossible, but whatever. I'll just unleash him on the villages."

"I don't think that is a good idea," Selene said from overhead. She was hiding in the ceiling like she always did whenever someone came to visit.

Grom and Nalgid's people had built what Benny called a Viking longhouse. It was just as the name implied a building about fifty feet long and twenty wide. It was large enough to host gatherings or to receive guests, but we didn't use it for anything else.

At the far end of the building, raised on a sort of podium, were mine and Benny's thrones. The others had insisted on the second throne, figuring someone as powerful as a God Beast should have one as well. The little ass liked the idea from the start, but after sitting in it a few times, the novelty had worn off.

"Should Legs and I come along?" Benny asked. "I was thinking of like...doing nothing all day. Maybe do a round of the fields and the mine entrance?"

"Well, you can do that when we're back, Benny," Emma said excitedly. "Shouldn't a big, strong guy like yourself be protecting us anyway? And you'll probably get to see...what was her name again? Lumila?"

"No, it's Ludmila. And don't. Just keep it to yourself, alright? Thanks."

Benny had fallen in love after visiting the first village a few times, and the lady in question had blown him a kiss in passing. Ever since he'd been smitten and head over heels in love. It was good seeing him care about something else than Legs and killing stuff.

"You do you, Benny. As long as she doesn't mind all that fur, you could even...you know?" I said, giving him a wink.

"Besides, they're just jealous. That fiery orange hair and the freckles are cute."

"Cute?" Emma, Sonya, and Jeanette said at the same time.

"You think she's cute?" the swashbuckler demanded.

"Yeah, tell him!" Emma said, getting up into my face. "I mean, she's cute, sure, but don't you already have your hands full with us?"

I sighed and shook my head.

"Benny, come on, big guy. Let's go find Mortimer."

"Don't you dare walk out when we're yelling at you!" Sonya shot after me. "We're not done yelling."

"I don't think he's even listening to us," Emma muttered.

"Of course he is, but he also knows how much you hate it when he acts like he doesn't," Selene added as she dropped from the ceiling. "I'm going with him. You can sit at home all day and sunbathe. Or whatever."

"Ugh, I hate it there. The cart ride is uncomfortable and the people stare at us funny," Jeanette protested.

"You sound like a petulant child," Emma jabbed. "But that's nothing new."

"She's got you there, Jeanny," Sonya chuckled. "Speaking of which, where's Elvina?"

I shut the door behind us, drowning out their voices. Usually, I didn't mind their fooling around and mock-arguing and whatever it was that they were doing, but today I felt different. This unease was breathing down my neck, and if something did happen, I wanted to be as far away from the village as possible.

Despite there not being any more of us than the people we arrived with, there were a few new additions to the buildings. Instead of slapping workshops onto their homes, we'd built what everyone just called 'the workshop'. And oh boy was it a beauty. The building was about a hundred feet long and just as wide with a smelter, a forge, a smithy, a monster processing corner, and even a weaver and tailor section. Whoever wanted to work, could do so inside the workshop and had everything on hand.

A small barn had been the second thing we built over the last two months and then proceeded to plant all the saplings. There were four different types, and according to Ferid's wife, who was a fanatic about all things fruit, they were mostly a perfect match to grow in close proximity.

I didn't know much about growing any kind of vegetable, fruit, or even flowers, but that's why I made it all up by killing a lot of things. Mostly monsters...

The third addition was a 10-foot-tall wall that surrounded the entirety of our small village. Due to the buildings being stretched out across a larger patch of land, just the wall had taken us three weeks, but it gave us a semblance of privacy. Also, the first group that had tried attacking our wall, found that Elvina's traps did more than a good enough job of protecting us.

I found one thing strange, though. They knew we had two God Beasts, and yet they still came. Sure, their attacks had been half-assed at best, but they had still attacked.

Lastly, we built the Viking longhouse as Benny called it, and it only took us a few days. The insides left a lot to be desired as we barely had any decorations.

The dwarves and elgar used their craftsmanship to carve images from our home into the wood, covering the walls and furniture with depictions of Greystone and the true Gods. The longhouse was slowly turning into a bastion of the old days. Probably the last in the world at that. With all the time lost between our departure from Greystone and our arrival in this new land, I doubted that whatever we had left behind resembled home anymore.

"Legs!" Benny yelled as we made our way toward Mortimer's shop. They were living together with Mano and his wife, who was late in her pregnancy and if all went well, we would have our first newborn.

The War Weaver came skittering across the park, as we

called it, which was just a green patch of land around which we'd left the trees intact. There were ten benches and some larger seats made for the elgar, so we could all gather to cook some meat under the starry sky or just hang out. It was a great idea that had come from none other than Selene.

Legs screeched as he tackled Benny and the two rolled across the ground, fighting each other. Despite getting his ass handed to him several times, the spider never gave up fighting for dominance in their awkward War Beast relationship. Unfortunately for the War Weaver, Benny knocked the shit out of him, tackling the spider to the ground and ripping one of its legs off. After staring at the leg for several seconds, he started beating Legs with his own leg.

"Enough, Benny. I think he got the point, and besides, who will pull the cart?"

"I will," he said proudly, standing over Legs and holding up the limb triumphantly. "What? It will grow back in a minute or two. What are you bitching about?"

Legs screeched some more, so I made my way over to Mortimer, unable to listen to them.

"Mortimer!" I yelled, stopping just outside the store. Mano was inside, polishing some of the equipment we'd stored there, while Rafika, his wife, sat on a chair in the store and seemed to be explaining something to him.

"What is it? I'm bu—sy...alright, they're at it yet again."

"Just ignore them. Do you want to come to visit Garm Village?"

"Well, of course I do. What do we need?"

"Food and supplies in general. Clothes? The fabric we ordered? All kinds of things. We're taking the big cart."

He eyed the two War Beasts and after several long seconds, looked at me. The merchant had a flat expression, but I knew what was going on in his mind. Ever since finding out about the two, he'd been somewhat reluctant about their presence, and even though it had become much better over time, the feeling was still there.

"I have a few minutes, I guess? His leg is still...detached."

"As I said, don't mind them. Coming?"

"Yes, of course. I need to...never mind. I'll place everything inside the guild storage." Mortimer hurried into his store, spoke to Mano and Rafika quickly, and then disappeared into the back, probably telling Callina that we were heading out.

I sat down on the bench in front of Mortimer's store and looked out onto the lake. It was shimmering in the morning sun, seeming so serene and fantastic, almost as if we were living in another world. Most of the fish were larger than me, and the monsters swimming at the very bottom were just as dangerous as Benny was, but they kept to themselves for the time being.

Benny finally jumped off Legs' back and ran a circle around the spider, who was getting back up. When the pangolin was done, he kicked Legs and pointed off toward the carts. We had stored them in the barn and only used either of them when visiting the villages. For some odd reason, the Godveil wouldn't allow us to store fabrics and some of the other things we needed.

Mortimer walked out of the store and sat next to me.

"I'm ready. How long will we be?"

"Depends on your haggling," I said with a smile.

"Alright, put all the blame on me, will you?"

"Well, I know you like the pressure, and besides, you'll get to unload some of the armor and weapons you had Mano polish. The duke's people won't sell any to the villagers, so it's a good source of income."

Mortimer sighed and slumped into the bench we were sitting on.

"I don't like to visit the villages, though. Everyone's worshipping Tan'Malas and it makes my skin crawl just remembering what happened back in Greystone. And now we have to—no, never mind. I'm good."

"If it's any consolation, none of us likes the situation, but it's just as Banxi told us. They've never known anything else. You can't blame them for accepting Tan'Malas' truth as the only one."

Mortimer picked a small pebble and tossed it in the lake's direction.

"You have a point."

"I know as theirs is not the only truth," he said frowning.

"We know that, but they don't. We need to learn to accept the way things are now."

I was quick to hand out advice I had a problem following myself. Tan Malas's reign over this part of the world wasn't something I could digest all that well, but I had to show resolve and try my best to calm the others. After all, we hadn't run into any animus or dark magic users yet. Most people worshipping the False God in the villages around us were just that, people.

"Or maybe they need to learn," Mortimer said, getting up. "But you're right. We better learn to accept what we can't change and move on. We still have each other and—"

"Hold on," I said. "You might be on to something here, Mortimer."

"What do you mean?"

"Maybe they *do need* to learn."

"Learn what, Cade?"

"Why wouldn't it be possible to change their views? When we came here we saw that Tan'Malas was considered the only God, but that's just because nobody knew any better. I haven't yet stepped into a village here that wasn't miserable. Whether it's the duke's taxes or the ignorance of their God, the villagers aren't happy. That much I know.

"What are you saying? That you should teach them about our Gods? Cade, with all due respect—"

"Not me, Mortimer. You. You and Sonya and even Emma. You could teach the people of this land that Tan'Malas isn't the only God, that there are other, better gods which won't be silent when they call for them in prayer."

Mortimer's expression shifted from serious and

confused to excited.

"Teach the people about Tan'Ruad, Tan'Drak, and Tan'Aria? Me? It's like...I'd become a priest," he mumbled, rubbing his chin.

"Priests are usually filthy rich," I said grinning.

"Well, if for no other reason," he said as a wide smile formed on his face. A second later he turned serious again. "No, Cade, this shouldn't be something we joke about. We're talking about reviving the True Gods in a strange land. If our hearts aren't in it—"

"Mortimer, relax. I know your heart is in it. How couldn't it be after everything we've seen?"

"A priest," he muttered, looking over the shimmering lake into the distance.

"I even have copies of the Book of Tan'Ur. This...This could be done, Cade. We could bring the people together. Stand against Tan'Malas once again. Eventually."

"You'll need a church or a temple or something, bro," Benny said as he scratched his nose. "You can preach all you want if you don't have anything to show for it."

"A temple," Mortimer said in a hushed tone as his eyes lit up. "Yes, I have a bunch of blueprints I thought I'd never even need. We could build it, Cade. We could make this work."

"We could," I said.

The idea shed hope on an uncertain future. If this thing worked, we could restore power to the True Gods, harm Tan'Malas, and make the lives of everyone around us better. But it could also attract attention from the rest of this place. Taking unoccupied land was one thing, but spreading your religion to others could prove very dangerous in the long run.

I didn't want to mention my concerns to Mortimer or the others. He seemed enthused with his new calling as a priest and all in all, I thought it was a good idea. With the True Gods at our side again, we'd establish a much stronger position in this new land.

"Say, what do you think about Lady Emma? She's a

priestess of Teonia," Mortimer said, grabbing my attention again.

"Wait, don't say it," I laughed. "You want her to be the grand priestess of this new temple?"

"Umm, yes. What do you think? With such a beautiful and strong head priestess, people would probably flock to us!"

Benny snorted and fell over on his back, laughing as if he'd lost it. We both stared at him for a moment, and Mortimer finally seemed to understand why the pangolin had seemingly gone mad.

"I just proposed that...one of the ladies becomes...a physical symbol and...I do apologize, Cade. Please forgive me."

I shot the older merchant a wink and offered Benny a hand.

"Come on, let's go. We'll talk about it later, although... Emma! Sonya!" I yelled. "Come here please!"

The door to the long house swung open almost immediately and all four girls rushed out.

"What?" Sonya yelled back. "Miss us already?"

Emma nudged her with an elbow.

"Always. Join us? We've got an interesting idea."

"Me too!" Jeanette said as she hurried toward us. "You're not leaving me behind!"

"Or me," Selene added, using her shadow skills to arrive before Jeanette could.

"That's not fair!" my black-haired swashbuckler protested. "I don't have any movement skills!"

"Tough luck," Selene chuckled. "So, what is this about? What kind of idea are we talking about? Having sex in the open? Oh, hey Mortimer."

"Lady...Selene," Mortimer mumbled. "You sure have changed over the last months."

"That she did," Jeanette said as she slapped the elf's ass. "She's trying to get Cade to sleep with her, and I don't like it."

"Trying? You have no idea, do you?" Selene laughed and dodged another slap, then slapped Jeanette's ass.

"Yeah, I thought that was supposed to stay between us, Selene?"

"What? You don't want me to share the best sex I've ever had in my life?"

"Best and only one, I'd say," Benny snickered. "I could smell your blood."

"Benny!" Selene hissed. "You little—come back here!"

The pangolin hurried off, his small legs carrying him much faster than anyone would give him credit for.

Legs let out a small screech, drawing our attention. He'd pulled the big cart along and it now sat there next to him.

"You've got a point, big guy. Come, we'll talk on our way there."

CHAPTER 2 – BELIEF

"Sonya, it's really up to you in the end," I said watching Legs prepare to pull the cart, "You and Emma, of course."

"I'm so happy you decided to do this," Sonya said, "Reviving the power of the True Gods in this land...It's the best idea you had in a long time."

"Thanks," I said flatly.

"Emma has the personality and the looks, that's what's important for the role. Of course, I'll be in the back pulling her strings if you know what I mean," she said with a mischievous grin.

"Pulling my strings?" Emma laughed, "You better watch your tongue before the high priestess!"

Though Mortimer wanted Emma to play the role, I had to bring it up with Sonya first. She was the one with the greatest knowledge of the Gods and if she wanted to be the face of our new endeavor, I was willing to offer her the position first.

"Unlike Jeanette, this isn't going to be easy," Sonya said.

"Hey!" the swashbuckler protested, "What was that for?"

"Good measure," Soyna grinned and the rest of us laughed.

Jeanette took the joke and joined in.

"Emma, you understand the responsibility you'd have?" I said steering back the conversation."Well, it's not like I'm against it," Emma said as Legs finally started pulling the cart. "But are you sure that you want people to...worship me?"

"Pfft! Who would want to worship your tiny ass?" Jeanette jabbed. "You need some meat on there, love."

"This is just fine, thank you very much," Emma retorted and poked her side. "Besides, it looks like you gained a few pounds."

Everyone aside from me gasped. I just shook my head and grunted. Benny's eyes met mine and he looked ready to lose it, but I shook my head just a tiny bit. He picked up on it and looked away, his back rising and falling quickly.

"You take that back!" Jeanette snapped. "Or I will—"

"You'll do what? I'm the high priestess now. You can't even touch me."

"No, you're not! At least not yet, so come—here!"

Jeanette threw herself at Emma and started tickling, poking her ribs, and tussling her hair.

"No! Not my hair!" Emma cried, pushing Jeanette off her. "You're a bitch sometimes, you know that?"

"I love it."

"Enough," I said, raising my voice just enough to get the point across. "All that's fatter is your pussy, babe," I said with a wink. "Everything else is just fine. Don't let Emma say otherwise."

"Yes, yes, whatever," Jeanette mumbled, looking away.

Selene tapped a finger on the side of the cart and cleared her throat.

"So, what's the plan, Cade? You want to build a temple in Garm Village and have Emma stay there?"

"No, not in Garm Village. We would do it in our own village," I replied. "Probably near the eastern exit? Or we could even place it outside the village wall so they would feel safer and more secure."

"False safety is better than no safety, right?" Mortimer said absently. He didn't meet our eyes and just stared off into the distance.

The first stretch of our trip would lead us across open land. We had Legs and Benny clear the land of trees for half a mile toward the nearest village in the north, and a bit less to the west toward the mountain range and south heading to the sea. The lake to the east of New Greystone was a natural deterrent so at least we didn't need to bother with that side.

The road was bumpy but considering we didn't have any people who knew how to make a good road from scratch, I was happy with not having to wade through thick forest. Besides, the dwarves had made the cart extra sturdy, especially the wheels. That's why we needed Legs' big form to pull it.

Another thing that I really liked about the cart was how they'd made benches on the side closest to Legs and halfway down the middle, then upholstered them so we would have a somewhat comfortable trip whenever we had to get supplies.

"Well, yes, in a way," I said, unsure if I really agreed. The people of the nearby villages weren't stupid so they'd be able to figure out what we were doing, but it only took one person...just one converted that would hopefully then start a landslide. "I want to make a test today first, then we can decide on where to put a temple."

"Oh? What test?" Emma asked curiously. "Tell us."

"You and Sonya will corner a poor fool and try to convert him. Let Sonya do the talking, and you just look pretty."

"He didn't just say that!" Emma yelled and then shot Sonya an incredulous look. "Did he?"

"He did."

"That's so sexist, bro," Benny said as he nudged me with his claw.

"Sex—what?" I asked, and this time I really wanted to know what the word meant.

"Sexist. That's like...when you discriminate against women."

Emma, Sonya, and I snorted at the same time, and I just shook my head.

"Benny, I have four...wives, so to say. I love women obviously. Does that seem sexist to you?"

"Man, where I come from...You have no idea. Look, bro, you just said that Emma just should stand there and be all pretty like."

"Yes, because Sonya knows the scripture better than all of us combined and Emma has strong charisma, the tandem can work wonders."

"Oh," Benny and Emma said in unison.

"Like, okay. My bad," the pangolin added. "I'm just looking out for the ladies, alright?"

"All good, Benny. Just don't get any wrong ideas, my man. You know how much I love my girls, and if I was a sexist, as you put it, they wouldn't be around. Being soulbound wouldn't help in that regard."

"I agree for once," Jeanette said and put an arm around Selene. "So, can I watch next time?"

I sighed and turned to Mortimer.

"So, are those blueprints in the storage? Or at home?"

"Storage. Do you want to see them?"

I nodded and held my hand out. He offered me a stack of ten blueprints, and I went through them quickly. Seven were way too small and consisted of barely anything more than four walls and a ceiling. One of the remaining three was way too big, and it said it was a type of temple that ran for 150 yards in length. Then there were two smaller buildings, which were also called temples on the blueprints, but they were much smaller. The first was 60 yards in length, while the second sat at 35 yards.

I studied the smaller one. It looked very similar to both larger versions but instead of being a square, it was roughly oval-shaped. The ceiling sat at 20 feet so there was enough room for even Benny to join us if we ever got to using the thing.

The double entrance looked similar to that of our main building, but larger and with a hint of flair. Both the walls and the doors were carved but I couldn't make out what. Inside there was a large rug that ran from the entrance to the far end of the building with a row of six benches sitting to either side of it. At the far end, there was a slightly raised platform with a round, desk-like dais that surrounded most of the platform. And behind all that was a room that we could use for various purposes.

I handed the blueprint to Sonya, who studied it for a long

moment.

"This could work. It's big enough, and we already have most of the necessary materials, but I still have no idea if it makes sense."

"Makes sense?" Emma said. "What do you mean? I thought we all said it was a good idea."

"She probably means that it's too small. Why not make something bigger and better from the start?" Jeanette asked. "That's like settling for a small dick when you can have a big one."

Benny cleared his throat and then wiggled his eyebrows.

"So...I wonder why I'm still single then. I've got quite the —"

Selene kicked his knee, and he winced.

"Hey, that's so not cool! I was just...joking."

"I somehow doubt that," she said with a mock glare. "Anyway, we'll tell Ludmilla that you were flirting with taken women."

"Cade? Help me out, bro?"

I shook my head in mild amusement.

"You brought this all on yourself, Benny. Sometimes you talk too much."

"Well, sometimes you guys don't talk enough! Why do I have to always be the one to brighten the mood, man?"

Legs screeched in support and stopped for a moment, turning his body sideways to face us, let out another screech, and then he returned to making his way up the slight slope. Garm Village was about two miles away and it wouldn't take that long to get there, even while riding the cart.

The two War Beasts did a great job cleaning a path straight toward the village, so when we crested the hill, I could see the small settlement. It was walled in with wooden logs reinforced with mana and steel. Grom had tried punching the wall once just for fun and found his strongest punch didn't do much more than bruise his hand. It was one of the things we wanted to trade for, but the village mayors of both villages we'd visited outright declared that we'd be considered hostiles if we tried to pry it from them. I didn't want that. Not yet at least... Hell, not ever if I could help it.

"Jeanette, Selene, you will join us. They're outright afraid of you two, so that should speed things up."

"I'm getting the feeling you're being...sexist, was it?" Jeanette teased.

"You've just been pushed to the back of the line, Jeanette," Selene said with a flat stare. "From first to last. How does it feel?"

"Wait, what? I—Cade! Don't you dare do that!"

"I didn't say anything, but she might just be right there. Selene could take your place."

"Finally!" the assassin said excitedly. "I want you all to be there when we—"

"Information overload," Benny grunted. "And we're almost there."

He was right. Time sure passed quickly when playing around. The 15-foot tall walls quickly approached along with the four soldiers standing guard at the entrance. They were sitting and playing a card game. By now the whole village knew that we weren't a threat, so they just ignored us most of the time. Even the God Beasts, though I always caught them watching from the corners of their eyes.

Just as the village's storage silos peeked over the horizon, I could hear the familiar sound of battle.

"Faster, Legs!" I ordered not even considering backing off or scouting ahead.

When we reached the walls of the village, we found a group of four guards engaged with an ox-sized black boar. Its tusks were already red with human blood. One of the guards was pulling back another, the wound to his side had pierced his armor and blood was gushing from it.

I used [Shadow Stride] to close the distance to the giant boar, leaped onto its back then shoved both my blades into its spine. The simple action opened two long deep gashes across its back. The boar groaned in pain, then staggered and tried to shake me off, but I wasn't giving it any chance. I dug my blades back down again, not even needing to use any skills, and it dropped, breathing heavily. One of the guards walked up to it and stared at me as if asking for permission.

"Go ahead," I said and got off the boar. The guard waited and leaned in, slicing its throat. The enormous head dropped into a pool of blood.

"That was...thank you, good sir!" the man who slit the boar's throat said, offering me his hand. "The thing came running after some of the villagers," he said and glanced over his shoulder toward the wounded man. "Vendir managed to save them but got caught in its tusks."

I turned to Emma and she nodded, already hopping off the cart. The others followed after her.

"He'll be alright."

"We're so damn lucky you came just now. We owe you a big debt."

"Don't worry about it," I said.

"But I do, good sir. We...aren't very well equipped to handle these kinds of monsters. They're becoming stronger and stronger, while the Duke, he...never mind."

Benny jumped off the cart, transforming into his Blood Beast form. He helped remove the improvised harness from the War Weaver's back and then put it on. The harness adjusted to his body as it was made from special materials the dwarves didn't want to talk about. It was probably expensive and their way of thanking us for bringing them along, so I didn't push.

The guardsmen watched him do it with a mix of awe and fear and I knew Benny enjoyed every bit of it.

Once Emma was done healing Vendir, the men returned to their post around a table set next to the main gate. A game of cards and several small empty glasses told me the boar had interrupted them in the middle of their usual guard duties.

"Come, join us, have something to drink," their captain

said.

"Gentlemen," I said, throwing four golden coins onto the table. "Mind getting the gate for us? We're not here to drink, but thanks."

They hurriedly pocketed the coins, as this was one of the only ways of getting a currency we accepted back at our own village, and honestly, we cut them good deals. At least those who didn't act out or behaved like assholes.

"Kills a boar with one strike and he doesn't feel like it deserves a toast?" one of the four asked.

He was seated closest to me. All four wore yellow surcoats with black stripes along the length and decently looking gray and silvery armor. I knew he was the captain by the additional stripe on his chest. Their weapons of choice were swords and maces. Shields hung from all four of their backs. It was a staple of being a soldier, after all. Good shields could protect the wearer even from lower-tier spells.

"You toast," I said flatly, "But if you do feel like helping me out, do you mind answering a question?"

The captain shot the other guard an angry look to which he smacked his lips and looked away. I didn't know any of their names, and their faces were very ordinary, forgettable even. Plus, they rotated in and out every week, going from one village to the other, and then back to the city. Most of these guards were conscripted from the villages and they were eager to protect them.

"Depends on what you want to know," the captain replied.

He had a small insignia attached on the breastplate, that of a sword and a mace. I never bothered asking what it meant as I didn't deem the soldiers important enough.

"Are the inquisitors out?"

Instead of the captain, the other guard spoke again.

"No, they're in the village. Why? Are you going to try and do something?" he asked hurriedly, shooting to his feet and putting his hand on the butt of his mace.

"Sit back down," I said coldly. "You do that again and you'll end up as peacock did this morning."

"P—peacock?" he stuttered, doing as I said. Another well-known fact was that we'd beat anyone senseless if they behaved inappropriately, and almost drawing a weapon on me fit that description.

"Gordon, shut your mouth," the captain ordered.

"Ven—something? Ventarilo?"

"Ventil Volarna," Sonya said from the cart. "The Duke's third cousin he said? Unless he lied."

The captain's jaw dropped as he looked past me and to Sonya.

"You beat up...Ventil Volarna?" he asked incredulously.

"Boss, I think a drink's in order," Vendir said. The blood on his surcoat was still wet, but the wound had closed. "Ventil needed a good beating."

"Shut up! You can't be heard saying that, you fool! You've got a family and kids!"

Their officer's eyes darted to me as he held his breath for a moment.

"Hear what? I didn't hear anything. All he said was if I'd be interested in having a drink with you guys. Just get the gate for us and I'll take you up on the offer."

The soldier he just reprimanded and the one sitting next to him shot up and hurried toward the gate, opening it. They stood at attention and had wide grins on their faces. Interesting. If the soldiers weren't happy, then the ordinary folk must be even less so.

"When do we meet?" Emma asked. "Do we really...do it?"

"Have Benny join you. Worst case, have him eat the inquisitors."

The officer tensed again and was about to speak, but he shut up.

"We...heard nothing."

"Good man."

It wasn't a slip of the tongue, of course, as I knew what

his initial reaction would be. He didn't like the inquisition either. Sure, it should have been obvious from the start, but...sometimes I was pretty dense.

I raised my hand to stop Benny from pulling the cart into the village and turned back to the captain, leaning in so I could whisper.

"Do you really believe in Tan'Malas?"

To my surprise, he didn't gasp or cry in outrage, he just stood there and eyed me as if trying to decide on something. After a tense moment, he sighed.

"Tan'Malas is our god," he said, "Of course I believe in Him."

"Of course you do," I said, keeping my eyes locked on his.

"Is there something you want to tell me, sir?"

"Your parents," I said, "They worshipped Tan'Malas too, have they?"

He nodded.

"Your grandparents and those before, has it always been Tan'Malas they prayed to?"

He shifted in place, looking over his shoulder.

"My grandfather used to tell me that his grandfather prayed to...Why are you asking these questions? You'll get us all in trouble."

I put a hand on his shoulder.

"I will share nothing of what you said, you have my word. All I ask of you is honesty."

There was visible turmoil within him and yet that was a good sign. Some people seemed to know about the old belief, that was apparent. I doubted they knew much, if anything at all, but sowing a seed of doubt would be a great start. A seed that we would see grow.

"What do you want me to say? That my great-grandfather believed in other gods than Tan'Malas? Perhaps he did, but those gods are dead now, aren't they? Now it's the Dark Lord that gives us our powers, meager they might be."

"They're not dead...I didn't capture your name."

"Samel," he replied instantly.

"A fitting name. I'm the embodiment of what the True Gods have to offer. Your great-grandfather was right. I ask you to listen, to think. Nothing more."

Samel took a look at the other guards, their faces were struck with fear. They had been subjects to the forces of Tan'Malas for so long that even thinking about other gods caused them visible distress.

I had to tread carefully.

"I will listen," Samel said and turned to the table, pointing his hand to one of the chairs.

"I'll listen, too," Vendir said.

"Gordon? Rodrick?" Samel asked the other two.

"If we must, captain."

I nodded and faced my War Beast friend.

"Benny, you can go. Good luck and see you in a bit. I will drink as...fast as I can."

I blew the girls a kiss each and then sat down next to the officer and his guardsmen.

"My name is Cade, Samel, and I'm going to tell you something...you probably won't believe it, but all I'm asking for is to keep an open mind. Nothing else. Can you do that for me?"

Samel pulled a bottle from his storage and another glass, he poured me and the other men a glass each and finally one for himself.

"What is it?"

"It's called rakia. Very strong stuff. Don't overdo it. And please, do go on, Mister Cade."

I took a sip and shook my head as it hit me like a slap.

"Shit, this is strong," I muttered. "Maybe we shouldn't be drinking before we've had our chat."

Samel emptied his glass, smacked his lips, and burped.

"Good stuff. Please, go on."

I eyed him for a moment. He seemed like a totally different person before he drank that stuff and after. Sure, it was possible that he'd already gotten drunk, but that wasn't it. He was paying attention for the first time since we started talking. Like real attention.

"We come from a faraway place, Samel. A very, very distant land where...your current god isn't the only god. What's more, he's considered evil where I'm from and I've seen what he does with dead monsters and soldiers. We fought against him and lost."

"As anyone else has in the entire world, Mister Cade. That is what our scripture tells us."

"Oh? And do you know more about the scripture?" I asked curiously. If he could tell me more, then we'd know how to approach the ordinary folk about the matter.

"I know the Tan'Malicron by both heart and mind and remember just about every page of the holy scripture. My parents forced me to learn them when I was a young child. Some of it has faded but not all. What would you like to know?"

"Everything you can tell me."

CHAPTER 3 –
SPREADING THE FAITH

"We always knew Tan'Malas wasn't the god our forefathers worshipped," Samel said. "There are stories out there of numerous other divinities, stories carried by word of mouth from one generation to the other."

"Fairytales," Gordon said with his arms crossed over his chest.

Samel continued ignoring the grumpy guardsman.

"All we ever knew, what our parents and grandparents knew, was the word of Tan'Malas taught to us by his priests through the Tan'Malicron and upheld by the Order. The only true god is Tan'Malas, the destroyer of the so-called false old gods."

"What kind of god is Tan'Malas?" I asked, "What has he brought you, your family, your village?"

Samel bit his lower lip and looked away.

"I'm not the only one, you know?"

"The only one what?"

The captain was still insecure, scared even, of the conversation we were having.

"Who finds fault with the Dark God."

"Captain!" Gordon said slapping the table.

"Shut up, Gordon. You of all people should be silent now. Do I have to remind you of what the inquisitors did to your son?"

Gordon spat on the ground looking furious, but he refrained from speaking further.

"The Church of Tan'Malas and those who work for him

have grown bold as of late. The people of our villages aren't doing that well. Sickness finds us often and so does madness," he said, staring off into the distance for a long moment.

"Prayer brings nothing and yet the inquisitors keep pushing us. Prayer shouldn't come by force."

"I feel the same way," I said, genuinely curious about hearing where he was going with the retelling. "I will tell you something interesting once you're done," I said and pulled out a bottle of the special stuff the dwarves distilled. The name eluded me, but that didn't matter. The reddish liquid seemed to be a favorite of the guards as they started drinking happily. I'd treated other guards to it before as well and they'd been willing to pay good for a few bottles.

"Yes, so, where were we?" Samel said, smacking his lips. "This is good stuff. Do you think we could—never mind. Where are my manners?"

"I have another one on me that I'd be happy to part with. Tell me more. Tell me of the faith."

"Yes, well it is said there are 13 pillars of Tan'Malas that uphold his faith across the world. Every pillar controls one region along with a small army of sub-pillars as they call themselves. Every sub-pillar has control over a small army and a dozen of inquisitor's chapters."

I raised a finger to stop him.

"Wait a second. Pillars. That sounds like they're generals of the Order, or am I wrong?"

"Exactly. They were the original 13 that had sacrificed their kingdoms or their cities during the re-awakening. We don't have any more information on those very events, so don't bother asking," Samel said as he took another sip, savoring it. I pulled the second bottle from my storage and placed it on the table in front of them.

"Who are the pillars?"

Samel shook his head.

"I do not know exactly, Mister Cade. We only know of three names: Lemas, Bardeen, and Zekan."

The hairs on my neck rose as if I were a cat.

"Where can I find the pillars?" I asked, and he could feel the crackle of power coming off me. "Where does that pillar called Zekan reside?"

"I...do not know. Bardeen and Zekan are names we heard of from sub-pillars and dignitaries. I don't even know if Duke Volarna knows anything more than I've already given you."

I took a deep breath and let it out slowly, then breathed in again and breathed out.

"So Lemar is this region's pillar?"

"Yes, he is, but he lives far away from here from what I heard, in a city called Luferson Castle. It is a huge city with an even larger wall that encases it. I also heard that it's impenetrable."

"Throw a big enough spider at it and it will fall, trust me," I chuckled, nodding to Legs. "But yeah, this isn't what I hoped to hear at all, Samel. Not at all.

"So, this Lemar? Know anything about him?"

Samel shrugged as if defeated by the mere thought of the pillar.

"He uses a spear and shield from what I know. He's as tall as your hairy God Beast, they say, but I never laid eyes on him. Maybe one of the inquisitors knows more?"

He stared at me for a moment and lowered his glass.

"I can't help but think you know much more than I do."

"Depends on what we're talking about. The days of past? The days before Tan'Malas won? Yeah, I can tell you more about that. But first, tell me more about the sub-pillars. Tell me about the villages, and the Duke's city. I want to know more if I want to help."

Samel smiled, cocking his head as if studying me.

"Are you serious? How do you think you can help, Mister Cade? There's not even a score of you."

"Trust me, it can be done, but first—"

"Yes, yes. Garm. Well, the four of us rotate between Garm, Tazul, Znica and Balan. There are four more squads that do the same. They don't want us to guard just our own villages and stress how no village is our home, that the only home we ever need is Faith, and Faith encompasses the whole world. You've been here more than once, so you should know that Garm Village only has about twenty soldiers on any given day and another fifteen inquisitors and zealots. It's not like you can't take them if you wish so.."

"No, I don't. Not the soldiers, anyway. What I want to do is...to get rid of those who stand between you and your family, your peace, and your beliefs. Once they're dealt with, we can change things. That's why they need to go, if you get what I'm saying."

"The Duke won't like that. If the inquisitors don't report back all of a sudden—"

"I'll deal with the Duke in time," I said and smiled.

It wasn't my words that compelled Samel to open up to me and speak of treason to a stranger, no, it was the power that radiated from me. Something none of these guards, villagers, or even that fool they called duke had felt before. That, and the fact that these people had been pushed to their limits. A drowning man will grab onto any hand. Luckily for them, I had no other intention than to pull them out.

Samel turned toward the other three soldiers and glared at them.

"You heard nothing, understand?"

"Is there any more of that red stuff, Mister Cade?" one of the guards asked.

"I'll send some over when we're home later. One each sounds good?"

The three soldiers perked up at that and grinned.

I turned back to Samel.

"Where is the closest sub-pillar?"

"Two stay with the duke as far as I know, and they do monthly rounds of the villages. One of them was here the other day...Danara. She's very strong and vicious. Uses a whip made of darkness and controls several thousand..."

"Thousand? Soldiers?"

"No, they're not just soldiers. They're shapes made out of pure darkness, bone, armor, and anything they were made of before...they turned to darkness. No one knows where they came from, but those dark ones have no fear, no anger, and no self-preservation instincts. All they do is kill, kill, kill. And follow orders. I've seen them fight once. It wasn't pretty."

"For the other side, I guess?"

"Exactly. It was a massacre. No, wait. I think you're misunderstanding. There was a dungeon break and monsters kept pouring out. They were sent instead of the army to deal with it. We were told to just watch and learn."

It made sense I figured. Keep everyone in check by demonstrating what happens if they don't. Spreading the true faith made even more sense after hearing all this. I should have asked around much sooner.

"If you hear any ruckus from inside the village, screaming or clash of steel or something, pretend you're deaf."

Samel just nodded, but then put his hand on my arm.

"You promised...information?"

He was right. I'd forgotten about it all as I listened to his part.

"We were there when...hmm...this doesn't make any sense. When did you say that Tan'Malas's faith spread across the lands?"

"Hundreds of years ago. It was way before my great-great-great grandfathers ever lived. Why do you ask?"

"Because we were there when a massive army of monsters and people made from pure darkness attacked, rolling over the city of Greystone. We escaped...narrowly. But that doesn't make any sense. It's only been two months since we got here."

Samel looked as if he was about to ask me if I'd gone nuts, but he frowned instead.

"Tell me more. What was it like back then?"

I decided to be honest and tell him about my past. Not

everything, but enough to give him an idea of how things were back then.

Quest Received: <u>Spreading The Faith I</u>

Description: The Gods of Old have been forgotten and are in a state of slumber. Revive the belief in the Old Gods.

Status: 0/5 Converted Believers

Reward: The continued existence of the Godveil.

NOTE: The Godveil is losing its power and will soon stop to exist, and if it does, you will lose all your powers.

"Shit," I cursed. "This is not good."

"What is? Did something just happen? I could feel some kind of power coming off you," Samel said worriedly.

"Do you know what mana is?"

He shook his head.

"No, I do not. Does mana have anything to do with your religion?"

"Yes and no. Mana allows us to be so powerful, and it is part of the Godveil, which is something the gods of old created to allow people to become stronger so that we could fight the monsters scouring our lands. Wait, is that why you're so...weak?"

"Weak? Our Captain here is—"

"Enough," Samel said. Or Captain Samel as the other soldier just called him.

"Tell me, Samel," I said, leaning in closer. "What would you do for real power? Power like ours."

The man visibly gulped and looked over to his subordinates. None of them said anything, but an understanding passed between the four.

"We shouldn't do this," Gordon, the same soldier who just defended Samel hissed. "It might as well be, well, I don't

34

know! But that's my point. We know nothing about them aside from what he just told us. And do you believe all that? Do you —"

"Enough. I won't repeat myself again. Sit there and drink until it's over."

Samel could feel it too, and just as I was about to speak, a loud crash came from within the village and was accompanied by a deafening roar. Benny was kicking ass. I focused on the mana signatures, and they were so weak that I could barely feel them. One disappeared, then another, and a third.

"It has started," Samel whispered. "Will the other soldiers—"

"No, I'll make sure of it." I focused on any other mana signatures and found the soldiers all grouped up inside a building. *"Everyone, don't kill the soldiers, only the inquisitors, and zealots. Keep an inquisitor alive if you can."*

"Already done that," Selene replied. *"I disabled him. Jeanette and Benny are having fun."*

"Don't torture them, alright? Just get rid of them all—no, wait. Try to leave them alive. I want to see if we can try and convert them."

"Convert?" Sonya asked. *"What do you mean?"*

"Didn't you get the quest?"

"No, what quest?"

I sighed and shook my head.

"Never mind. Just do as I said. I'll be there in a minute."

Benny let out another roar and all battle ceased after that.

"I think that's my cue," I said getting to my feet and giving Samel a curt nod.

"Wait. I want to hear more about your old gods. Do you think you could tell us?" he asked sounding hopeful.

"Then come on in. Join us for another little chat."

I wanted to kick myself as I had no idea what I was even doing. Ever since I started my conversation with Captain Samel, I'd been hoping to get my hands on some information we previously didn't have, but this...

It had turned into something I felt I had little control over. The inquisitors and zealots were dying and the Order would find out soon. And though I wasn't too worried about them, I could hardly anticipate what the real repercussions of our deeds could be.

It is what it is now, I thought to myself, strengthening my resolve. We did what we felt was right, and that was all I could do in the end.

We made our way into the village where a massive crowd had gathered around the girls and Benny. Two inquisitors were hog-tied, and Selene sat on one of their backs. Seven zealots were dead and strewn about in pieces. Their outfits were different enough that I could make them out even at just a glance.

Inquisitors were equipped with full plate breastplates and pads but no helmets and browner than yellow surcoats while those of the zealots were yellow with black stripes. They were fully encased in armor, including helmets. Of the five inquisitors, only two remained, and from the twenty zealots, there were only thirteen left. I figured that was more than enough for what I had in mind.

"Good people of Garm Village," I said, raising my voice and putting all focus on me. "You all know me and my generosity in trade. It is very unfortunate that it had to come to this, but the religion of Tan'Malas is a false one, and his tools need to be...taken out. No one will harm any of you or the good soldiers that are...trapped? Benny? Really?"

The Blood Beast shrugged as he dropped one of the choking zealots.

"What? I had to stop them from joining in, right? I figured collapsing the building was as good a way as any, bro."

"I guess you're right," I chuckled. "Anyway, I will ask of you for one thing only. Listen to my people this one time, let them preach about the true old gods, and after that, you can send a message that we've killed some of these idiots and taken the rest. You can even request the help of a sub-pillar to rid these lands of our evil ways."

I looked around the gathered people. There were over three hundred of them, I knew as much as that's how many of them there were according to their mayor.

"Mister Cade! This was not what we agreed on!" the mayor, a woman in her early thirties snapped at me. She had a mane of white hair that hung loosely around her shoulders and piercing orange eyes, which was the oddest thing I'd ever seen. Even in a world where monsters were commonplace... She wore a long, woven beige smock dress that fell to her ankles and a yellow belt that was wrapped tight around her waist.

"Mayor Najla," I said with a light bow.

"Mister Cade!"

"Yeah, Mister Cade," Jeanette said with a hint of venom. "Why are you being so hostile to that young woman? She's in distress because of you."

"Oh, I could totally see him go after her," Emma laughed.

"She's his type. Big tits, small waist, tall," Sonya added with a chuckle of her own.

"Ladies, please. We're not here to—please, not now." I focused on the mayor and tried one more time. "As I just said, we're not here to hurt anyone. Things just...happened. And exactly what happened?" I asked, turning to my girls.

"Sonya started talking about Tan'Aria and one of the inquisitors attacked her without so much as a warning. Poor fool is over there," Jeanette said, pointing to a dismembered corpse.

"Benny?"

"Yeah, me, bro."

"Good. Thank you for protecting the ladies."

"Any time, bro. You know I'm all good for it."

"Yes, so please transform back. You're scaring the people."

That wasn't necessarily true because they were all

waiting to see what was going to happen next. There was no outrage, no screaming, yelling, or throwing rotten vegetables and fruit our way.

"You have no idea what they will do to us! They will say we were accomplices!" Najla yelled, clenching her fists. "The duke will have no choice but to have us all executed!"

"Not if we protect you," I said flatly. "Look, the Gods of old have bestowed a quest on me, and I plan to fulfill it, no matter what. And to do that, they have granted me—"

```
You have received a minor sculpture of
Tan'Ruad, Tan'Drak, and Tan'Aria.

Note: The statue can be used to grant
Godveil powers to all believers.
```

Now that was interesting. The gods, seeing I was serious about their quest, had granted me a very effective tool, one that would definitely help me get started.

"What is it? You look surprised," Emma asked as she put her arm around me as if telling Najla to back off. Jealousy. Can't say I like it, but it showed how protective she was of me. I would do the same and more if I'd been in her shoes.

"Yeah, I just got an interesting gift from the Gods, one that will help us show these fine people that we're telling the truth."

I looked around for a moment, looking for the best spot to put the sculpture. Despite the 'minor' in the name, it was easily ten feet tall and six wide, depicting the three deities in battle armor and wielding weapons. Tan'Ruad held a spear, or at least I figured it was him as the statue's face looked older than the other guy's, who held onto a sword and a shield. Tan'Aria had a staff in one hand and a mace in the other.

I made my way across the square and stopped right in the center where the ground had been paved with stone tiles, and placed the statue there. The people around me gasped and even started chatting excitedly. Their not having access to the

Godveil made me realize how good we had it with all the extra storage space. We technically didn't need the cart, but we'd done so not to stir suspicion, despite them having seen us fight and use spells and abilities they couldn't.

"These are the True Gods! Tan'Ruad, Tan'Drak, and Tan'Aria! Tan'Malas is the evil half of Tan'Drak the Destroyer! For all this time, you have been praying to a malicious god that only cares about enslaving the entire world and forcing every living creature to worship his name. The dead, man or woman, monster or beast, are turned into mindless soldiers that only know how to kill, kill, and kill! We fought them back in our homeland, and I can tell you, there is nothing benevolent about him!"

"So it is true?" one of the villagers called. "It is true that he isn't the only one?" The man was older, probably somewhere in his sixties but looked still fit enough to do manual labor.

"There is so much that I wish to tell you, but we do not have the time now. Listen carefully. I need one person who will take the leap of faith and touch this statue. He or she will get access to the Godveil, which is a power beyond your wildest dreams. We just need one person to convert to the true faith of old, and they will be the living proof that we are telling the truth!"

The crowd grew silent, which I'd figured would happen. It was one thing indulging one's curiosity, but when it came to actually doing it, that was something else entirely.

"I will do it," Captain Samel said, walking up from behind me. "I have no family that will miss me if something were to happen."

"Nothing will happen to you, good Captain, at least not today."

"Then I will be the first!" he said, raising his voice so everyone could hear him. "Be my witnesses!"

He stepped up to the statue and held his hand out, placing it on an indentation at the center of Tan'Drak's shield.

The captain glowed for a brief moment, just like we would back in Greystone, and then he gasped, pulling his hand away.

"By...no, not Tan'Malas...by...the old gods?" he exclaimed, sounding unsure of what he must have seen or heard. "What is this? What are these words? What is this class thing?"

"So, it worked," I whispered, offering my hand to the soldier. "Alright then, let me explain how it all works."

CHAPTER 4 – MAPS

It took me a good while to explain everything, during which time Benny had helped dig the soldiers out of the collapsed building. They had joined the captain as their superior officer, but they all looked pissy. Sure, I understood that their pride had been hurt, but their attitudes bothered me to the point I wanted to sacrifice one to the almighty Benny. He had already drained all the corpses dry of blood, but he could always have more.

"Mayor, can we start loading the goods? I will leave this statue here while we head to Balan Village, that way everyone can decide for themselves if they want to become stronger, healthier, and live much longer."

"Hedor," the mayor said, glancing over her shoulder. "Arrange for the goods to be loaded while I talk to our guests."

"In private?" Selene asked, still sitting on the unconscious inquisitor. "I don't think that's a good idea. He might do something to you."

"Exactly. He's a vicious...love maker," Jeanette added hurriedly. "I don't think you'd be able to take him all...in."

If any of the villagers had taken us seriously, they now sure as hell didn't.

"Alright, I think I've had it with you two. Next time you're staying home, cooking and cleaning. And you better do a good job," I said with a mock growl.

"Yes, Daddy," Jeanette purred and I died just a little bit inside.

"Jeanette, go make sure they're loading up everything correctly. Benny, stay with those...freaks," I said pointing to the captives. Selene, make a few rounds about the village and scout ahead."

"Will do, *but can you punish me tonight?*" she added through our mental link. *"I've been a bad girl and I feel that you should punish me."*

"So you did it on purpose?"

"Of course."

I sighed inwardly and turned toward the others next.

"Emma, Sonya, Mortimer, tell these good people more about the gods and the Godveil, about loot, which surprisingly worked for just about anyone now and not just those with a looting ability, skills, and classes. The whole thing."

"Will do, boss," Mortimer said and turned toward one of the larger groups, raising his voice. "Good people of Garm Village, today is truly a blessed day! As you've witnessed firsthand—"

I shut his voice out and followed Mayor Najla toward her manor house. It sat at the edge of the village and was encased in a wooden log wall. A small gate led us further onto her estate, if I could even call it that. The manor house was only a bit smaller than the allotted plot of land on which it stood. It had four tower-like corners with a large wooden door at the front. The outside looked as if it was mostly made of wood and some other materials I didn't recognize. The windows were made from thick, blurry glass.

What I found most interesting was the large clock set above the door. It clicked loudly as the second hand made its rounds. We used the Godveil for measuring time in Greystone and of course the sun's movements. Some mages could conjure time-measuring instruments here and there but I had never seen a contraption as large as that.

"And there I thought you'd never invite me in," I said as she pushed the door open and strode into her home.

"It's not a social visit, so please, don't. Also, I won't be offering you a drink either as we need to have a serious conversation."

I followed her into the manor house and was surprised

to see how minimalistic it was. The last few times we talked out in the square, but not this time. I figured she wanted a personal favor or something since we were doing it in private.

"That's...harsh," I said, eyeing my host. "Should the mayor be dressing so pretty?"

Najla started to say something but stuttered and closed her mouth, took in a deep breath, and then tried again.

"Your tactics won't work on me, so please, don't. Now, please follow me to the lounge room," she said with a hint of embarrassment. "I didn't call you here to talk in the foyer."

I smiled at the way she said it and followed after her. The entrance had no decoration other than a shelf with some small trinkets and a painting of the lake. It led toward a staircase just ahead of us, and to the right was a door, which I figured would lead to the pantry, kitchen, or storage area.

The door on the left was wide open, and I could see it was the lounge. Inside was a small sitting area with two upholstered sofas and a lounge chair. A rectangular, wooden coffee table sat between them. Four more paintings hung on the walls, and several cabinets and more shelves lined the walls with small pottery and busts. They were similar yet different enough to be distinguishable from the kind of art people had appreciated in Greystone.

Najla studied me and my reaction, but I liked to think I did a good job of staying as blank as possible. I looked around for a moment and then took the lounge chair to her surprise.

"You're sitting in my chair."

"Do you want to sit in my lap, mayor?"

"Your—lap? What do you take me for? One of those harlots you call wives?"

I stared at her flatly, which caused her to take a step back.

"You shouldn't talk about my girls like that, mayor. I'm not the forgiving type. Speak, why are we here?"

Najla sat across from me, crossed her legs and arms, and then pursed her lips.

"What will it take for you to stop coming to our village?"

"I don't understand. You don't want to trade with us anymore?"

"You misunderstood. We still want to trade, but not here. If we even survive what's to come, I don't want to see all that we've worked so hard for be destroyed. Sure, we don't have much to offer, but we produce a lot of food, we breed animals, we have weavers, leatherworkers, and even—"

"Look, mayor, you don't need to convince me about anything, but I do feel an obligation to warn you. Our fight is with the followers of Tan'Malas. The dark one won't even feel a dip of a few hundred, or even a thousand followers, so what's going to happen is that we'll convert anyone who wants to the one true faith, give them the means to fight, and then be their bulwark."

"So you want to fight for people you don't know?"

"No," I said firmly. "My fight is with Tan'Malas, it always has been. Every man, woman, or child I free from his bonds is a victory. That said I do want to learn more about the people living here. If we—say, do you have a map of this place? We haven't gone past the lake and the village to your west, Balan."

"Why do you want a map?"

"Please, indulge me. I will pay you handsomely."

"No, I don't want to."

"Why not?"

"Because I do not have any need for your coin."

"What about power?" I asked, leaning in closer. Her bright orange eyes were so strange that I couldn't help but keep staring.

"Power? What kind of power?"

"You will age very slowly, your body will be much stronger, and you will not get sick unless someone inflicts some kind of disease on you. There are many more benefits, but also one great downside."

"What's the downside?"

Najla stood from the sofa and walked around the table, sat down in front of me, and leaned right up into my face.

"If I die, you will die too, but for as long as I am alive, you will live a much better life."

"And this crusade? Won't it get you killed?"

I shrugged, scooting over to sit even closer to her.

"Only a pillar has a chance against me. You haven't even seen what we're capable of, mayor. The world has changed for some odd reason, but it has also grown weak."

"Weak? What do you mean?" she whispered, biting her lower lip. If I didn't know better, I'd think she was trying to seduce me or something.

"Everyone stagnates with a lack of worthy opponents. If you only get to fight someone weaker than yourself, or if you throw countless numbers at an enemy, they will sooner or later succumb. Two of my friends are truly immortal and they're much stronger than the rest of my group combined."

"I see. That's...would you mind if I kissed you?"

I smiled but wasn't sure what to reply. Sure, she was great-looking, but I wasn't *that* desperate.

Her hand shot forward, and I could have stopped her if I wished to, but I didn't. Before the knife in her hand even made contact, I'd spotted it and was about to swat it away. Instead, I held back and let her stab me. The knife tip broke as it came in contact with my armor, and Najla cried out.

"What is—it should have pierced your side!" she hissed, hurrying to get away from me.

I slowly got to my feet as she hid behind her sofa, squeezing the hand she cut against her chest.

"What in the name of the Dark One are you people?"

"Najla, Najla...that wasn't very smart. Why do you people keep thinking of us as equals? We are not your equals, and for all you know, we're just as godly as Tan'Malas. Now tell me, why would you try something stupid like that?"

"You...You'll get us all killed. The Order, they'll..."

She didn't finish the sentence, but I made a mental note about it.

"Killed? No, it won't come to that," I sighed seeing her

cower like a little girl behind the furniture. "You're as brave as you are stupid."

"What? You can't blame a girl for trying," she sneered. The glare in her eyes was more than I could take at that moment, so I grabbed her and used [Shadow Stride] to appear back outside. I grabbed Najla's ass and swung her over my shoulder, then strode right across the village square and to where Emma and Sonya were preaching to a small group.

I noticed the captain and most of the other soldiers standing to the side, talking animatedly. Mana radiated now from them, the raw power at least five times what it had been. Sure, they were all weak and low-level compared to us, but that could all change. However, I had an ace up my sleeve, namely the two dungeons I still hadn't placed. We would have to try them out and see what they would spawn, so I'd use the land south of our village as a testing ground.

"Does anyone want to sell me a map of these lands? The first person to bring me one gets a 500 gold credit with our store. For a single map that I can get my hands on in Balan Village."

A dozen people hurried off presumably toward their homes to get a map, while others stared at me accusingly, even with anger. A young child lashed out, throwing a small pebble at me.

"Let her go! You monster!"

It bounced off my armor and clattered to the ground. A woman, somewhere in her mid-twenties, grabbed the child and pulled it to her chest.

"I'm sorry, please! I beg you!"

It was only then that I noticed Najla was still hanging off my shoulder.

"Right, my bad," I said, lowering her. My girls were shooting me evil stares, especially as my hand brushed against her ass.

"That was so unnecessary," Sonya said. *"You could have just lowered her, you know?"*

"Yeah, what she said!" Emma added. *"We know you like ass, but come on!"*

I looked at the mother holding the small child in her arms and went to a knee.

"I'm not going to hurt your kid, but you, lady, need to teach your kid not to do that. If I was an asshole, you all would be dead now."

The woman gasped and fell to her knees, sobbing. Many of the people in the crowd let out breaths of relief and I couldn't help but try and put myself in their position. What if it had been me hanging off someone's shoulder or watching my child getting murdered?

"What do you people really take us for, huh? That we're heartless monsters?" I muttered, but those closest to me could hear every word.

"Of course we do! You've killed the inquisitors and—" Najla started to say, but the captain cut her off.

"Enough," he said, raising his voice. "I have been saved by this man and his friends. Come here!"

Captain Samel grabbed Najla by the hand and pulled her toward the statue, pressed it against the indentation, and stepped back. The mayor cried out and then fell to her knees, screaming and pulling at her hair. I wanted to step in and help her to her feet, but he did that for me.

"Hey! Get your shit together!" he snapped. "And stop throwing a tantrum!"

I had seemingly totally misjudged the mayor, and she was far from the woman I'd seen in her. Instead, she was like a child that just broke her favorite toy.

More people gathered around the statue and started going through the process as I stood next to my girls, watching them intently. Benny and the prisoners were still off to the side, while Jeanette and Mortimer were busy overseeing the goods being loaded. That only left one person.

"Selene?"

"Yes? Miss me already?"

"Always, but that's for another conversation. Is everything in order?"

"Yes, of course. I think we're fine for now. Do you want me to come back?"

"Please do."

"Is everything alright?" Grom asked.

"Sure is. We had a—"

"We didn't have a little scuffle, as you were about to say," Jeanette chimed in. *"You told us to kill those poor Tan'Malas' fanatics."*

"Ye what?" Nalgid asked. *"Do we need te prepare?"*

"No, we don't, and Jeanette, don't spread panic. I've got it handled. Elvina?" She still didn't respond, which was unlike her. *"Does anyone know where she is?"*

"I haven't seen her," Callina said. *"But I can go out to look for her. She said something about taking a stroll around the lake."*

"Be careful, love," Mortimer said. *"We're almost done loading the cart, but Cade needs us to visit Balan as well."*

"Don't tell me you can't keep your hands away from him for such a short time, sister?" Emma asked. *"I never hear you scream. Maybe you should join—"*

"Hey! That's my wife. Cade already has the four of you," Mortimer protested.

"But none of it is official," Selene added quickly. *"We should make it official, right? Have a big party and stuff? I wouldn't mind being the first wife. I'll carry your first child with pride."*

"Hey!" both Sonya and Emma said at the same time.

The crowd around us was silent, staring at us as our facial expressions changed and we snorted and laughed. I didn't bother explaining, especially as Jeanette hurried through the gate.

"We're done!"

Two of the men who'd gone off to get maps earlier arrived then, pushing past the crowd to get to me first. The first stumbled over his feet and fell on his face, giving the second man enough time to get to me first. It was surprisingly well-drawn, almost as if he'd been doing it his whole life.

I studied the map, seeing a large lake at the center with a river running south into the sea. At the most southwest point was our village, which he'd marked with a question mark. Garm Village was northwest of it, with Balan going even further west. A village we hadn't visited yet, was at the very top of the lake, Znica Village. It looked larger than Garm and Balan. On the very far east side of the lake was a town, Tazul. Further south across a branch of the river, was Motar Village. Northeast of Tazul was the duke's city of Volarna. It was truly large even on the map, so I figured it could be close to Greystone in size. Maybe a bit smaller.

The entirety of the land surrounding the lake was surrounded by tall mountains, and there was only one mountain pass, or rather, one road that led out of the valley. I figured that the pillar lived somewhere across the mountains, which suited me just fine. There was one thing I knew for sure: nobles and those in power didn't like going to out-of-the-way places to take care of minor nuisances.

"As agreed," I said, offering the man my hand. "Do you want credit or gold? If it's credit I'll add 100 on top."

"Deal, good sir! Thank you very much! If there's anything else you need, I will do it!"

I shook my head.

"No, this is good for now. Mortimer, write the man a 600 gold coin credit note. Everyone else, we're—"

Quest Completed: Spreading The Faith I

Description: The Gods of Old have been forgotten and are in a state of slumber. Revive the belief in the Old Gods.

Status: 5/5 Converted Believers

Reward: The continued existence of the Godveil.

NOTE: The Godveil has stopped
deteriorating and losing its power.

Quest Received: Spreading The Faith II

Description: Continue to help spread
faith in the Gods of old.

Status: 5/50 Converted Believers

Reward: Totem of The Old Gods

NOTE: Shields any place of worship from the
prying eyes of Tan'Malas and his followers.

"Now this is very interesting," I whispered to myself.

If the totem could really prevent anyone from locating us directly, we would have a much easier time attracting people to our temple of worship. And seeing we already had five people, it was only a question of time when that number would rise to 50 and beyond. The one thing that we couldn't do was to force people, as it wouldn't count. Belief was a choice and not a decision made by someone else.

"Captain," I said, turning to Samel. "You've become a believer?"

"Yes, sir. Along with four of my soldiers, even Gordon, I guess the rest will follow soon. Once they open up their minds and hearts, they will see the truth. It's truly all we've ever wanted. Freedom from darkness."

"Then you will have it, I promise. Please guard the statue and allow anyone who wishes to receive a class and be connected to the Godveil to do so. Also, keep an eye on the mayor, but let her write that message and send for help. I truly don't mind if they send an army this way, we will kill them all."

The captain didn't seem so sure about my words, but he nodded and straightened.

"Sir, I thank you. Truly. This is all I've ever wanted and more. I will do my best to serve the Old Gods."

"Good. Now, is there anyone here who knows how to read and write? I need something copied."

CHAPTER 5 – GUILD DUNGEONS

Despite what I had originally wanted, we didn't go to Balan and instead returned home with our captives tied up behind the cart. I didn't want to give them any stupid ideas, and despite Benny and Legs being there among others, I knew fanatics didn't mind dying for a cause they believed in.

We ended up spending several hours in Garm Village, which was more than we'd planned. Still, I considered it a total win. We had test subjects, we had our first believers, and we had all the stuff we needed, including fabric, wheat, and some other stuff we'd ordered. All it had cost us was some store credit, tools, weapons, armor, and processed monster corpses.

Captain Samel's group of soldiers was steadily converting, I could see as much by the rising number of believers. I guessed it would be much easier to convert them than the ordinary folk as once they received a class, everything became all too real. The civilians didn't need to fight the monsters or other soldiers so they couldn't appreciate or understand the difference a class brought, not to mention all the Godveil notifications that would appear in their minds.

Elvina waited for us outside the village walls when we arrived. She didn't look very happy, which made me want to go out and have a chat with her right away. I'd taken her to this place without any real choice, so it only made sense that she was lonely and grumpy.

"What are you going to do with those guys?" the silver-haired helfar asked. She didn't wear her usual pants and bustier but instead had opted for a long, flower-patterned dress. I had to say her look took me by surprise.

"They're test subjects," I said, putting a hand on the side of the cart and jumping off. "Legs, can you take the cart to the workshop? I'll tell them to unload it. Benny, would you mind staying with our... guests?"

"Sure thing, bro," the pangolin said as he jumped off the cart as well, stumbled, and almost fell. "Shit. These short legs, man." He turned back to his Blood Beast form and grabbed the rope the zealots and inquisitors were tied to. "Follow and don't try anything stupid. I'll eat you."

The captives didn't speak though the expressions on their faces were full of malice and misplaced arrogance. We were nobodies to them and they were the servants of the greatest force in the world. What harm could we do to them that they couldn't reciprocate? Well, they'd soon learn.

The girls jumped off the cart as well, and Mortimer also stumbled, but Jeanette caught and steadied him.

"You got to ease up on the food, Morty," she joked. "Callina will leave you for—"

"Don't joke, please," the merchant said with a dignity he probably didn't feel. "We've been together for many years. A few pounds aren't going to—"

"Just kidding, big guy. Go get your woman," she jabbed, pushing him away and chuckling.

"I swear, one of these days someone's going to beat your ass," Emma mumbled. "You're overdoing it, Jeanette."

"Oh, who asked you, man-stealer?"

"Man-stealer? If anyone's stealing men then it's—"

"Shush. You're both embarrassing Cade," Sonya said, raising her voice. "Jeanette. Plug."

"No!" The swashbuckler ran off after Benny. "Wait! I'm coming with you!"

"See what you did?" Selene said, nudging Sonya's side. "Anyway, I think Elvina needs a minute with Cade."

"Always tactful," Emma said. "Come, I want to do your hair, Selene. It needs some combing."

The elf pushed her hands through her hair and scoffed.

"No, it does not!"

"Sure does," Sonya said, putting an arm around her waist and leading her along. "Let's get changed. We don't need to wear battle gear while in the village."

The girls hurried off toward Brahma's Rest as Elvina just stood there, shifting from foot to foot. I wasn't quite sure how to approach whatever it was that bothered her, but I would do my best.

"How are you feeling?"

"Not so very good," she whispered. "You? It's been a busy few months."

"It sure has, and I know I haven't really given you much attention. Things have been, busy, yes. Do you want to go for a walk?"

"Sure. Where to?"

"Anywhere. Do you have a favorite spot?"

She finally looked up at me and met my eyes, tucked a loose strand of hair behind her ear, which then fell back down on her face again.

"I do. There's this nice spot near the mines."

"Alright, let's go."

"Wait, are you sure?" she asked, taking a step back and raising her hands as if in defense. "It's about twenty minutes on foot for us."

"Doesn't matter, and why are you so jumpy? What is it?"

Elvina shrugged her shoulders and remained silent. I didn't want to push it, so I didn't say anything either. At least not for a few seconds.

"Lead the way?"

"Sure. Come on," she said and ran ahead of me.

I didn't need much to catch up to her as my agility and dexterity were much higher than hers. We didn't speak for several minutes, so I enjoyed the view of the silver-haired strider elfar in a patterned dress. I thought it was something I'd never see in a thousand years.

"That dress looks great on you."

Elvina almost tripped over a large branch as I said those words.

"Don't startle me like that!"

"What? I mean it. I really do. You look cute. Much cuter than I'd ever seen you."

She didn't say anything for a long moment again and picked up speed. It wasn't my intention to flirt or to try and get in her panties...wait, was she even wearing them? Luckily, my mind was faster than my mouth this one time and I didn't make a comment, instead focusing on the terrain around me. It would be very embarrassing if I tripped while staring after her.

The forest wasn't so overgrown as it had been when we just arrived. People must have just left it to overgrow and not bothered with it. In a way, it made sense. Why would a village like Garm send people out to cut the trees down near the sea?

"Hey, stop for a moment," I said, spotting a nice little area amidst the cut forest. There were several large rocks placed on top and around each other as if they were forming the entrance to a cave.

"What is it?"

"I want to try something out. We have access to two guild dungeons. I want to put one here. It's far enough from the town and the mine that it shouldn't prove difficult to deal with."

"Wait, what? A dungeon? I mean you can create an open-world guild dungeon?"

"One that summons monsters, yes."

Elvina froze, started to speak, but then her mouth closed.

"What if it goes wrong?"

"Then we get rid of them. Come on, buff us," I said and opened the guild menu. There was a separate tab called Guild Dungeons, which had two different options. The first was called a Minor Guild Dungeon, while the second was a Major

Guild Dungeon. They looked like a swirling monstrous well entrance, dark, deep, and wet.

I read the first description.

• The Minor Guild Dungeon, Level 1 (0/250), will keep spawning monsters at a rate of 1 per minute and up to 100 in total.
• The level of summoned monsters ranges anywhere from 25 to 35.
• The dungeon will accumulate experience points from defeated monsters and level up once it reaches 100 . The level and rarity of summoned monsters as well as the rarity of dropped loot will go up with every level up.
• The rarity of summoned dungeon monsters ranges from common, uncommon, rare, to mini boss.
• The monsters can drop level 1 monster cards, equipment with 1 or 2 enhancements, upgrade materials, and monster ingredients used for crafting.

There were definitely some interesting things in the description like how the dungeon could level up after enough monsters were killed, or that it could spawn mini-bounty hunts, it would give us loot, and the total of monsters summoned wouldn't pass 50 and swarm the entire southern part of the valley.

I went through the second dungeon description next.

• The Major Guild Dungeon, Level 1 (0/100), will keep spawning monsters at a rate of 1 per minute and up to 50 in total.

• The level of summoned monsters ranges anywhere from 40 to 55.

- The dungeon will accumulate experience points from defeated monsters and level up once it reaches 100 . The level and rarity of summoned monsters as well as the rarity of dropped loot will go up with every level up.

- The rarity of summoned dungeon monsters ranges from common, uncommon, rare, mini boss, and mini bounty.

- The monsters can drop level 1 or 2 monster cards, equipment with 1, 2, or 3 enhancements, upgrade materials, monster ingredients used for crafting, and War Beast Eggs.

I read the descriptions to Elvina, and she was equally excited about them, mostly about the possibility of getting War Beast eggs. Now that we didn't have people to pull on, getting a menagerie for Benny was the only real way of expanding our forces.

Elvina picked the pile of large rocks to place the dungeon, and I did as she asked. It was as good a place as any.

"The other one, the minor dungeon, we can put that closer to the water. This way we can create a natural barrier and protect our mines as well."

"And not just the mines, but also our south."

"Agreed, though it could get dangerous with people going back and forth toward the mine."

"We could have someone escort them. There are enough of us around."

Elvina shrugged.

"There's two War Beasts in our village, and then there's us, the girls. We're more than capable of handling these monsters and then some."

The silver-haired strider's mood seemed to have

improved greatly after mentioning monsters and dungeons to her. I guessed it was a sort of coping mechanism that she used not to think about her problems, about the loss we all endured, and even about her uncle.

Do you wish to build the Major Guild Dungeon?

[Yes] – [No]

I chose yes and watched the stones form around the dungeon, growing until the mound was about fifteen feet tall and as wide. The inside of the dungeon was dark as, well, any darkness I'd ever seen. Something stirred within, and I lunged away just as a feral cat-like monster with thick black fur, long claws, and a monstrous snout jumped out.

"It's a Snout Shredder," Elvina said, raising her crossbow and unleashing a single skill. A massive bolt the size of my arm appeared locked in place and then flew straight into the creature. "Yes, definitely," she whispered as the bolt pierced its neck, and passed right through.

You have received 0.3 experience.

Great. At 0.3% per kill, I would only need to kill over three hundred of these higher-level monsters to level up. That number would exponentially grow with every new level. Still, since I was at level 53, grinding out 7 levels wasn't that bad.

The monster, to my surprise, dropped a monster card. I picked it up and snorted. It was an ordinary Dodge I card. Still, it would help someone else who didn't have any equipped cards. Nothing else dropped, but the corpse remained. I placed it in our guild storage and turned back toward the dungeon.

Elvina seemed ready to kill anything that came out, so I stopped her.

"Let me place the other dungeon first, then I want to see that place you told me about."

"The one at the mine?"

"Yeah, that one. Now, where should I put..ahh, there's a

nice spot."

I gathered several of the felled trees and placed them in a rough half-circle, then built the dungeon in their midst. The trees expanded and merged until they had created a fifteen-foot-tall wooden portal surrounded by a cracked log. It looked much less imposing than the second dungeon, but that didn't matter. We needed the monsters.

"Do you want to wait? And see what comes out?" I asked, and she shook her head.

"I want to show you the place."

I looked at the two dungeons one more time and saw more monsters getting out, but they didn't attack us, and instead spread out across what looked like a red, glowing field. I hadn't noticed it right away, and maybe it hadn't even been there moments before. The red field spread easily some hundred yards in every direction.

I watched the monsters a minute longer, and it was just as I thought. The moment they touched the border of the red field, some kind of force pushed them back, not letting them leave. That was fantastic.

"Elvina? Can you see the red border surrounding the dungeons?"

"What red border?"

"So you can't. Good. Then anyone who wants to hit us from the south will have another thing coming."

"Whatever you say. Can we go now? I'm not in the mood for killing more of those things today."

"Sure. Let's go."

I followed her for several more minutes, running and jumping, and finally using [Shadow Stride] once we got to the spot. It was a small cliff that overlooked the valley, and I could even see our village from there, the mine, the dungeons, the lake, and far away in the distance, Garm Village.

To my surprise, there was a small sitting area complete with two benches, a small table, and even blankets.

"Is this where you've been staying over the last weeks?"

She nodded and sat on one of the benches, wrapped a blanket around her, despite it being warm outside, and stared out toward the lake. I remained silent for a while, just letting her settle in and enjoy the view. It was truly remarkable, I had to admit, and how golden rays of sunshine caught the surface of the lake, creating a shimmering effect.

"I miss him, Cade," Elvina said after a long moment. "I miss him so badly, and even after telling myself that it would be alright and that he had to do it, I just come here to cry and be by myself. I think about him and why he did it, why he sacrificed his life, and...it was for nothing in the end. That's the part that really hurts. He died for nothing."

She had a point, but I wasn't going to tell her that. The Shadow Sage was a lot of things, but a fool wasn't one of them. He had character, power, confidence, and poise. With some luck, I could become just like him one day.

"I liked him. A lot. He helped me several times and listened to what I had to say," I started. "If it hadn't been for him, I don't know if Emma and I would have made it. Everything seemed lost when we returned to Greystone after Zekan massacred my friends. Sometimes all it takes is just a small nudge or a nice word, you know? And that's what he did. He made me realize everything would be fine one day, and it was."

"That's who he really was," Elvina chuckled. "He'd try to help everyone, and that's exactly what got him messed up with the wrong people. At least they're all dead now, right?"

"Not everyone," I muttered.

"What do you mean? No, wait, us. We're still alive, obviously. Maybe some other people survived too? This is definitely not the place that teleport scroll should have brought us."

"And how do you know?"

"Because uncle told me about that place all the time. It was mostly desert and the family stronghold was built around an oasis and—yeah, that doesn't matter anymore, does it?"

"I guess it doesn't, but things aren't as simple as you think. Look, I had a talk with the captain of the soldier detachment. He told me about 13 pillars of Tan'Malas, and one of them...is called Zekan."

Elvina gasped and dropped the blanket she'd been holding around herself.

"What are you—Zekan? Pillars? Cade, what are you talking about?"

I let out a deep sigh and handed her the second blanket.

"I think you might need this after I tell you what I've found out. Things don't look very good, Elvina. And I'm afraid that I've overplayed my card."

"Okay, then talk to me. What did you find out?" she asked, taking the second blanket and tucking herself in.

I started with everything Samel had told me, then the mayor, and the general situation in Garm Village, as well as the new quests. Even though she'd started out terrified after I mentioned Zekan, a weak smile graced her beautiful face once I was done.

"That only means we have one way forward, right?"

"Right, and I will need you there with me. Think you can do that? Become one of us?"

"Sleep with you? What will that do to help us?" she yelled.

"Not sleep with me, silly. Bind with me. Both our powers will go up. You'll share 10% from each of the girls. Speaking of which, I need to step up my game and get the intimacy with Emma up."

"Intimacy? Game? No, never mind. Yes, the girls told me all about the soulbinding thing, and I've been meaning to mention it, but I'm afraid."

"Of what?" I asked, already having a suspicion, but I wanted to hear it from her. Giving someone else reign over your life wasn't an easy thing to do, especially if you didn't have strong feelings for them. Emma, Sonya, and Jeanette were one thing, Selene...was different, but Elvina was just someone who'd been whisked off along with us and forced to adapt.

"What if you get yourself killed? I don't want to die because of someone else."

"And that's totally understandable, so I'm not going to force you. If you ever decide that you want to take the next step, even if it's a baby step, you know that we're all there for you, right? And yes, I've noticed how you've distanced yourself from the girls. It isn't just this place, but even during dinner or breakfast, hell, you're so late that I often don't even hear you coming home during the night."

"I know," she whispered and looked away, clutching at the blanket. "I'm just trying so hard, and nothing's working. I hate this place, I hate that we had to come here, and I hate that I don't have anyone to kill!"

So that was it...With someone like the Shadow Sage as her uncle and guardian, and considering her overkill traps, Elvina had gained a desire for murder. It wasn't the worst trait, but definitely something that I'd need to keep an eye on.

A soft breeze carried Elvina's sweet scent. Her chest rose under the blanket as she took in a deep breath. She had covered herself up to her chin, but that somehow made her more irresistible. I almost succumbed to the notion of kissing the white naked skin of her neck, but shook the thought away.

"So you want to go to battle?"

"Of course! That's what I was raised to do!"

Elvina shot to her feet and threw off both blankets, staring at me with her piercing eyes. She suddenly seemed determined and angry.

"What are you planning to do with those prisoners?"

"Convert...them or something?"

"I want to try out my torture rack. Will you give me one of them?"

"To torture?"

"No, to coddle," she muttered. "Of course to torture. I want to know more about this world. I want to know where I can fight their kind."

I smiled wryly and shot her a wink.

"Well, that shouldn't be a problem. They'll be here sooner rather than later, Elvina. I want to take out the sub pillars and all the fanatics in these lands. Care to help me?"

"Will you bind me?"

"If you want to," I said with a wink.

The silver-haired strider put her hands on her hips and smiled.

"Alright, let's do it."

CHAPTER 6 – INTERROGATION GONE WRONG

Elvina was visibly nervous, but so was I. This time things were a bit different, as she had shown absolutely no interest in being with me. We had enough time, though, or so I hoped. Given that our bodies were nearly indestructible and that aging wasn't really a thing, I could see us becoming a thing.

"It's pretty simple, alright? I will initiate the prompt, and you will accept. It would be smart if you remained seated, though, as the rush of power could knock you out."

"Okay," the strider said simply and sat, taking in a deep breath. "You can go ahead."

I selected my Soulbound card and sent her a request to bind with her. A small jolt of pleasure and power shot through me, and I knew she accepted then. For her, it was a much stronger surge.

"I—what is—wait I can—feel them?" Elvina gasped. "W—what is this? You didn't tell me that this would happen!"

"What the—what is this?" Jeanette cried over the mental link. Both Elvina and I could feel her distress.

Emma was next.

"Why can we feel each other now? What did you do?"

A notification popped up before me, and it wasn't going to make the girls happy, not at all.

```
Hidden Quest Completed: Soulbinding 101
```

Description: Find and Soulbind with three different races of the opposite gender.

Status: 3/3

Reward: Increased sensitivity and intimacy between the Soulbound, Raise all stats 1

"*So, about that,*" I said and read the hidden quest. "*No more binding other races, I get it. My bad.*"

"*You had to,*" Sonya said. "*It's okay. We'll learn to live with it, but I have to say, by Tan'Aria, Jeanette here has some complicated feelings. And Selene? Don't get me started.*"

"*Hey, keep that to yourself!*" Selene retorted. "*I don't wish to talk about my feelings so everyone can listen in!*"

"*Please, enough,*" I said, cutting them off from any further yelling. "*We'll talk about everything tonight after dinner, alright? The day is still long, and there's a lot to do. Alright?*"

The girls agreed and I sighed and slumped further into the small wooden bench.

"Are you alright?"

Elvina nodded hurriedly but she seemed to be having trouble breathing as she gasped for air.

"I—just give me a minute." I was about to scoot over but she held her hand out. "Give me some space."

I did as she said and looked away onto the lake, checking my stats after the new soulbinding. The whole process was a bit anticlimactic, but whatever. As long as it still worked, I was totally fine with no explosions and rainbows.

My eyes first moved to the free stats, which I hadn't used in a while. I had a total of 26 spare points to use on any stat point. All my stats were more or less balanced aside from strength, which wasn't one of the main class stats, but I found that the stronger I was, the easier I could punch through someone or something with my daggers. After another quick glance, I decided to follow my guts and added them all on strength. My armor shifted instantly and slightly expanded to hold in my now-larger muscle mass.

CLASS CARD			
Name	Cade	Race	Human
Level	53	Experience	38%
Class	Assassin	Sub-Class	Plague Revenant
Strength	172	Stamina	172
Agility	178	Dexterity	181
Charisma	128	Free Stats	0

A grin spread across my face as I couldn't hold it in. Those stats were totally insane and far beyond anything I'd ever imagined. Just the stat points from my girls added between 40 and 60 points per different stat. Then there was the ring of life that added 15 points to all stats, special and upgrade effects on my gear, that also added a nice chunk...

I checked my special stat growth next and was happy with some of the increases, but not so much with others. Dodge had gone past 80%, which meant that with all the dodge buffs I got from the girls, I would be insanely hard to hit. Sure, I wouldn't be able to get away from skills or spells that innately had to hit, but other than that, I loved my overall survivability. The rest of my special stats had gone up as well, some only a few percent, others a bit more, but all in all, I was satisfied.

SPECIAL STATS			
Accuracy	166%	Dodge	82%
Critical Hit	56%	Critical Damage	175%
Defense Penetration	28%	Physical Resistance	54%
Magical Resistance	52%	Debuff Resistance	66%
Debuff Accuracy	95%	Debuff Effectiveness	71%
Debuff Duration	153%	Attack Reach	159%

"*Hey, Benny,*" I said over our link. "*I want to wrestle your ass when we're back. You should see my stats, boy. I think you're going to cry."*

"No! You're cheating! You're a bad, bad man, bro! You're using the power of your ladies and call it your own! That's not how power should work!"

"Hey, calm down, you little shit. What are you yelling for?"

"Oh, sorry, my bad. I was just yelling at some of our prisoners. My bad."

"Are they misbehaving?"

"No, but one shat himself and it stinks."

"Fuck's sake. Callina? Could you prepare the prisoners some food, please? Nothing special, just the most ordinary food you can make."

"No, she can't! She's busy now, with me! Hah!" Mortimer cackled.

"Shit, they're so totally fucking," Sonya chuckled.

"I bet you tonight's fuck that he won't last another 2 minutes," Jeanette laughed.

"More like 1 minute," Selene said. *"I can feel the fluctuations in his mana. He's about to—"*

"Three minutes," Callina sighed. *"Please, give him some credit, ladies."*

"Oh, she can speak and make love at the same time. That's a good trait to have," Emma chuckled.

"Girls, is it just me, or can I hear your expressions now as well?" I asked.

"I can hear them too. Jeanette's laughter is annoying," Selene replied and a mind-speak war broke out then as all the girls started arguing. My mind felt as if it was going to explode, but I let it go on for a minute. They needed to release all that tension, but after a second thought, there were better ways to release it all.

"Hey, I have an idea," I said, raising my mental voice, which just worked strangely. *"Shut up for a moment and listen. Tonight we'll have a wrestling match between the four of you. The winner gets to—"*

"I'm so going to win!" Jeanette said, interrupting me.

"*Maybe, maybe not. Now keep it down, my head's about to explode. See you in a bit.*"

I glanced at Elvina, but she was still looking away and lost in thoughts, so I used the time for yet another issue, or rather, several issues.

"*Nalgid?*"

"*Bossman? What can I do fer ye?*"

"*I need a dungeon or a prison. Think you can help me with that?*"

"*Sure, sure. I heard ye wanted a temple. What about that?*"

"*That's the second issue. I want that temple built. A big one.*"

"*And ye want my clan te do it all?*"

"*Of course. We'll all pitch in if you want, but I know how protective you are about building stuff.*"

"*Hah! Ye got that right, boss man. When and where?*"

"*Tell you in a bit when I'm back. Out here with Elvina. Was having a chat and stuff.*"

"*Okay. Talk to ye when yer back.*"

It was a short conversation, but that's how dwarves liked it. They weren't the chatty types, at least not very often unless they had something to drink beforehand. We learned to accept each other's flaws and mannerisms, otherwise, things wouldn't be going as smoothly.

"*Grom?*" I said next, wanting to give him a heads-up.

"*Cade? Is everything alright?*"

"*Of course, big guy. We will need stone. A lot of it.*"

"*For what? If you don't mind me asking. We were just about to have lunch.*"

"*No, not right now, Grom. Hell, man. Go eat. Talk to me when you're done.*"

As was usual for the big elgar, he didn't respond and probably went back to eating. I eyed Elvina, who had just stirred out of her stupor, and put my hand on her knee, squeezing gently.

"Wh—what are you doing?" she cried, jumping to her

feet. I stood as well.

"Let's go. We need to get that torture rack of yours set up."

"Rack? Are you talking about my breasts? Benny calls them racks as well when he's talking to Legs."

"No, I—what? He does? Why? That doesn't make sense."

"He's your pet, not mine. And okay. Let me stash the blankets away and tidy this up."

"Sure. I'll help you."

We stopped to check the monsters before we headed back, and despite the Godveil's description, they were all of the lowest rarity and near the bottom with levels. That was good, though, as those who needed the practice would have a place of relative safety to fight the monsters.

Elvina killed a few, and so did I, but nothing aside from their corpses dropped. And a few monster ingredients. Once we were done putting them away in the guild storage, the two of us made it back to the village. There was no one to be seen as they usually spent their days in the workshop, mine, or just at home.

"Benny?"

"What is it, bro?"

"Where are you guys? Did you eat the prisoners?"

"No, we're up at Brahma's Rest. They're behaving."

"Okay. Be right there," I replied and pointed up toward the small hill. "They're probably eating. Benny took them to the main building."

"Don't tell me that we'll have to give them our rooms or something."

"No, not your rooms. Just your time. Come on."

We hurried up the hill and found them all sitting on the ground, but the rope had been untied. They were busy eating meat from wooden plates. It was the most readily available source of food, so I didn't mind. As long as it wasn't fish. Those things were dangerous to catch, and we only sent Benny down into the water.

"Gentlemen," I said.

"Yo, you're back. Does that mean I can go now?"

"Sure thing, Benny. Go enjoy your free time. I'll call you if I need you."

"Legs!" he roared. "Meet me at the lake!"

A loud screech came from the village's east. The War Weaver appeared as he ran through the forest and jumped over the wall, tried to skid to a halt, but fell over onto his side. Benny rushed over to him and helped the spider back up, patting his bulbous body.

It was a comical sight, one that made me chuckle and momentarily forget about the prisoners. They, however, remained seated and just ate in silence. The door to Brahma's Rest slammed shut, and I figured it was Elvina going inside as she wasn't there anymore.

I took a deep breath and eyed them for a moment. None of them were wounded anymore, and I figured Emma must have healed all fifteen.

"Listen up as I won't say this again. If you try to run, you die. If you try to fight, you die even worse. If you try to hurt one of my girls or any of my friends, you will suffer torture worse than any you could have ever dreamed of. If you understand, just grunt or make a noise as you're eating. Don't want you to talk with your full mouths."

Most of them made some sort of noise, and I nodded appreciatively.

"Alright, see? We're getting along already. Now, you two are in charge?" I asked, pointing at the two inquisitors.

The right one raised his hand.

"I am," he said defiantly. He had a tattoo of a spear across a shield on the top of his scalp. It was black with a golden, glowing outline.

"Name?"

"Feros."

"Rank?"

"R—rank?" He exchanged looks with the man next to

him and then shrugged. "I'm an inquisitor," he said with a judgemental grin. These guys were used to obedience and had little experience being on the other side of power. I was eager to give them a taste.

"Okay, so that's one rank. What other ranks are there? Both below and above you."

I pulled a chair from my storage and sat across from him, pulled out a bottle of the red stuff Samel liked, and handed it to him. I wanted to see how far manners and respect would take me before I did anything harsh. Feros reached out carefully, but when he saw I wasn't going to do anything to him, he took the bottle and nodded.

"Thank you. Can I?"

"Sure. Take a sip."

He popped the bottle open and took a healthy swig, then cursed.

"Shit! This is strong! What is it made—no, never mind. So, ranks, you say?"

"Ranks I say."

"So you don't know about the ranks of the Order?"

There it was again. The Order.

"Have you been asleep for the last few centuries or something?"

I gave him a wry smile. Despite being manhandled by a War Beast, despite ending up a prisoner, his arrogance never faltered. No wonder, the servants of the Dark Lord had ruled unopposed for so long that they felt invincible.

I let him think like that for a little while longer.

"Let's say I'm not a local."

He smirked.

"Fine, stranger. Here's how it works. The lowest rank is an acolyte. They usually serve as aides until they become strong enough to fight. Then there are the zealots, which are these guys," he said, nodding to his right where the thirteen were seated. "I am an inquisitor, just like Rezak here." He nudged the man sitting on his left. "There are the interrogators

71

who are above the inquisitors, and there's usually one in every town or village. Ours...died last year, and still hasn't been replaced."

"And their interrogations? I doubt they're peaceful."

Feros shook his head.

"No, they're not. Interrogators are trained by sub-pillars, who are at the head of smaller armies stationed in strategically important places."

"Like the capital city of a region?"

"Or places of importance like mines or mountain passes. Lastly, there are the pillars. They govern countries, or huge regions and are—"

The other inquisitor, Rezak, elbowed him and the two shared a look.

"What does it matter, Rezak?" Feros said, "People know this, it's not a secret. What do you think he'll do if I tell him about the pillars? Defeat them?"

"We shouldn't talk to our enemies, no matter what it is about," Rezak retorted.

"It's simple, Rezak. If you don't tell me, I'll kill one of you and then have the other tell me. If neither wants to, I'll just find another inquisitor. Or interrogator. Or whatever."

"We are ready to die for our god Tan'Malas!" Rezak cried.

I pulled out my kris and jammed it into his mouth, then stored it back away as he fell lifeless to the ground. The extended mana aura around the blade had ripped through his brain and the back of his head, killing him instantly.

"You were saying, Feros?"

The man gulped as he stared at the corpse of his co-inquisitor, then looked to the bottle in his hand, drank some more, and gulped again. The thirteen men and women sitting to his right looked as if they were frozen, none of them moving.

"Go on, eat. I'm not going to kill you unless you're stupid. And if you're stupid, you deserve to die anyway," I said, then turned toward the wall. "Benny! There's a corpse here for you!

Stock up on blood if you're running low!"

"All good, bro!" he shot back. "I'm trying to get Legs to go fishing with me, but he's being a little bitch, yo!"

"Good luck! And catch me one of those red ones! They taste good!" I shot back. "So, we were talking about pillars."

"Yes, pillars. They're...at the very top of our religion."

His eyes darted back and forth between me and the dead inquisitor at his side.

"Which is an army, more or less, right?"

Feros nodded.

"It is much more than that, but yes, it is an army that defends our belief in Tan'Malas."

His words became laced with venom. Rezak's death didn't sit well with the inquisitor, nor should it.

"And the ordinary soldiers? Say the duke's army. What about them? Do you work together?"

The bald man shook his head.

"No, we don't. They never interfere with whatever we do unless we tell them to. Nobody," he said stressing the word, "Interferes with what we do."

"It all boils down to fear, doesn't it, Feros? It's your most important asset."

The inquisitor grunted.

"Of course it is," he scoffed, "It is good to fear the Dark Lord. It gives you purpose."

"Like it gave purpose to the mayor when she tried to stab me?"

Feros smiled.

"She is brave."

"And stupid."

"You truly know nothing of our faith, do you? How can someone like *you* be so completely clueless? The Dark Lord encompasses the whole world. His word orders the sun to rise and set, the winds to blow, and the seas to ebb, and yet here you are."

There was disgust on the inquisitor's face.

"A true god, isn't he? Tan'Malas."

"Of course he is," Feros barked through clenched teeth. He had shed all pretense at civility. Decades of authority growled through him, trying to claw their way back to their rightful place.

"Both you and your god are blinded by the same things, power, and fear," I said, locking eyes with him.

I felt the interrogation slipping out of my hands, but it wasn't my doing. Feros might have indulged me at first but at the core of his being, he was the same as Rezak who now lay there in a pool of his own blood.

"And what would you know, stranger? None of these people here would know peace if it wasn't for the Dark Lord and the Order. This entire continent suffered nothing but war until it was united under his name."

"United? Fear doesn't unite. It only masks the truth."

"You speak like a librarian, but you're a killer at heart."

I couldn't say that didn't sting. I never thought of myself as just a killer but now that he said it, I could understand why people would see me that way.

"I am," I said playing along, "And you should keep that in mind when I ask you questions."

He snorted and looked away. My patience was thinning quickly. Too quick for a proper interrogator. Perhaps I wasn't cut out for that line of work.

"You see these men and women?" Feros said, nudging toward the zealots. "They'll all die before they turn traitor. So ask your questions, use your tools, torture us, kill us. Do what you think you need to, but you'll never shake our faith."

"I was there when your god escaped imprisonment," I said, trying another angle. Feros' eyes widened.

"He was locked in a war with the True Gods, destroyed my city, and killed thousands. You might find it hard to hear this, but Tan'Malas is nothing but Tan'Drak's aspect. A fragment of a god, nothing else. His power is fickle, but his dreams are big. It's no wonder weak-minded men like you flock to his teachings."

"Heretic," the inquisitor hissed, clenching his teeth and then spitting on the ground. "How dare you…"

He was seething but there was a visible confusion on his face too. I assumed I said something that I *shouldn't* have known. Something that people outside the inner circle were supposed to be ignorant about.

"Where is the pillar of this region?" I asked, more or less knowing I had missed my chance.

"Heretic," Feros repeated, the words dipped in poison, "Who are you?"

"Answer my question, Feros."

He spat on the ground a second time. Yap, the only way I'd get anything out of Feros or the zealots would be to utilize torture, but I wasn't really confident that would get me anywhere either.

"Who are you?" he asked again, raising his voice.

I got up from the chair and sighed.

"I'm a heretic, Feros. You said it right. The greatest of all the heretics you met. I saw your god up there above the city, Feros. With these two eyes, I saw him struggle against the True Gods. And I will see him struggle again, struggle and fail."

"You will burn for those words!" Feros glanced at his zealots and then back at me.

He kissed the back of his hand and traced his fingers down from the top of his head to his chin.

"The pillar needs to know of this," Feros said, his hand tensing around the bottle.

"Don't do anything stupid. There are far worse things that can happen to you than death."

All thirteen zealots threw their food my way as one and jumped to action as Feros started glowing. I had my dagger back out in a second, but three of the zealots had jumped in between us.

"The fuck?" I cursed, stabbing through them and pulling the dagger back out. I couldn't use any of my shadow skills as the inquisitor was leaning his back against the wall.

I pushed the three dying men aside and was tackled by two more. Or rather, they tried to tackle me but it was as if they'd hit a mountain. I couldn't use any area of effect spells either as I'd kill the man.

Shit, shit, shit!

The glow intensified and a beam formed over his head, moving upwards into the sky. I came to a split decision and used [Blade Storm], the only area of effect attack I had that could deal enough damage to kill them all instantly. Blades of mana formed in the air around me, cutting into all the zealots and the lone inquisitor. Bodies fell apart around me, and the blue beam that had been reaching for the sky dissipated, dying before it could fully connect with the clouds.

"Hey, what's going on, bro?" Benny asked over our link. He had some tact at least, and asked me directly.

"I don't know, man, but I think I might have fucked up."

CHAPTER 7 – BUILDING A TEMPLE

"So, there is no way that you could have left just one of them alive?" Elvina yelled. "You promised!"

"Well, if you want one so badly, then let's go and get one!" I snapped back. "I'm sorry to have treated them like humans and—"

"That's not it! I didn't get to try the torture rack!"

"Torture rack?" Emma and Sonya asked a the same time, and Jeanette just snorted, which turned into full-blown laughter. Only Selene wasn't finding it amusing at all.

We were seated around the bar, drinking and yelling at each other. Thanks to the quick intervention, no one had seen the pillar of light. No one but Benny and me. So far.

"Why don't we decide on what blueprint to use, alright?" I asked, pulling the two smaller temple blueprints from the storage. Personally, I liked the smaller one more but it made sense to go with the middle temple. If it worked, then I'd be happy to build the smaller one on the cliff where Elvina had brought me.

"Middle one," she said, leaning in to see better. "I don't think we'll ever need that big one."

"Middle one," Sonya and Emma said in unison, looked at each other, and then started chuckling.

"They're so annoying," Jeanette muttered. "If they looked alike, at all, I'd think the two were twins."

"Hey, what do you say about dying our hair?" Emma asked Sonya. "Maybe you could—"

"No, no way. I'm not doing," she said and pointed at

Emma's hair, "That. It doesn't look good on me. I already tried once."

"Oh? Tell me all about it," Emma said as she scooted over to sit next to the black-haired beauty.

"I guess this meeting is—"

"No, it is not," Selene said, interrupting me. "There's the matter of making things official."

"That you're sleeping with Cade?" We already know that," Jeanette said. "It's only a matter of time before he starts banging the helfar."

"I'm not *the helfar*, I got a name," Elvina retorted without looking up from the blueprint. "And the more I look at this, the more I like it Cade."

I stared at Jeanette, but she just smirked in response.

"One of these days I'm really going to keep you at the back of the line. That's a promise."

Her mouth dropped open and a scowl made it up on her face, but then she just looked away, huffing and puffing. I didn't enjoy being an ass, but Jeanette worked the bar for way too long. Not only did she have a foul mouth, but she'd also become pretty rough around the edges. Especially with other women.

"As I was saying. The ceremony."

"What ceremony, Selene?" I asked, unsure what she meant.

"The marriage ceremony. I don't think any of us is going to be chasing down other men, so we might as well make it official."

"Oh, oh! Yes! I like it!" Emma said excitedly. "Once the temple is complete! We can have a ceremony and all!"

"I like it too," Sonya added. "The Gods will look more kindly on us if we bond for life."

"We're already bound for life, Sonya," Jeanette muttered. "We're soul-bound, but I like the idea. Hell, maybe we can even invite our newly converted. How many do we have anyway?"

That was a very good question. I pulled the quest up and checked it.

Quest Received: <u>Spreading The Faith II</u>

Description: Continue to help spread
faith in the Gods of old.

Status: 23/50 Converted Believers

Reward: Totem of The Old Gods

NOTE: Shields any place of worship from the
prying eyes of Tan'Malas and his followers.

"I have no idea if this is good or not, but we're at 23 already."

"That's good, I think? Just imagine if someone were to show up to a small village where you lived all your life, and said that you believed in something evil," Sonya said, trying to explain her view on the matter. And she was right.

"I've got a more important question," Elvina said. "Where do we put the temple? I'm not sure if we should put it anywhere our enemies could get to easily."

That was another valid comment, and it made me think. Sure, the newly converted would maybe feel safer if the temple was further north, but no, we wouldn't be able to keep it as safe. Not only that but if we put up traps, they couldn't tell friends from enemies. An idea struck me.

"Hear me out before you start yelling, alright?" I said, tapping the counter. All five pairs of eyes landed on me. "So, what if we start a new village just south of ours?"

"What is our village called, anyway?" Jeanette asked. "I'd like to be able to tell people where I was from."

"New Greystone?" Sonya proposed.

"I like it. You girls?"

Emma smiled and hugged the black-haired beauty.

"I knew there was a reason I took you in!"

"Took me in? I thought Cade took me in," she said, hugging the priestess back.

"I did, but only thanks to Emma. Anyway. Jeanette?

Selene? Elvina?"

"Sure, whatever," Jeanette mumbled. "New Greystone. Well, it has a ring to it."

"I'm fine with the name," Selene said, sending me an impish smile.

"Yes, I like it too," the helfar said. "Temple. Where?"

"We put the temple inside New Greystone and expand the wall toward the south. Make just enough room for say...200 new people?"

"There are over a thousand people up in Garm, and would they even want to move?" Sonya asked. "If they remain in Garm, they'll still be able to claim innocence. I doubt Tan'Malas' people have a way to check them."

"Unless they use torture," Jeanette said. "Which is very likely after what our love did here. He literally sliced them up."

"Which Benny then had to clean up, might I add," Emma chuckled. "Oh, he wasn't happy about that."

"Well, tough luck. I had more important matters to attend to," I said, picking up my glass and drinking down the amber liquid. "So, what do we do? I don't want to push anything on you girls."

"I'm okay with adding new people as long as they can contribute in a way," Selene said. "Considering Garm Village is self-sustainable, I vote yes."

"Me too," Elvina added. "But I don't think they'll want to. They're too afraid, and once they stop being afraid, they won't need to move."

"Then we can just put the temple within our walls and rearrange it. Once we feed the blueprint, we can always make it smaller or whatever. We got a clan of dwarves."

There was more than enough space once we removed what we'd called the park. It got moved closer to the water, which bothered no one. We all stood around the space where the temple was going to be built, and I held the blueprint out, studying it. The Godveil would allow me to see how the temple would look like when finished, though it was a translucent image.

"I think it looks best if we have the temple face toward the northeast," I said, rotating the image.

No one else could see the temple, so I handed the parchment to Nalgid, who would be in charge of the building process. Grom would have been the go-to guy if it wasn't for the Blackforge Clan, but despite us being here for over two months, he was still all over his wife and using every moment to catch up with his sons.

"Yes, yer right. It looks marvelous like that. Half of the temple will show over the village walls. Anyone with half a mind will know what it is."

"And it won't obstruct anyone's view," I added. "It will be as if the temple was always part of the village."

"Agreed," Ferid said as he held the parchment in his hand.

They passed the blueprint around so everyone could have a look. It was a funny sight to see all of their families outside as they usually didn't like the sunlight that much. Their shoulders were wide, arms bulging with muscles, and every one of them sported a beard. Aside from the women, that is, and some of the sons had some real height. Dwarves were mostly a head shorter than the average man or woman, but the Blackforge Clan almost looked as if they were just bulked-up humans.

"So we all agree?"

They nodded in agreement, letting Nalgid speak for them.

"What about the prison?"

"Don't need it for now. Temple first."

"Aye, alright. Set the foundation. I want to see how much time we'll need."

I pushed some mana into the blueprint and accepted the building prompt. A foundation about two feet in height appeared out of nowhere, taking up 60 yards in both length and width. Above it was a notification of the necessary amount of raw materials.

I read over the list.

```
NAME: Medium Sized Temple

DESCRIPTION: This blueprint allows the owner to
  set the foundation for a generic medium sized
temple that can hold up to 500 people at a time.

     NECESSARY BUILDING MATERIALS:
         WOODEN LOGS: 1,500
         STONE BLOCKS: 2,500
          STEEL BEAMS: 120
```

"Shit, this is going to take a long time," I cursed, reading the list out loud.

"What ye think us for?" Nalgid hissed. "Children? We will have this ready in two weeks!"

"Just over a week if we help as well," Grom said.

"We will help too," I added. "But I won't solely be focused on this place. We need to go to Balan as well, and I want to scout the other villages. See if we can get our hands on some other inquisitors. Maybe even a sub-pillar?"

"I would like to go with you," Merek said. "My skill set is similar to Grom's, but I am much faster. And you won't know I'm there."

"Agree," I said. "Anyway, you can start, Nalgid. Once the temple is up, you can do a building for yourselves. I know you mentioned a—"

"No, not that. We want a second home near the mines. It's bothersome te go back and forth 5 times every day. That fine with ye?"

"Totally. Also, since we're already here, I wanted to mention the monsters to the south. We built two open-type guild dungeons out there. The more we kill, the higher their level will go, and the better rewards we'll start to receive. Their levels are pretty low and—"

I continued to explain everything that we knew, and everyone seemed much more excited about killing monsters than building a temple. Still, it needed to be done.

Quest Completed: Spreading The Faith II

Description: Continue to help spread faith in the Gods of old.

Status: 50/50 Converted Believers

Reward: Totem of The Old Gods

Quest Received: Spreading The Faith III

Description: Continue to help spread faith in the Gods of old.

Status: 50/250 Converted Believers

Reward: Aura of the Believer

NOTE: Aura of the Believer is a passive buff that raises all stats by 5 points for 24 hours for those who pray within the assigned temple.

"Things are progressing a bit faster than I assumed they would," I said, reading the third quest from what was set up to be a long-ass quest chain. I didn't mind a long chain quest, of course, as it seemed that the rewards went up with every completion.

"This aura is basically a permanent and passive buff," Merek said. "We need more of those, especially to train all the newly converted."

"Not just that, Merek. We need all the buffs we can get our hands on. Once they come in numbers, even an ordinary converted will become a capable fighter after a few days of hunting monsters."

"Exactly what I—wait, I'm not so sure of that. Is it better

to have a mass of weak fighters, or a very strong one?" he asked, and I knew what he was going at. "You should hit level 60 as soon as you can, Cade. That's when you'll hit your last evolution, and from what I know, the rise in stats is really steep."

I stared at him for a moment, and then at Sonya. She was the only person we had with area-of-effect spells. They were pretty basic and part of her elemental orb, but that didn't matter.

Judging by the soldiers and even the inquisitors we met, the duke's forces were relatively weak. In comparison to Greystone's knights, or even the city watch, the armed men and women of Volarna were little more than a meat shield. If my assumption was correct, anything that had magic energies to it could kill a dozen or two of the duke's men with ease.

"Sonya should be at the top of the list then. And Elvina with her traps. They're the real muscle," I said, and meant it. The helfar had gotten us out of several sticky situations with her insanely creative and deadly traps. I sure wouldn't want to be on the sharp end of that stick.

"Let's agree to disagree. Anyway, what about you, Nalgid? What about your family? Do you want them to grind some levels?"

He grunted and cursed and spoke to himself for a long moment before he finally sighed. I figured he was talking to his family, but didn't know what about.

"Ferid, Mirna, and I are already over level 50. All of our kids are over level 40, and with so many of us, yes, ye can see where I'm going with this."

"He's right," Mirna said. "Let us deal with this first, then we can think about getting stronger. What is the spawn rate of the dungeons?"

"One monster every minute for both dungeons."

"They're both at full capacity then," Elvina said. "It's been a while since we got back."

"And you'll be fine without me?" I asked, looking the

crowd over.

"What? Yer not me mother, boss man. I've been alive two or three of yer lives. Go be the boss and let us do this. Clan, get yer axes. We'll first finish with the logs."

"We will start cutting stone," Grom said with a nod.

"And we'll just look pretty, or something," Jeanette mumbled. "What do you want us to do?"

"Keep an eye out on the north," I said and then looked at Selene. "Do you want to join me? We need to have a chat."

The sound of axes slamming into large tree trunks could be heard even as far as the dungeon spawn points. Monsters filled the entire clearing, and a smaller number were roaming the forest surrounding the clearing we'd used.

We stood on the small rise west of the monster-filled area. Selene snuggled up against me, which was nice but felt odd as I still wasn't used to seeing her as one of my girls. It was almost a dream come true having her on board, though, as she brought something different to my little group of lovely ladies. She was an elf. Sure, our bodies were almost identical but for the ears, which were elongated and had sharp ends, the fingers, which were a bit longer than those of humans, and their hair that seemed to shimmer even when there was no sunlight.

"So, you wanted to talk?" Selene asked. "What about?"

"Us. I wanted to make sure you want this. Jeanette can be annoying and she's needy, but Emma and Sonya make up for that I guess."

The elf watched me with her silvery eyes, pulled her hairband free, and shook the ponytail away. Her hair had grown somewhat and hung halfway down her back.

"You're beautiful, you know that? Even more so than any other I've been with."

"Shh, don't. They'll hear you," she whispered mischievously.

"How come? The girls are back in the village."

Selene shook her head.

85

"Not you, but my heart. They can feel what I feel now, right? What if my heart keeps beating so hard, they'll know."

I put my hand on her cheek and leaned my forehead on hers.

"Back when we met, remember? I never thought we'd end up together. You were a bit stuck-up and unapproachable."

"And you were on an arena high having won a few battles. I despised the guard duty, but who knew you were actually stronger than me?"

"See who kills the most monsters?"

"No fair," she whispered, pursing her lips. "I don't have any area-of-effect attacks. You do."

"I won't use them."

Her breath was warm on my lips and it was hard to hold back. My lips brushed against hers and my arm snaked around her waist. I slid it down the tight pants and squeezed her firm ass.

"N—no, not here. I'm dirty and...you'll need to wait a few days."

"I don't mind if you're—"

"No! Not...dirty. I want to be clean."

I pulled away from her and sighed. She had the right to choose where and how, so pushing any further would be stupid. Still, I had an idea why she was so adamant about not being intimate. Selene was just as petty as Jeanette and wanted to rub it in the other woman's face. Very well, I would indulge her this time as my fiery swashbuckler had been a bit mean to everyone around her lately.

"Alright, sure. I will oblige, my beautiful killer."

"Speaking of killing, no AOE's?"

"No AOE's but for my debuff. That one will help you just as much."

"Deal! The winner gets bragging rights for a month!"

I grinned as she shot off like an arrow, running down the steep slope and using her shadow skills to get ahead of me.

"Shit, she really has a nice ass," I whispered and rushed

down after her.

CHAPTER 8 –
MOKRA CLAN

Three days passed of continued monster farming while the others dealt with the temple. I would come and go when all the monsters were dead, which didn't happen that often, and help with small things as they wouldn't let me anywhere near...well, anything really.

To make the steel beams, we needed a foundry, and since there wasn't enough room in the workshop, Nalgid decided it was best to extend it along the entire length so there was enough room for both the foundry and anything else we might need later down the road.

Progress had been steady, and thanks to the elgar's great skill with cutting stone blocks and having plenty of resources nearby, it felt as if the temple was rising out of the ground on its own.

Selene had been avoiding me, but the other girls hadn't, which worried me. At first, she was pushy, but then backed out and spent more time by herself or with Elvina. I decided to give her two more days before I brought it up, not wanting to be pushy myself.

An interesting thing happened after the dungeons had leveled up. It only took a day to get them both to level 2, after which monsters started randomly dropping currency alongside loot. It wasn't much, and the most coins one dropped had been 32, but it added up because of how quickly the monsters respawned. It took both dungeons under two hours to fully repopulate, and as I wasn't killing them using my AOE skills, I constantly had something to kill if I didn't push it.

The pieces of gear I acquired over the first three days would have been enough to outfit about 50 starter soldiers like Samel was. Their gear was ordinary, but the one the monsters dropped had minor enhancements. The added stats and boons the gear provided wouldn't automatically make them much stronger, but it would give them a good edge against anyone of the same rank.

Late during the third day, and sometimes just before evening, a small caravan of carts came rumbling down the road north. I had instructed Benny and Legs to use their free time to work on the road, flatten it as much as possible, and get all the larger chunks of stone out of the way while filling up any holes. They'd managed to get the first 500 yards or so done, and it was layered with white cobbled stones which Legs had rammed into the ground by slamming his belly down on the cobbles. It was a smart use of his body and weight.

A thrumming noise reverberated from the direction of Garm Village, and I knew what it was immediately. Banxi was flying one of those planes again.

I finished resting and hurried to the northern gate to meet our guests. The small plane landed on the newly-built road, breaking both wheels as it wasn't flat enough, and skidded to a halt some twenty yards away from the wall.

"Banxi! What the hell are you doing here? I told you not to come—"

"Unless I had made a decision! And, oh boy, did I make a decision!" the goblin yelled back from the plane's cockpit.

The glass windows from last time were missing, but since he had a mask on, I figured the wind hadn't bothered him so much. The plane wouldn't fly again, though, at least not short a total rebuild, I could see that much.

"Everyone, Banxi, and a small caravan have arrived. Come to the northern gate and give them a welcome if you are free," I said over our mental space.

Elvina had leveled it up and gained a new ability for

her [Mental Space] skill. She was now able to create rooms for different people who wanted to communicate without bothering others, instead of talking one-on-one and then relaying messages. It was a game-changer as I could now talk to all the girls without anyone else hearing what we had to say.

I pushed the gate open and stood there at the entrance. Benny and Legs were coming our way, I could feel it by the tremors in the ground. They were too heavy not to feel at the speed they were going. Seconds later, they appeared around the lake and stopped nearby, changed to their smaller forms, and joined us.

"Banxi! You came back!" Benny yelled as he ran toward the goblin steampunkist as he called him. The goblin backpaddled with a wry smile on his face. Even the friendliest of words brought little comfort when one met Benny riding the giant spider. Legs bore his giant appendages into the ground, dirt, pebbles, and dust almost swallowed the goblin before him. The pangolin used the inertia of the sudden, violent halt to jump off the spider's back.

"Banxi! My goblin bro, got any good news? Did you ask around if there's any God Beast for your pal, Benny?"

The goblin coughed and then brushed the dust off his shoulders and face. He looked up at the pangolin.

"In fact, I did ask one, and she almost ate me. Not that you'd want her, anyway. She walks on four legs and doesn't have a tail."

Legs let out a loud chittering sound which I learned meant disapproval.

"It would be so weird to see her genitals all over the place," he added grimacing.

"So... why did you ask her?" the pangolin asked.

"Because I had no one else to ask, duh! It's not like Mokra is teeming with God Beasts."

"Don't you mean Volarna City, you little shit."

"No! We call it Mokra! Us goblins I mean."

I sighed, already annoyed by his mere presence. He was

one of the good sorts, I could bet my boots on it, but there was something about that goblin that made me want to stick my head in a bucket whenever he opened his mouth.

"So, yes, we decided," he said, jumping down his small plane and landing with a half-graceful flip on a knee. "We will accept your rule, great Cade, killer of inquisitors and many other things."

I grunted at his proclamation.

"Where did you hear?"

"Oh, don't worry, we only heard about it in Garm Village. I figure the message will last for another week at least?"

"Right, right. And you're ready to become enemies with your duke?"

"Duke? Hah! Those fools didn't even allow us to work on bombs! Imagine that!"

I stared at the goblin and thought about what he just said. Bombs. No sane person would allow anyone to work on bombs under their roof. However...

"How many of you are there? And how big does the bomb place need to be?"

"The Mokra tribe is twelve strong. I have three wives and eight children!"

"Three? And... that worries me, Banxi. Wait, Mokra tribe? You called said damned city was called Mokra!"

"I think you're missing the point, bro," Benny said. "That guy has three wives, you know?"

"And you're a God Beast, so what? You jealous I got myself some tail and you didn't?"

"Hey, I got a tail, dude!" Benny protested. "And I can also eat you in a single bite, so don't push it, you little pipsqueak."

"Pip—wait, what even is that?"

"Focus, Banxi. Mokra?"

"Ahh, yes, well, I feel that the city should be mine and not that of Volarna, that fat bastard. Anyway, I'm not interested in your kind. I'm not quite... tall enough, so there won't be a 4th wife any time soon."

I snorted, unable to hold back as he said that.

"As if we'd let you," one of his wives said from behind him, but he chose to ignore it.

"Right. So, it's just because you're not quite tall enough, huh?

"Among other things," he laughed.

"I can see that. So, twelve is just fine. We can get you a place to stay in the village but if you're going to work on bombs, then you'll have to do that far enough away that you don't blow us all up."

"Blow you...up? What do you think me for? That bunch of dwarves? Or that giant...whatever he is?"

"Banxi. You've been with us for a few days, yes, but don't push it. I like your eccentric approach to advancement, but there are some limits—"

"A hundred yards in every direction. I think."

"A hundred yards? What do you mean?"

"That's the blast radius. Don't you think it's fascinating? I mean, do you even know what a true bomb even is? We pack a lot of—"

"Hold on, Banxi. I've seen fireballs the size of...that building over there during the siege of our city. Remember? I told you about it. You want to tell me you can create a device that could outmatch that?"

"Yes, yes, but that's not the same! Mages, bah! I read about your mages and what they could do. Ancient hogwash is what it is. What do mages know about fires and explosions?"

I opened my mouth, thinking it was a legitimate question, but Banxi continued.

"Nothing! Spells and magic are for primitives. Ancient tomes and rituals, that's...That's for savages, not for learned individuals like myself. Here, look at this," he said, producing a tiny charcoal black ball from a pouch.

"Wha—"

Before I could finish my question, he tossed the thing at my feet and it exploded with a loud bang. It didn't do any damage but was enough to startle Legs who raised his front feet with a loud shriek.

"Easy there, big boy," Benny tried to calm it.

"See that?" Banxi said smiling.

"Don't. Do. That. Again," I said as seriously as I could.

Banxi locked eyes with me for a moment, unsure of whether he had crossed a line, then coming to the conclusion that he hadn't, the goblin continued.

"Now imagine that thing scaled up by a thousand! Ten-thousand! A million! What mage can compare himself to that, I ask you? No mage. None."

"Alright, I get it you—"

"And that's not even all! I have a special ingredient! A fire that can't be put out and I'm willing to make these things for you! Now, have you heard about that? No? Of course not. A mage casts a fireball and boom! Fire! Toss some water on it and poof, gone! But this baby, oh boy, this baby burns like crabs, ever had those? Not really pleasant. Burns night and day, can't eat, can't sleep, can't fuck, all you want to do is dip your balls in ice water."

I groaned, already feeling a headache setting in. Banxi could ramble on like a man on a breaking wheel.

"Banxi, regarding the war effort, we got it, alright? I don't want to kill everyone, you crazy goblin, I want to convert them."

"Convert them to what?" he shot back, getting back to his feet. By then, his family had gathered as well as my girls, Merek, Grom, his family, Mortimer, Callina, Mano, and Rafika.

"There's food left over from this morning," Callina said, waving at the group of goblins. "We also have some good booze to go with it. Do goblins even drink?"

"Hah! Do we?" Banxi laughed but then went quiet. "Well, we drink grog. If you have any? If not, we have enough for a few weeks."

"Grog?" Jeanette asked. "I've never heard of it and I used to have a bar."

"Mushroom booze, lady. Speaking of which, we'll need to infect a small part of the forest with fungus or they won't grow."

I sighed.

"Was that the second reason why he kicked you out?"

"That's preposterous!" Banxi cried. "Kicked me out? The greatest inventor of our age? Well, yes. He did."

"And there go all your big words that you kept spouting on our way here, husband," the middle of the three gobla, which was the correct way to address female goblins, said. At least it was according to Banxi. She was larger than her husband by half a head and wider in the shoulders, which were covered by dark blue hair, as opposed to Banxi's bald scalp.

"Copta! Shut it! You're one to talk! Khubba, Usvee, greet our new friends."

"By the hob lord's balls, there are a few really big ones," one of his other two wives said and waved, which was just...odd. She was as tall as the first wife but slender with short brown hair and deep-set eyes.

"Yes, I'm sure you'd like to go to the hob, wouldn't you, Khubba?" the third gobla said, which made her Usvee, the petite red hair. She was even smaller than Banxi and looked exceptionally frail.

The three lady goblins wore dresses that could, in a different reality, maybe rival those of my own girls. The sons and daughters wore yellow and black pants, and jackets, with white shirts and brown boots. All in the color of the duke's house.

"Da'r? Where will we stay?" one of the larger goblins asked. He must have been the oldest son, or at least looked like it with his spiky mohawk haircut.

"If you don't mind sleeping in the foundry or the workshop, you'll have a roof over your head right away. If you rather wait a few days, we'll have your new home built."

"New home? Da'r?" one of the smaller gobla asked. She had red hair, just like her mother. Or so I assumed that she was Usvee's offspring.

"Yes, new home. We'll be staying here for a while. Okay? I promise it will be nice. And you'll be able to play with that small God Beast. He's nice. In a weird way."

Benny glared daggers at the newcomer and bared his teeth, which turned into a smile as the young gobla stared up at him. The tribe as a whole seemed to take their situation rather well, which allowed Banxi to do great things for the village like getting running water and building a sewage system. Or so he'd promised.

"So, how about we get some food in your bellies?" I said, motioning for the gate. "Welcome to New Greystone."

"Hah, it's a name as fine as any," Banxi snorted. "We'll take you up on the workshop offer."

"Good. Grommasch will help you settle in once you've eaten. Come on, let's go."

A short while later, everyone was seated around the four dinner tables in Brahma's Rest. We'd mixed up with the newcomers, and everyone was having a good time. Emma, Sonya, Jeanette, and Selene were chatting up Copta, Khubba, and Usvee. They were animatedly chatting about a topic they all had in common: being part of a harem, as they called it.

Banxi wasn't letting me listen in as I found it all rather fascinating. They had everything planned out, when, who, what, and where. Each of the gobla's had their own tasks that they fulfilled, and Banxi was the crazy inventor who took care of them. The kids were almost like slaves from what I gathered and each of them, despite being pretty young, was already working.

"Say, Banxi, I will be honest with you, alright?"

"Yes, sure, go, speak," he said hurriedly.

"I need everything you can give me on, well, everything around this place. How much do you know?"

"Me? Everything," he said with a devilish grin. "But it'll

cost you."

I took one of the knives and slammed it down on the table.

"Cost me? What exactly?"

The little brown-green bastard didn't even so much as flinch.

"If you think I'm afraid of a little knife, you don't know goblins."

I shrugged and pulled out my kris. It glowed like a miniature sun as it was upgraded to +9. Mana extended from the blade and crackled as I lowered it onto the table.

"Okay, I can see when I'm beaten," he mumbled. "I want to prospect the lake with the help of your God Beasts."

Now that was something I wouldn't have guessed in a thousand years.

"The lake? Why?"

"Because the fool believes a comet struck this valley a long time ago and that there are special minerals down there," Khubba said. "He wants to build a—what was that thing called again?"

"A mecha!" Banxi said proudly. "That's short for a mechanical suit since you already seem so very interested."

I looked over the group of humans, elgar, elves, and goblins that were seated around the tables and eating a late lunch, and no one seemed to be bothered by what he just said.

"Mechanical suit? For what?"

"So I can fight on the front lines!" he exclaimed proudly.

"There's a much easier way to get there," Sonya said, shooting him a smile.

"You mean that convert to another religion thing? Yeah, I'm not interested in that. I always knew there was something off with the whole Tan'Malas thing. I used to pray, you know?"

"Pray? What are you talking about, goblin?" Copta, his wife said, "I saw you pray once when you bet half our money on pig racing."

"And I lost!" Banxi said as if that confirmed his point,

"Tell you what, I don't really believe in anything!" he said and crossed his arms.

"Fool," Copta said this time. "Haven't you seen how strong those soldiers are now? They were fighting like there's no tomorrow!"

Banxi waved her off and looked away, embarrassment apparent on his face.

"Hey, tell me something, goblin," I said, picking my kris back up and holding it in front of me. "What do you think how hard it would be for me to kill you with this kris? Or how hard it would be for Sonya to cast a [Fire Pillar] inside this building and kill everyone?"

"You with your knives and daggers again. I don't believe, and you can't make me!" the goblin yelled, gritting his teeth.

"Leave him," Copta said again. "He's a fool, he only starts believing fire is hot when his arse is lit up."

"Damn you, gobla! Shut your mouth! I'm not afraid of death!"

Copta yawned as if bored with his angry retort.

"I've got an idea, Banxi, but first, I want you to tell me more about the villages and towns surrounding the lake. Then you will tell me about Volarna?"

"Yes, yes. What do you want to know?"

"That's more like it," I said with a smile and leaned on the table. "So, tell me about the duke's military power."

"Alright, that's a fair question I guess. He's limited to 1,000 soldiers in total. From what I know, about 200 of those are spread across the villages and towns, with the rest sitting on their ass in Volarna. They're just a bunch of bullies if you ask me, a bunch of thugs that harass the weak and steal from the people of this region to fill the duke's coffers. He's a pig that one, and I'm sure he'll be coming for you with all his power. You ignored a summons, after all."

I thought for a moment and shrugged. From what I'd seen so far, the soldiers weren't going to prove difficult to deal with, not even if all of them attacked at once. They didn't have the Godveil, but we did, and that did a lot to tilt the scales to our side.

"What about the others? The religious fanatics?"

"The Order?"

"Well, if that's what they call themselves. I heard it in passing several times but nobody cared to explain. Not even the inquisitors and zealots we captured."

"Yeah, that's what it's called. The Order has over 10,000 soldiers in this province alone, but the thing is that most of them are...hmm, how should I explain this? Imagine it like a coin. The Order consists of two distinct groups," Banxi explained as he produced a small keg from his storage and poured himself a drink. "Oh, my goodness, is this good! Do you want to try?"

I shook my head.

"No, Banxi. Two groups?"

When I asked the question, seemingly most conversations around the tables stopped and everyone listened to us.

"You have the fighting force, as well as the group that runs all daily operations for The Order. They're ordinary humans, not much better trained than the duke's soldiers, but the dark soldiers...oh, boy. That's why I've been developing this special type of bomb. I call it the Banxi Buster!"

I stared at him flatly, which elicited a scowl on the goblin's face.

"What?"

"Nothing, Banxi. Anyway, tell me more about The Order. I've seen their daily activities group, as you called them, and they're nothing. I could kill a thousand of them by myself. What do you know of the others? The dark soldiers as you called them."

"Man, oh, man. Yeah, I've only seen them twice with my own eyes, but never in battle. However, from what I've heard, and I have heard a lot mind you, because see, these big ears aren't just for decoration," he said rapidly, pointing to his ears,

"They can't be killed with steel, hence why I developed this eternal fire. Well, not eternal, but you get what I mean. It burns until there's nothing left to burn."

I did like the notion of having more tools available to fight Tan'Malas' army, so we'd first have to see the bombs in action before I made any decisions.

"Sure, that's at least something. Anything you know about the sub-pillars?"

He sucked in air through his sharp teeth and shuddered.

"Now those are some hard-ass clowns, I tell you. They do not joke around, you know? The subs are all about torture and death. How strong are they, you want to know, and I have no idea. My best guess is that they're as strong as a hundred of their soldiers. Maybe less? Maybe more?"

"So you don't know? Alright, come on, I want to show you something. Your family can get settled in the foundry's spare rooms."

"You heard the man! Finish up and go get the carts, you lazy bastards! And you three, help them."

"I've had enough of pulling a cart for a whole lifetime," Usvee protested. "Why can't the big guys help?" she asked, nodding toward Grom.

"Yeah, they can," I said. "Grom, could your sons do this for me? I want them settled in as fast as possible," I added, giving him an urging look. He understood what I meant and grunted in approval.

"We will take care of it," he said after a moment.

"Thank you. Now, Banxi, let's go. We can talk some more along the way."

CHAPTER 9 – WENDIGO

Two more days passed before the Mokra tribe got their new home. It was the upgraded guest house that I'd stored before leaving Greystone. Every floor was basically an apartment for itself, so they had more than enough room to make themselves comfortable in whichever way they liked.

I was close to getting to level 57 by the time the goblins finished building what they called was a watchtower. The building was made from stone and looked like a fifteen-by-fifteen-foot narrow tower that rose about a hundred feet in the air. The very top was double as wide, giving the goblin ample space to play around.

At the very top of the tower sat what Banxi called a prism. It was one of his inventions that allowed us to see as far as Garm Village when looking through a piece of glass within a long tube, conveniently positioned just above a comfortable chair. If anything, the goblins knew how to ease their daily burdens...

After giving me brief instructions, Banxi busied himself by setting up a small workshop of his own. He preferred to spend most of his free time sitting up in the tower and tinkering away at new things. Considering the space was large enough to hold a workbench that spread across all four walls and had built-in cabinets underneath, as well as shelves above, he had a lot of room to store his works of art, as he called them.

I pulled the tube toward me and looked into the glass, putting my hand on a small gear Banxi said would help focus the image. At first, everything was blurry, but after several turns of the small gear, the image became gradually clearer. Another gear would, as he called it, zoom the image in or out.

Oh, boy, did I have fun with it. At least for the first ten minutes. The prism would allow me to zoom in close enough on Garm Village's square to see if my statue was still intact. It was partially obstructed by a building as well as by people milling about.

Next, I focused the prism on Najla's home but all I could see were the walls surrounding the manorhouse. On the second floor, however, was a balcony and behind it what looked like a bedroom.

I felt my heart skip a beat as I spotted movement within. Najla was standing next to a closet and going through her clothes, throwing them down on the bed, ripping them apart, and screaming. I couldn't hear if they were silent screams or those coming from deep within, but I could see the anguish on her face much clearer than I cared to admit.

I changed direction and zoomed out a bit so I could see the entirety of the village. The gears and prisms were slow to turn and adjust, so I had a minute before everything had reset to its original state.

Having seen the crowd near the statue, I pulled up the quest counter.

```
Quest Status: Spreading The Faith III

Description: Continue to help spread
        faith in the Gods of old.

Status: 163/250 Converted Believers
```

Alright, things were moving along smoothly. That was good. Had Najla's raging anything to do with the converted, or was it something else? Maybe even bad news as it had been a while since the incident with The Order. I really wanted to know as I kind of liked the woman in a strange way.

I looked into the tube again and saw the village had slowly zoomed out. Beyond it were farm fields and a small stream, while even further were the hills and mountains that fully encased this small patch of land. It was almost large enough to be called a province.

I steadily moved the prism to Balan Village, eager to see if anything had changed since we visited a few weeks ago. The first thing I noticed was how the villagers were busy putting up a wooden log wall all around the small village. Barely 500 people lived there from what I'd heard, though most were in their best years and healthy as could be. That could have been one of the reasons why they'd started the village just recently. I didn't think it was older than a year, maybe two. There had barely been any wear and tear on their buildings, and the crops hadn't even ripened yet.

I focused the lens on the Balam Village's center square. A small crowd was gathered there, and among them were two inquisitors and a dozen or so of zealots. They were arguing with the soldiers, who after a minute of protesting finally backed down, revealing a man, woman, and two youngsters kneeling with their hands tied behind their backs.

I tensed, my hand instinctively moving for my daggers as one of the inquisitors, a short, tubby man with a balding head and a thick mustache addressed the crowd. His mannerisms and the way he looked at the crowd told me exactly what was going to happen. Before I could have made it outside and to the gate, the zealots pulled the four to their feet and executed them while standing.

My hand tightened so hard around the steel-looking tube that Banxi smacked me with a hammer.

"Shit! What was that for, you little asshole?" I cursed, looking down at the goblin.

"You damaged my far-seer! Bastard, do you know how hard it is to make one?"

"No, but I guess it's not more expensive than a life. Or four lives."

"Four? Why are you being so specific?"

I handed him the far-seer as he called it, and the goblin let out a string of curses.

"Executions, huh? They usually do that to entire families to make sure there's no one to avenge the dead. I guess they have you to thank for their deaths."

"Me? Because of what happened in Garm?"

"Why else?" Banxi hissed. "Executions are rare. Manpower is short in these parts if you haven't noticed!"

I closed my eyes and let out a deep sigh.

"Can any of your kids do this job well enough? Keep a look out around the clock?"

"Yes, they can," he said, going back to his rearranging the work benches. "I will have one of them take the next six hours. By the way, we expect to be paid for work. That's how you motivate a goblin, not through food or trinkets."

I stood from the chair and straightened my armor, pants, and sleeves as we stared at each other.

"Two gold coins per shift, and every time they have an important message, another five coins to the messenger."

"Deal. Get them started. I need to take care of those zealots."

"Wait, don't. It will only get even worse if you do!" he snapped, stopping me. "You know nothing of this place, so listen to me! You're strong, but I don't think you realize how strong the darkness soldiers are. The Order will retaliate, and if they can't kill you, they will kill everyone in the villages."

Banxi was dead serious and even poked me with his finger.

"You're strong, right? I saw you kill those monsters with ease, but what about everyone else here? What if they come when you're away or something, huh? What then? Will you be alright if they kill my family? Or that of the dwarves?"

His words stung, and I knew he was right, but there was no way I could just let it slide, not like this.

"Then what do you suggest?"

"Nothing. At least not yet. Patience."

"Cade, you need to see this," Selene said over our mental link. *"Our first mini-bounty spawned."*

"Be right there." I looked at Banxi and smiled. "We've got a mini-bounty spawned out back. Do you want to come and watch?"

He shook his head and pointed to the work benches.

"I've got a lot of things left to set up, boss. Also, you wanted me to get you hot running water, heating, and sewage all as soon as possible, well, I can't get to that until everything's set up. You go have fun and forget about what you saw, boss man. Don't tell anyone, as that is your burden to bear as the boss. The man everyone looks up to, alright? And I'll deny we had this conversation if you tell anyone."

"Heh, who would have thought you had such nice words to share, Banxi?"

"Oh, shut it, please. You will see the real me soon enough. I have to keep up appearances, right? And again, don't do anything stupid you might regret. They don't come cheap?"

"Cheap? Regrets you mean?"

"Yes. Any time we lose something important, we'd give the whole world just to get it back, so keep that in mind. Is someone else's life worth losing one of your wives? Or that of your God Beasts?"

He was right, and despite already knowing all that before he even said anything, we sometimes needed to hear something we might not like to come to terms with it. This was one of those situations, and from a goblin no less.

I stuck out my hand and waited for Banxi to take it. He did so hesitantly, and I shook it.

"Thanks, Banxi. I'll deal with it one way or another and repay them one day."

A heavy weight pressed down on me as I made my way down the countless stairs. Life wasn't cheap, no, it should be priceless, but those with power often forgot that they also had a life to lose. I would just file it for a later date and repay them several times over for all the misery they caused.

Emma, Sonya, Jeanette, Benny, Merek, and Legs were waiting for me downstairs.

"What's up, bro? Do you need us all to kill that thing?"

I looked over the group and then toward the southern gate.

"Who called you here?"

"Selene did," Emma replied. "She said you need us to help you kill a mini-bounty."

"Huh, really?" I muttered. "I should be able to take care of anything myself. What got her so worried?"

"Let's go check, bro!" Benny said excitedly as he jumped on Legs' back. "Anyone else? Merek dude? You said you wanted to try Legs out."

The stoic spearman glanced up at the building-sized War Weaver for a moment, studying it, but then shrugged.

"Yeah, what the hell. Why not? It's not every day you get to ride such a magnificent creature," Merek said. Legs offered one of its limbs to the man and helped pull him up. Benny took over and then helped him sit between the scaly protrusions up top.

"Thank you," Merek said, holding on to one of the scales and trying to position himself comfortably.

"You two look so ridiculous up there," Jeanette said.

"And you're just jealous of Legs' beauty," Benny shot back, which brought a scowl to Jeanette's face.

"What is it with everyone picking on me over the last week?"

"Maybe you should learn not to talk shit to everyone," Sonya said with a wink. "So? Do you want us or not? We were helping Mirna with something."

"*Selene? What kind of monster is it? Why did you ask everyone to come?*"

"*Because I don't think you're strong enough. Just come already. We'll definitely need magic as well. And hurry up, please.*"

"And there we have our answer, love. Come on."

We made our way south and found Selene sitting on the small hill we used to overlook the southern part of the valley. She pointed toward the monsters down below as we arrived.

There was a monster below that was actively killing and eating other monsters. It was about as tall as Benny in his bigger form I figured.

Its entire body was black and resembled that of an oversized human with a thick torso and firm but thin, hooved legs. Antler-like horns sat on top of its elongated head.

The creature was shrouded in an eerie, unsettling aura. Burning orbs sat where the eyes should be, showing off a dangerous amount of mana residing within the creature. A tangle of inky tendrils hung from its frame, the skin a sickly ashen black and stretched taut over its limbs.

Long, gnashing fangs protruded from its gaping maw, stained with a dark red liquid. I figured it was the blood of the monsters that it'd eaten.

"That thing looks like a wendigo, bro," Benny said as he jumped down from Legs' back. The Blood Beast landed with an otherworldly grace, making barely any sound.

"You know of them?" Emma asked.

"Yes, my Lady. They're born from humans, usually those who'd died under brutal circumstances and they feast on flesh, becoming more powerful as they absorb their victims' powers."

"Great," I muttered. "Do you want to take it on?"

"Yeah, sure, bro. Legs, come on."

The War Weaver wouldn't move from place, almost as if it was rooted to the ground. Legs screeched then and he sounded distressed.

"Hmm, he's afraid," Benny said. "That's weird. Alright, I'll try to fight it myself. Can you all buff me?"

"Elvina? Where are you?" I asked, holding my hand up to stop him. *"We could use your buffs."*

She replied almost instantly.

"Where do you need me?"

"At the monster dungeons. And bring some traps with you, just in case. Mana based preferably."

"Oh? What's this about? I was just finishing setting one up

at the northern gate, something new I came up with. Give me a few minutes."

"A monster even Legs is afraid of. We're waiting for you to buff us before we attack."

I couldn't see any kind of information on the creature other than its level, which was 60. It was devouring another of the monsters as we waited there. Unease was creeping up my body and I felt as if a shiver ran down my back. That stag-and-human-like monstrosity sure didn't feel as if it was an ordinary being. It had a great amount of mana stored inside its body, but did it have a way to release all that power?

"Everyone, buff up as we wait for Elvina. Benny, you go in there and test the damned thing. If it's as dangerous as Legs thinks, then you bolt but don't fucking come anywhere toward us. Lead it away and jump into the water. I have no idea if such a creature will even be bound with the Godveil's dungeon borders."

"Alright, bro. Don't worry. I'll do as you say."

The pangolin wasn't as calm as moments ago as he seemed to finally understand that something was wrong. Sure, he was almost immortal, but that didn't mean he couldn't get hurt or feel pain. That was the one drawback of immortality: pain was endless.

I pulled Benny aside just as Elvina arrived and put my hand on his large, furry back. He half-winced and moved his body aside as if to make room for me, then sighed in relief. It was a bunch of emotions I hadn't seen in him since our first days together when we just joined the arena.

"Listen, the moment you make contact, I will hit him from behind. Alright? You're not alone."

Benny suddenly grabbed me with his large, meaty clawed hands and almost crushed me in a Blood Beast hug.

"I love you, bro. I mean, bro love and all, not like, you know. You're almost married and stuff, so don't get me wrong, hah!"

"I...feel very fond of you...as well, Benny...I

can't...breathe..."

"Oh, shit!" he cursed and released me. "Sorry, bro."

I could feel the warmth of Emma's healing spell wash over me. She stormed over to the big, furry Blood Beast and slapped his arm.

"You enjoy bullying the weak?"

"W—what are you—hey, bro, she's saying you're weak."

I looked at Emma, who now had a sheepish look on her face.

"Sorry. Didn't mean it like that, love."

"I know you didn't, but that means punishment. I'll have to slap that fine ass of yours around a bit later."

"Ugh, I don't need to hear that, bro."

"Neither do I," Merek mused. "Though I find it highly interesting that you feel like making babies in times like these."

"Making love, Merek, not babies," I said with a grin. "Alright, Benny. Go get 'em dude."

"Hah! You called me dude, dude!" Benny yelled over his shoulder as he ran down the hill. "I'm expecting you!"

I did as I had promised and charged after the big guy. The wendigo, as Benny had called it, stopped chewing on the monster it held up in its claws, and threw it aside.

I focused on my target and felt two of my skills that hadn't procc'ed a long time activate: [Mark of the Hunter], which lowered all of the wendigo's stats, and [Predator], which raised my dexterity and agility. Before I was halfway down the slope, I slapped on [Dark Presence], which lowered the accuracy and dodge of any enemies within 30 feet, and [Plague Domain], which inflicted a random debuff on any enemy within a 55-foot area. I was as ready as I could be, fully buffed by the girls.

"What the hell are you doing?" Sonya yelled after me. "You ass! If you already want to fight, then let us join in!"

I could feel their movements behind me and even a few hissing voices, but I tuned them all out. The moment

Benny made contact with the wendigo, I would appear behind it, and...the Blood Beast went flying backward as our target released some kind of mana blast.

"Shiiit!" Benny cried as he flew past me and slammed into the hard, rocky ground.

I didn't stop running, because if I did, I wasn't sure if I'd want to attack again. Activating [Shadow Stride] just as I came into range, I disappeared from place and appeared behind the creature, my daggers already angled downwards.

"Die, you piece of shit!" I yelled, launching a [Backstab].

My mana-infused, glowing daggers slammed right into its back but seemed to do little as the wendigo just staggered a step forward, and then bent its arms so it could reach for me. Black puss oozed from the wounds, unlike the other dungeon-spawned monsters which just disappeared into smoke.

A fireball struck its chest and almost toppled the black creature on its back. The limbs moved unnaturally, and the right leg bent at an impossible angle to stay upright on its feet.

I pushed off its back and lunged out of the way as Merek charged with his spear and shield at the ready. The spearman glowed for a moment, and then the wendigo froze, only its clawed fingers and the antlers on its head twitching.

Benny suddenly came flying and landed with his feet outstretched on the wendigo's chest. The creature slammed into the ground, flesh tearing and bones breaking. Before it could even react, Benny started ripping into it with his hands, ice forming at the tips of his fingers that froze the gaping wounds solid. The ice shattered, ripping out even more of the flesh.

A renewed mana blast sent Benny flying for the second time, but this time his chest looked as if it had been caved in. The pangolin cried in pain as he flew for over 50 yards. Legs caught him and the two went tumbling down the hill.

My first debuff struck the wendigo then, or at least it should have but the bastard was immune.

You have failed to inflict the (Cripple
II) debuff on Cursed Wendigo.

The wendigo turned toward me, staring with the two burning coals sitting in its eye sockets, and then cocked its head. I felt a chill running down my spine as its lips curled upward in a sneer. The eye sockets glowed for a moment and I could feel mana building up within its body.

"Sonya!" I yelled, but she was already on it, and a split second before the blast hit, she cast the [Arcane Shield] spell, protecting me from a single attack. The blast dissipated, giving me time to jump in again, but Merek was there, his spear glowing like the sun for a brief moment.

"Die!" he cried, his arm moving at incredible speed, jabbing the tip of his spear into the wendigo's leg. The attack disintegrated flesh and pierced bone, splitting it. The wendigo roared in pain and fell on its hands.

I used [Shadow Step] to appear behind its neck, activating [Blade Storm]. The skill wasn't that useful when it came to attacking single targets, but this monster wasn't ordinary. Even when hitting the flesh and blowing it away, nothing seemed to work until Merek had touched the bone.

Benny roared again from somewhere off to my right, and I could feel his thundering steps vibrating through the ground.

"Merek! Step back!" I yelled and the spearman lunged back as far as he could and knelt, angling his shield so he could deflect what he assumed was an incoming attack. "No, further! Protect the girls! No one else comes close! Girls, back!"

He nodded and obliged, and so did Selene and Jeanette, who were about to join the fighting. Elvina was still setting up a magical trap, but she abandoned it now that Legs was also joining in.

Both Benny and his companion rushed the wendigo, the former roaring in anger and the latter screeching in rage.

I quickly dashed aside and jumped backward, then strung in [Shadow Step] so I would make it far enough not to get smashed. Legs was twenty feet tall and if he stepped on any one of us, we'd probably be dead, no matter our high stats.

Three of the War Weaver's spiked feet slammed into the wendigo while Benny pulled at the one remaining good leg, clawing and ripping until it came free. A strange thing happened then as Legs pulled away with a shriek as the pangolin's [Blood Field] came alive. The Blood Beast lifted the massive leg and started hammering the wendigo's head and chest, breaking bone and smashing flesh. Black blood sprayed all over his arms and legs, but he didn't seem to mind.

Legs screeched as if angered by the hairy pangolin getting all the fun and pushed Benny off the monster. In turn, the Blood Beast slammed the freed leg into the spider's closest limb. Probably remembering their last encounter, Legs stepped away hurriedly as the mist started covering the three limbs closest to Benny.

Panic set in as I knew just how dangerous he could be if the berserk state took over. I had to do something quickly, or we'd all be in danger, but what?

"Benny!" I yelled. "Snap out of it, you little shit!" It was the first thing that came to mind, and the second was to charge him and stab my daggers into his neck. He wouldn't die, but maybe he'd need enough to recover and by then the berserker state would be over.

"I'm already out of it, man! Hold on! Legs is being a little bitch! Just need to smack him one more time!"

I cursed under my breath as a range of emotions I didn't think could possibly come all at once washed over me: relief, anger, anxiousness, and a dozen others.

"Stop fighting and finish off the wendigo! It's already caused enough trouble for such a low level!"

I looked for Merek's towering shield and found a glimmering dome covering Emma, Jeanette, Selene, Sonya, Elvina, and him.

"You girls safe?" I yelled, only remembering that I had our mental link after the matter. Unfortunately, I had to admit that I failed the group a little. No one got hurt, and nothing bad happened, but I'd underestimated this monster. That only meant one thing: mini-bosses, bosses, mini-bounties, and bounties were going to be much stronger and harder to beat than the weak stuff we'd fought in Greystone's area.

> Congratulations! You have received
> 243 experience.

> Congratulations! Your guild has
> killed a Cursed Wendigo.

> You have received 500 Guild Favor.

> You have received 5,000 Gold Coins.

I stared with my mouth agape as I read the message. The creature had given me enough experience points to hit level 60. Oh, shit, I wasn't ready for this, not in a long shot.

CHAPTER 10 – PESTILENCE LORD

"Hey, hey, hey! What was that?" Sonya yelled as she stormed over to me. "You glowed! Just like Benny and Legs did during their evolutions! Tell me! Did you just hit level 60?"

Everyone went silent and all eyes focused on me. I couldn't find any words for a response, so I just nodded and gulped down the knot that had formed in my throat.

"I have."

"Then tell us! What have you become? What did—wait, you haven't evolved yet. You just got a choice of what you want to evolve into!" Sonya said again as everyone gathered around me.

"Hold on, give me just a second." I Walked over to the cursed wendigo's corpse and looted it. That head was going to look magnificent on our wall. Even though it was dead now, it still gave me the chills, almost as if it was about to jump out of the storage and attack us again.

"Hey, talk to us, Cade!" Emma demanded as she started shaking my arm. "Tell us! What happened?"

The problem was that nothing had happened other than the four reward notifications. Perhaps the Godveil didn't have enough power to let me evolve, or...the compendium.

"I think we need to go home first. And no, I didn't get a new class or sub-class, no stats, no nothing. There's something I need to check first."

"Would you mind if I stayed here for a while?" Merek asked, cleaning the black goo off his spear.

"These 3 levels rekindled my wish for getting back to

level 60, and I only have 4 levels to go."

After seeing him fight, yes, please. He'd not only frozen an insanely powerful monster, but he'd demolished its leg with a single skill and protected the girls after that.

"No, please. As far as I'm concerned, you've earned the right to hit 60 next. We'll come up with a schedule now that everyone's pretty close."

"Thanks. I'll make sure not to let you down."

I took in a deep breath and let it out again as I took in my girls. They were worried and anxiously awaited what was going on with my evolution. So was I.

"Come on, let's go home. I need to consult the compendium."

"Can Legs carry you, bro? He said you were very brave and stuff," Benny asked with a wide grin.

I looked up at the War Weaver and shrugged.

"Yeah, sure, this time. Girls? Want to join me?"

"No, no way," Jeanette replied hurriedly. "I don't want to fall off and hit my head and die or something."

"Drama queen," Selene mumbled. "You need to learn and enjoy the moment. I'll join you."

"We're going too," Emma said excitedly, holding Sonya's hand.

Elvina walked next to Jeanette, explaining something about a trap while the latter pretended to care. Benny had turned into his smaller form and sat atop Legs and in my lap. He'd earned a pat on the head, and with him in his pangolin form, that...tool of his wasn't going to be all over me.

The spider easily stepped over the village wall and then lowered us in front of the temple. I jumped off and helped the girls. Sonya jumped in my arms playfully, and so did Emma, while Selene slid down the body and landed gracefully.

"Everything alright? We heard some booming coming from the dungeons but Banxi said it was all fine," Grom asked. "You look beaten up."

"Yeah, we're good, Grom, thanks. There was this

monster I'd never seen before, and it was causing us some trouble. Nothing the deadly duo couldn't handle."

"Hah! Deadly duo? I like it, bro! Can you guys call—no, Legs, they can't call us the deadly trio. My dick isn't big enough to take monsters on by itself. You should—oh, shit. Yes, sorry about that."

"Benny, thanks for taking care of that thing. You too, Legs," I said instead of berating them. "You guys saved the day."

"Sure did!" Sonya said, patting him on the head. "So, Cade. Now. I don't want to wait any longer."

"Neither do I," Emma added. "Go, go, go! I think I'm going to pee myself or something if you don't go now."

"Grom? Do you want to join us? And tell me, how's the temple getting along?"

He scratched his long, elgar beard and gave me a 'meh'.

"Two more days? One? I don't know. It depends on the forge. The dwarves are really giving it their all, I have to say that, but I need to compliment my sons as well. They've been cutting stone for days on end."

"And I'll reward them for that, I promise," I said, trying to put an arm around the big guy and give him a friendly pad on his back, but he was too tall and big so it ended up looking a bit awkward. "Anyway, yeah. This whole situation is making me feel awkward. It's as if you guys want this more than me."

"You don't seem to want it bad enough," Jeanette mumbled. "And what was with that monster? Why was it so strong? Is it this place? Or because it is a guild dungeon?"

"That remains to be seen, but I bet you it has something to do with the dungeon having already leveled up," Sonya said. "We're killing monsters at a too-high rate, though unless we do, we can't get that sweet experience and loot."

I looked up at the watchtower and the prism. We could potentially use it to search for other dungeons or monster-infested parts in the valley. Maybe we could even start hunting the large monsters deep inside the lake.

I pulled the interface up to check the dungeon's

descriptions.

- The Minor Guild Dungeon, Level 3 (308/5,000), will keep spawning monsters at a rate of 1 per minute and up to 120 in total.
- The level of summoned monsters ranges anywhere from 25 to 37.
- The rarity of summoned dungeon monsters ranges from common, uncommon, rare, to mini boss.
- The monsters can drop level 1 or 2 monster cards, equipment with 1 or 2 enhancements, upgrade materials, and monster ingredients used for crafting.

- The Major Guild Dungeon, Level 3 (7/2,500), will keep spawning monsters at a rate of 1 per minute and up to 75 in total.

- The level of summoned monsters ranges anywhere from 40 to 57.

- The rarity of summoned dungeon monsters ranges from common, uncommon, rare, mini boss, and mini bounty.

- The monsters can drop level 1, 2, or 3 monster cards, equipment with 1, 2, or 3 enhancements, upgrade materials, monster ingredients used for crafting, and War Beast Eggs.

Not much had changed in the dungeon descriptions. The most noticeable was that the maximum levels had gone up by 2, the number of total monsters summoned at any given time, and very minor changes to possible loot.

"I think that was just a freak accident, maybe even because of the major dungeon going up to level 3. Could as well have been a milestone reward," I said, closing the dungeon interface.

"How far away are we from the next level-ups?" Selene asked.

"Well, the requirements skyrocketed, so at least a few days? A week? I'm not in the mood for calculating stuff right now."

We reached the Brahma's Rest by the time I was reading the descriptions and we'd thrown some speculations about the wendigo back and forth, but it didn't help anything as no one had any idea how an immortal mini-bounty could have spawned. At least it would make for a good trophy...

We gathered in the altar room. It was packed to the brim with everyone present making me feel like a priest of Tan'Ruad holding mass in a crowded temple.

I took the compendium from Brahma's hand, flipping it open. Despite being as thick as my fist, it always opened on the same page: the one meant for the person opening it. This time, the page looked different. It had two options laid out for me, or rather, evolutionary paths.

I read them out loud one after the other.

Soul Manipulator

As a Soul Manipulator, you will harness the very existence and concepts of souls. Manipulate and sacrifice souls to weave intricate webs of power, control living beings, or imbue souls into non living constructs.

The Soul Manipulator, aside from receiving a wealth of soul oriented attack and defense spells, abilities, and skills, is also a versatile plague master. In battle, you can afflict your foes with crippling spiritual and physical ailments, sapping their strength, making it your own, or seeing them consumed.

Pestilence Lord

As a Pestilence Lord, you harness the primal forces of pestilence and decay. You will become a master of manipulating and sacrificing any living being you encounter, even causing afflictions with your mere presence once you are strong enough.

The Pestilence Lord has full command over afflictions in combat, blanketing the field with death and decay. Nothing you encounter will remain standing if you wish it so. Crippling curses will destroy your enemies and restore your life power at the same time. Command over life and death is at the tip of your fingers.

I read the text once more for myself, and then a third time. The second option looked just like an upgrade to my Plague Revenant class, while the first might have something to do with my Soulbound monster card. Both options looked tempting, but the problem I had with the Soul Manipulator was that it seemed to focus too much on other people's souls. Having linked just five to myself was already way more than I would have ever wished for, but—no. Did I like what the Pestilence Lord evolution read? No. Command over life and death, yeah, sure, I was an assassin, someone who'd killed many people already, but keeping it up close and personal was the one thing that kept me from wanting to become a maniac in the first place. If I could kill people at my will without even having to come close to them would lose that effect and, probably, make me numb to death.

"So," Sonya said, breaking the silence that had ensued after me reading the two descriptions. "Talk about ominous."

"And dangerous," Emma muttered. "I'm not sure I even want you to evolve. All that talk about sacrificing souls and control over life and death...and...yeah."

"I like the second one, bro. I figure it's just a more advanced version than what you have right now. And Pestilence Lord sounds fucking cool, dude."

"Cool, huh?" I whispered. "It all depends on what end of my dagger you are. I don't think our enemies will think I'm cool, Benny."

"And that's my point! We want them to tremble. Fuck them and their inquisition! We'll destroy them all!"

"Wait, wait, wait," Selene said, raising her voice and slapping her hands. "If these are the same types of soldiers as back when...in Greystone, you know? Debuffs didn't work on them."

She was right. I'd totally forgotten about that. Debuffs only worked on the living, and our enemies were...what exactly? I had no idea.

"Don't we have the light potions? And a ton of points to buy more?" Elvina asked, joining the conversation as well. "We could buy 30 potions with the remaining deity favor, and we all have a bunch of potions as well, so...that's a lot of uses. And each use lasts 30 minutes. If we can't win a battle in that time, it's probably a battle we can't win."

"You are right," I said. "Going with your logic, we would have enough for a long time, but what once we run out? Will we be getting deity points here? We don't know."

"Hey, you're forgetting something, bro," Benny chuckled. "Once everyone is level 60, you won't have to take on that burden by yourself. We all will be much stronger, not just you."

"He's right, love," Sonya said, taking over. "What you need to focus on is staying alive, and I think that debuffs and buffs and life steal are the way to go."

Benny shuddered and even fell to the floor, rolling like a ball.

"This is so exciting! You're literally the epitome of an OP character, man! And I get to be your bro, like. This is awesome!"

I sighed, nudging him with my foot.

"You're talking crap no one understands, Benny. Get up. And maybe it would be a smart thing to go outside. Just in case something happens?"

The girls hugged and kissed me, all but Elvina, of course.

"See you in a bit, alright? Everything will be fine," I whispered to Emma as she was last. "Go with the others and wait for me outside. I can't use the compendium unless it's here."

"Don't do anything stupid. Please."

I kissed her, our eyes meeting just before I pulled away. Sonya pulled Emma along and gave me a small wave. It was one of the hardest moments in my life. What if I became a lich or something? Stranger things had happened, and we'd heard all kinds of stories growing up. Sure, nothing bad *should* happen, with a heavy emphasis on the word should. Knowing my luck...well, it wasn't that half-bad, so maybe things would turn out well?

"Brahma, be kind," I whispered, pushing some mana into the compendium and activating the evolution prompt again. "I choose Pestilence Lord."

"That is a wise choice," a voice spoke into my mind. I recognized it as belonging to Brahma. *"Your surprise is unwarranted, human. It is only natural that I should address one who makes it this far. There aren't many level 60 assassins left in the world."*

I froze at that statement, my breath catching in my lungs.

"Not...many?"

"Only eighteen souls bear the class of assassin in this world today. Does that trouble you, young one??"

"Trouble me? I have no idea where we are, what this place is, why everyone is worshipping Tan'Malas, or what happened to my home. Tell me, please!"

Brahma let out a deep sigh, and I could feel a chill creeping up on me. The entire room seemed to be getting colder with every passing second.

"I can not tell you much, Pestilence Lord, but seeing you have enough favor with me, I will tell you at least something. The world you've once known doesn't exist anymore, the people you've known are all gone, and the place you called home is now the domain of...an old acquaintance of yours."

"An acqu—wait, is it Zekan? How do I get there? Where even are we? Please!"

I could practically feel Brahma shaking her head.

"That is all I can give you for now. Become my champion and purge evil in my name, sacrifice those who kill others, and I will tell you more. Now, why don't we begin with a little demonstration of the first Pestilence Lord ever?"

A jolt of deathly cold and pain surged through my body as a scene began unfolding in my mind. A lone man in a black hooded cape stood on a hill looking down on an army of thousands. Behind him sat what looked like a War Beast, the skeleton of a snake with bony wings. It was curled up in a coil and loomed over the figure protectively. Its mouth moved as if the two were conversing.

The army started moving as one, row after row of soldiers in dark, shiny armor strode forth with shields and maces in their hands. Some had swords or cudgels, but most wore maces. A thought crossed my mind. Swords didn't do well against bone monsters and the undead, but heavy and spiked weapons did. Was that army created to subdue that winged snake? Or maybe it was just a coincidence...

The hooded figure climbed atop the War Beast's head and raised a long blade, one that was easily twice the length of my Birds of Prey dagger. A mass of green, purple, and black glowing tendrils flowed around the weapon, easily extending ten feet beyond the sharp point. With a single gesture of his blade, the snake shot down the hill, half floating and half slithering as its bony wings flapped uselessly.

Thousands of magical shields appeared in front and around the soldiers, bright mana erupting from their bodies and creating a golden barrier that was visible to the naked eye. Countless elemental and mana attack spells flew toward the charging duo and harmlessly passed by them or exploded against a dome that covered the hooded figure. Every spell that made contact with the dome simply corroded or turned to dust.

The figure raised his sword and swung it in a straight downward arc. A wide fan-shaped blast shot out toward the lines of soldiers, and halfway toward their target, the surge of mana turned into a black mist that slammed into his opponents' army, killing the first few lines of soldiers almost immediately, and inflicting terrible pain on those who weren't as lucky. The armor turned brittle and shattered, flesh turned to mush, and bones disintegrated.

The hooded figure swung his blade again, and a second burst of mana flew toward the army, releasing a green fog that spread so quickly that I couldn't even see the soldiers anymore. It went twelve lines in and only disappeared as the magicians in the back lines cast a gust of wind. The scene stopped there and suddenly flashed quickly through my mind, speeding up and stopping at the very end where the hooded figure stood amidst the defeated army. Everyone was dead.

The pain disappeared along with the image of the hooded figure and his winged snake as I gasped for air. A chuckle filled my ears, and it wasn't one of the good kind. What also lingered was an aftertaste of what I was going to turn into. With such power...yes, I would be able to protect everyone and destroy any army that stood in my way. It was a means to an end, one that I'd happily sell my soul for.

"That was the last battle of the first man to ever become a pestilence lord. Now tell me, do you regret your choice after witnessing such brutal death and destruction?"

"No," I said through a ragged intake of air. "I don't regret it as long as I can protect my friends and family. I would even become the most hated person in this world, Brahma."

"Good, good. You will now undergo your evolution, Pestilence Lord. It will depend on you how much of your humanity

remains afterward."

CHAPTER 11 – SCABS

I came to my senses on the altar room's floor. It was cold and hard, and my body was barely able to move. The bones in my body felt as if they were about to break when I tried to stand. A thundering booming reverberated in my mind, disorienting me. I fell to the ground again and passed out.

Something warm and soft caressed my skin and I felt as if I was floating on a cloud. A weightlessness had taken over, removing all the pain I'd felt earlier. I slowly opened my eyes, only to see the flickering of warm, gentle lights. Candles were lit all around me.

"He's awake," a voice spoke softly. "Cade? Can you hear me?"

My dried, heavy lips parted as I forced a string of words out.

"Where am I? What happened?"

The last thing I remembered was talking to Brahma, who had warned me that the evolution could take away my humanity. I passed out after that. Did I fail and lose all that I—

"You're upstairs. We had to pry the armor off your body and cut the clothes away. It was all glued to your body."

My hearing wasn't that good, so I barely registered the words as if through a blurry haze.

"Sonya?" I asked and reached for the voice. My hand landed on something soft.

"Yes, that's me," she said as she leaned in and tried to help me stand. A second pair of hands joined her and I sat upright.

"How are you feeling?" the second voice asked. I knew it was Emma as her golden hair passed through my voice.

"I feel like...shit," I muttered. "I feel as if someone has trampled me over."

"And you look like the part," Jeanette's voice came from behind me. A pair of new hands touched my back. A light sting jolted through my body. "Hold still or I can't cut off this dead skin."

My eyes had adjusted enough by then to see Sonya and Emma standing to either side of me. Selene was sitting on the edge of the bath, her legs, and arms crossed over her chest. When our eyes met, she looked away and I couldn't help but feel agitated. What was going on? Why was Jeanette cutting off dead skin?

"Can someone tell me what you're doing? Jeanette?"

"Yes, but you should take it one step at a time. Emma's been healing you all day. Remember when you guys saved my life back when I came to your guild home?" Sonya asked, wrapping her hand around mine. "This was more or less the same."

"So I was wounded? How?"

"Oh, be quiet just for a minute, alright?" Jeanette hissed from behind me. "Just another minute and we'll show you everything."

I took in a deep breath for a long moment, holding it in as I felt her blade scraping against my back. It didn't hurt so much as it was an unpleasant feeling.

I waited while staring at Selene. She was acting strange and I didn't like it. I held my hand out for her and she hesitantly slid into the water. My black-haired assassin was naked and still holding her hands over her chest as if embarrassed.

"Come here," I said, trying to smile but the corners of my lips felt as if they were glued together.

"I—am sorry," she whispered. "Forgive me."

"Forgive—what?"

"I was afraid and...just sat there. I won't be afraid anymore. It's you, right? Cade? Is it really you?"

"Of course it's him, Selene," Sonya said and I could feel the exasperation in her voice. "Who else would it be?"

"Well, I didn't know that, did I?"

"Finished. You can look into the mirror now," Emma said, producing one from her storage and handing it to me. The smile on her face was genuine, but she seemed too tired to even stand properly.

"Look, Cade, your body was in a mess when we found you in the altar room," Sonya explained as she took the mirror from Emma and held it in front of me. "We've done the best we can, and it should heal just fine. Give it some time, alright? Hell, maybe you even need to absorb someone as your class description said."

I looked into the mirror and saw something that I hadn't expected to see. My short, black hair was still there, as was my face, but it was covered by little cuts and scabs that were already being covered by fresh skin.

My chest and arms looked much worse. They were covered by thick black and red blotches that made me think back on the wendigo, who'd also been banged up badly but recovering.

"Were they growths? Or just rotten skin or something?"

"Both? I don't know, they were disgusting, but the moment I cut through them they just turned to muck," Jeanette explained.

I couldn't help but look down at my pelvis, just to make sure everything was in place. Luckily, it was. The girls seemingly found it amusing as they chuckled. Only Selene was still afraid.

"Do you want to leave, Selene?" I asked. "No hard feelings. I'll be myself soon enough, alright?"

The elf bit her lower lip, gulped, and then threw herself at me.

"I'm sorry! I'm so sorry. It's just that—I don't know. I was afraid and felt as if you'd turned to something else and—"

I hugged her, placing a kiss on her forehead. The long, pointy ears wiggled at that, which made me smile. Her naked skin was pushing against mine, and I couldn't help but wince. I was full of cuts despite the rapid healing process.

"I'm not going anywhere, alright? I'm fine."

Selene pulled away from me, looking up into my eyes and nodding.

"I'm sorry. Do you want to get out? Here, let me help you."

"And I'm the one who gets to clean shit all by myself while the others go off to fuck. Just great," Jeanette mumbled.

"No one's going to fuck. I can't even sit or lay down, babe. I'm in pain, by Tan'Ruad."

"Well, you won't be in a bit. Emma's been healing you for hours. It's odd how you haven't sealed up yet."

"Sealed up?" I snorted. "It's not like I'm leaking, Jeanette."

"No, well, you know what I mean. Ugh, whatever. Also, you're welcome. Now get out, I want to see if those cuts on your ass are closing up."

I shot her a wink and got out of the bath with Selene's help. She held my hand and steadied me as I was still on shaky legs. As the water dried from my skin, I could feel the pain lessen and the wounds healing. Emma cast another spell on me, just in case, and Sonya grabbed a thin, smooth bathrobe that she helped me get into.

"Do you think it will be like this for all of us? Or just Cade because he's an evil killer?" Emma asked. "I kind of don't want to have cuts and scabs all over. I'm too pretty for that."

"You would be just as pretty if you were scabbed all over, love," I said, holding my hand out for her to take. She did and I pulled her into a gentle hug, the smooth, thin fabric doing much to ease the pain.

"Hey, I forgot to mention, you don't have any nice clothes right now. Usvee and umm, two of Ferid's daughters are making you three sets. They should probably be finished soon. It's been a few hours since we measured you."

"All of you," Jeanette purred as we made our way to the bedroom. "And I think you've grown, but I'm not sure. I'd have to feel you inside me first."

"Didn't we agree that I...could be first?" Selene asked weakly.

"Just ignore her," Sonya said, giving the swashbuckler a mock glare and mouthing 'plug'.

"Ahh, whatever. I'm already used to it, so just bring it on, witch."

"Oh, you're so fucked!"

Sonya tackled the brunette onto the bed and they burst into laughter, giggles, and crystal translucent toys.

"At least someone's having a good time," I said, raising an eyebrow. "You two have become...fond of each other."

"If you mean each other's pussies, yes, we have," Sonya said and stuck her tongue out. "She's a squirter, so I have fun teasing her."

"Sonya! You promised not to tell anyone!" Jeanette protested, slapping the black-haired magician's ass so hard it reverberated off the walls.

Sonya gasped and stared at Jeanette with her mouth wide open.

"You know, his dick would fit in there just fine."

"Ahh! You're so getting it!"

I felt a surge of mana washing over the room, and Jeanette gasped, then fell almost limp onto the bed. Her legs were spread a moment later and Sonya was sliding two fingers between her still-wet lips.

"N—no! Not with mana! Sonya!"

Emma sighed and led me over to the one comfortable chair we had in the bedroom, pulled the robe off my shoulders, and placed it on the chair.

"Why don't you check what changed? Can you read it out loud to drown out Jeanette's moaning?"

"Yeah, sure, though I don't mind her voice a bit," I said, winking at the swashbuckler.

"Love you, lover."

"Love you too, babe."

I pulled up my class card, and it had changed drastically. After hitting level 60, I had 14 free stats left, so I pushed 8 into strength to get up to an even number, and the rest into stamina.

CLASS CARD			
Name	Cade	Race	Human
Level	60	Experience	38%
Class	Assassin	Sub-Class	Pestilence Lord
Strength	200	Stamina	208
Agility	218	Dexterity	221
Charisma	148	Free Stats	0

SPECIAL STATS			
Accuracy	176%	Dodge	92%
Critical Hit	66%	Critical Damage	200%
Defense Penetration	33%	Physical Resistance	64%
Magical Resistance	62%	Debuff Resistance	100%
Debuff Accuracy	150%	Debuff Effectiveness	100%
Debuff Duration	200%	Attack Reach	159%

"That was kind of to be expected," Sonya shot over her shoulder as she was already busy 'punishing' Jeanette.

"Not that hard! Come on, be gentle!" the swashbuckler grumbled. "I don't like it when you act all tough!"

I sighed inwardly and moved on.

"Yes, it was. Now it makes sense how all those high-leveled nobles and the King's Guard were so strong. Just a hundred of me could take on an army. How damaging is that for morale?"

"Damaging or not, sit, please," Emma said, pushing me down. "We need to check if your best part is still functional while you go through all your stats," Emma said as she nodded toward me while eyeing Selene. "Go on. Didn't you say you wanted to be the first one?"

"B—but I have never—done that!"

Emma sighed as she pushed me down. I'd remained standing as I didn't want my elf girlfriend to feel uncomfortable...or future wife? We were still out on that...

I sat and Selene went down on her knees as Emma pulled her hair back into a ponytail and tied it with a hairband.

"Are you sure you want to, Selene? Especially when I'm rambling about stats? That's not so romantic."

"Oh, shush, you," Emma retorted. "We all want to know how strong you've just become, right? We want to know if our chances of survival just rose or not."

"They definitely did, love. Alright."

"Good. And you, go on," she whispered in the elf's ear. "It's just as we told you. Take the tip in your mouth and...just like that."

Selene's eyes were focused on mine as she lowered her head between my legs, taking my cock in her hand and kissing the tip. A jolt of pleasure ran up my body as everything was amplified when Sonya released her mana blanket. I gripped the armrests as Selene's lips slid along my entire length. Her free hand cupped my balls and massaged them as she started bobbing her head back and forth, never removing her eyes from mine.

"Keep going," Emma whispered, still holding Selene's hair and guiding her head, pushing it a bit too far down. The elf gagged and tried to pull away, but Emma held her down. "It's all good, don't stop. My first time was just like it."

My devilish priest's hands slid down to cup one breast and the other went between Selene's legs, sliding into her wet pussy. The black-haired elf cried in surprise and squirmed, trying to get Emma to stop, but gave in only several seconds later.

"Oh, you like this, huh?" Emma said with a mischievous smile. "Sonya? Can I get one of—ahh, thanks."

She caught what Benny called a crystal dildo and slid it between the elf's legs. Selene tensed and her teeth sank into my flesh just a little bit before she caught herself.

"Emma," I grunted as my cock felt as if it was about to explode. "Don't push her...if she can't, oh lord, Selene!" I cried as she dug her nails into my balls and circled her tongue around my tip with every dip of her head. Her lips tightened and she sucked harder. That in combination with Sonya's mana blanketing almost drove me to almost cum that quickly.

I pushed Selene away and pulled her in for a kiss.

"Turn your ass around," I whispered. She just nodded and turned, lowering her rear, lips glistening and ready for me to enter. I slowly guided my tip between her legs and felt a wave of pleasure erupt inside I finally got to make love with Selene in front of the other girls.

I glanced over to Sonya and Jeanette. The latter had her face buried in a pillow while her ass was out, another of Sonya's dildos sticking out of her pussy and a plug stuck in her ass.

"Fuck me! Harder! Please, Sonya!" the swashbuckler begged and moved her hips in rhythm with Sonya's movements. More mana left Sonya's hands and entered Jeanette's body, forcing her to squirt with every movement of her fingers.

Selene looked away as if embarrassed, but Emma forced her head around and pushed the elf's chin up. She leaned in close and stuck her tongue into Selene's mouth, exploring her as she bounced off my hips.

I really didn't feel like talking about my stats when I was being drained of my most precious resource and the whole atmosphere felt odd, but both Sonya and Emma yelled at me when I stopped.

"My special stats went up...by 10% and...oh, shit, this is so good. Can't we do this...later?"

"No!" they yelled in unison.

"Ugh. You two are the worst," Selene yelled.

"They sure are, babe. Anyway, the rest went...up to their maximums...anything debuff-oriented is top."

My golden-haired beauty suddenly pushed the elf into me and spread her legs apart.

"You're so done for," Emma said with a wink and knelt in front of us. She leaned in and traced her tongue along my cock and Selene's clit, twirling and sucking.

Selene's fingers dug into my hands, causing me pain, but I ignored it and thrust my hips as fast as I could. Emma's fingernails dug into my balls, squeezing and massaging them, causing me pain and pleasure in equal measure. The pressure in my cock was too much to hold back. For a second I blacked out from the pain, but I felt her spasming around me and heard her screaming. Emma pulled away as we came together, giggling as Selene hid her face in her hands.

"That was intense," Emma said as she pulled the elf off me. "Come on, let's get you cleaned. You're all sweaty and you're...dripping." Emma traced her fingers over Selene's pussy, wiping some of the cum off and putting it in her mouth. "Good. You don't taste like death."

I snorted at her jab.

"What? You thought I'd be cumming little death soldiers or something?"

It was Emma's turn to laugh.

"So, it looks like you can go some more," she said, sitting hurriedly in my lap and guiding my member between her legs. "Fuck me next."

CHAPTER 12 –
NEW POWERS

Congratulations! Your intimacy with
Emma has risen to level 2!

Reward: Emma will receive 5 to all stat points and
both share and contribute 10 from and to all other
pack member's stats.

"Oh! This is so good! I wish you'd brought me to level 2 much sooner!" Emma said excitedly.

"Level 2? What are you talking about?" Jeanette asked as she lay atop Sonya. Her hand was between the other woman's legs, her middle finger sliding in and out of her still. The sound she made was pretty loud in the deafening silence that had ensued after we'd all come multiple times.

"My intimacy with Cade went up to level 2 and I get more stats from all of you. And oh, Tan'Aria! My stats! I'm so strong now!"

"Intimacy, huh?" Sonya whispered. "So, if we go by seniority, I'm next? And do you have a way to check?"

"Hold on, let me check," I said, opening my class card again and then my skills, and finally monster cards. There, under the soulbound card, I saw the names of the women who entrusted their souls to me.

Monster Card: Soulbound

Emma: Level 2, 00
Sonya: Level 1, 59
Jeanette: Level 1, 82

```
Selene: Level 1, 27
Elvina: Level 1, 00
```

"So, I'm the highest?" Jeanette asked and finally stopped sliding her middle finger in and out of Sonya, who protested by squeezing her tights around the swashbuckler's arm.

"Don't stop," Sonya moaned. "Just a little bit more. And look, he's watching us."

I indeed was watching the two and could feel my member start pumping blood again.

"You two have no idea how much I want to take you again but we need to get cleaned, have dinner, and...do a bunch of other stuff like checking what new skills I have and...stuff?"

"Stuff?" Emma asked suspiciously. "What do you mean by stuff?"

"Well, there's this...thing."

"Thing?" Selene snorted. "You're being surprisingly vague, which can only mean one thing. As usual, you're going to do something stupid."

"Mhm," I mumbled and finally got off the chair. Selene was seated on the ground and in Emma's arms, which brought me unspeakable comfort and joy. If they could get along well, I would be the happiest man in this new place.

We bathed, again, and this time it didn't hurt as all the scabs were gone, and the cuts had healed over. It had been an odd moment seeing myself in that state, but sometimes we needed a reminder of what we had. It was easy to lose things and watch it all burn, but building up and finding that which you can hold dear was much harder.

The sound of heavy footsteps resounded from the staircase just as we were drying off. A familiar voice called out from the central hallway on the second floor.

"The new clothes are here."

It was Mirna, the dwarven sister of Ferid and Nalgid. She was an interesting one, and I'd definitely want to spend some more time with her. For a dwarf, she was amazingly well built with toned arms and legs, large breasts, and long orange hair that went well with her paler complexion. Unlike her brothers and kin, she didn't wear armor. Instead, she wore what I could best describe as a smocked waist red and white peasant dress. It was too small for her, that much was obvious as her breasts were pouring out from the deep cleavage, and her waist, though not nearly as wide as most dwarves I'd seen, struggled against the tight fabric.

"Why don't ye come out, boss man? I want te try them on ye meself."

"He's naked," Emma said as she slid on a dress of her own over her head and wriggled into it. Who cared about underwear, right? Well, not me. I liked her just fine like that.

"So what? He's got nothin I haven't seen yet. Come on, no need te be shy."

The girls started laughing but not in a mean fashion. They found it rather interesting how the dwerna didn't care much about my humbleness.

"I think she'll jump him right away," Jeanette said, shooting me a wink. "Maybe you can add another one to your pack, as the card called us."

"No, I...don't think I want anymore," I whispered so Mirna wouldn't hear me. Hell, I didn't mind her being a kind-of-tall dwarf, but damn, she'd crush me with those arms and hips.

"I think she should get a reward," Sonya said. "If she did a good job with the clothes, you could...just do as she asked."

"Hey, Mirna?" Jeanette called. "How good are the clothes? He won't come out naked unless they're the highest of quality."

"Oh, by me brother's beard, I'm te best in the village! Just come out ere already!"

To hell with false modesty. Four naked women were all over me not even an hour ago, so yeah.

I stepped out of our bedroom with my member out on full display. Mirna, to my surprise, didn't even look down once. Sure, she'd seen all of me, but she wasn't gawking or playing around and produced three sets of clothing that she held out. The girls joined me in random states of undress and looking even more excited than me.

"What do we have here?" Sonya asked, taking one of the outfits and pressing it against my body.

From what I could see, all three were more or less the same in my eyes and consisted of white and black shirts, black and dark gray pants, an overcoat, a coat, and two pairs of shoes. Now, I had no idea how they made them, I didn't care, and I wasn't planning on asking. The material looked expensive, felt soft and comfortable to the touch, and I'd make sure to repay her. That's all that mattered.

"Do ye need some underwear? I made some just in case, well Usvee did. Said te new boss man needed te finest to protect his jewels."

"Oh, I like her even more now!" Emma giggled. "Thank you, Mirna. I mean it!"

"Yes, yes. When I need a favor meself, you will repay it, yes?"

"Of course, Mirna. You have my word. Is there anything I can do for you now?"

"No, no, I'm fine. I just need ye to say that ye owe me."

Owing someone could be something that could potentially cause me harm, though I knew that if any one of them tried to do something stupid, well, let's say that it would be the last thing they did. However, I was pretty sure none of them would be as stupid.

"Yes, I do owe you to a certain extent, so once you know what you want, I will give it to you."

"Good, good. A man's worth as much as their word, ye know?"

I eyed the dwerna for a long moment, the way she stood there, stared me down, and honestly looked very, very...pretty in her own way.

"Yes, I do. Tell me, how far along is the temple?"

"Almost done. Me thinks we just need a few more hours.

That's also why I came here. Definitely not to see ye naked, though I like what I see. If ye know what I mean?" she said and wiggled her eyebrows.

"Oh, Tan'Ruad! No! She's got the hots for you!" Jeanette laughed. "Oh, oh! This is so awesome! Why not add another exotic?"

"Add another—" Mirna started to say, but then gasped. "Hmm, I wouldn't say no. Probably. Maybe," the dwerna said hurriedly as her cheeks reddened. "I'm going now."

"Hey, wait, why don't you stay for a little bit? We could show you how we—"

"No, no, I'm good. Thank ye, lady, but I'm good. Now, if ye'll excuse me."

Mirna turned about, remembered she was still holding the underwear, placed them on a nearby chair, and hurried out. The girls started giggling, but I didn't find it as funny. When Jeanette asked her, she genuinely seemed interested in at least staying for a little longer, but then got flustered and left.

"You need to be nicer to her. I think she wants to hang out with your girls, and I don't blame her. You're all awesome, and fun to be around. She has no one but her family."

"Hmm, you might be right there. And I like her too," Emma said as she swung the clothes over her shoulder. "Promise. I'll try to spend more time with her."

"*We* promise," Sonya added hurriedly. "Besides, I need some new underwear as well. It's getting breezy during the nights."

I pulled her close and slid my hand up her dress, squeezing her ass.

"And you're not wearing any right now."

"I never wear underwear. Isn't that just how you like it?" she whispered, her breath hot on my neck.

"Hey, hey, no, enough," the swashbuckler pushed between us. "I think we've all had enough for one session."

"Talk for yourself, skank," Sonya grinned. "I only had him for a bit."

I sighed and turned to Emma.

"Help me dress? If I stay here any longer, I won't get anything done."

"Well, it's technically night, so...we could go back?" Selene proposed with a weak smile.

"You want to come with me later tonight? I want to go somewhere. Test out my new powers. You could keep me company."

"Rude," Sonya jabbed. "Alright. Let me help you, too. I'm rather curious to see what the evolution brought you."

A short while later, the girls sat around the bar, drinking and chatting about sprucing up the place. I pulled a swig, drank my amber liquid, and then made my way into the altar room. The compendium sat there in Brahma's hands, waiting for me. I picked it up, pushed some mana into it, and felt a cold wave of power pass through me.

The skill page came alive in my mind, and instead of the previous plague revenant skill tree, I now had two: Pestilence Lord and Patron. I opened my new evolution first, where I found two more skill trees. One was of the plague revenant and the other of the pestilence lord. Since I wanted to keep the best for last, I started with the revenant's passives.

Congratulations! Due to your evolution into Pestilence Lord, the skills Mark of the Hunter and Predator have merged into Apex Predator.

NOTE: All learned Plague Revenant passive skills have been upgraded to level 5.

PASSIVE CLASS SKILLS

Name: Apex Predator, Level 1
Effect: Lower the stats of all enemies within 50 feet by 15 while in combat. The debuff can not be blocked or negated.

```
Name: Biohazard, Level 5
Fffect: Raises debuff accuracy by 20
and debuff effectiveness by 35
```

I now only had two passive skills, and one of them gave me stats that were already maxed out. Still, I appreciated the Godveil's intent. One major change was the loss of skill descriptions. It's not like I missed them, but for some reason, the Godveil decided not to grace me with the short explanations.

There were two more new passives under the revenant tree that I had unlocked after leveling up. I paid for both and upgraded them to level 3 straight away.

```
Name: Sapper, Level: 3
Effect: Lower the resistance stats
of all your enemies by 12  in a 50
foot radius while in combat.
```

```
Name: Stolen Power, Level: 3
Effect: Absorb 0.5  total stats from
every debuff afflicted enemy within a 30
foot radius while in combat.
```

The two new passives were extremely interesting, not only because they raised my chance of inflicting damage even further, but also because my stats would rise even further when fighting large groups of debuffed enemies.

I checked the support skills next.

```
Congratulations! Due to your evolution into
Pestilence Lord, the skills Shadow Step and
Shadow Stride have merged into Fade.
```

```
NOTE: All previously learned Plague Revenant
support skills have been upgraded to level 5.
```

```
SUPPORT CLASS SKILLS
```

```
          Name: Fade, Level: 1
   Effect: Move instantaneously in a 30
      step radius in all directions.
          Cooldown: 10 seconds

     Name: Dark Presence, Level: 5
 Effect: Reduces 25  dodge and 35  accuracy of
  any target within a 30 step area of effect.
 Cooldown: 300 seconds, Duration: 200 seconds

     Name: Plague Domain, Level: 5
   Effect: Inflict 2 random Level 2 plagues
    every 20 seconds to all targets within
         a 30 step area of effect.
 Cooldown: 600 seconds, Duration: 200 seconds

        Name: Nightveil, Level: 5
 Effect: Cover your body in mist and become
    100  invisible while hiding and 50
  invisible while moving within darkness.
          Cooldown: 30 seconds
```

In all honesty, I liked the new movement spell much more than the previous two. A 10-second cooldown was more important than the distance it could take me. The other three skills had received upgrades and now lasted longer, were more effective, and would allow me to hide better during the night.

There was only a single new support skill that I'd unlocked by hitting level 60 within the skill tree, but it was a good one. Again, I upgraded it to level 3 because I had the funds. With a stack of over 15,000 coins, I'd let myself indulge in some upgrades. The only reason why I didn't upgrade them to level 5 was so I could help the girls upgrade their own skills further.

```
      Name: Extend Senses, Level: 3
 Effect: Release a burst of mana that will create
  a 100 step domain around the user, allowing them
```

to sense any movement within the area of effect.
Cooldown: 60 seconds

The new support skill I'd just gotten was going to help me in many more ways than I ever thought possible. Being able to sense any movement within that hypothetical dome was priceless.

I moved to the active class skills and was again hit by the same message.

NOTE: All previously learned Plague Revenant
active skills have been upgraded to level 5.

ACTIVE CLASS SKILLS

Name: Quick Attack, Level 5
Effect: Quickly attack the target five times in
rapid succession. Raise critical hit 25 and
critical damage 35 if attack target from behind.
Cooldown: 15 seconds

Name: Leech Strike, Level 5
Effect: Strike the target and inflict a (Leech
Life) debuff and drain the target's health.
Cooldown:60 seconds, Duration: 20 seconds
(NOTE: Leech Life   mends minor
and medium wounds.)

Name: Backstab, Level: 5
Effect: Attack an enemy from behind and attempt an
assassination. If the attack fails, inflict the
debuff (Cripple II).
Cooldown: 45 seconds
(NOTE: Cripple II lowers the target's
dodge by 36 for 5 seconds.)

Name: Plague Strike, Level: 5
Effect: Attack with a plague imbued
weapon and inflict (Plague II). Add a

2nd debuff with a 50 chance.
Cooldown: 30 seconds
(NOTE: Plague II lowers all the target's
stats by 16 for 15 seconds.)

Name: Plague Fang, Level: 5
Effect: Deliver a single, powerful attack
that will always inflict (Poison II). Add
another random debuff with a 50 chance.
Cooldown: 40 seconds
(NOTE: Poison II drains the target's life
by 1.5 every second for 15 seconds.
The effect is stackable.)

Name: Blade Storm, Level: 5
Effect: Attack an area of effect with a
mass of mana infused blades, and inflict
(Bleed II), and add a second stack of
(Bleed II) with a 30 chance.
Cooldown: 45 seconds
(NOTE: Bleed II drains the target's life
by 0.5 every second and lowers all stats
by 8 until the bleeding has stopped.)

Name: Plague Storm, Level: 5
Effect: Attack an area of effect with a mass of
plague infused daggers and inflict (Plague II).
Add up to 2 extra, random debuffs on all targets.
Cooldown: 60 seconds

I was a bit overwhelmed just reading the upgraded
versions of my previous skills, and to top that off, I had two
more new attack skills. As with the others before them, I
invested in getting them up to level 3 right away.

Name: Dagger Rain, Level: 3
Effect: Blanket the target area with daggers
made from plague mana, inflicting (Bleed

II or Plague II) on every target.
Cooldown: 60 seconds

Name: Assault, Level: 3
Effect: Inflict a crippling attack on the target,
inflicting (Mangled II) and increasing own attack
speed and defense penetration by 1 for every
next successful attack. Stacks up to 10 times.
Cooldown: 150 seconds, Duration: 30 seconds
(NOTE: Mangled II lowers the target's
speed by 40 for 15 seconds.)

The decision between which of the two skills was better would be a hard one. If I had to make it, that is. Both were fantastic and served different purposes. One would serve to try and break a group of soldiers or monsters, while the other would be perfect when I had to fight one-on-one again. Like with the wendigo.

"So, let's see what good old Brahma has given me," I whispered once I was finally done with my old evolution.

I had a nagging feeling that many people felt the same way and immediately wanted to discard the old, but I had to remind myself that I wasn't a maxed-out pestilence lord, but one who just hit level 60 and though my new powers were more than I could hope for, I still had a long road to go before they fully unraveled.

I returned to the previous page where both skill trees sat and then went into my new evolution. There I found one passive, one support, and three active class skills. I started with the passive and support ones.

Name: Corrosion, Level 1
Effect: Increase Defense Penetration
by 10 whenever attacking a debuffed
target. Stacks up to 3 times.

Name: Pestilence Aura, Level: 1
Effect: Inflict 50 retribution damage to any

target within a 15 step area of effect.
Cooldown: 300 seconds, Duration: 60 seconds

The two skills were no game-changers by themselves, but they were incredibly useful and tailored to what I'd become. And my fighting style. Considering they were only level 1, I couldn't even start to imagine how strong they'd be one day.

The three active class skills were next, and I honestly couldn't say much when just looking at their names, though the battle I'd seen play out in my mind was a good starting point.

Name: Pestilent Wave, Level: 1
Effect: Attack a large area with a wave of pestilent mana that will knock all targets off their feet and inflict (Plague III). Add another random Level III negative effect on all previously debuffed targets.
Cooldown: 120 seconds
(NOTE: Plague III lowers all the target's stats by 21 for 15 seconds.)

Name: Pestilent Storm, Level: 1
Effect: Create a storm using pestilent mana to ravage every target within the area of effect, and inflict random Level III debuffs every time they are hit. Stacks up to 3 times.
Cooldown: 300 seconds

Name: Onslaught, Level: 1
Effect: Unleash a deadly combo of up to 5 attacks on a single target, inflicting (Mangled III) and (Numb III) with a 30 chance. Chance goes up with every successful attack.
Cooldown: 240 seconds
(NOTE 1: Mangled III lowers the target's speed by 50 for 15 seconds.)

(NOTE 2: Numb III lowers the target's
attack power by 50 for 15 seconds.)

If the first two skills hadn't already impressed me, I
surely would have been by the three active battle skills that
followed. Two were area-of-effect attack skills, and the third
was a single-target attack skill. And everything dealt level 3
debuffs, which was just the cherry on top.

The last thing I needed to check was the Patron Skill
Tree, so I flipped back to the page in question. There I found
two 5 different tiers of active and passive skills, one each for
every type and tier. Only the first tier wasn't greyed out.

Name: Guild Communication
Effect: Allows for guild wide
communication between all members.
NOTE 1: Guild Communication between all
members is instantaneous and automatic
within all communication rooms.
NOTE 2: Guild Officers, Vice Leaders,
and Guild Leaders are the only members
who can create guild rooms.
NOTE 3: No one aside from the Guild Leader can
force themselves into a communication room.

Name: Guild Convergence
Effect: Send out a guild wide teleport
invitation that will be active for 10 seconds.
All the guild members who have accepted the
convergence call will be teleported to the Guild
Leader after the 10 second timer is over.
Cooldown: 24 hours

Congratulations! Do you want to activate Guild
Communication?

"Yes, please," I replied and tensed as a strange sensation
washed over me. It was similar to Elvina's [Mental Space], but

not as intrusive on the mind. The prickly sensation I'd felt back then wasn't present, and I could clearly feel the room within my mind. Sure, it wasn't that hard to speak within the different mental spaces the helfar had made for us, but it had to take some kind of toll on her body.

"Can everyone hear me?" I asked, using the guild room.

"Yo, what is this, bro?" Benny was the first to speak.

"Does this mean I don't have to keep my [Mental Space] up any longer?" Elvina asked.

"Why are you still in the temple room? Come have a drink," Jeanette said, and then the guild room communications blew up when everyone started talking to one another.

"Hold on! Shut up for a moment!" I said, stopping them all from flooding the guild room. "I will create several rooms and then designate the room owners. Grom, you and your family get one. Nalgid, you and your clan get one. Banxi, you and your family get one too. Speak in there exclusively unless there's a guild emergency. This new communication skill isn't something that I can shut off as it's Brahma's gift."

I proceeded to tell them about convergence as well and how no one should ever accept the teleportation request unless I told them so explicitly.

Once the rooms were created and I had handed over the room ownership to the people in question, I created several more. One was for Mortimer, Callina, Mano, and Rafika. I then proceeded to make one for myself and the girls, one with the addition of Elvina, Mirna, Benny, Legs, Grom, Nalgid, Banxi, and Merek. The War Weaver showed up as a possible participant in the guild communications options, so I threw him in to feel more included. I named it the Leadership Room.

The next communication room I called The Hang-Out, and added everyone in there as well. If anyone wanted to talk to the other guild members within that communication room, they could do so. Everyone had the option to temporarily mute a room as well, which meant that they wouldn't receive any chat while inside that room.

Lastly, I created a Battle Room but remained there just by myself. That one would be used whenever we went to battle and the participants would change most of the time.

"Elvina," I said over the main guild room. "Please remove all your mental spaces. We can use the guild communication options now."

"Alright, and...doing them one by one...and...done."

I felt the tiniest pull at the back of my mind and then the mental link that had been there for months disappeared.

"Thank you. We will still need you to open mental spaces with people who aren't part of the guild, but for now, you can rest."

"You have no idea how hard it was to keep the spaces open at all times. I already feel much better. Thank you, Brahma."

I suddenly felt shitty for not giving it any thought before and cursed at myself.

"*Elvina? I'm sorry. I really am, alright? I'll make it up to you. I promise,*" I said over my newly gained guild communication skills.

It took her a moment to respond.

"*I don't blame you, but there was no need for you to ask about my skills, so please don't go there. And I'm fine now.*"

"*Alright. At least join us for a drink?*"

CHAPTER 13 – TESTING THE WATERS

It took me a good while to explain all of my new skills and upgrades to the ones I already had from before. The girls were just as excited to hear about them as I'd been exploring what my new evolution had entailed. What's more, I felt the urge to try them out on live targets, and no, not Benny or Legs despite them being mostly immortal.

"Anyone know how to get past the level 60 barrier? Level 41 was easy as there were enough people to kill back in Greystone, but here? They don't even have levels."

The girls shook their heads one by one, and despite everyone being nearly there, we had no idea how to get past it. I doubted any of our other guild members knew. Maybe one would know...

"Merek? Any idea how to get past the level 60 bottleneck?"

"No," he simply said. *"I never asked as I didn't think I'd get there in my lifetime."*

"Alright. Thanks anyway."

"Merek doesn't know either," I said with a sigh.

"I could have told you that," Selene said, perking her ears up. They wiggled cutely for a moment. "We've talked about it before, but information like that is closely guarded by the nobility. Or was, in this case. We would have done Giovanni a great favor to get that kind of info."

"Too bad we didn't kidnap any of them bastards," Sonya whispered. "They'd come in handy right about now."

"Hold on," Emma said, putting a hand on Sonya's. "Would you sleep safe knowing one of them was around? I sure wouldn't."

"True. Whatever. As long as we all hit level 60, I don't think we'll have anything to fear from the followers of Tan'Malas. Aside from the big bad dark one himself."

"I'll drink to that, Sonya," Jeanette said and raised her glass. "Cade? Want to get that intimacy up to 100?"

"No, not tonight, love," I said with a wink. "I'm going out to test my new skills on the dungeon monsters, then I have something else in mind."

I told them what I saw up in Banxi's watch tower, and that I wanted to learn more about the situation in the other town. Also, now that I was strong enough to become a menace to the enemy, maybe they would stop killing civilians. Even more so when I could pop up out of nowhere in the middle of the night and end them with ease.

"That's good, I like it," Emma said. "Unless we protect them, people won't believe in the Old Ones. Why would they want to convert if there's no one to protect them?"

"I agree. We need to set an example, Cade. Both in Garm and Balan villages. Maybe even that town northeast of Garm?"

I shook my head and even felt a pang of guilt. We couldn't overextend. Not yet.

"Znica, right? We can't stretch that far, even if I'd be happiest to attack Volarna right away. We'll need to lure the sub-pillars and their armies out in the open. And I need to test my new powers. Come on, want to join me out back?"

"I wouldn't miss that for anything in the world!" Jeanette exclaimed, drank whatever was left in her glass, and shot to her feet! "Come on, what are you waiting for? A written invitation?"

Emma and Sonya joined her, equally excited. Selene was a bit more subdued, and I could swear I saw a hint of jealousy in her eyes. Seeing someone within the same class evolve before you and into something extremely powerful. Yeah, I understood very well how she felt as I'd been there most of my earlier life. The last few months were more than overwhelming in many ways, so I'd need some time to process it all and sincerely hoped that my body wouldn't start falling apart because of all the plagues I'd be unleashing.

Benny was outside, running after Legs, who'd turned into his smaller form. I had no idea what they were doing, but they looked to be having fun, and that's all that mattered.

"Big guy? Want to check out my new skills?" I yelled after them. The two skidded to a stop and tumbled over each other, got back up, and rushed over to us.

"Yes, bro!" Benny cried as he clung to my leg. Legs did the same with my other leg as he screeched happily.

Since it was already late in the evening, I didn't see anyone outside as we made our way toward the temple. I wanted to check on the progress before we went down to the dungeons. Mortimer and Mano were sitting outside the temple on a bench, admiring the building and whispering something about the ship. I was about to greet them when Mano whispered about how he wished he hadn't come to this place because he'd become useless and a burden.

That couldn't be further from the truth. If he did nothing else in our lives, the man was instrumental to us escaping Greystone's waters, and that's something I could never repay him. I filed his complaint away for later and added Mortimer to that as well. We hadn't spent any time together lately, but that's more because I was busy with anything from killing monsters to, well...fucking.

"Definitely need to make more time for my people," I muttered as we approached the two. "Mortimer. Mano," I said in greeting. "Enjoying the evening?"

"Oh, boss man," Mano said and hurried to his feet. I put my hand on his shoulder and pushed him back down.

"Sit, my friend. Enjoy the evening. Do you guys want a snack? Something to drink?"

I immediately pulled out one of our whiskey bottles from my storage and handed it to the ship captain.

"Drink, guys. You will have to get your own glasses or

share. I don't have any with me."

"Why?" Mortimer asked, nodding to the bottle.

"No reason. I figured you guys could use a drink. Nothing else. Anyway, we're heading out to the dungeons to test my new powers. I'll catch you guys later, alright?"

Mortimer and Mano sat there in silence for a long moment and just waved as we made our way toward the southern exit. Everyone remained silent, but Selene took my hand in hers and squeezed gently.

"I heard them too. It can't be easy," she whispered as Elvina and Sonya rushed ahead.

Jeanette and Emma walked behind us and talked about the intimacy level. There wasn't much our resident priestess could tell her, but she kept pushing.

"Say, do you want to go out with me tonight? When I leave for Balan? You could keep me company."

"I'd love to. We don't want any horny women to jump you when you're most energetic, right?"

I snorted at that and put my arm around her.

"Horny elven women? Or women in general?"

"Oh, you tease," she chuckled. "I'm joking, of course, but really, you could use someone to have your back, right? We never know what your new powers or just the evolution could have done to you."

"Very true."

"And because of that, I accept. Just the two of us."

Emma slapped my ass and pushed into me.

"What are you two whispering about?"

I put my free arm around her waist and pulled her in for a kiss.

"Nothing special. So, what do you think? Will I be able to kick their ass or not?"

"The monsters?" she asked. "Of course."

"Hey, me too!" Jeanette exclaimed, grabbing onto me from behind. "Carry me!"

I let go of Emma and Selene, grabbing the

swashbuckler's rear as she hung off me, and squeezed.

"Soft. You need to work out more, babe."

"Oh! You! My ass is just perfect! Ask Sonya if you—wait, I know what you're doing. It's not funny."

"I'm not doing anything," I said squeezing again. "I like the way it feels, you know? Soft is good."

A short while later, we arrived at the dungeon spot. Elvina and Sonya were talking to Merek, who looked pretty beat up and tired. Emma cast a healing spell on him, and then another, which seemed to do wonders for the man. He straightened his back, stretched his arms, and offered our priestess a big smile.

"Thank you, Miss Emma. Cade."

"Merek. What level are you at?"

"I just hit 58. One or two days and I should be done. Thank you for asking."

He placed the big shield on his back and strapped the spear to it before sitting down on a big log that wasn't there the last time. Must have dragged it there in his free time. The girls joined him, and Selene pushed him almost over, forcing the spearman to scoot over to the end.

"Why are you here if I—"

"Yes, you may," Selene replied, nudging his side with her elbow. "My man here wants to try out his new skills."

Merek looked at her funnily and then smiled. I knew that the two were more like brother and sister, so I wasn't bothered by their closeness. If she hadn't been soulbound to me and I couldn't read her feelings, then I probably would have been jealous. Luckily, there was no interest in the other man.

"Can I stay and watch too?" Merek asked, and I nodded.

"Yes, you can. In fact, I'm counting on it. If something bad happens, you need to protect them."

"What could possibly happen with you around?" Sonya said, shooting me a wink.

"Yes, that's exactly what I'm afraid of. Alright, let me get into position."

I looked out at the monsters below, but since it was already dark, I couldn't see them all. There was some light coming off the moon, but not enough to light up the forest. It didn't matter, though, as I had a bunch of AOE attacks now and I didn't need to see the monsters in order to hit them.

I opened up with [Dark Presence], [Plague Domain], and [Pestilence Aura], all three skills covering the area around me with debuffs and a retribution skill that I wanted to check out. My passive, [Apex Predator], activated on its own as I approached the nearest monsters. It needed a 'be in combat' trigger, but since my other support skills already lowered their stats or counted down to inflict debuffs, the predator skill had its necessary activation requirement.

I activated [Fade] and jumped into the midst of a group of around twenty dungeon creeps. Some stood on two legs, resembling Banxi in a way but they were larger and more muscled, while others looked like oversized wolves. They belonged to the same class of monsters, feral gaars. Strong and aggressive but lacking any special abilities. Among them was a 10-foot-tall tortoise-like creature with a massive shell on its back that promised some resistance.

"Here goes," I whispered and activated [Pestilent Wave].

A green mass of mana gathered before me, and I recognized it from the scene that had unfolded in my mind. It shot forth and slammed into the monsters, knocking over half of them down and enveloping them in a green mana fog that inflicted them with [Plague III] and hit them with more debuffs than I could count. The creatures roared and screeched, some in pain and others enraged by the sudden powerful attack. My power rose by at least 15 points across the board as debuffs stacked and then rose some more. The debuff [Sapper] and [Corrosion] activated, lowering their resistances and increasing my defense penetration by 30%.

The monsters that survived the initial attack grabbed

forward, trying to reach me, but their charge was slow and painful. A few steps into their assault the plague tore through what little resistance they had. Their fur steamed with toxic death as it penetrated their bodies to the very core. Flesh and bone boiled them from the inside. The smell of death spread spread on the soft breeze carried from the sea.

"Shit, now I understand," I muttered. "Just the debuffs are killing them with ease."

I could hear the girls and Merek talk excitedly. Honestly, I could understand their excitement as I felt overwhelmed by it all. Such power shouldn't be available to ordinary people, or adventurers in my case. No, wait, I was no ordinary adventurer anymore. The old gods had made me into one of their...servants? Was that what I was? In all honesty, I could have had worse masters than the three that created the Godveil...

There were no experience gain notifications, only coin drops, a single monster card, a Dodge I no less, and the usual monster corpses. Of all the creatures surrounding me, I'd had hoped at least the tortoise monster would prove hard to deal with, but no, it died just as easily.

I used [Fade] to emerge inside another group of monsters that had been out of my range. The same debuffs immediately hit them, and I followed up with [Pestilenct Storm] next to check how it would activate. A purple and black and green orb rose from within and hovered some ten feet above me, crackling with deathly energies. It turned into a fog-like state and slammed down as if an explosion had hammered the ground. The fog expanded all around me just as tendrils very much like lightning started destroying everything around me.

My powers increased again but not as much since this skill was significantly stronger than the one I used minutes ago. The knockback effect was great, but this was pure death, and after several seconds of utter destruction, all that remained were monster corpses.

I was so dumbfounded by the sheer strength behind the

attack that I just stood there for a long minute, just imagining if I'd been as strong during the Greystone siege as I was now, could I have made a difference? The reasonable answer was no, but there was a tiny hint of guilt that wouldn't leave.

"Hey, got anything else to show off?" Jeanette yelled from where they were sitting.

"Yeah! It's not like we're jealous or something!" Sonya added. "An assassin class out-damages a magician in area of effect attacks! That's just great!"

I knew they were just joking, but she was right. Even though I wanted to reason with myself that everyone could have gotten this evolution with a bit of luck, I sincerely doubted it. There was more at play here than I knew, and Brahma could possibly have those answers. Benny had once joked that something must have brought us together as we all had special classes, and he was probably more right than I liked to think.

"Hold on, I got one more AOE I want to try out, then two more single attacks."

I turned toward the forest and eyed the monsters roaming within. There were only about a dozen or so from what I could see, but that was more than enough for me to test out the last new area skill. I walked up closer and made sure I was within range, then activated [Dagger Rain]. To my surprise, both my daggers appeared in front of me, but they were made from mana. Two daggers became four, then eight, then sixteen...Within seconds, there were over a hundred mana blades hovering all around me. Once they finished forming, a single mana dagger slammed into the area I'd chosen, and the rest followed, shredding the trees and monsters alike. Dozens of debuff notifications appeared in my mind as the attack didn't kill them outright but rather maimed them. Some died immediately, others suffered before they were vanquished, bleeding out; their life force slowly drained away.

"This is brutal," I whispered as a feeling of exhilaration

washed over me. "Thank you, Brahma. And the Old Ones, you too."

I meant it. Sure, maybe I didn't sound as sincere since I was a bit blown away by my new evolution, but yes, I'd make it up to them.

Several monsters made it out of the forest, limping and snarling to get at me. I was too strong for them to do me any harm on a bad day, even less when they were almost dead.

I stepped up to the closest one and equipped my physical daggers, then used [Assault]. Both of my blades glowed a vicious purple and then shot out at the monster coming toward me. It was slow and walked on two legs, but it was hunched over with long arms and clawed hands. It didn't have eyes or a nose, only a mouth spread across the entire head.

My daggers caught it in the same spot, sending the monster flying backward and killing it. A second monster was already in striking distance but I still had enough room and time to activate the last skill I wanted to test out, [Onslaught]. Considering the creature was half-dead, I didn't know how many combos it would take, but I sure hadn't expected it to die with the first attack. It was empowered with pestilence mana that exploded inside the monster as my blade slid into its side, almost ripping its torso in half.

The stench of death assailed me again. The powers I commanded felt overwhelming. A whole new world of possibilities opened up before me, changing the outlook of our future. I relished in it, let it course through me, but at the back of my mind an alarming thought clawed at me.

Could I truly remain who I was with so much power at my disposal?

I breathed out hard trying to push away the smell of decay left in the wake of my destruction. It was a reminder of the nature of this power. If I ever grew used to the smell of death, that would be the day I crossed a line.

"Merek, you can take over," I said, glancing over my shoulder. "I think I've wasted enough of these things."

The spearman got to his feet and hurried over toward me.

"Thank you for leaving the higher-level ones," he said, shooting me a grin that said he knew I had no idea what I'd just killed. Not that it mattered. Ten levels more or less didn't make such a big difference when it came to my new skills. I was a freaking monster.

"Any time. So, girls? What do you think?"

CHAPTER 14 – ARBITER PELIS

The girls were patient, but also excited after seeing my potential for destruction. Not only that, but they wanted to join me and Selene on our trip to Balan.

"That's so not fair, you know? I don't get why you can't admit that you're a possessive, controlling...man," Jeanette protested.

"Possessive?" I snorted. "Well, maybe, but I also want you to stay alive."

"I don't believe I'm saying this," Sonya started, "But I agree with her for once. We should go out and destroy things together more often. Not just when push comes to shove."

"I quite like it like this," Emma said. "I don't have to focus on keeping people alive. See, I have to carry that burden around every time we go into battle. What if someone dies because I fumbled a spell? Who will you blame?"

"I'd never blame you," I said.

"No, you wouldn't blame me. You would never say it, I know that. But you would think it. If Emma was faster, if Emma had used a different spell, if Emma..."

Tears welled up in her eyes, and I had to admit that it was the first time I'd seen her upset like that since losing our friends and family to Zekan. Not only that, but I hadn't given her role any thought. We all relied on her so badly that it had just become second nature to expect our wounds would be taken care of.

"I—I'm sorry," I said. Just like anyone else, I had a hard time apologizing as everyone liked to think they were right. So did I, but this time...yeah, this time I was dead wrong. "Come here."

I pulled her in for a hug and kissed her forehead. Sonya embraced her from behind, and Selene joined in. Jeanette was last. We all knew the swashbuckler wasn't a fan of hugging and comforting people. She could scream better than any of my other girls, but she was totally lost on the small things. I wasn't much better, either...

"There's this saying I once heard," Sonya said. "It's going to get a lot worse before it gets any better. We've escaped one war to be thrown into another one."

A notification popped up, startling me and breaking the magic of the moment.

```
Quest Completed: Spreading The Faith III

    Description: Continue to help spread
         faith in the Gods of old.

    Status: 250/250 Converted Believers

    Reward: Aura of the Believer

NOTE: Aura of the Believer is a passive buff
 that raises all stats by  5 points for 24 hours
 for those who pray within the assigned temple.
```

Another notification followed right after.

```
Quest Received: Spreading The Faith IV

    Description: Continue to help spread
         faith in the Gods of old.

    Status: 250/1,000 Converted Believers

    Reward: Establishment of a New Religion

NOTE: After establishing a new religion, you
 will be able to assign a divine priestess who
 will become the voice of the Old Gods, and with
```

that, will gain a special class. Prophet.

"Hey, is everything alright? What is it?" Sonya asked worriedly as I tuned out for a moment to read the note.

Things were getting interesting on the religious front. People were starting to convert at a greater speed than I thought they would, and the rewards were becoming more and more interesting. However, things would definitely become more dangerous down the road, that much was clear. If we got the attention of Tan'Malas himself...yeah, I wasn't looking forward to that.

"We've converted 250 people so far, so I got a new chain quest. That's all. We need 1,000 people now."

"That's good, right?" Emma asked, wiping the tears from her face. "We're helping to restore faith in the old ones."

"Not just that, Emma dear," Jeanette said, drawing attention to something that wasn't just a byproduct, but rather the whole reason why we started doing this. "We get to keep our powers and the Godveil."

"Exactly," Sonya said excitedly. "It's already proven to have our best interest at heart, so yes, I figure it's a very important byproduct."

"Byproduct, huh? I think we're the byproducts here. Strange how it survived without worshippers, but I guess even one is enough for a god to exist? As long as someone believes in them, they should stick around, right? Will they be at full power with a single believer? No, but still."

"I'd be more than happy if you were my only follower," Emma whispered seductively. "What if I become your head priestess? You would have to take better care of me, right?"

I chuckled, unable to withstand the way she said it.

"Well, you're the only level 2 so far, so I think I'm doing a pretty good job, my lady."

"Cade, can we go already?" Selene said, sounding a bit annoyed. "If we wait any longer, dawn will catch us."

I sighed theatrically and did a little bow to the girls.

"Duty calls, fair maidens. I bid you farewell, and until we meet again."

They all snorted and laughed as my elven assassin and I kicked up a dust cloud behind us.

"No sex," Jeanette said over our direct link. *"I want to hit level 2 next. Or Sonya."*

"Your wish is my command, fair maiden. Do watch out for that black-haired demoness. She might level you up before I do."

"You wish! I'm not letting you off so easily. Take care and don't do anything stupid, alright? I didn't come all the way here to lose you and die like a sad widow."

"Don't worry. See you soon."

Selene noticed I wasn't responding as we accelerated, jumping and leaping at a break-neck speed. If my body wasn't that strong, I wouldn't even dream of daring to go as fast. Strangest of all, she was keeping up, though I wasn't going at full speed.

"Did you say something?" I asked, shooting her a glance.

"Yes. I asked if you had anything particular in mind at Garm and Balan?"

I thought for a moment, the cool night air buffeting my face as the wind picked up. The stars were hidden behind thick clouds, though it wasn't so cold. Just a typical night.

"Need a drink?" Banxi yelled after us as we sped through the southern gate, moving straight north.

Mortimer and Mano still sat there on the bench, but they were laughing and enjoying themselves, lost in the chatter. Nalgid and Ferid were wrestling inside a circle made by their children. They had bandages wrapped around their naked torsos as they struggled to take each other down. Even Ferida was busy wrestling the female side of the family.

Grom and his sons stood off to the side as well, pointing at the two dwarven brothers. It was good to see them so lively.

"Everyone, be good tonight! I'll be away until tomorrow morning!"

"Alright, boss man! Good luck!" Nalgid yelled as he

wrestled his brother to the ground. Seconds later, we'd left the village and were running toward Garm Village. I was looking forward to seeing what had happened over the last few days and what the good captain was doing.

Selene kept quiet for most of the run there, and so did I. My biggest fear was that something might have happened to the few people I knew from the village. Considering what I'd seen happen in Balan from atop the watch tower, I wasn't so sure that the Order wouldn't do the same in Garm as well.

We arrived at the village shortly and found the gate closed. That wasn't anything strange in itself, but coupled with four new guards that wore gear more alike to that of inquisitors than ordinary soldiers, now that put me in a state of vigilance.

We hid inside a copse of trees and knelt, keeping low so they wouldn't see us. Selene's hair was black, and her battle gear was very dark so there was no way they'd see us. We, on the other hand, could see them very well as there was a brazier burning off to the side of the gate. They were huddled up there and seemed pretty cold.

I closed my eyes and took in a deep breath, focusing on using a borrowed power that I hadn't felt since coming to this place. [Light of Tan'Ruad]. Despite being a passive skill, I felt that I needed to use mana actively and reach out. Perhaps the Godveil wasn't as strong as we hoped it would be after regaining some new believers.

I added Selene to the battle room so we didn't have to talk out loud or focus on the direct link.

"I got a hit inside the... oh, shit. It's not just one."

Selene switched over to the battle room as well.

"How many?"

"I don't know," I said. *"Thirty? Forty? I can't count them as something's interfering, but they're all grouped up."*

Selene shifted from kneeling on the cold ground and sat down on a small rock.

"So, I have an idea, but I don't think you're going to like it."

162

I turned toward her with an already deep-set frown.

"You're not doing anything stupid, alright? I do that crap."

"Nope, not this time." She reached for my cheek and then leaned in, kissing me. *"Trust me, it's a good plan."*

I sighed, kissed her back, and placed my forehead on hers.

"Let me hear it."

A short while later, Selene rushed out of the thick brush and headed straight for the gate. Her hair was disheveled and she had thin cuts all over her arms.

"Help! They're after me! Help me!" she yelled and the four guards jumped to attention at once. They looked sleepy earlier, but now they were wide awake.

"Huh? What—who are you? Stop there! Stop or I will attack!" one of the four men yelled.

I couldn't really make out any details as it was too dark. I had tried focusing my sight on them, using the passive my Third's Eye provided, but it didn't work quite well. My best bet was to try it out during the day and see if something was really wrong with the Godveil or if it was just me.

Selene fell to the ground as if struck from behind. She cried out again and looked over her shoulder panicky.

"No, they're coming! Help me!"

The man who'd ordered her to halt took a step forward but then cursed loudly and motioned his men forward.

"Get that woman! Get her inside! We can always interrogate her if she's suspicious!"

The three men rushed forward, grabbing her by the arms and pulling her back up. I did my best to imitate a roar, which ended up sounding like a half-scream and cry, but whatever, I was no monster with a strong, loud, rumbling voice.

One of the three stumbled over his feet, fell, and cried out. The other two struggled to pull her along, barely making

163

any progress. Since I didn't have any real long-range skills that could kill any of them while still giving the survivors reasonable doubt that it was a monster, I used something Banxi and Elvina had cooked up.

The third guy who'd fallen, struggled to his feet as I aimed a small crossbow-like launcher. It held a single, small vial that would explode on impact, but not with fire. The vial contained a toxic liquid that would burn through his back and come out the front, eating away at his insides. The strange acid was very useful for infiltration missions as it made almost no sound on impact and the victim would die before they could cry out in pain.

I took in a deep breath, and pressed the trigger, launching the vial into his back as he ran toward the gate.

Fear of the dark.

The vial struck just below his neck and bit through his armor, skin, and flesh, exploding outward. His entire body dissolved right in front of his companions.

Selene let out another scream that echoed in the silence of the night, and within seconds, the gate was being pushed open and more zealots were rushing out.

"Is it them?" a voice rang out over the ruckus. "Tell me!" The voice was shrill and high-pitched, but definitely male.

"P—pillar! I—"

A man with long yellow hair, that seemingly floated around him, walked out the gate flanked by two hooded Tan'Malas cultists in black robes. The smell of incense filled the air coming from the censers in the sycopanths hands.

The man in the middle had sickly pale skin that looked as if it was changing color in places. A black, spiked armor encased his body, and the hilt of a long sword stuck out from behind him.

"Arbiter Pelis!" he told the soldier in front of him. "When will you fools remember?" he roared, slapping the other man's cheek with the back of his hand.

To my surprise, the other guy's head came flying off.

I grimaced at the show of unwarranted force. The Pillar had revealed himself finally. It was hard to read his power, but judging from the beheading smack, he certainly earned his place in the Order.

Selene, acting up again, screamed even more, and one of the two guards holding the assassin up grabbed her mouth and hissed.

"Oh, they're so sweet," she said through the battle room. *"This zealot is telling me to be quiet or the arbiter might kill me. I'll do as he says for now, and once they settle down, I'll do as we planned."*

I glared at their backs, already imagining a hundred ways to kill them.

"You are one bad elf, you know that? I already want to rip their arms off and beat them to death with their own limbs."

"Stop!" the arbiter yelled as he looked over at Selene and the two retreating zealot guards. "What happened to that...puddle over there?" he said, pointing at the poor sod I hit with the acid vial. The arbiter walked over to where his remains were and prodded the skull with his boot.

"I—I don't know, arbiter. A monster roared from the forest and then his chest burst open and...he turned into that."

I took a moment to study the newcomer. I'd finally come, more or less, face to face with one of the upper echelons within the Order. He didn't seem all that impressive, and the mana within his body was, well, mostly absent. There was something else within him, though, but I had no idea what it was. The type of power coursing through him was something I'd never felt before, not even back during the siege of Greystone.

I looked past him and studied his guards next. The two cultists to his side had no mana signatures. They were Tan'Malas priests and I assumed their powers were in reading scripture rather than battle. The zealots guarding him didn't look like anything special either aside from wearing full body armor. I couldn't even see their faces or if they were male or female. Not that it mattered as anyone who wished us harm would die either way. One thing that did catch my eye, was how the air seemed to shift around them, displacing the glow coming from the brazier. All light was absorbed by a dull darkness that seemed to want to hide them from prying eyes like mine.

"And the woman?" the arbiter asked. "What is with her? Let me see."

Pelis walked over to where the two guards who were holding Selene upright and grabbed her chin.

"She came out of—"

"Yes, yes! I know!" Pelis snapped. "Go get some shovels and buckets. I need that pile of bones in there to study what could have killed him so quickly," he said, nodding toward the town. "I will take this young weird creature in myself. The ears are quite peculiar. I've never seen any—ohh! Now I understand. You belong to that new group, don't you?"

"Umm, do you want me to intervene?" I asked, unsure of what to do.

"N—no! I...ran from a ship! Slavers! They wanted to sell me in...what was that city called again? I...don't know. I was supposed to go to a duke. Yes!"

Pelis snorted, obviously amused by her trying to get out of the predicament. He turned toward the forest and eyed the darkness. It would surprise me if he could see in the dark, but I had no idea what kind of powers Tan'Malas had bestowed on the Order.

"Maybe, maybe not. We can check your story tomorrow morning. If you're really a runaway slave, we will take you back to the duke when we return to this province's capital. And if you're lying, well, let's just say that death is the least of your worries."

Pelis grabbed Selene's arm and pulled her along as his guards fell in line with him. The surviving duo walked back into the town as well, only to come out several minutes later with shovels and a wooden wheelbarrow. I felt bad for them in a way, but that feeling quickly disappeared when I heard them speak. It was as quiet as could be and I'd snuck up on the gate, kneeling not even ten steps away from them.

"What do you think he's going to do to her?" one of the two asked. Both had ordinary, unremarkable faces but one was a bit shorter than the other and walked with a slight limp. He was the one who hissed at Selene.

"Fuck her? Kill her? Who cares? She's a sinner, and all sinners need to be punished! That long-eared woman, did you see what she looks like? Her breasts were hanging out, and her entire neckline..." he grunted to himself, shaking his head.

"Yes, yes, and you ogled her every second. I bet you want to fuck her yourself, huh?"

The two burst into laughter and started shoveling what was left over from their friend. Now, I wasn't someone who could just sit still and listen to some assholes talk shit about my woman, so, I got up from the darkness, walked up to them, and slid my kris into the shorter man's spine. Since the blade had extra reach, the tip exited through the chest, opening him up from both sides. He fell limp to the ground, blood spurting from the two holes. Before the other guard could even comprehend what just happened, I used [Backstab] on him. I didn't have to, but I wanted to. Both daggers came down between his shoulder blades and down his back. With a twirl of my bird of prey blade, I cut his head off.

"The only one who's fucked is you, poor idiots. Men of God? Yeah, right. Now, what do I...ahh, right."

I picked the head up and held it up in front of me. His eyes and mouth were wide open and frozen in terror. Good, that's just how I needed him.

"Selene? What's your situation?"

It took her a moment to respond, and with something I wouldn't expect after his showing earlier.

"Pelis and I are having dinner or early breakfast? Or whatever you want to call it. He's trying to get me to admit I'm, well, who he thinks I am."

"Is he showing any sense of hostility?"

"No, not yet. If he does, I'll shadow jump out of there, don't worry."

"Where are you? What building?"

"The mayor's place. She's...cooking."

"Distressed?"

"More than. She was beaten badly. I think she isn't one of them after all, Cade. So, what now? I have a feeling you want to do something stupid instead of going through with the plan."

I chuckled, still standing there in the brazier's light and holding the soldier's head by the hair.

"Well, yes. Where are those armored soldiers? I want to pull them out of the village."

"All over from what I could see when he led me toward the manor house. I can play decoy just as agreed."

"Nah, you enjoy your food. Just sit tight, and if you can, escape with Najla do it. If not, then...wait, is the statue still in one piece?"

"Yep, it is. Pelis complained that no matter what he did, he couldn't destroy it. Anyway, you were saying?"

"Sorry, got sidetracked. Take Najla with you if you can and run once the fighting starts. Enjoy your food, my little elf. And I'm so going to spank you for this. I can't stand to see another man touching you."

I could feel her inner turmoil and knew I'd made it even more awkward than it already was. Still, I thought it better to put things out in the open than to suppress them.

"Stupid idea, I know."

"It's good that you know. Now, let the fun begin," I said, finishing our conversation and lobbing the head over the gate. I was sure that I'd thrown it hard enough when people started yelling and screaming.

"Cade? What did you do?" Selene asked, and I could feel a hint of urgency coming from her.

"I killed those two guards that touched you and threw one of their heads toward the village square. Eat up and leave.

See you soon."

CHAPTER 15 – SPLIT DECISIONS

It was odd talking through the battle room and it felt a bit more intimate than through Elvina's mind link. Not that it was a good thing, but I could feel some of Selene's emotions as she spoke.

"Really? A head?"

"Yep, a head," I said and made my way around the wall.

In my best-case scenario, I would miraculously manage to lure them all out and take care of them in one fell swoop, but I had no idea what they were capable of. Their powers were something I didn't know anything about, yet, so I needed to tread carefully.

Once the first group made their way outside, I'd sneak in and single out a few. After all, the fully armored soldiers couldn't hide from me even if they tried. The [Light of Tan'Ruad] would find them even in the deepest darkness.

I used [Fade] to get through the stockade wall and appear inside the house on the other side. The smell of sickly sweet iron hung in the air as I faded in. I took a step backward, wanting my back to the wall, but almost stumbled over something, and caught myself on a chair.

"What the f—" I stopped myself from cursing, but felt sick to my stomach.

Beneath my feet were a man, a woman, and two children. All dead. Their throats had been slit, and their hearts torn out.

I sat on the chair for a moment, watching the dead family lie there in a large pool of blood. They were discarded like trash, just thrown onto a heap.

I took in a deep breath and pushed it out through my nose, then inhaled the sickly stench again. I didn't want to forget this. The best way to burn a scene into your memory was to become a part of it, and by inhaling what remained of them, I did just that.

"Selene? Have you seen any of the villagers? Where are they?"

For a long moment, she didn't respond. I got worried something might have happened, but there were no emotions of distress or anything coming off her.

"Something's wrong. He's looking annoyed and angry. One of the soldiers just came to report to him, but I have no idea what they said. He has anger issues, that much is clear."

"Selene. The civilians. Where are they?"

"I...don't know. There were a few outside in the village square, but...I haven't seen any others. And I can't sense anyone either. Just Najla."

A feeling of dread washed over me and I almost fell off the chair. She was right. I couldn't feel any mana signatures either. Not those of Captain Samel, Hedar, Ludmilla, or anyone else.

I opened my quest window

Quest Received: Spreading The Faith IV

Description: Continue to help spread
faith in the Gods of old.

Status: 0/1,000 Converted Believers

Reward: Establishment of a New Religion

NOTE: After establishing a new religion, you
will be able to assign a divine priestess who
will become the voice of the Old Gods, and with
that, will gain a special class. Prophet.

"Listen to me, Selene. I think that they killed everyone. I'm

sitting next to the corpses of a small family. Pelis is a wicked bastard, and he needs to die. Take Najla and get the hell out of here."

"Alright. When?"

"I will walk out into the village square and call him out. The moment they make a move, you two get out. Drag her along if need be and go south. I'll tell Benny and Legs to come get you."

Selene remained silent for a long moment. I was about to speak to her again when she replied.

"Alright. This definitely hasn't gone as I thought it would. I had no idea everyone is—"

"Keep up the act and wait. We'll talk about this fiasco later."

I mentally switched to our main guild room and took in a deep breath before I spoke.

"Listen up and don't interrupt me. I know that it's late and that most of you are probably asleep or about to sleep, but that will have to wait. One of the arbiters is in Garm village, and they seem to have killed everyone here aside from the mayor. Benny, I need you and Legs to pick up Selene and the mayor, and then escort them to our village. I'm going to kill these bastards in the worst way possible."

Everyone remained silent even after a minute passed.

"Benny?"

"Yes, bro?"

"Did you understand what I just said?"

"Yes. We're about to leave New Greystone. Sorry, you said to be quiet."

"Wait, Cade," Emma said then. "Maybe there are survivors? And they need help?"

"We're coming whether you want it or not," Sonya added.

"Yes, we're coming!" Jeanette said next.

I sighed inwardly.

"Why can't you ever just do as I say?"

"We always do what you say, but not this time, so just let us help you!" Emma said again. "Benny, wait for us. We want a ride on Legs' back."

172

"I'm coming too," Merek chimed in. *"I want to make sure no one gets hurt. Just in case."*

I decided that it was better to accept than fight them on the matter. Besides, Emma was right. If there were any survivors once the fighting started, I would need someone to protect them.

"Alright. Hurry up. I don't know if they can sense me or not."

I made my way up the stairs, making sure I made as little noise as possible. Who knew if the houses were in use or if they were empty? It was always better to act safely than regret a stupid mistake.

There was no one upstairs, to my luck. I didn't want to kill anyone before it was time if I didn't have to. That arbiter guy could find out something was wrong.

I slowly made my way down the hallway and into what looked like the bedroom of the dead couple. It was empty but for a large bed, two closets, and a nightstand on one side of the bed. There was a large window just across from the entrance, but it had its curtains drawn.

"Let's see," I whispered, stepping over toward the window and pushing aside just enough of the curtain so I could peek down onto the street.

I couldn't see all of the village square but just enough to find a bunch of still-alive people huddled together. I figured there were no more than a hundred of them, maybe a bit more, and they looked terrified.

A score of armored soldiers were arrayed to one side, but I couldn't see past the building that obstructed the view of the opposite part of the village square. There were probably just as many if not more keeping guard there. It got me thinking. I already knew about the Order's ranks, but what about their soldiers? They all looked identical with their black armor and the darkness that surrounded them, but was there any difference in fighting power? Rank within their ranks? Were there different types of soldiers?

"I should have asked," I mumbled and then pushed some

mana into the [Light of Tan'Ruad] skill to try and see if there were darker blotches or if they were all the same.

It took a second, but once the skill activated and the familiar feeling from back in Greystone hit me, I could both see and feel a subtle difference. It was hard to put into words, but some blotches had a different shade. They pulsated brighter than most of the blotches, creating a strange mix of pure darkness and semi-bright points of light.

"We are heading at full speed," Emma said over the leadership room. All of us, including Merek and Legs were in that room already, so we might as well use it.

"Alright. Selene, get ready. I'll be—"

"He's frowning hard," she interrupted me. *"Something's off. He either knows you're there, or he's feeling you guys approaching."*

"Is he still seated?"

"Yes, but he's about to—Najla is serving us tea. She's barely standing on her feet."

"Alright. Just a few minutes more," Emma said again. *"We can see the village in the distance. Do we attack right away?"*

"No!" I said hurriedly, not wanting them to make a stupid move. *"Benny, you're the only one going in. Kill everything outside the gate, roar, and charge into the village. Kill every fully armored soldier. Understood?"*

"Yes, bro."

"Good, little brother. Let's see what you're made of."

"Hah! You called me little brother! Love it!" Benny said excitedly. I could feel his happiness even outside the gate.

"Cade? He just mentioned something about sacrifices. I think you need to hurry!"

The word 'sacrifice' rang in my ears, and I felt as if it had flipped a switch. Nothing had changed since Greystone and the Valtorian attack. People still did the same horrible things as back then, and I fucking hated it.

"I'm going in. Benny... kill them all."

I activated [Dark Presence] and [Plague Domain] and

used [Fade] to appear in the village square. My passive, [Apex Predator] screamed in my mind as it hit over fifty armored soldiers at once, and two large groups of civilians. The moment everyone fell under my passive debuff, [Sapper] activated as well, lowering their resistances, and then [Stolen Power] siphoned a minuscule amount of stats from everyone present. With over 50 soldiers drawing their weapons and activating their own buffs and throwing debuffs my way, a hint of panic fell over me. It lasted only for a single heartbeat, though, as a singular message kept on repeating itself in my mind.

```
You have resisted a debuff.
You have resisted a debuff.
You have resisted a debuff.
```

I could feel a large enough stat boost to know that these armored soldiers were on a different level than the zealots or the duke's guards. They were the real deal. Making a split decision, I raised my hands as if in surrender, my daggers tucked away safely in my storage.

"Pelis!" I yelled. "Come out so we can have a chat!"

My voice carried all the way to the manor house, which was only about fifty yards away from where I stood. And since it was the middle of the night, I had no doubt that the arbiter would hear me.

Strangely, not one of the soldiers attacked me. I was still reaching out with the [Light of Tan'Ruad] skill, just in case there would be any changes. There were none. It was as if they were soulless constructs, puppets waiting for an order.

I looked over the civilians who were mostly tied up and guarded by the armored soldiers. Some of them were already dead and just lay there among the others. It filled me with rage that kept on boiling, threatening to spill over. If I lost it, all these people would die for sure, so I needed to play for time.

"Pelis! Come out!" I yelled again, this time even louder. "Come out or I'll destroy this whole village to make an example!"

That second part was an improvisation, but the poor civilians didn't know. It was better no one did just to keep appearances up.

"*He's coming. Do you want me to run?*" Selene said over the leadership room.

"*No, not yet. Once he's here talking to me,*" I replied, seeing the dark armor and yellow hair appear in the manor house entrance. The arbiter held himself with dignity, his chest stuck out and shoulders squared. He wasn't that tall, but his posture made him look much larger.

You have resisted a debuff.

Interesting. Was it a skill? Or a passive like mine? Whatever the case, I was pretty sure that he had an effect on people just like I did. For a split second, his demeanor changed as he came into my apex passive's range, and took a step back. His expression soured as he raised a gauntleted hand and pointed a finger at me.

"So you're the unfortunate fool who dared to question our authority."

I chuckled, motioning for him to get closer. He took one step forward, eyeing me carefully.

"Arrogant blasphemer," he said through his teeth, yet there was no judgement in his voice, no, it almost felt like he was amused. "Do you know you're in the presence of an Arbiter, you dog?"

"It can't be helped," I said coldly. "You're in the presence of your betters, arbiter. Come, I want to have a chat with you. I think you'll be very much interested in what I have to say. And don't worry, I'm alone. Do you think I can't get through your armored soldiers? They're in the square, in the buildings around us, on the roofs, in the alleys... I would feel safe if I was you."

The fool actually smiled at me and put his hands on his hips as if telling me 'I wasn't afraid all along, now what?' and just stood there for a long moment. There it was. If he truly felt he was safe, he'd never offer me the courtesy of words. Despite his bravado, the arbiter was careful. He was looking at something he didn't truly understand and acted accordingly. Pelis was careful, which spoke of his intelligence, either that or he was afraid. It was hard to tell.

"Yes, well, you need to understand something. The moment you visited these poor sobs, they were destined to die. You should have stayed away and minded your own business. And do tell me, that woman I have inside? Who is she to you?"

"A slave!" I said, raising my voice. "She ran, so I want her back. Is that going to be a problem?"

Pelis's expression turned to one of genuine mirth. He snapped his fingers and then lowered his hands. The armed and armored soldiers lowered their weapons as one and just stood straight as an arrow.

"They are linked to your mind?" I asked, staring the arbiter right in the eyes. I didn't fear the man nor his soldiers as no power radiated from them, at least not any power I could quantify. It was probably a good thing or I might have started laughing. He reminded me of that bastard Zekan, curse his soul, and that didn't go in his favor at all.

"Why do you want to know?"

"No reason. Just curious."

"Well, then, why don't you come in for a drink? I just might have the one you're searching for."

I smiled and nodded, making my way toward him.

"Is she in there? A woman with pointy ears and black hair?"

"Yes, she is. But wait," he said and crossed his arms. There it was again, the debuff notification.

```
You have resisted a debuff.
```

"What is it?"

"I'm almost there, bro. Just give me like...30 seconds or so," Benny said over the leadership room.

"Ah," he said, "You're the one who settled south of here,

aren't you?"

I shook my head slowly.

"No, I'm not. I came by ship. It's moored near the river east of here. Does that matter?"

He blew air out of his nose. Annoyance was plastered all over his face.

I felt a sudden pain enter my skull and then vanish just as it had appeared. Shivers ran through me and I tightened the grip on my weapon. Something had broken into my mind, like a foreign thought rummaging through my memory. It was brief but extremely uncomfortable.

"What did you do, arbiter?" I said through clenched teeth.

"Foolish," he said, eyeing me up and down, "I expected more of you. Let me explain, I have this skill that allows me to read anyone once a day. The Dark One must have guided me because I hadn't yet wasted it on those peasants," he said with a shrill voice. "See, you're lying," he added confidently, "And to an arbiter no less. A sin for which we tear out tongues and eyes, yet you intrigue me I must say." He smacked his lips then pointed to the entrance door of the house, "Come, let's have a chat. Just you and I."

"Oh? You can read minds as well?" I asked with a wry smile. *"Benny, hold it. Everyone, stop for now,"* I said over the leadership room. *"I want to sit down with this guy first, get as much as I can out of him."*

"Are you sure?" Emma asked. *"We can take them, right?"*

"Yes, we can, Emma, but all the villagers might die. No need to be hasty. Just sit tight."

The arbiter eyed me curiously as if trying to decide on something, and then chuckled dryly.

"I was given free reins over this matter, and I intend to get to the bottom of it all. Come, join us for a drink. I won't harm you or your friend, though I have to give you points for trying to pull a fast one on me. Why, though?"

"Can you do me a favor?" I asked, replying to his question

with one of my own.

"Speak."

"Don't kill any more civilians before our conversation is over. If another one dies while I'm here, I will kill you personally. Can you do that for me?"

Pelis studied me for another moment, this time seemingly trying to figure out whether I was being honest. I was as serious as could be and no skill in the world could say otherwise.

"That will depend on you, newcomer. Now, come in before I change my mind. I think we've got a lot to talk about. Oh, and that head? Was that you?"

I smiled wolfishly.

"And so much more. Now, why don't we have that drink? I've got a million questions and all have your name written on them."

CHAPTER 16 –TRUTH FOR A TRUTH

Najla stood behind Selene, who looked frightened. When she saw me enter, the elf sighed and sat, pulling the mayor to sit next to her.

"This was getting exhausting," Selene grunted. "You really need to learn how to treat a woman better. I almost killed you myself when I saw her face."

Pelis froze in place, then took a step back and stepped into me.

"Wait—what—"

I pressed a knife into his back, just deep enough for the idiot to understand what was going on. I didn't even have to penetrate his armor, which honestly looked pretty good, since my daggers could reach much further thanks to the layer of mana encasing it.

"I don't think you realize what is truly going on, Pelis," I said, pushing the tip of my dagger further into his skin. The arbiter winced and took an involuntary step forward.

"W—what are you—hold on now! Are you threatening an arbiter? I will have the soldiers kill all the civilians if you even so much as touch me again!"

I used his short threat to think about how to move the conversation forward. If it had been me in his stead, further violence and threats would only be counterproductive, but if I...

"Please, sit, Arbiter Pelis," I said, stashing my blade away and walking over to where Selene was already seated. "Did he hurt you?"

She shook her head but glanced over at Najla.

"Emma needs to have a look. I don't think she's in good shape. Inwardly I mean. Maybe even a broken rib or internal bleeding." My elf assassin turned back to Pelis and glared at him. "Men who hurt women are cowards."

"Yes, I quite agree, love," I said, leaning my elbows on the table. "Selene, could I please bother you for a drink? Wait, can you get us all a drink? Najla, join us. Pelis won't hurt you anymore."

The arbiter scoffed at that, but he too joined us, taking what I figured was his previous seat. His look promised pain if she misbehaved, more of what she'd already tasted. I pulled my dagger back out and placed it in front of me on the table. If anything, he looked amused by my attempt at intimidation.

"You do know I'm no pushover, right?" Pelis said, tapping his finger against the table. "I'm not the same as those weaklings from the Duke's army, I'm an arbiter."

"You mentioned that," I said flatly, showing him just how much I cared about his title. Truth be told, I'd felt the amount of power pushing back against my dagger when I tried to break the skin on his back. He was strong, that much was clear to me.

"Then why all this charade? And why don't you tell your friends to come to the village? Yes, I can feel them, and not just that," he said, seemingly not caring for their presence.

"There's no need. At least not for now. So, do we talk first, or do we fight right away?" I asked, taking the drink Selene set in front of me. Najla was still standing to my side, refusing to sit down so I pulled out a chair and nodded toward it. She accepted reluctantly.

Najla had finally done as I'd told her, and it wasn't sitting right with Pelis, it was clear in his murderous glare.

"How about we exchange some information first? The winner gets to leave smarter. Isn't that how war is played? To the victor go the spoils? Or something like that."

I snorted, finding his rambling mildly amusing. He was

right, though, the only reason why I was willing to talk to him was to get my hands on much-needed info.

"Sure. How about we alternate questions, one-for-one with a gentleman's agreement? I go once, you go once. Deal?"

I raised my hand and held it out for Pelis, who stared at it as if I had a disease. Still, after a long, uncomfortable moment, he shook it.

"Go ahead. I will know if you're honest."

"And what about you?" I asked, staring back at him. "I can only hope you'll be man enough?"

Pelis shrugged and pulled his gauntlets off, then placed them on the table. His breastplate was next, and then the rest of his armor.

"I have no idea where you're from, newcomer, but we don't lie here. Why would we? There's only one true god, Tan'Malas, and only we have the power to rule this world. Even if I tell you everything you want to know, it still won't change a single thing."

"Maybe, maybe not," I said, taking a sip from my glass. "So, why don't we start?"

"Sure, sure. Go ahead, newcomer. Let's see what you open up with."

I had used the time since sitting down to come up with a few questions, things that I really needed to know before I could proceed to kill this bastard and his soldiers.

"So you're an arbiter? That's below a pillar, right?"

"Yes, I'm what you would call an arbiter, newcomer. You truly know little of our world, or am I mistaken?"

"No, you're not," I answered, "But I learn quickly. My turn." He opened his mouth to protest but then blew more air through his nose and gestured for me to continue.

"Your soldiers, there are different tiers. I want you to tell me about the tiers from weakest to strongest."

He seemed to be taken by surprise, which was a good thing. Now, if he only decided to be smug enough to try and indulge my question, I'd be one happy man.

"There are four tiers," he started, taking a swig of his drink as well. "The first tier are the animus, they're the basic armored soldiers you can see outside. Well, most of them are. Then the next tier are the beles, which is a stronger version of the animus. They are capable of using basic skills, spells, and abilities Tan'Malas has granted us, bless his holy name."

"Holy," Selene snorted, sounding very much like me minutes earlier. "Sorry, continue."

"Yes, as I was saying," Pelis continued, shooting her a venomous glance. "The third tier are the cardes, and they can both think and act for themselves, they can lead smaller groups of animus and beles, and possess greater powers than the first two tiers."

"Interesting. I figure you have—never mind. I'm not wasting my question. Please continue," I said, almost asking a second question to an answer I most likely already knew.

"Oh, that was close. Do waste a question next time."

"Only if you do, arbiter Pelis," I mused, raising my glass again. It was good stuff, though I had no idea what kind of drink it was. The green liquid was strong with a hint of both sweetness and bitterness to it.

The arbiter smiled wryly and shook his head in amusement.

"The last tier are the deces. They can even lead smaller armies on their own and follow directives to a much greater degree than the cardes. That's as much as you're getting. For now."

"Fair enough," I said, tapping my fingers on the table smugly. I'd only noticed two types of dark blotches when feeling for the armored soldiers' powers, so I didn't think he had any of the stronger tiers. "Your turn."

"Right, right. So, where do I even start?" Pelis said with a chuckle. "Ahh, I got it! So, tell me, where are you from?"

That was a simple enough question, one that already gave me an edge in this verbal fencing match.

"Greystone City."

"Greystone? I've never heard about it. Tell me more of the place," he said, throwing his yellow hair back. "Oops. That was a second question, wasn't it?"

I smiled and nodded.

"Greystone is a...was a great city situated on the coast and had a majestic river running right through the center. A million people lived until...they didn't."

Pelis shot me a curious gaze, "How could I have not heard about a city of that size? And what do you mean by until they didn't?"

"My turn," I said. His face scrunched up and he almost recoiled as if finding the very thought of me cutting him off insulting. It was in a way. "I want to know the approximate number of animus, beles, cardes, and deces in the dukedom."

Now it was his turn to stare at me flatly as if the question hadn't even rattled him. I knew what he must have been thinking, and it wasn't pretty. He wanted to know where I came from and what made me so interesting, but all I cared about was the power base within Volarna.

"Roughly 10,000 animus, about 3,000 beles, 100 cardes, and 20 deces. I'll add some bonus information since you seem to be so interested in our military capabilities. A group like this is called a valens and is the smallest of its kind. Here, I'll spare you a question. A valens is commanded by five arbiters, of which the strongest is called the high-arbiter, who is in control of the entire valens. Now, come, ask me something more interesting."

"It's your turn, Pelis," I said, seemingly ignoring him. His right eye twitched as he leaned his side and left elbow on the table, staring at me. If looks could kill, he'd have done so a hundred times over.

"I've decided that I don't like you, newcomer. What is your name, anyway?"

"Cade of the Bloodmoon. What is your rank within the five arbiters?" I asked.

"Fourth. Who is the strongest of your group?"

"Me. Using numbers from 1 to 10, rank all five of you arbiters."

"Vestila is a 4, I am a 5, Danara is a 5 as well, but Meras is a 7. Balog is a 10, obviously. He's much, much stronger than I am. Even the four of us couldn't take him on."

"Good, good. Thank you. I figure you're being honest with the speed of your responses," I commented.

"Of course. If I want to expect an honest answer, it is only fair that I do so as well. See, this is all becoming more exciting by the moment. If they even knew I was telling you all this, I would be killed, but I don't think I'll lose to you, Cade of the Bloodmoon. Now, me next." He paused for a moment, sipping on the green liquid and then pushing the glass over to Najla. She looked up at me and I turned to Selene. The assassin put a hand on Najla's shoulder and pushed her back down, took the glass and walked off to refil it.

"Thank you," Najla said in hushed words.

"Don't worry about a thing. You're not dying today, that's a promise."

"Which you shouldn't have made," Pelis roared. "You are looking down on me, Cade of the Bloodmoon. You should take a step back and look where you are."

"Where's that exactly?"

He smiled smugly.

"In our domain. Now, tell me, Cade...how many of you are there that come close to you in power?"

I shut up for a moment and tapped the side of my chin as if I was counting.

"I'd say 7 of us. Maybe eight, but they're definitely weaker than me. Just making sure so you can calculate your next question."

Selene pushed a filled glass to Pelis, who took and raised it to the former mayor.

"Thank you, dear. I knew there was a reason I left you alive," he snickered.

Selene tensed and was about to snap when I put my hand

on her leg and squeezed.

"Don't, Selene," I said over the leadership room. *"As for the rest, I know you're anxious to hear what's going on, but give us a bit more time. We'll start fighting very soon anyway. Make sure you're ready."*

No one said anything, which showed how much they'd improved. Everyone knew about the danger we were in and didn't want to interrupt anything important. Or at least I thought so.

"Bro, Legs wants to go in and save those people, you know? I want to as well. Just let us. I think I can disable them all with my blood mist, but I'll need more blood after that."

"Hold that thought."

"Hmm, an interesting question now, Cade of the...I'll just call you Cade if that is alright?"

"Go ahead, but it's my turn now."

"Wait, what?" he protested, slapping the table with his open palm. "I didn't ask—oh, I did. Very well," he said, the anger apparent in his eyes and on his flushed face.

"I want to know all about your valens' arbiter powers."

"Oh, no, that's not something I can tell you. We keep our powers close to our hearts and rarely show each other anything. Ask another question."

"Alright, then tell me about your powers in particular," I said, making sure to stay on topic and keep him off guard. If he was focused on one matter, then he'd be easily blindsided by a trick question.

"Boring question, but alright. As you already know, being that you have the same type of powers as us, the Darkveil provides us with certain types of powers. They are all similar in their origin, essence, and execution, but it depends on how *we* deliver that power. See, I use a two-handed greatsword, so my powers will manifest within my sword. You use daggers, and they are your power outlets. Am I right?"

"In a way," I replied simply. He didn't need to know anything beyond that.

186

"Tell me," I started and he tsked me.

"You keep interrupting me, Cade. That's not very honorable of you."

"Honorable? You asked me if you were right, and I replied."

Pelis gritted his teeth and slammed his fist on the table.

"You are taking this too literally! I want to stop here, so that's it for my powers. You're not getting anything else."

"Can't do. You asked a question more than me, Pelis. Now listen, if you want to say you're a man of honor, you will answer one more question. Am I correct to assume that we'll need light magic to defeat your animus and beles?"

Pelis froze, his fingers hovering just above the table.

"How did you know that? Which traitor told you? I will have their head right now!"

"Is that another two questions?"

"Yes, damn you! Tell me how you know!" the arbiter snapped but suddenly looked unsure if to go through with the questions or not.

"Not a traitor, a deity. We used to worship them back in Greystone. They're minor gods that help us with many things: farming, smithing, even tailoring, or making love. Now me. Why did you kill the people of this village?"

"Deities? There are no deities beyond Tan'Malas," he said, sounding insincere. He knew more than he was letting on.

"Why did you kill the people?" I repeated.

Perhaps he knew of other gods, perhaps he was just playing with me. In any case, I had to push on with the things that mattered at the moment.

The surprise previously showing on his face disappeared and was suddenly replaced with what could only be described as joy. He pushed a hand through his yellow hair and chuckled slowly.

"Why? That's simple. The number of believers in this village had dropped when I returned from my meeting with the other arbiters. A little birdy told me how they were all starting to have a change of heart and wanted to change their faith," he said, raising his voice. His pitch also grew and he almost sounded as if he was shrieking. "Being the good man that I am, I sent them to meet their new gods! Also, I sacrificed them so I could make some of my soldiers stronger. Now, you have one more question and this mockery is over!"

"Alright. Where are the other arbiters stationed?"

He scoffed again as if he had hoped to get a more exciting last question.

"I'm disappointed, but I guess that can't be helped," he said with a deep sigh. "Vestila is in charge of Balan, Danara is in charge of Znica, Merars of Tazul, and Balog of Volarna. Motar is without an arbiter as Balog killed him the other day. We're expecting a new one to arrive any moment now."

I picked the glass up again and drank whatever had remained.

"Selene, take Najla out and meet up with the rest. Go."

The elf placed her hand on the mayor's shoulder, and the two disappeared from where they'd been sitting. Pelis didn't look alarmed, if anything, he just looked pissed as his face screwed up in a sneer.

"I don't like you, Cade of the Bloodmoon. I don't like you at all. Come, let us do battle, and before you even think of running, I will kill the remaining civilians if you do. Their screams will fill the night and you will—"

"I'm not running anywhere, Pelis, but I do have a proposal for you. If you let half of the civilians go, I will let you have a free one."

"A...free one? I do not understand," he said as his eyebrows scrunched up together.

"You can hit me once, and I won't fight back. If I survive, you let the other half go, and I will give you another attack. Then we can start fighting. I will not run away or use any movement powers that will let me escape an attack. I will take the attacks head-on. What do you say?"

Pelis, for lack of a better word, seemed to shiver in

excitement.

"Ohh! That is fabulous! I couldn't have asked for a better birthday surprise! You know, it is today and no one remembered. I feel...sad. Maybe I shouldn't have killed so many people tonight...but no, we will do it like this. There are 392 villagers left. For every attack you take, I will let a hundred go. Survive four, and the last hundred will earn their freedom. But that's only if you manage to survive long enough."

I stuck my hand out again, and this time he grabbed it without so much as a change on his face. Pelis was excited, but so was I. If we could get 392 people out alive, then I'd be happy to take some of their pain.

"I agree."

"Deal!" he said excitedly, squeezing my hand much harder than was called for. I didn't squeeze back and instead, I let him assume he was stronger than me. It definitely hurt, which meant that the bastard was on a much higher level than I'd originally thought. I was confident I could take him, but I promised myself to be careful. I knew little of this land and even less about the arbiters and the cursed Order.

"Then let's do this, Pelis."

CHAPTER 17 – ARBITER VS PESTILENCE LORD

We stood outside on the village square, just in front of the manor house. The terrified villagers surrounded us in three groups, with the last one slightly smaller than the others. An unwilling audience that could hardly comprehend what was about to go down.

My girls stood to the south of the square together with Merek, Benny, and Legs. There was apprehension on all of their faces except for Benny. The pangolin shot me a casual wink. His relaxed, larger-than-life attitude was a refreshing and welcome sight. The arbiter's dreaded troops were equally spread out around the northern side of the village center.

Pelis and I faced each other. He held his greatsword firm with both hands, and I was meeting him with my daggers. They looked comical compared to his oversized lump of steel, but I knew they were good enough to take on anything short of a unique masterpiece.

The atmosphere was dreadful with the civilians trying to hold back their panic and keep quiet, while the animus and beles just stood there, unmoving like a black, armored wall.

"How do we know the duel is going to be fair, bro?" Benny said as he stood right behind me, giving Pelis the evil eye.

"How? I've got you here. They do anything beyond what we agreed on and you kill them all. It's simple as that, Benny."

The pangolin shot me a wide grin.

"Yes, yes, so very dramatic," Pelis said, taking a step toward me. His body started glowing, and as it was a passive, my [Apex Predator] immediately hit him, followed by [Sapper] and [Stolen Power].

"I'm sorry, Pelis, those are skills that activate automatically, so you'll just have to deal with it."

I checked my status screen quickly and saw that just two debuffs had added between 2 and 3 stat points. That was a moment where I came to realize how utterly I'd underestimated him and this whole situation. Whatever. If I survived his first hit, I'd know what we were finally dealing with.

"I don't like it, but I will...accept it," Pelis said, readying himself. "As per the agreement, here I come!"

A black mass appeared around him, like an extra layer of armor. His oversized sword took on the black glow as well. I tensed, tightening my grip on both daggers as he lunged for me. The blackened blade came down in an overhead swing, and I moved to intercept it, crossing both blades above me. Mana coated both the kris and the bird of prey, and slightly bent my knees. The sword came crashing down, making contact with both weapons. In all truth, I barely held on to the kris, as it was a much weaker weapon than the other dagger. A wave of power slammed into me next. My feet dug an inch into the graveled road, but I held on.

Pelis lunged back, obviously afraid I might counterattack or hurt him in another way. I didn't even have the time to think of a counterattack as I hadn't been expecting such a strong blow. To say he rattled my bones was a pretty fair expression.

"Hah! You really did it! You took my attack without trying to hit back! A man! You're a real man!" he laughed madly. "Choose whatever group you want. They're yours."

I didn't bother choosing and held up a single finger.

"First group. Once they're safe, I will take your next blow."

Pelis seemed genuinely amused by the whole situation, and he even had four of his armored men and women gather two chairs and a table from a nearby home.

"Come, sit. Rest a minute as the civilians go. Let them out. First group only."

Over fifty of his animus stepped aside, and then pushed the whimpering civilians on their way. Not one of the soldiers made a sound other than the moving and clanking metal.

"You might wonder why I'm doing this most likely," Pelis said, leaning his elbow on the table. "But listen. When there's nothing else to do in life, you take what you get. And you..." He grinned, "You're something else. Balog would kill his maker just to get his hands on you. I figured if I could play with you first, then I'd have one up on him."

"Don't worry, I'm fine. Just a bit surprised by his power," I said to my group in the leadership room. *"If the next three attacks aren't much more powerful than this, I'll take them, and then we kill them all."*

"I see," I said after the quick message to my people. "Is it fair to assume that none of the other arbiters are like you?"

"Precisely! I'm as unique as they come. Well, not as unique as those God Beasts of yours, but they're not that rare further up north and to the east. One of the pillars has over twenty of them I've heard."

"Over 20 God Beasts? As strong as my companions?"

"Maybe, but you don't have to worry about that as you won't be leaving this place alive. Anyway, what was I—ahh! Yes, the other arbiters. Let me tell you, some of my fellow arbiters wouldn't have even talked back, and one certain arbitress would just attack you straight away. Balog? Who knows. You're lucky to run into someone as reasonable and merciful as me," he said, eliciting no reaction from me. He was joking. To him, the massacres he caused, the deaths and suffering, all of it amounted to a joke.

"So, ready for the next attack?"

The group of civilians had already made it across the square and were hiding far behind our defensive wall of God Beasts as these people called them. There was so much to do in this land. So much I wanted to build, create, make better for us and the people living here, but we just didn't have the time because of people like Pelis.

We stepped back to the center, and he prepared again. This time, he held his blade off to the side, the sword tip leaning against the gravel below our feet. He charged again, bringing the sword up and slashing toward my left side. I angled both daggers and ducked as his blade made contact. The power behind the attack made me stagger and I almost fell.

Pelis laughed yet again and clapped his hands like a child at a circus seeing some break-neck stunt. Well, I was probably very interesting to him, but he wasn't to me. Angling my daggers had made his attack go over me, though not before some of his black aura crashed into my hands. I thought that I'd heard a finger or two breaking, but when I looked down at my hands, everything was fine.

I took a deep breath as I stood and gathered myself.

"Group two, go."

I sat back down next to Pelis, who was seemingly amused beyond reason. His mouth was wide open and his eyes bulged out of their sockets.

"That was good. I mean it. You took one of my stronger skills."

"It was nothing," I said nonchalantly, but I didn't really feel that way.

"Maybe, maybe not, but how were you able to dodge? I was sure I'd get you. My skill had an additional attack speed modifier."

I was about to ask what he just meant, but then figured it out on my own. It was just a different way of saying the skill added extra attack speed to his, well, attack. I knew the only reason was the passive my Third's set gave me. Perceiving the time at 107% gave me just enough wiggle room to make minuscule changes to my movements, which in this case turned out to be just what I needed.

Of course, I wasn't going to tell him any of that.

"Pelis, are you sure we can't just let these fine people go? I'll be happy to kick your ass and send you back to Balog. There's no need for you to die."

His mood took a shift for the worse as he glared at me, then shot to his feet and pointed at the center of the square.

"You and I will fight to the death! Now! Take all those filthy peasants! You can have them! All I care about is your head!"

I didn't rise to his tirade, at least not at the speed he was expecting, and slowly stood and straightened myself.

"Pelis, are you sure? Are you really letting them go if I fight you? Just like that?"

"Yes, now stand!" he hissed, stepping away from me and pacing back and forth. "Get up! I want to fight you!"

I held my right hand up.

"First the civilians, and then we fight with everything we got? Deal?"

"Deal! Oh! You have no idea how much I want to hurt you right now. And I thought we might even become friends, but you had to go and hurt my pride! Well, no one has ever done that and lived to tell about it! No one insults me and lives!"

"Recall your animus and bcles," I said, finally taking him seriously. "Now."

Pelis tsked and motioned his hand toward the armored soldiers. They stepped aside, letting the remaining civilians go. Men and women, both old and young, children of all ages, they knew very well what it meant to be oppressed by maniacs like Pelis. All they cared about was to run away and make it out of the lion's den alive. The two groups pushed past us and joined the other civilians we'd already saved.

"Buff up!" I said, raising my voice so Pelis could hear me, but then switched to the leadership room for the follow-up message. *The moment all buffs are up, Benny, you go in. Legs, stay behind, and protect the girls with your limbs and body. Kill anyone who comes your way. Merek, Jeanette, and Selene, you're the last line. Don't let them kill Sonya and Emma.*

"As if you even need to tell us," Jeanette said as their buffs washed over us. More dodge, speed, critical hit and damage, all stats... I didn't even bother reading all the buffs as Pelis' animus and beles started preparing for battle.

"Najla!" I yelled, hoping she would hear me. "Get them all out of here! Go into the forest so you're not in the way!"

The arbiter smiled at me and even winked, then he pulled his sword back around and charged along with more than a thousand armored soldiers.

My body moved almost on instinct as I used a darkness-devouring elixir that would allow us to deal true damage to the soldiers. I slashed through the air, releasing a [Pestilent Wave] that formed almost instantly before me and then surged outward. It slammed into Pelis and his army of reanimated darkness, knocking the first several rows over. To my great surprise, the attack was so effective that the ensuing wave of pestilent power ate through the animus. Dozens of suits of armor fell to the ground, but more of the mindless creatures jumped over the chunks of steel and spread out around the square as if to bypass me.

"No, you will not!" I yelled, using Fade to move about twenty steps back, and readied another skill, [Pestilent Storm]. It formed overhead, purple, black, and green tendrils slamming into the village square, devastating anything they touched.

A two-handed sword that was taller than me, came right for my head. I activated [Backstab], which teleported me into Pelis' shadow. Both my daggers bounced off his thick armor. I kicked off, forcing him to stumble into Benny's raking claws. The arbiter angled his sword and caught the attack. He was sent flying toward me just as I finished using my support skills, including [Pestilence Aura]. If Pelis got a hit in, he'd receive half of the damage back, which was still something.

Notifications flooded my mind, and I just kept pushing them away as debuffs took hold of the horde, while deflecting more than a few debuffs of my own. The arbiter had some nasty skills, I could feel them, but my resistance was too high for him. If I had to guess, he was all brawn.

Using the moment he flew at me, I followed up with [Assault]. Out of all certain debuffs, I needed to lower his speed so I could evade his attacks. Even the seven percent time dilation wasn't of much help against someone of his caliber especially because his minions were at large and could intervene in our battle.

My blades connected with his side as he flew past me, drawing two deep gashes. The (Mangled) debuff activated, lowering his speed for 15 seconds by 40%.

I took a single second to glance at the girls. Merek stood about ten steps away from them, holding his spear and shield at the ready as a red glow encased him. The mindless armored soldiers were all focused on him, trying to break past his defenses as Sonya used her limited area of effect spells to devastating effect while Emma focused on keeping him alive. Selene flashed in and out, cutting through the enemies with ease.

Elvina finally appeared as well with a monstrous contraption in tow. It looked very much like the wall of death that'd shot countless bolts at the Valtorians back in Greystone, but it was mobile and seemed to follow her. She quickly assumed a good tactical position and set it up. Bolts flew first into the right flank, penetrating the armor and exploding once they'd struck the bodies beneath. The cart turned to the other side just as I felt a surge of power coming from my right.

"Cade of the Bloodmoon! Enough!" Pelis roared, slamming his sword into the ground. Ten-foot-long stone spikes coated by darkness shot out from the ground and went straight for me. I raised my kris and targeted the beles that had stayed behind and were using ranged weapons and minor spells to attack me and Benny. I used [Dagger Rain], showering them in scores of mana blades that formed above their ranks and crashed into the 200 or so second-tier soldiers.

I used Fade to slip past the closing spiked attack and

passed it by entirely, appearing right above him with both of my daggers pointed at his face. Just before my body started dropping, I used [Onslaught] and felt my body stiffen. I halted in mid-air and then crashed down into the arbiter, stabbing, cutting, and slashing at his face five times in quick succession. My debuffs went through.

```
You have inflicted the (Mangled II) debuff
   on Arbiter Pelis, lowering the target's
          speed by 40  for 15 seconds.

You have inflicted the (Numb II) debuff
   on Arbiter Pelis, lowering the target's
      attack power by 40  for 15 seconds.
```

My [Plague Domain] finally kicked in and I was immediately hit by a shower of [Stolen Power] that increased my main stats by over thirty points each. [Sapper] and [Corrosion] reactivated, going up to their maximum number of stacks in a heartbeat, lowering our enemies' stats even further while raising our defense penetration by 30%.

I kicked out and Pelis caught my leg, but he grunted in pain and was sent staggering to the side. That little moment was more than enough to finally end the battle. More than half of the animus were dead while almost all beles had been hit with my mana daggers, dying almost instantly. The sheer number of attacks, my auras, support debuff skills, and the number of debuffs I could dish out in mere seconds, had just shown me how dangerous such a skill set was. Fight me alone, and he'd be at a disadvantage as I was a pure debuff class that focused on stealing even the will to live. If he sent in an army, I'd just drain their stats and inflict massive damage with just the random debuffs.

Emboldened by my success, my girls and Benny started playing more aggressively. The pangolin Blood Beast charged where the enemy ranks were the thickest and released his blood cloud. It utterly devastated his targets. The bloody mist infused both with the dark elixir and so many buffs, while the enemy was hit with just as many debuffs, that I had no doubt he'd been able to win this battle all by himself. Still, experience points were coming in, though not many. And then there were the sweet, lovely deity favor points.

"Coward! Fight me fairly!" Pelis screamed as he pushed out of a mass of dented armor and broken animus.

He grabbed one of the mangled bodies and held it up in front of him. One moment, the animus was there, and the other it was gone, turned into a dark swirling mass that then entered his body. All my stat points rose across the board by two points. Pelis grabbed another two of his animus, and they too turned into a dark blob that he absorbed.

"Alright, this is getting scary," I muttered and switched to the leadership room. *"Guys! Kill as many of those things as you can! He's absorbing their power!"*

"Need help, bro?" Benny asked, standing with his chest puffed out and with a wide grin. One moment he was there, and the other he was flying past me, slamming into the side of a building.

Pelis glanced over my shoulder and a foreboding grin crawled onto his thin lips.

"Hah! Took you long enough, you wicked—"

"Shut up or I'm gone!" a female voice snapped back. I looked over to where the voice was coming from and saw a woman wearing a black armored battle dress with her arms crossed standing there. Two golden horns that circled downward sat atop her head, making her look like a monstrous ram on two legs. In her left hand, she held a sword whip, while in the other a long spear.

"Right! Thank you Danara, my savior!"

The woman stepped toward him, raising her whip

sword. She struck him across the face, leaving a deep cut behind. Her bob-cut hair was very similar to Pelis' in color but a bit darker and it had a hint of orange.

"If you want my help, then show some gratitude and stop groveling! I'll never become your woman! The only reason I'm here is because I don't want to have to kill all my villagers like you did, fool!"

Benny groaned as he pushed away part of a wall that had collapsed on top of him, and stood, brushing the rubble off his muscled, hairy body. He looked at Pelis and then at the newcomer.

"That was so not cool, you know?" he said, giving the woman called Danara the middle finger. "Anyway, two on two, bro? I kind of want to smack her around a bit. She hit me pretty hard."

"I guess so, Benny, but do you really want to hit women?"

"Well, yeah. I mean, I'm all about loving women, but she's not a woman. That crazy chick is a God Beast. She might even be similar to me." He paused for a moment, staring at her, and then gasped. "Shit! It isn't considered bestiality if you fuck something that's kind of the same species, right? It's like--no, never mind."

Pelis and Danara shared a look and then studied Benny. I knew exactly how they felt, as Benny could go off on a tangent unless stopped.

"So...what? Do you want her for yourself? Legs will kick your ass."

"Nah! Right, Legs? You know I love you, bro!" Benny shot over his shoulder and the spider let out a happy screech.

"Hmm, I don't think this was very smart after all," the horned woman called Danara muttered. "You can have them both, Pelis. I'm off to--"

"Oh, you're not!" Benny snapped, taking a step toward

her.

"Like my friend here just said, neither of you are leaving this place alive."

"Unless you want to become my lover, yo!" Benny said excitedly, pointing a hairy finger at Danara.

"Now that escalated quickly," Selene mumbled as she appeared next to me. "We're done with the remaining armored soldiers. What do you want to do?" she said just loud enough so the two could hear her.

"Hold on," I said and visibly relaxed. "Are you an arbiter or a God Beast?"

"What's it to you?" Danara hissed. "You better watch yourself, or I'll stab your thing!"

"Ohh, I like her, bro! Let me at her!"

CHAPTER 18 – SMACK MY BITCH UP!

The rest of my girls, along with Merek and Elvina, joined us. There were only a handful of animus left, and Pelis was eating them like there was no tomorrow. The helfar lifted her crossbow and shot two of them dead, but it didn't help as he just ate their corpses.

"That's so nasty," she said, stowing her weapon. "We made sure these other ones didn't leave any bodies behind, but I guess ordinary bolts won't do it."

"No, and that's fine. I need to see what the arbiters are capable of anyway. So, is everyone fine?"

"More than fine," Sonya chuckled. "I'm almost level 58. These animus didn't give that much experience, but there were a lot of them."

"Ohh! I'm only 57. That's so not fair!" Emma said with a hint of disappointment. "You were getting all the kills."

Sonya stared at her flatly with both hands on her hips.

"Emma, just how exactly did you plan on killing them to get more experience points?"

Now it was my turn to stare at them.

"Girls, now is not the place," I whispered. "We're about to kick their assess, as for you, I think it's better if you wait with the civilians."

"Why?" Jeanette protested. "I want to fight, too."

"And you just did, didn't you?" Selene mumbled. "Come on. Give the man some space."

"Smack my bitch up," Benny whispered rubbing his hands and grinning. As usual I had no clue what he meant by any of it, "Ta-na-na-na-na! Smack my bitch up! T-n-n-n-n!"

"What...are you doing?" Pelis asked as he absorbed the last animus. I'd counted thirteen in total, which I figured wasn't that bad as my stats had only risen by about 30 points across the board. Sure, that was about 150 stat points in total, but there must have been some kind of maximum he could absorb, I was sure of it.

"My brother here is singing if you already have to know, but don't ask what. I have no idea," I replied, giving the blood beast a questioning look.

"Prodigy, bro! Firestarter! No good! Smack My Bitch Up! Voodoo People! Come one, don't you—oh, right. Wish you could hear them, man. I need to get my hands on some instruments so I can learn how to play music and shit."

I sighed. Scatterbrained Benny sometimes shifted in and out of worlds it seemed. Benny was...special.

"Whatever, Benny. I still have a bone to pick with that scumbag arbiter. As for you...ask the girls if they can accept a female God Beast."

"Hey! You're assuming two things!" Danara yelled. "Firstly, I don't like furry people! And secondly, should you really underestimate us?"

Benny and I stared at each other and then burst into laughter.

"Alright, yeah, that was funny as shit, bro. Anyway, you ready? My claws are itching."

A thick, bloody mist spread outward in a cone, focusing on Pelis and Danara. His muscles tensed, and then the Blood Beast shot forth like a furry projectile, heading straight for Danara.

I sighed inwardly and activated my [Pestilence Aura] again. Several debuff notifications appeared in my mind, and I pushed them all aside as I readied myself to attack. He was now stronger than during our first clash, but I didn't worry about the outcome and headed straight for him.

Pelis reacted a little bit faster than I thought he would,

swinging his greatsword in a wide arc, releasing a wave of darkness that exploded as it hit my body. I was sent flying backward, barely absorbing the dark energies with my blades. The force of the attack made me step back but also gave me a few precious seconds to see what my pangolin beast was up to.

Benny was yelling at Danara, who in turn just cried and threw insults his way. It distracted me way more than I thought it would as I couldn't help but imagine the fear she must have felt. Seeing a Blood Beast coming for you after saying he wants to make you his bitch, and then even singing something about smacking a bitch up, yeah, that could unnerve even the godliest of God Beasts.

"Benny! Behave!" I yelled, charging back into battle.

Pelis didn't look good, though. He was sweating, his face pale, and his body was trembling. I opened up with a [Pestilent Wave], engulfing the entire village square in death and decay. It wouldn't kill him, but if it distracted the arbiter even for a few seconds, I'd be happy.

I used [Fade] to close in on him, appearing to his left and hitting him with [Plague Fang]. It was a powerful, single blow that pierced his armor.

```
You have inflicted the (Poison II) debuff on
  Arbiter Pelis, draining the target's life
     by 1.5  every second for 15 seconds.
```

More spikes rose from the ground all around him, and one clipped my leg, creating sparks as steel and steel-hard rock met. I knew that a fighter with his durability and power wasn't a great match-up for an assassin class, but I was so much more than what I used to be and wouldn't die from a single attack unless it cut my head off.

```
          You have resisted a debuff.
          You have resisted a debuff.
```

I had no idea what the debuffs were as the Godveil didn't show me, but it was probably bleeding or something similar.

Instead, several more notifications replaced the resisted debuff ones, showing me just how much of my own debuffs were going through. Pelis, who had a strength that was somewhat higher than mine, wasn't able to do much. He struggled as I sliced him open with relative ease.

The whole situation was a bit off as Benny sang and howled, trying to corner Danara, who was doing her best to keep him at bay. Little did she know that our Blood Beast was nearly indestructible.

I used [Fade] to get out of Pelis' range as he started glowing brightly. His shoulders exploded and dark tendrils rose from inside. They grabbed the oversized sword and swung it at me, releasing three more waves of dark power, all hidden within a single attack. I blocked the first, but the next two struck my right arm and my hip, drawing deep gashes in my armor and skin. The only reason why I hadn't taken the waves in my face was probably the 7% time dilation that came with the Third's set of gear.

Pelis let out a guttural roar that cut through the night and two more dark tentacles broke free from his back and propelled him in my direction. Cobblestones and chunks of hard soil flew in all directions from the power he released with that single lunge, but I didn't sit still. The arbiter had already seen the way I fought, but I still had a few things, like more of the deadly vials Elvina prepared for me.

I jumped to the side and behind the ruined building where Benny'd crashed into a minute ago. The crossbow I'd used outside the village was just perfect for someone with greater reach than me, so I deployed it without regrets. Screw fighting fair when your own deities and gods had almost lost all their powers, while those of your enemy were at their peak.

I loaded a vial-tipped bolt and released it as Pelis landed. The vial struck his chest just as he turned toward me. The glass container exploded, releasing its content. His dark armor started hissing and dissolving right away. The four tentacles covered his chest and started wiping away the vial's content, a special acid we'd made from the wendigo's corpse.

I thought about shooting another vial for a brief second, but it would be a waste. Pelis was already falling to his knees when I stashed the crossbow away and pulled out my daggers. I used one more skill to finish him off, [Backstab]. It was more than enough to finish someone already on his knees and dying.

I appeared behind the arbiter and suddenly time seemed to slow down almost to a halt.

```
   Do you wish to sacrifice Arbiter
    Pelis Fejner to the Old Gods?

            [Yes] - [No]
```

There was no further explanation, just a prompt. I had never experienced anything like it. If I didn't choose to sacrifice him, I probably wouldn't get any direct rewards, but that didn't matter so much as letting the trio of gods get their hands on someone with a lot of dark power.

I accepted, which was the only reasonable decision as I didn't want to piss off the gods. Besides, they'd given us quite a few interesting special powers that made life easier. Considering our mission, more would follow. I was sure of it.

Bright white light erupted from Pelis' body, burning the dark tendrils away in mere heartbeats, leaving a dried-up husk of the former arbiter. It was both anticlimactic and spectacular at the same time.

```
   Congratulations! You have sacrificed an
     Arbiter of Darkness, Pelis Fejner.

   You have received 1,000 Guild Favor.

   You have received 2,000 Deity Favor.

   You have received 3,500 Patron Favor.

   You have received 5,000 Gold Coins.
```

The rewards weren't exactly something to brag about,

but the gold coins would come in handy to upgrade Merek's new skills once he hit level 60, or those of the girls. It didn't matter really as we would all get our turn upgrading our powers. All it would take was some time and a little bit of risk.

A strong gust of wind blew in from everywhere at once, carrying away Pelis' ashen remains. The oversized sword and all of his armor remained on the ground, which was something I hadn't expected. I was glad to see it in any case. Sure, it would need to be upgraded and fixed from the ground up before anyone could use it, but considering how much of a beating Pelis took wearing that armor, I was sure that the suit had been worth the battle.

A loud crash echoed from where Benny had run off. Danara crashed into the village center's fountain, utterly destroying it. She'd grown double in size and had dark, leathery wings sprouting from her back. One of the two horns was chipped, the very tip missing. Her armored battle dress was torn in places where Benny had probably tried to get her with his claws.

The arbiter roared in rage as she shot out of the rubble and slammed into Benny. She still held her sword whip and spear in hand, attacking him with a ferocity I'd rarely seen before. Danara really wanted to hurt him, but no matter how many times she cut and pierced his skin, nothing changed. Despite their very similar size, he was much stronger.

"Are you—is he playing with me?" Danara roared again, but this time she looked at me. "Why isn't he fighting me at his full power?"

I shrugged and sat down on a piece of broken-down wall.

"Because he would kill you, it's that simple. And I have to be honest, I think he likes you...though that's kind of really weird since he just met you and all."

"Oh, please! He already knows me," the God Beast said, wiping blood from her face. "We met," she added, nodding at Benny who snarled at her licking his upper lip.

"You met?"

"I'm Ludmilla," she said narrowing her gaze at the werewolf.

"Hah! So that's why you smelled so familiar!" Benny laughed. "Ludmilla, this is awesome! I had no idea you were so damn hot when...I mean you're hot in your human form but this?"

First I thought Danara would impale Benny on her spear for his words, instead she seemed taken aback, confused even.

"You blabbering idiot," she said.

"Come on, Ludmilla, this isn't you. An arbiter for the Order? You told me you loved this place!" Benny said.

She looked around at the devastated village square. The bloodied tiles and walls, the destroyed houses and the many dead. Sadness washed over her.

"Don't tell me who or what I am," she said, her voice weak and full of guilt.

"Danara, why don't you just stop before more blood is spilled? There's no reason to fight us anymore," I said.

The God Beast didn't say anything. Her eyes wandered over the dead until they took in the frightened survivors hiding behind the rubble.

"I knew there was something odd about her, man," Benny said finding himself next to me. "I told you, like, I was attracted to her beyond reason. Turns out she's a God Beast!"

"Which begs the question of how she's able to be human and beast at the same time," I said, eyeing Danara, or Ludmilla as she was known in her human form. "Would you care to explain, lady?" I asked. She had my curiosity piqued, that much was clear.

"I don't want to," she replied, her voice a hint weaker than moments before. "I...that's something you don't need to know."

She thumped the butt of her spear against the wrecked stone tiles of the square, wrenching her eyes away from the people of the village and focusing on Benny again.

"Now fight me, beast!"

"You'll die," I said flatly.

She groaned loudly with frustration. The tides of battle weren't in her favor. Pelis was dead and she was fighting a losing battle surrounded by enemies. I could sympathize with the feeling, luckily for her we weren't out for mindless slaughter like some others who I had the misfortune to meet.

"Do you *want* to die?" Emma asked as she leaned against me.

"You know, I was an enemy to Cade and Emma as well," Sonya said, nodding at me and the golden-haired beauty. "We became friends rather quickly, and as you can see, we're a diverse bunch. Benny likes you, and that means we can learn to like you too given time."

"Also, we don't even need to get along with you as long as Benny does and you don't cause trouble," Jeanette chimed in. "See, I can't stand these girls, but I love Cade, so I tolerate them."

Sonya snorted, then burst into laughter.

"Oh, you're so going to get it tonight!"

"No, I'm not! I have decided that I won't be bullied!" Jeanette hissed. "You're a bully."

"I think Sonya's right, Jeanette," Emma added. "You're so fucked tonight."

"They're doing it again," Benny said, lowering his voice. "Cade?"

I sighed and stood back up again.

"Girls, this is Benny's moment and choice. If he wants to...smack her...up or something, and then the two can work it out, let them. I don't think she likes it that much with the Order or she'd be fighting much harder."

I knew I was right. Despite her power and rank, Danara wasn't as steeped in dark energies as Pelis was. She was powerful, there was no doubt about it. Not many creatures could take on Benny for as long as she did and live to tell the tale, no matter how much my weird otherworldly friend restrained himself. Danara, as she was known while transformed, cleared her throat.

"You know that I can hear you, right?"

"And that's the whole point, Danara. Are you ready to die tonight?" I asked again, eyeing her. "Because we came here tonight to kill everyone and everything responsible for this massacre, including the troops at Balan."

She tensed and took a step back.

"I never agreed with Pelis' methods," she said.

There was a clear struggle within her. The Order must have recruited her for the powers she wielded, not because of how fanatical about Tan'Malas she was. Just went to show how blind the powerful could be. They say you can't put a price on loyalty. That's true, some people can't be corrupted by power and I sincerely hoped Danara was one of them, for Benny's sake if nothing else.

"Come, everyone. I want to check up on the survivors. Benny, you do what you feel is right. Either kill or talk to her, see if she'd be willing to stick around."

I then turned to Danara and pointed my dagger at her.

"I guess you're in a really awkward situation. Stay loyal to those monsters we destroyed and die, or turn a new page in life. Maybe help rebuild, make up for what you've done. You're a God Beast, if nothing, you'll live long enough to atone for your service to the Order."

Danara seemed lost in thought after my words. The spear in her hand suddenly dropped to the ground and she sat down on a large chunk of stone that was once part of the fountain.

"Choose carefully," I said and turned to Benny. "Both of you."

Ignoring my remark, Benny rushed over to her.

"Ludmilla..." he muttered, kneeling next to her. She shuddered as Benny lowered a hand on hers.

"Wait, what about the loot? The armor and the weapons from those animus?" Merek asked, kicking one of the suits of armor for emphasis.

"Later. Give them some space, and we need to tend to the villagers. Things are going to get a lot darker before they get any better, Merek. We need to continue converting people or we will lose the Godveil."

"Hey, just one small thing," Elvina said hopping over to me. She seemed much more excited than I imagined she'd be after another slaughter.

"What?"

"Don't beat yourself up, alright? The Godveil will give us all a better life, including the converted. Don't you even dare think that you're doing this just for yourself or for the guild, okay? I know that look you just had, and it never leads to anything good."

"She's right, love," Emma said, pushing past Elvina and putting her arm around me. "Don't overthink it. We're doing good things here, well, minus Pelis killing all the people...and yes, I know what you're thinking, but you can't be everywhere at the same time. No one can."

They were right, all of them, but somehow I couldn't help but feel like an imposter, someone who was working for his own benefit. A part of me cared more than it should.

Before we arrived, there wasn't nearly as much death, that was simply a fact. In trying to help these people, we managed to have entire families killed and it was hard to not feel guilty. On the other hand, we were preventing not only the suffering of those among us, but also trying to save all future generations under the boot of the Order, and yet...

One of those things was the cold hard truth, the drying blood under my soles, the massacred bodies around the square, while the other was an idea, a noble one, but no more tangible for it.

Pelis was dead and it brought me little comfort. The trail of death left in the wake of our arrival was crowding. There would only be even more and I knew that if I ever wanted peace for my family and friends, for the people living here, I'd have to curl my fingers around the throat of every single member of the Order until there were none left.

I found comfort in that. Whether it would bring me peace was a different question. Perhaps after everything I didn't deserve peace, and that would be fine too. At least the others would finally live a worthwile life.

"I know, don't worry, ladies, but I do appreciate you keeping my mind straight. These are dark times," I said and smiled, trying not to show too much of the struggle within me. Emma didn't smile back, she simply leaned her head on my shoulder for a moment then kissed me gently.

Good enough, I thought. *This is good enough for me.*

We made our way out of the village to a ruckus behind us. Benny and Danara were at it again, fighting and roaring. I didn't know what the village would look like once they stopped fighting, but...then it all went silent and a crying moan pierced the silence. I stopped and was about to say something stupid when Emma shushed me.

"Right, love. I think we got our answer," I chuckled.

"Ohh, she's a screamer alright. I doubt Benny will have to watch that big thing of his with her being a beast as well and stuff."

Sonya and Jeanette giggled, but Selene and Elvina remained silent, just giving them odd glances as we hurried along through the darkness. Najla and a group of others stepped out of the forest to meet us. She'd been crying as her eyes were all red, and she hadn't been the only one. Legs loomed over them protectively, and I looked up at the War Weaver, flashing him a warm smile.

"Good job, Legs. I appreciate you."

The spider let out a soft purring screech-like sound that I knew was him saying his thanks.

"Wh—what happened? Where is the arbiter? Did he run? Will he—" the former mayor started to ask but I stopped her.

"No, he won't. I killed him, Najla. He will never hurt a living soul again, but I don't think it's smart to go back to the village aside from getting the most basic of necessities. There's God Beasts fighting out there still, I don't think –" Another bestial moan resounded in the night.

"I know *that* kind of fighting," Jeanette said and laughed.

"In any case," I continued, "There's nothing to protect you there anymore."

I knew I've put them in a difficult situation. They either had the choice to go back to the village where two God Beasts were duking it out, one way or another...or come with me, though I could hardly shelter them all. My Godveil showed 392 of them; a whole village basically. Our resources would dry out in days.

"Then what do we do? We have nowhere to go! We will all die! And the other villages are regulated, they will know even if we all spread out across—"

"Stop and listen, okay? Just give me a moment."

She shut her mouth and did as I said, nodding once. I could see she was annoyed as much as she was afraid, and that was a good thing. As long as no one panicked, we'd be fine.

"Listen to me!" I said, raising my voice to be heard over the ever-larger gathering crowd. All four groups that I'd saved earlier huddled together, watching me in both anger and hope. "I can offer you shelter back in our village, or you can stay here and in your homes. However, I will not be able to stay here and protect you. Best-case scenario, I have one of my God Beasts stay for a few days and make sure you have a chance to run!"

I stopped and let it sink in. Having Benny and Legs stay in Garm was a spur-of-the-moment thing, one I probably should have thought out better, but what was it that I could actually do for all the villagers right now? Not much.

"If you want to move into our village, I need to know so we can start preparing facilities! Our temple will soon be done and with that, the power of our Godveil will increase. Everyone will be able to become stronger, get a class, level up, get skills, and fight these bastards! If you choose to move into New Greystone, you will be free but obliged to help the village!

There is no currency, and there are no free meals! You work, and you get fed! You get clothed, and given armor and weapons so you can level up and protect yourself and your loved ones!"

I stopped again, letting the next part sink in as well. Their expressions shifted from anger and hope to doubt. It wasn't an easy thing being told that in order to live, people would have to uproot their lives, their rules and ways of living and move under our wing. And what guarantees did they have? None other than my word.

"Lastly! Whoever moves to New Greystone will have to convert! It will bring danger, but me defeating Pelis so easily should tell you enough. Both of my God Beasts are even stronger than me, and my friends here can take on an army by themselves, so fear not."

I stepped back, motioning for the rest to join me as the crowd broke into a murmur and people started exchanging thoughts.

"Hell yeah!"

The roar came from the village and was quickly followed by another roar of sheer excitement. The villagers were startled. Mothers pulled their children closer to their chests and men looked nervously around, trying to find a way to comfort their families.

"I think Benny and Danara came to...a conclusion," Jeanette said, shooting me a wink.

As weird as it might sound, it brought me relief to know the God Beasts were done with their...battle.

"Be calm, this is a good sign," I said. "Najla, take charge. You are their mayor, make sure people do what's best for them," I said as my eyes met hers. She stared hard for a second, but then shook her head.

"I have no idea what to do! I don't even know what I want, how can I ask them to make such a hard choice?"

"Then go back to your homes. I think it's safe for now," Sonya said, trying to keep her voice gentle. "Sleep for a few hours and process what has happened. We will stay in Garm until dawn, right, Cade? We can see who wants to convert then and come up with a plan."

Najla took in a deep breath and let it out slowly.

"Very well," she said and turned toward the crowd. "Everyone! Listen to me!"

CHAPTER 19 –
FAMILY PROBLEMS

It took us about half an hour for everyone to return to their homes or take residence in the homes of their neighbors. Legs was stationed outside the village and a few minutes to the northeast where the enemy would come from if they were to attack. Benny and Danara were roaming the woods, to the east and north, and would stay outside for the rest of the night.

The girls and I had settled into the manor house with Najla, who was busy taking a bath. Jeanette was raiding the liquor cabinets along with Selene and Sonya, while Elvina, Emma, and I sat in the living room. My golden-haired beauty sat next to me with her head leaning on my shoulder. She was snoring softly. Healing the villagers and Danara had taken a lot out of her.

Neither Najla nor the other people from Garm Village liked that the golden-horned arbiter had joined our group so to say, but that was one thing I wouldn't give anyone but Benny and Legs the right to vote on. He'd bested her with ease, which didn't mean much as he was just that overpowered, and she'd agreed to become his mate. There was a glint in her eye when they announced it and I couldn't help but imagine the two going at it yet again, breaking down trees and cracking rocks.

"What do you think of my vials? They did good, right?"

I smiled at Elvina. She truly had done an outstanding job there, and I sincerely hoped that she'd continue to do so. The vial had eaten through Pelis, who was something like a minor god to these people.

"Yeah, they did just great. It's one of the things I wanted

to talk to you about. I guess this time's just perfect since everyone's busy with something."

"Yes, sure. What is it?" she asked, making herself comfortable. The helfar had shed her combat dress and now sat there wearing an almost sheer golden nightgown. It barely reached her knees and folded up the side of her hip. The little minx knew I could see it all but just sat there and smiled back at me.

"Is there a chance you could do this permanently? Just make traps and contraptions we can use? Vials of death and the like?"

She shrugged and looked off to the side where the other girls were drinking.

"Maybe, maybe not. I like my freedom."

"And you'd get to keep it. Just make sure we have the means to kill the big bad guys with as much ease as we can. Every time we fight it out with the arbiters, there's a chance someone can die."

"You had it all under control," Sonya shot from over at the bar.

"I did, love, but that wouldn't matter if he'd been the one with the acid vial, right?"

"Totally. You want a drink?"

"Do you even need to ask? What kind of woman are you?" Jeanette snapped at her. "Let me make it."

"No, you won't! I can make a fucking drink by myself, butt-plug!"

"Oh, you take that back!"

Elvina groaned as she shifted in the upholstered relaxing chair. Her wings were in the way even though she'd folded them.

"Anyway, as I was saying, I need more trump cards. Fighting fair is for idiots, especially when other people's lives are at stake."

"Well, I have about 14 more left and there's enough wendigo for 20 more or so? But honestly, I wanted to try some other stuff. Banxi is pretty good with alchemy and all these mix-and-match processes."

"And you're getting along with him? I know he can be a bit strange and hard to deal with, but—"

"No, no, he's fine. It's his wives I have a problem with. They're jealous and annoying. As if I'd ever want to lay with a green, leathery—ugh!"

I chuckled, finding it genuinely amusing. If I didn't know better, I'd think she was into goblins.

"I'll talk to them, alright? The goblas are usually pretty nice, but you need to understand something."

"Oh, and what's that?"

"You're as beautiful as can be, and no, I'm not trying to get into your panties."

"I'm not wearing any," she said with a smirk and spread her legs just far enough that I could see she was telling the truth.

"Hey, is that one stealing our man?" Jeanette asked incredulously. "Why don't you plug her, Sonya? She just said she aint wearing any panties!"

"She did, didn't she?" Sonya said with a mischievous smile.

Elvina pressed her legs together and pushed into the chair.

"No, you're not doing the nasty to me! Cade! I don't want them anywhere near me!"

I sighed and looked over to the trio, who found everything obviously very amusing.

"They're just teasing you. Anyway, what did you say you wanted to do with the rest of the wendigo's body?"

"I—are you sure? Sonya and Jeanette are looking at me funny."

"Yes, I'm sure. Go on."

Elvina took in a deep breath and let it out slowly, her eyes never leaving the others.

"I was thinking of making some accessories. You

mentioned how he shrugged off most of your debuffs?"

"That's right," I confirmed.

"Well, what if we could raise our debuff resistances? Just in case. Wouldn't that be a good thing?"

"And the trophy?"

"Will stay intact. I think they finished it yesterday but wanted to do some more work on the antlers. Varnish and some stuff. I'd use his bones and...I don't know. We'll see. It's just an idea, so I have no idea if it will even work."

"It's a good one if you ask me," Sonya said as she joined us and handed me a tall glass filled with a rose liquid. Bubbles were rising to the top. "Yeah, I have no idea how it's called. The label read CHAM. Whatever it is."

I took the glass and she sat to my other side, careful not to wake Emma up, which I appreciated immensely. Our resident priestess needed some rest. Hell, we all did, but she in particular.

"Well, you have my blessing, Elvina. However, please refrain from teasing me by not wearing any panties. You heard Danara, now you can imagine just how hard you'll scream if you stir the dragon."

The girls stared at me flatly for a moment, and I could hear Selene and Jeanette stop doing whatever they were up to, and then a collective laughter broke out.

"Stir the dragon? Really?" Sonya asked as she leaned in and kissed me.

"Hey, I'm just saying. All of my stats are higher now, so yeah, stir the dragon and find out what happens."

Selene and Jeanette joined us then, hurried over and sat in one of the other leather upholstered sofas.

"I'd like to see you try," Elvina said defiantly. "I've outlasted better lovers than you."

Sonya snorted, some of the cham drink leaving her nose.

"You're full of shit, El," she laughed and wiped the liquid from her face. "I can feel you're still a virgin. And Selene can even smell it. Don't even go there."

Elvina's mouth snapped open as if to protest, but then she just stared at the elf, and then the brunette magician.

"You...can?"

"No, of course not," I said with a sigh and slapped the inside of Sonya's thigh. "Don't tease her, Sonya. Not everyone likes to get plugged."

Now it was Jeanette's turn to protest.

"I don't like it! I just endure because Sonya makes these weird noises and squirts whenever she plugs me!"

"That...is disturbing," a new voice said from the doorway. Najla stood there, her wet orange hair hanging down her shoulders. All she wore was a slightly too-large bath towel wrapped around her body.

"Jeanette? Can you please make her a drink?" I asked. "I think she needs one just as much as we do after today."

Emma stirred awake, and I wiped the drool from her face.

"Do you want to go sleep in a bed?"

"N—no, I...want to hear what you're all talking about. But please, Najla, can you get me a blanket? I'm cold."

"Cold? Wait, that doesn't make any—"

"I'm just over exhausted, Cade. Don't worry."

"Fine. If you want to stay up and listen in, be my guest. Speaking of which, there's something we need to discuss, Najla."

"Are you telling her about—the thing?" Sonya asked guiltily. "Maybe we should wait and not pressure her?"

"It's not pressuring her," I said, motioning for Najla to sit across from me on the table. She did as I asked but pushed the towel down her knees.

"He's not interested in your body right now, girl," Emma said. "Well, not in the way you'd like him to be. See, he told us about this new...quest that our Godveil has given us. Let me read it to you."

Quest Received: Spreading The Faith IV

Description: Continue to help spread
faith in the Gods of old.

Status: 0/1,000 Converted Believers

Reward: Establishment of a New Religion

NOTE: After establishing a new religion, you
will be able to assign a divine priestess who
will become the voice of the Old Gods, and with
that, will gain a special class. Prophet.

Najla stared at Emma and then at me for a long moment before she finally gasped as if understanding what we were going at.

"You want Emma to become a prophet? But who will heal people if she changes...to that thing you called other class?"

Our smiles never wavered, and after another long moment, she apparently understood our intention. Her expression changed from one of mild amusement to shock and utter horror.

"What are you—no! I'm not—I hate you! The only thing you gave my people is death and—no!"

I gave her a moment to gather herself, and Emma took the woman's hands in hers.

"I don't know you, but I can tell people, and you don't seem like someone who's been getting along well with both the village and people like Pelis. Am I wrong?"

Najla's lips quivered and before we knew it, she broke down and started crying. It was an awkward moment, one where I wanted to try and comfort her, but despite all my good intentions, I didn't think it would be appreciated. Emma did a fine enough job, and Sonya sat on the table next to Najla as well.

"Listen, we never wanted anyone to get hurt. We've lost so many people we used to care about back home and fled to this place. Seeing your people getting killed by a maniac... We all know exactly how it feels because we were once in your shoes. If anything, we want to see the suffering go away along with those causing it."

"And we're also putting our lives on the line, aren't we?" Emma added, her voice full of sympathy. "We can do most of it alone, but not everything. Someone from here, from this place, needs to guide them. We can show them the miracle, but you need to show them the way. You need to remind them that there's a greater power out there than that of Tan'Malas, and that together, we will win."

Emma had such a calming effect on Najla, who just stared at her with a look of admiration.

"But...how do...wait, no...I mean...is there such a thing? I've heard the village speak. Those who converted seemed so sure of it all but it was hard for me to accept it. All I saw was the danger such things brought with them. And I was right..."

"The Order's doing is nobody's fault but their own. The slaughter they caused should tell you all you need to know about what the worship of Tan'Malas truly means. The Old Gods are not only a better way, they are more powerful than the Dark One and we are living proof of that."

"More powerful than a real god?"

"Hey, hold on, let me tell you something," Sonya said, taking over. "Look at me." She placed her hand on the former mayor's cheek and gently pulled her face around. "Tan'Malas is not even a real god, no, he's only an aspect of Tan'Drak, one of the three Old Gods. He was banished never to return. The only reason why he managed to come back again was that a lot of people did a lot of very bad things. Tan'Malas took hold of the darkness in people's souls, and he reanimated all the dead people and monsters killed by humans all across the world. He's no all-mighty god, he's just an aspect of one. A very bad aspect."

I stood corrected, it wasn't only Emma who could preach, but Sonya as well. For a moment I wanted to choose one of the two for the prophetess class, but I remained silent. They were buttering Najla up for that role, and in all honesty, she was used to talking to crowds and motivating people, problem-solving, and having them get along...

"Najla, let me ask you just one question, alright?" I said, leaning closer toward her and staring the young woman in the eyes.

She nodded hurriedly.

"Yes, what is it?"

"What is it that you desire? Truly, deeply, and from the bottom of your heart."

She stared back for a long moment, chewing on the inside of her mouth and lips. It was hard to keep eye contact with her as the orange-haired beauty had a fierceness despite the vulnerable state she was in.

"I want everyone to know that...my family weren't traitors. I want everyone to know that what they did was...for the good of the village. They never sold anyone out, and used all their wealth to bribe the corrupt Order to look the other way."

She gasped, pulling away from me.

"You! What did you—why did I even—"

Najla shot to her feet and rushed out into the hallway. I could hear her loud footsteps carrying her to the upper floor, and then the loud slam of a door closing.

We all sat in silence for a good long minute. The only sound was of Jeanette sipping on her drink. Not many things affected her, which was good in a way, but she also had very little tact.

"So? Looks like you won't be getting in her bed any time soon."

"As if I need to add another one. You four are insatiable," I mumbled. "Not that I mind, of course."

"Of course you don't. You've been ogling Elvina for the last ten minutes, and I can't say I blame you, lover," she jabbed. "Now, if you could only look at me that way as well, I'd be very happy."

"Stop being a bitch, Jeanette," Sonya muttered. "He's been with you more than with the rest of us because you're so pushy. Just appreciate it for what it is."

"I need some fresh air," I said, getting to my feet. *"Benny, can you ask Danara if there are any other arbiters or other scum in Balan? I still have this indescribable itch to kill someone or something."*

It took him a few seconds to reply over the leadership room.

"Yeah, there are a bunch of zealots, inquisitors, and even an interrogator. They arrived here with Pelis. Do you want to kill them? That was her question, not mine."

"I do. Ask her if she's got a problem with that?"

"Nope, already did, bro. She doesn't care anymore, she says. All she wants is for me to do her in—"

"Enough, Benny. Just go...do whatever you want, but keep an eye out, okay?"

"Sure, sure. When I had to listen to the girls screaming all the time and stuff, I was quiet, but now that I got some tail, you can't even be happy for me. That's just...you hurt my feelings, man."

"Oh, shut up. You'll tell me all about it over a drink, alright?"

"Mean it?"

"Mean it."

"Alright! Love you, man! Talk to you!"

I chuckled inwardly as there was no way I could get mad at the pangolin badger. Unless he tried to kill me or the girls, or something. Now that he got his hands on someone like him, I figured he'd only do even better.

"You talking to Benny?" Selene asked. I hadn't noticed her standing next to me.

"Yes, sorry. I'm going to Balan. I want to clear them all out before dawn. Want to come along?"

"Of course, just take the elf with you. Again," Jeanette

mumbled. "It's getting annoying. I'm just as fast."

I held my hand out to her and the swashbuckler grabbed it.

"Then come with us."

"I don't want to. I'm tired. I need rest. Wake me up when it's dawn, girls."

She put her legs up and lay on the sofa, snoring within seconds. Emma and Sonya shared a look and then giggled.

"Elvina? You staying with Emma and Sonya?"

"No, I want to come with you, but without Selene. Just us two."

The elf, to my great surprise, put her hands up as if she'd been defeated and sat back down.

"Just no fooling around out there, alright?" Emma chuckled. "I don't want to feel another woman's lust and emotions right about now. I'm too exhausted."

I leaned down and kissed Emma's forehead, then did the same with Sonya and Selene. Despite Jeanette being asleep, I kissed her as well. It felt wrong not to include her, even if she was bitching for most of the time.

"See you soon, girls. Try to talk to Najla later on when she calms down. We don't want to force her, but if she can accept that burden, things will be a lot easier."

"Will do," they replied in unison, and the golden-haired beauty snuggled up into Sonya.

"Let me dress up quickly. I'll meet you outside?" Elvina said.

I winked at her and made my way outside into the last few hours of the cold, dark night.

CHAPTER 20 –
THE MESSAGE

I sat on the wall separating the village square and the manor house when Elvina walked out. She wore a new white dress I'd never seen before and I had to admit it looked fabulous on her. Her chest and arms were bare with golden lace running just above where her nipples were, barely containing her ample breasts. The golden filigree ran down to her navel, where it spread out across her waist, pinching the fabric tight. Two long slits ran up her legs and ended up on her thighs, which made my eyes linger for a moment too long.

"What is it?" she asked weakly. "Something wrong?"

"Did the girls see you in that?"

"They did. Why?"

"You want an honest answer?"

She nodded slowly.

"I already know what you're going to say, and no, I don't have any panties on."

She slid the front part of the dress aside that almost reached the ground, but she held her hand between her legs.

"I have no idea what to think of you, Elvina. I don't like playing games, but I also know you came here against your will. I made a promise to the sage, and I intend to keep it to the best of my abilities, but these mixed signals...they're becoming frustrating."

"You think? Imagine how I feel when you fuck one or more of the girls? Their feelings are projected onto me just because I'm part of your...whatever this is called. Can you blame me?"

I did something I knew would only cause her even more heartache, and hugged the helfar. My chest pressed against hers, and my arms were crossed around her back. I could feel her wanting to pull away, but after a moment of half-struggle, she sighed and put her arms around me as well.

"Ass."

"I'll take that as a compliment. Anyway, if you want me to do things with you, all you need to do is ask. Besides, it's not as if you're unpleasant to look at. I'd dare say you've got the—" I leaned in so no one could overhear us, "—Best body out of all five."

"Liar. I think it's Selene or Emma. They're gorgeous."

"You all are, and saying otherwise would be a lie. So, what do you think? Want to do some exploring?"

She took my hand and pressed it against her tight stomach, letting it linger there for a few seconds as she looked into my eyes. Her hot breath was laced with drink, which made me wary of the whole situation. I didn't know how well she could handle any kind of stronger drink, so I had to tread lightly.

"Are you drunk?" I whispered, lowering my free hand down her back and cupping her ass. "If you are, then nothing can happen tonight."

"Drunk on desire, yes."

I activated [Fade] and moved us out of there, and even though I wasn't able to clear the full distance to move outside the village, we were far enough for the girls at least not to see us.

I picked Elvina up, both my hands on her rear and her legs tightened around my back. The white dress moved up her hips, and my hands slid down to cup her soft, pale skin.

"What the hell are you two doing?" Selene out of all people demanded over the leadership room. *"We can feel Elvina. She's like an animal in heat!"*

"Told you she was going to try and seduce him," Jeanette added. *"It's not as if he needs much. I bet she just slid her dress*

226

aside again."

"Shush, you have no idea what's going on. Elvina and I are just talking and things are getting emotional. Go drink and rest or whatever you're doing."

Elvina smiled smugly and kissed my neck. I had to admit that I was getting aroused by her closeness and my hands on her soft skin. She moved he hips, lowering herself just a tiny bit so she pressed down on my manhood.

I suddenly felt very exposed while holding her up in my hands and standing outside. Lights burned in windows, and people seemingly weren't able to sleep after what they'd gone through. I could imagine most of them just sitting there and trying to come to terms with what had happened or talking it over with their families. Trying to decide on what to do next.

I lowered Elvina to the ground and gave her an apologetic smile.

"Not here, not now. It's neither the time nor place."

She looked away, her cheeks burning red as she nodded.

"I...will go back inside. Can you go alone?"

"I can if you want to stay."

"Then take these," she said, casting [Matchless] and [Absolute] on me, raising my skill power and resistance. I should have enough time to get there and deal with the zealots before the buffs are over.

"See you in a bit. Now go, but don't fight. They'll probably pester you about just now."

Elvina nodded again but then hugged me tight for a moment. She smiled, winked, and hurried off, the white dress fluttering behind her.

"Shit," I cursed under my breath. "Is this even considered cheating anymore when there are so many of them?"

We would have to talk about some ground rules, as I was starting to get a bit uncomfortable with the whole situation. With Emma and Jeanette, I was already emotionally invested, but Sonya and Selene had somehow just pushed their way into my heart. The ashen-haired helfar was doing the same now. It wasn't that hard to like someone who had such a great body and an interesting personality to go along with it. It's true that I only had eyes for extremely beautiful women and that could be interpreted in a number of ways, but I didn't give a shit. Whoever gave me crap for that could go fuck themselves.

I pushed the thoughts aside and focused on Balan. If there was an investigator stationed there, I needed to incapacitate him before he could try and warn the pillar. That was something I definitely didn't want, at least not right now. The other arbiters...well, that was another story entirely.

I made my way northwest, moving as quickly as I could, and faded in and out of existence every ten seconds. The feeling of wind rushing through my hair and the somberness of the dark affected my mood. Elvina's warmth was quickly replaced by anxiousness. I hated leaving the girls behind despite Benny and Legs being there to protect them.

Lost in my thoughts, I reached Balan Village and its partially built wooden stockade. Fires burned throughout the village, with zealot guards standing around the braziers. They wore the usual yellow outfits with black stripes, distinguishing themselves from the rest of the villagers. Shields hung from their backs and weapons from their belts. Strangely, none of them seemed on alert despite Danara not having come back yet.

I focused for a moment and pushed mana out into my surroundings, feeling for any followers of the dark God, Tan'Malas. One by one, I counted them slowly, making sure I got an approximate number, which came up to around forty in total. There were a few smaller groups where I couldn't distinguish between every blob of darkness, but that didn't matter much. A few more or less wouldn't change the outcome by even a single percent.

The strongest dark blobs were gathered in a small building on the far side of Balan Village. There were six of them if I counted right, and I guessed the inquisitors and interrogator were there. I'd like to strike them first, but I also didn't want the large group of zealots to run rampant and kill the villagers.

I hunkered down and faded into a shadowed corner near the stockade and two groups of zealots on guard duty. There were eight of them in total. I readied myself and focused on the right angle. All of them needed to die with a single attack, from which I'd proceed to the next nearest group.

I took in a deep breath and waited for [Fade]'s cooldown to hit zero, and then moved in behind the left group, using [Blade Storm] to get rid of them as quickly as possible. A few screamed as the mana blades tore at them, ripping their bodies apart. Just as I finished the attack skill, the last of the eight fell to the ground.

I immediately turned further into the village, already spotting the flames burning brightly ahead. Shadows danced along the streets, with only the sound of hushed whispers and the crackling of fire disturbing the silence. I eased along the sides of the buildings and made my way around the next group. There were five more zealots huddled in a circle, warming their hands. It must have been really cold as they were shivering. Had all the extra stats made my body more impervious to the cold? Or was it the debuff resistance?

I faded in again behind the group, and the moment the first of the zealots noticed me, I was already in the middle of cutting them apart. A part of me wanted to torture them a little, but I didn't want to risk it. At least not until I busied myself with the inquisitors.

A strange sense of foreboding hung in the air as I made my way through the groups of zealot guards and neared the small house the big dogs were hiding in. The closer I got, the worse the presence in the back of my mind was.

"I sure would like to have Selene with me now," I whispered, knowing very well just how much her scouting mattered. Then I remembered something I'd forgotten about because of all the fighting that'd been going on.

I activated [Nightveil] and felt a cold mist cover my

body and surroundings. Light seemingly bent around me and dissipated into the dark night.

That's better.

Still a bit distrustful of the skill since it only worked at 50% when I moved, I made my way around the last few buildings and finally entered the yard of the house they were huddled in. What met me there was something I expected but hoped wouldn't have to see. Over twenty corpses lay stacked on top of each other, and they all showed marks of torture. Deep gashes, missing fingers, hollow eyesockets, and even three heads sat neatly atop one pile of corpses.

I wasn't someone who should preach about morality and non-violence, but torture and mutilation for whatever reason had never been something I'd done. Even less against people who couldn't defend themselves. There was even a child's body among them...

I took in a deep breath and steeled myself, activating my debuffs and pushing the door open. There were five inquisitors in total and one interrogator from what I gathered at first glance. They all looked shocked to see me, which meant that they hadn't known I was coming. Unfortunately for them, they were too stupid to recognize the danger they were in.

I decided not to play around with them and launched a [Pestilent Wave]. It wasn't so strong as to kill them all outright...or so I thought. All five of the inquisitors died as the wave hit them, but not the interrogator. He was thrown back into the wall but didn't seem hurt. He wore sturdy, glowing armor that was covered in blood. There was even some of it on his face.

"You! You're that barbarian from south of Garm!" he snapped. The man had a remarkable face with strong cheekbones and a chiseled chin. His long white hair was tied in a top knot and one of his eyes had a deep cut running across it.

"Did *you* carve their eyes out? Torture them?"

"Torture who?"

"The civilians," I said, not wanting to play any word

games. "Did you torture the dead civilians outside?"

The interrogator snorted and shook his head as if in sadness.

"They're no civilians, they're cattle. We use them to feed our armies. Why would I care about their lowly lives?"

I ignored his jab. Power-drunk fools like him were usually narcissistic and viewed themselves as superior to everyone else. Well, two could play that game. Before I killed him, though, I needed to know something.

"Can you relay a message to Balog?"

"You! How do you—You're not supposed to know his honorable name!"

I just stared at him flatly, waiting for the fool to respond. When he didn't, I asked again as he was obviously a bit denser than I thought. Or he was pretending to be.

"Can you relay a message to Balog or not?"

The interrogator squared his shoulders and stuck his chest out proudly.

"Of course I can, but why would I—"

I faded in behind him, burying my daggers deep into his shoulder blades.

"Aargh! You ba—bastard why are—"

"Shut up!" I yelled into his ear and kicked him into the back of his knees. The man tumbled forward, and I stepped on his back. Using my kris, I cut off his left arm. He thrashed and tried to roll over, but I didn't let him. My strength stat was way too high for him to free himself. "I know that inquisitors can contact the arbiters. Can you do that too?"

"I—I can but—I'll lose my life!"

"Do you rather want to be tortured?"

I slammed my dagger down into the meat of his right arm and pinned it to the ground. His left arm was heavy and armored. In other words, it was a perfect tool to inflict both physical and mental anguish. I picked it up and proceeded to beat him with it, breaking both his legs. By the time I was done, he was barely conscious.

"Will you tell him?" I asked, leaning in closer so he could both hear and see me despite his body lying sideways at an odd angle.

"Y—yes—what do—"

"Tell Balog that I spit on his faith and on Tan'Malas. If he wants to fight, I'll be waiting for him. We'll meet him, the other arbiters, and his army outside Garm in five days. Tell him not to be late."

I brought my dagger down into his face, stabbing right through his one good eye, and plucked it out. No, he wasn't going to get off that easily even if I wanted him to be my messenger. He was one tough bastard, I had to give him that as over the next half an hour or so, he barely made a sound no matter what I did to him.

"Are you ready to go?" I asked, finally stopping and sitting on one of the now-empty chairs. The interrogator remained silent just as I had while cutting and mutilating him. "I take that as a yes. Go. I have had enough. Remember, five days in front of Garm Village."

As if he'd been waiting for my mercy, a bright blue light enveloped his mangled body, gathering power within. He grunted and even whimpered a few times as he readied himself to meet Balog. After a short while, a bright beam shot through the roof and dissipated into the night. His body shuddered for a brief moment and then relaxed.

I already had an idea of what to do with him and his underlings. About ten minutes later, I'd gathered all the bodies of the zealots, the inquisitors, and the interrogator in a heap. I made sure to put the worst of the bastards on top so everyone could see he hadn't gone out easily. I took a deep breath and raised my voice as loud as I could.

"Balan Village! Wake up! Now! Get up and listen to me!"

I waited for a long moment, but only a few candlelights went on in random windows surrounding the village. Repeating the same thing, I raised my voice even further, putting some mana into it.

"Get up! I don't have much time!"

Doors and windows started opening as people slowly made their way outside or peeked through the windows. Confusion was apparent on their faces, and why wouldn't it be? I awakened them in the middle of the night after what was probably a long day of watching their friends and family get tortured.

"Listen to me! I have killed Pelis and enslaved Danara! In five days I will kill Balog and the rest of the arbiters plaguing this land! See here! Your torturer! This fiend! I have plucked his eye, I have cut off his limbs, and I have left him to scream in pain until he couldn't take it anymore!"

I pointed at the interrogator and for emphasis slammed my dagger down into his chest. No more blood would seep out the wound as I'd already bled him dry.

"Pelis killed half of Garm Village before I could get to him and his army, but they are avenged. Today at first light, the survivors of Garm Village will have to make a tough decision, one that will either change their lives for the better or cement their demise once and for all! You will have to do the same! Join us! Believe in the Old Gods, believe in what is good and just, and I will keep you all alive! I will give you purpose! I will give you hope! Decline and you are on your own. I will not hurt you, no, I am not like them, but I will not rush to your aid. We all need to make hard choices today, and I have already made mine! I will give them war, and I will give them death! You have a few hours to make up your mind and come to Garm if you decide to throw your lot in with me! If you stay here, you will be mostly on your own!"

I was about to leave when a man in his early forties stepped up to me. A pair of large glasses sat on the bridge of his nose and his short hair was slick with sweat. His skin was a darker color than I was used to, and after looking around for a moment, I noticed he wasn't the only one. Back in Greystone most of the humans had been as pale-skinned as elves or the helfar, but not here. It was an interesting and welcome change.

"Sir, wait. Good man, please. What should we do? Tell us, please!"

I stared at the man, trying to look sympathetic, but it was harder than it had any right to be. How did you tell someone they had to do something or they'd die? Yeah, I didn't like it at all.

"Do you have a family?" I asked, holding my hand out. He shook it and nodded.

"Yes, sir. I do."

"Then do what your heart tells you to. If I succeed in what I've set out to do, all of you will be safe anyway. You can trade with us, hell, go and marry, make babies, grow crops, and hunt monsters. Do whatever you want to, but everything is much easier once you get access to the Godveil, the biggest gift the Old Gods ever made to this world."

I waited for a long moment until I could see the confused looks on everyone's faces. The Godveil was something we've known about our entire lives, but for these people, it was something new, something strange and elusive.

"I will tell you one last thing, good man. Once you have access to the Godveil, you will age much slower, your body will be much stronger, you will have more endurance, you will be more agile, and you will have access to classes that allow you to hunt monsters. You won't have to depend on the duke and his army. Trust me, there's a lot more where that is coming from."

I stopped again, giving them another minute to let that sink in. There was much more that I could tell them, but I also didn't want them to think I was pulling a story out of my ass.

"You have a few hours. If you want to join us, meet me in Garm Village."

"Wait, please," a woman pleaded, rushing to stand between the man and me. "If we decide to join, where will we stay?"

"In Garm," I said simply. "Over 500 people died there today, so there are enough empty homes. I can not protect three places at the same time, at least not until I get rid of

Balog. And yes, they will accept you, I guarantee they will. You will have to come for anything else."

With that, I faded out and disappeared into the darkness. I gave them a lifeline, now it was up to them to decide.

CHAPTER 21 – DAWN

I stayed away from Garm Village for about an hour. No matter how convincing I sounded, the only person I didn't convince was myself. It was like a puzzle I needed to solve, and the only thing that could solve it was time. So I took it for myself.

An hour passed quickly and I still wasn't much closer to getting my answer. Of all the people I had to see then and there, Benny and Danara hadn't even been on the list. They accidentally stumbled upon me as they chased each other through the forest. Both looked bloodied with deep gashes and cuts all over their bodies.

"Let me guess," I said as the two stopped and froze as if caught red-handed. "You two like it rough?"

"Come on, bro. It's not like that, but you know, when you're as strong and as big as me, there are certain expectations, you know?"

"Okay, I'll bite. What expectations?" I asked, taking in a deep breath and letting it out again as he puffed his chest out proudly.

"Well, rough sex, rough love, and rough...everything else!"

"Says who, Benny?"

"Says, well, me."

He was so full of shit that I had a hard time just not getting up and smacking some sense into him.

"You're not helping, big guy. Anyway, I see you've really hit it up with Danara?"

"We have," the former arbiter said. "I have proudly renounced all my ties with Tan'Malas and wouldn't mind if he struck me down here and now!"

I looked up at Benny, and he just shrugged.

"She's right, bro. I saw a good chunk of power leave her body, man. And yes, I know, how do you trust a former enemy that fast, but you did the same with Sonya, right? I was there."

He was right and I'd really done the same with a former enemy who'd, well, not tried to kill me, but she'd been partially to blame for my bad performance against Zekan back then. Not that it would have made any difference as he'd been just too strong.

"Danara, has Benny told you about the Old Gods yet?" I asked as an idea came to mind. She would be perfect to get the whole process started.

"A bit, why? If I may ask? And how do I address you? And what or who are you exactly to Benny?"

"Hey, hey, one thing at a time, girl," Benny said and put his giant arm around her. She looked even smaller with him just standing there next to her.

"I'm his brother of sorts, and you can address me as Cade."

"Alright, Cade, thank you for not killing me. I would have missed this crazy guy otherwise."

I offered them a smile and motioned for the two to sit. They did so on the ground and were still taller than me. Benny looked nervous but in a good way. It was good seeing him a bit flustered.

"Danara, we are from a different place than this one. There we used to believe in the Old Gods: Tan'Ruad, Tan'Drak, and Tan'Aria. They used to provide us with vast powers and a longer, healthier life. Well, that was before Tan'Malas was resurrected or...well, we have no idea what he was. Maybe he was in a deep slumber and just reawakened, but that doesn't matter now. All that matters is that if you want to be with us, be with Benny, you will have to be one of us. I hope you understand?"

Both eyed each other for a long moment. The pangobadger didn't look quite happy with my...demand.

"Do we really have to do this now, bro?"

"We do, Benny. If she's going to stay under our roof, I need to know she will stay loyal, at least to you if not us. I know I can trust you, but her? All I've seen so far is her attacking you, though being around us humans and pretending to be Ludmilla does go in her favor."

"Hah! See? She's one of us, man!"

"No, Benny, he's right. And hold on, before you go wild, listen to me, my furry beast. I will do this. I will do what he asks of me, and then I can prove I mean you no harm. No one, really."

"This is so not cool, bro," Benny spoke to me directly. *"Don't you trust me?"*

"I do, so that's why I'm even entertaining this idea. She could probably kill the girls if she got the drop on them. Do you want to risk that?"

"That's bullshit and you know it!"

For a moment, I could see Benny's rage push past the chilled persona façade. He really wanted this and probably figured I was the one standing in his way. So be it.

I took a deep breath and turned to Danara.

"Turn into your human form."

To my surprise, she did so right away, changing into the orange-haired, freckled young woman.

"I will do whatever you want me to, but don't take this away from me. From either of us. Please. I thought I'd never meet someone like myself, and then you people came along and Benny...well, he could talk and change form and...I like him. I really do."

"Then let me ask this of you, Danara...no, that's wrong. What do you want me to call you?"

"Ludmilla! They insisted I took a more menacing name and...just use Ludmilla, please."

I nodded, offering her what I thought was a disarming smile.

"Ludmilla, don't look at Benny and answer me just this question. Would you trust me if I was in your place and had a sudden change of heart?"

She shook her head, the long, orange-curled hair dancing around her face.

"No, I wouldn't trust you. And Benny, let me do this. I will do whatever I need to do, and if you give me a chance, show you in the long run that I really had no desire for whatever the Order is up to. What's more, I haven't gone to any of their meetings for months now. I don't care about them."

"But you still let the inquisitors and interrogators do whatever they wanted to."

The words came out of my mouth before I could stop myself. I didn't regret them, but Benny's betrayed and disappointed expression did sting.

"Because I didn't want to be found out," she said weakly. "I didn't want to risk my life over theirs, it's as simple as that, Cade. My life is more important to me than that of some humans, and I'm sorry to say that, but I'd do it all again. I didn't hurt anyone, but I also didn't stop any of them from hurting the villagers. Yes, I am guilty, but that doesn't mean I'm a bad person."

Benny took her small hand in his and placed the other over it.

"What do you want her to do?" he asked simply.

"Be the first to convert. If everyone sees an arbiter converting, they will be more open to it. If she does, convert, I will use some of my points to ask Brahma if what she said is true. Once the deity confirms—"

"You will do no such thing," he cut me off, raising his voice. *"I am telling you that I trust her, and so should you."*

I took a mental step back and closed my eyes, taking in a deep breath. Any more arguing could only worsen our own relationship.

"Alright, Benny, we'll do it your way. She converts once the sun comes up, and the two of you live happily ever after."

"Deal!"

"Ludmilla? Do you agree?" I asked her, wanting to hear her say it as well.

"I agree, Cade. Thank you, I mean it. I promise I won't ever betray Benny. You have no idea how hard it is to be different and...hated."

There were many questions I wanted to ask her, like how she joined the Order, or became one of the arbiters. She must have done something to deserve that spot and there's no way people like that would have just gifted her such a rank without asking something in return. No, there was a lot she was holding back, but I sincerely and from the bottom of my heart hoped that I wouldn't regret it. Benny deserved a mate, someone he could spend his time and life with, but only on the condition that it didn't put any of us in danger...

"I'll see you at the square in about...I don't know. An hour? Two? Whenever the sun rises. And where is Legs?"

"Securing the northern perimeter, yo. He fits in good with the trees."

"That's good. Keep an eye out on him. I don't want a jealous spider destroying our village in a jealous fit."

"Pfft! What are you even on about? Legs is my man!"

"Man or not, don't tell me I didn't warn you, Benny. See you two soon."

I made my way into the village and headed straight for the manor house. Lights were still on in most of the occupied homes I noticed. No one was getting any sleep, that much was sure. Not that I would be able to get any sleep if I was in their place. Hell, I was the one giving ultimatums and even then I couldn't sleep.

The girls' voices came from inside Najla's home. I could hear Sonya, Emma, and the former mayor talking, while Elvina and Jeanette were arguing on the upper floor. It didn't take long to figure out what the argument was about. All four of the girls had felt the helfar's little...escapade. Their argument must have gone on for a long time since Elvina sounded more annoyed than anything. The swashbuckler deflated as well from the sound of it, and then I could only hear Selene telling Najla something about duty and trust.

"Who knew Selene had such a way with words," I whispered. "She's strong, smart, beautiful, and deadly. Why not add eloquent to that as well?"

I headed in and closed the door behind me. The girls stopped chatting as they heard me come inside, which meant that I'd probably get a stern talking to. It's not like I wasn't looking forward to it. Sometimes we needed to argue so we could have great make-up sex.

"Ladies," I said entering the main living room. "You're still up. And everyone's dressed. Good."

"You didn't expect her to go out naked, right?" Sonya asked. "Maybe you'd prefer that so you could slide your hand up her dress. Just like you—"

"Enough. Please. I don't feel like arguing. I've seen some nasty crap out in Balan, so don't start."

I sat down on the lone relaxing chair and put my feet up on the edge of the table.

"Want a drink?" Selene asked, already on her feet. "You look like shit."

"And I feel just like it," I mumbled but nodded.

"What is it? What happened?" Emma asked as she scooted over to the edge of the sofa she was sitting on. Her hand landed on mine and squeezed gently.

I told them what I'd seen and what I'd done. It wasn't something I was proud of, but I justified my torture with the pain the interrogator had inflicted on the villagers. And truth be told, I would do it all again.

I held the glass Selene prepared for me in my right hand, swirling it around gently. The orange liquid circled as if it were a miniature whirlpool. Three small ice cubes clanked against the sides of the glass.

"I will do it," Najla said, breaking the silence that had ensued. "I will do whatever you want me to as long as you do this soulbinding thing to me. I want to live a long life, I want to be strong, and I want you all to protect me. Then I will do it."

"No, no way!" Selene and Sonya snapped at the same time. "What are you on about, Najla?" the elf assassin continued. "We only told you that because there's a chance you'll need the stat points!"

"Well, I have a right to haggle if I'm already going to throw my lot in with you guys!" Najla protested. "And besides, what's one more?"

"What's—you have no idea how hard it is for everyone to feel each other's emotions half of the time. And guess what? Whenever he's having sex with one of us, or even anything remotely like it, the others feel all of it!" Sonya said, raising her voice.

She was almost yelling, which was out of character for her. Still, I could imagine how frustrating it must have been to feel all those emotions belonging to someone else.

The first rays of sunshine peeked through the window as if telling us to cut it out and get back to the matter at hand. Alright, if that's all it was going to take, then yes, I would make her one of us.

"Well, then I'm—"

I put a finger to my lips. Najla didn't seem to understand for a moment, but then she just went quiet anyway, probably thinking I was going to follow it up with something.

"Najla and Danara will be the first two to convert. I figure that should get the ball rolling."

"And Benny agreed to do it?" Emma asked. "He was here earlier, all pissy because he figured you'd make her do something. Seems he wasn't wrong."

"No, he was. Danara, or Ludmilla if you will, is doing it of her own volition."

Najla coughed and grabbed the chair to steady herself.

"Ludmilla...is Danara? The Arbiter?"

I nodded concerned that they didn't know of such a thing.

"She never told you? No one?"

"No! Why would she...damn it, she's a God Beast! Is that correct?"

I sighed and walked over to the window that looked out toward the gate leading into the village square. People were already gathering and they looked just as I felt. Anxious and tired.

"I hope the people of Balan will be here soon as well, but I have no idea. Do you think the survivors will take them in?"

"Take in people...here? In Garm?" Najla asked.

"Yes, here. Into the empty homes of, well...the dead. We'd have a much easier time reinforcing Garm since it already has a wooden palisade and it's closest to Greystone. What do you think?"

Najla shrugged and tried to gather her thoughts for a moment. When she was done, a string of words I'd hoped to hear followed.

"We will do our best. It's not like there aren't enough homes to go around, but it's more about mixing in with them. We don't want them to fill the cracks between our homes. Let them take the western part of the village, the killings started there."

"Good, very good. So, why don't you ladies get ready while I wait outside? I need to find Benny and his new lady."

Outside, the sun was peeking past the tall mountains east of the dukedom and cast an eerie glow on the land. Birds flew overhead and chirped playfully. It was a truly magnificent morning, one I couldn't have enjoyed as much if I was still busy fighting or moping over my choices.

"Good morning, everyone," I said as I joined the gathered crowd outside the manor house. "Why don't we move this to where the magnificent statue of the Old Gods stands?"

The indestructible, stone sculpture I'd gotten from the Old Gods stood proudly at the center of the village square not even thirty steps away from where I was. It was the one thing that Pelis hadn't managed to damage, which only went to show

how important it was.

The crowd parted and did as I said while I waited for the girls to join me. A heavy silence had fallen over the village, but the sky was bright and a light breeze brought in fresh air from the sea. The moment was broken by Benny's laughter. He and Danara were enjoying themselves, which was a bit in bad taste considering what was going on. At least the two hadn't run off somewhere to howl at the moon and live happily ever after...

The door behind me opened and the girls walked out with Najla at the very front. She wore a long white dress similar to the one Elvina had on earlier but was much more modest and didn't show nearly as much skin.

More commotion came from the western entrance. Villagers from Balan had arrived, but not in as great numbers as I'd hoped. Maybe they would change their minds once they saw how much stronger their friends had become. Knowledge of the old ones and their worship came with a whole slew of personal boons as well, so there was that...

Hushed whispers broke out amongst the crowd, and some were pointing at Danara, while others at me or Najla. There was this warm feeling residing in my chest, one that told me things could still be alright, and that everything would turn out well. I had no idea if that was true, but a man could hope.

The girls stopped right next to me, and Najla turned to look a the crowd. She took them all in, and they watched her intently. After taking a deep breath, she turned to the Balan crowd.

"Is Mayor Downel still alive?"

"He's dead. Killed him and his family first," a man spoke up from the crowd. "They killed my brother and his pregnant fiancé as well! The bastards!"

Several of the people put their arms around the man who broke down then and there.

"Emma?" I said, nodding toward him.

"Hold on, let me try something," she replied and clasped

her hands in front of her. Several seconds passed and her body started glowing. The spell was called [Great Restore], and what it did was heal everyone in a large area of effect. A golden wave erupted from her body and encompassed the entire village square. Before the spell even finished, I could feel her mana drain rapidly. I stepped up just in time and caught her as she stumbled to the side.

"Easy now," I whispered, kissing her forehead. "You shouldn't exert yourself like that. I just wanted you to heal that man, love."

"I know but...everyone is just...they need to see that we can protect them," she replied, her voice barely as loud as my whisper. "We need to show them that they can depend on us, Cade. We can defend them, we can heal them, and we can provide for them. Happiness will follow, right?"

"You're so melodramatic," Sonya chuckled. "But you did well. Good job."

I shot Sonya a wink, thankful that she supported her over-the-top gesture.

"I hope everyone's feeling better," I said, pulling Emma to her feet and holding her upright. I scanned the entire crowd, trying to make eye contact with as many people as I could. "Is there anyone that still needs healing?"

"My son does!" a woman cried out from the Garm crowd. She pushed forward, carrying a young boy in her arms. "He isn't getting better! Please help us!"

I helped Emma over to where the woman stood and then picked the boy up from her arms.

"This is the darkness debuff that Selene had when I found her," I said over the leadership room. *"Use a potion, but make it just as dramatic. Maybe cast a small heal over him. We need to show these people that we will give it our all, and if it's just a small vial, the gesture will look small despite this being the worst case of debuff."*

Emma didn't say anything and instead just placed her hands on the boy's forehead and chest. As her debuff cleansing spell, [Minor Cure], activated, she hurriedly poured the darkness elixir into his mouth. The boy started coughing and I turned him over, face down. Dark liquid hit the ground and he started crying. Emma hit him with another healing spell, just to make sure he was alright, and then I returned him to his mother.

"Sam! Talk to me! Does it still hurt? Tell Mommy!"

The boy was probably five or six years old, which begged the question, how he got the darkness debuff? He shouldn't have been hit unless...they were just really unlucky.

"Everyone! I think we need to make a tough decision right now," Najla said, using the moment. "I have seen what the Order does to its people, even after we were loyal for hundreds of years! They never helped anyone, healed, or fed any of our people! All they did was take, take, and take! This man, Cade of the Blood Moon Guild, he and his guild have done more for us in these few days than the Order has in all their time ruling over us. With their help, I have no doubt we will be able to stand against the rule of the Order and the Duke... I swear that I will do everything I can to help you prosper and keep the good people of Garm and Balan Villages safe! What do you need me to do?"

Sonya put her arm around Najla and then stepped over with her to stand in front of the large statue.

"Place your hand on the indentation and repeat after me," Sonya said. Najla nodded and carefully lowered her hand on the statue. Sonya then said the same words I told Samel a while ago, the words all believers of our continent knew by heart.

"I believe in the Old Gods, Tan'Ruad the Maker who birthed this world. I believe in Tan'Drak the Destroyer who weighs life and death. I believe in Tan'Aria the Other who nurtures our souls. I believe in the power and wisdom of the Old Gods and bind my soul to their will. May they shed their light on me and guide me through the darkness. Their will is my will, their strength is my strength so that we may revive all that is good and banish all evil."

Najla repeated Sonya's vow word for word. A dull blue light rose from within the statue and engulfed her. The woman gasped and threw her head back. Tears formed at the corners of her eyes and slid lazily down her cheeks and neck.

A notification popped up in my mind. I opened it and smiled.

Quest Name: <u>Spreading The Faith IV</u>

Quest Status: 1/1,000 Converted Believers

CHAPTER 22 – VISITORS

"I...what is this? What—I can't believe it!" Najla cried as she grabbed for her hair. "Is this real? Is what these letters in my mind tell me real?"

"What does it tell you?" I asked with an excited smile. "What does it say under your class?"

"It says that I'm a priestess. What does that mean?"

Emma pulled her aside and started explaining things as she'd been in the same situation when she just got her class.

"Listen to me!" I yelled, raising my voice. "This is a joyous occasion as Mayor Najla has awakened a healing class! Come! Who is next?"

Danara approached along with Benny and turned into her human form. The transformation drew gasps from the entire crowd and many even recoiled.

"You! You've been living among us!" a woman cried, pointing her finger at Ludmilla's human form. "We thought you were one of us!"

"Stop before anyone of you says anything you will regret. She lived among you as Ludmilla because of that very reason. Is it so wrong that she wanted to be one of you? That she wanted to be accepted and be seen as an equal?" I yelled over the ruckus. "Has she ever wronged anyone here? If she has, I will take her punishment instead as she is now one of my people! Anyone who has ever been wronged, step up now!"

I looked over the crowd and waited tentatively, praying that no one would step up. After a long tense moment, no one did. I breathed an internal sigh of relief.

"Anyone at all?" I asked again. "No? Then proceed! The Old Gods will judge her best!"

Benny held his massive hand on her back, glancing around protectively as Ludmilla pressed her palm down on the indentation. Sonya helped her utter the words and though she struggled to get it right in one breath as Najla did, the God Beast eventually finished her vow. The same dull glow emitted from the statue, covering her entirely and then dissipated. Her reaction was very similar to Najla's, but the God Beast fell to her knees, weeping with her face in her hands. Benny covered her with his body, providing her with some privacy.

I knelt next to her and put a hand on her shoulder.

"Tell me what you see," I said gently, despite not knowing what exactly to feel. The counter had switched to 2 out of 1,000 so she must have accepted what she'd seen, but I still needed to know. At least the end result.

"It says that...I'm a Shifter Beast. There are so many words in my mind and so many things that I...what does this all mean?"

"Benny? Mind taking her away and explaining things?"

He nodded and picked her up in his arms, then hurried toward the manor house, disappearing from sight in seconds. I stood with an honest and large smile on my face, feeling absolutely fantastic with the outcome of both assigned classes. Sure, they wouldn't have gotten anything special if the Gods hadn't deemed them worthy, but I was still happy.

"So, who is next?"

It took most of the day until everyone who'd gathered converted. Some of them hadn't accepted the new truth within themselves even after seeing it with their own eyes, and they were stripped of their access to the Godveil. They'd quickly retried again and were offered a second chance. Somehow, even then some of them had managed to fail and see the truth. They were mostly from Balan Village and had picked themselves up and gone back. Hours later, though, they'd returned with the rest of Balan and had undergone a third change along with the newcomers.

As the number of believers surpassed 250, a sense of unease washed over me. The first people to accept our belief had vanished overnight in a disgusting exercise of violence and brutality. I clenched my fists instinctively until my knuckles hurt.

Never again, I thought to myself. I wouldn't let these people perish for my arrogance. We had good intentions when we converted the first bunch, but we were stupid enough to believe there wouldn't be repercussions from the Order. Good intentions, bah, even the best intentions needed a sword to carry them through in this world. 250 people paid for that lesson.

Sonya took me by the wrist and looked up at me shaking her head. I relaxed almost instantly. Somehow she knew or at least felt what was going through me.

"It won't happen again," she said. I smiled and nodded; the tension in my body disappearing.

"They can bet their asses on it."

As the girls and I sat in Najla's living room, a notification appeared in my mind, one I'd hoped I'd see.

```
Quest Completed: Spreading The Faith IV

   Description: Continue to help spread
          faith in the Gods of Old.

   Status: 1,031/1,000 Converted Believers

   Reward: Establishment of a New Religion

NOTE: After establishing a new religion, you
 will be able to assign a divine priestess who
will become the voice of the Old Gods, and with
    that, will gain a special class. Prophet.
```

Three more notifications followed right after.

Quest Received: <u>Spreading The Faith V</u>

Description: Continue to help spread
faith in the Gods of Old.

Status: 1,031/2,500 Converted Believers

Reward: Establishment of a Divine Military Cadre

The first two were prompts that stayed open within my mind, of which the first asked me to name the religion, while the second prompted me to choose a prophet.

"Divine military cadre," I muttered. "Say, is that something like the religious orders from back in Greystone?"

"Cadre? I think...yes. One of the older orders had been called a cadre. Why do you ask?"

I told them about the latest quest chain and the lack of any note explaining things. The girls got even more excited than I did.

"Do you know what that means, Cade?" Emma asked.

I was dumb when it came to certain situations, but not always. This was one of those times.

"A small military with the backing of the Old Gods. That means buffs and a guild structure but on a much higher level."

"Exactly. Buffs, buffs, and buffs!" Emma cheered. "See, I can't wait to—oh, hmm. What about the last quest's reward?"

"Yeah, we need to come up with a name for the religion, and I need to assign the prophet position. Najla? Are you still with us?"

She nodded excitedly as she shot up from the sofa.

"I am! But again, promise me that—"

"Yes, I will when the time comes. We already added Elvina a short while ago, so yeah, just give the girls some time. I'll bind you when the time comes."

Najla sighed but nodded.

"Alright. Well, I'm ready. Come on."

I opened the prompt and assigned her name, then accepted. A bright light shot out from her body, flooding the entire living room and passing through the windows. Benny came rushing in and Ludmilla followed with claws extended. Well, that was something new. I'd have to sit down with her and see what kinds of changes she'd undergone. Her body was a bit bulkier and her long hair was a bit darker orange now, almost red in a way.

"What is it? What—ohh, she's glowing like a supernova man! That's so cool!" Benny laughed, all anxiousness leaving his body as he relaxed. "Is it that prophet thing?"

I nodded, shooting him a grin but got to my feet to help steady Najla if she needed it just in case as she was looking down at the floor with her hair covering her face.

"Are you okay? Any changes?"

She took in a deep breath, let it out slowly, and then took in a breath again as she straightened herself. The moment I saw her face, I gasped and took a step back. There was a dull glow coming from her eyes that was so mesmerizing, that I got a debuff notification.

> You have resisted a debuff.

"What the—"

"Sorry, I just—I'll turn it off now."

The dull glow disappeared, revealing a mix of golden and red irises.

"Did anyone else just get that?" Selene asked as she pushed to stand next to me with her arms crossed. "Did she just glamor us?"

"Glamor?" I asked, never having heard the term before. I felt stupid for asking, but I knew the girls would never give me any shit for not knowing everything.

"Yes, sorry. It's a pretty rare spell so it's no wonder you never heard about it," Sonya said, joining us. The other girls formed a half-circle around the new prophetess. "Glamor spells usually try to persuade you into either believing the person doing the glamoring with your whole being or into adoring them and giving yourself up on a shiny platter. It's not very ethical, to say the least."

"Glamor, huh?" I murmured. "Did you do it on purpose?" I asked, staring at Najla.

To her credit, she was honest.

"Yes? I'm sorry, but I wanted to know what it did!"

"So you used it on us?" Jeanette hissed. "You could have hurt us! Or worse, make Cade get down on you!"

I barely refrained from rolling my eyes.

"Yeah, don't do it again, please. Now tell me, did your class change or is it a title or what?"

"Yes, my sub-class now reads Prophetess. Let me check my stats and—ohh, they're pretty nice at level 1 I figure from what you all told me. I'm over forty points on each of the stats and I feel...hmm, let me try something."

She bent over, her dress slipping down the side of her hip and revealing a long leg. Then, she grabbed the side of the sofa and just lifted it.

"By Tan'Ma—no, wait, that's wrong. I don't worship him anymore, do I? It's strange how this Godveil thing has such a strong influence on my mind. It's like I never even worshipped Tan'Malas. Isn't that almost the same thing as using a constant glamor?"

She got us there. However, in our defense, we didn't know how the conversion thing worked. I tried placing my palm on the statue earlier and nothing happened, but then again, we were already believers so...

"Skills, please," Emma said. "I want to know if they're similar to mine."

"I have a few and they can be considered very good if I'm nearby, or useless if I'm away. Do you want to know what they are?" she asked mischievously. I remained silent, not wanting to rise to her bait.

"I don't think it's the time to push, Najla," Ludmilla said. "You're becoming that same annoying bitch from before. And yes, I know, you told me to keep that to myself, but I don't feel like it."

"B—b—bitch? I told you to never call me that again!"

"And I told you not to act like a B-I-T-C-H!"

"Benny," I said, nodding to the door as the two women glared at each other. "So, skills?"

Najla sat back down and crossed both her arms and legs, then stared at Ludmilla's retreating form.

"I can't believe she just called me a bitch. That's so not nice!"

We all sighed as she kept on nagging for a good minute when I cleared my throat. She seemed to be lost for a moment, and I honestly wouldn't have minded if it wasn't such an important matter.

"Ahh, sorry. So, umm...let me start with...okay. I can share them, right? So you can read?"

"Well, yes," I said and tried to explain to her how it worked, but she held a hand up, and then several notifications popped up. They were unreadable. "Hmm, I can't read any of it. You?"

"Well...no...Strange. I could read them just a moment ago."

"Maybe we need to come up with a name for the religion first?" Sonya asked. "Any ideas?"

"I have one," Emma said. "Why don't we go with Trifurcism? Or something like that? Three main gods and all?"

"That sounds so stupid," Jeanette grunted. "Why don't we just name it Blood Moon? It doesn't need to be modeled after the three Gods of old, right?"

"She has a point," Selene said with a sigh. "I'm out of ideas, honestly. I'm not that good at naming things."

"Hey, I've got an idea," Sonya said, snapping her fingers. "Brahmaism. What better way to show your appreciation for Brahma and her generosity than to name a religion after her?"

I looked over at the girls, and they all nodded in support. All but Najla, who had no idea that Brahma was my patroness.

"Don't you think it's a bit...too much?" I asked, though found the proposal both reasonable and flattering. She had looked out for me when I needed it most, twice now, so yeah, maybe it was time to give back. They all agreed again, which made me feel...awkward. I didn't want to seem as if I was kissing Brahma's ass, though I'd much rather kiss hers than most I knew of...no, don't even go there.

She can probably read your mind, idiot!

"Okay, so Brahmaism it is...not. I'll go with The Old Faith. I think it's the best way we can honor the Old Gods and deities altogether."

I entered the name into the second prompt from earlier that was still open and accepted. Considering how Najla had almost blown up from the golden light mere minutes before, I figured something similar would happen, but nothing aside from a new notification did.

Congratulations! You have established
the religion of The Old Faith!

And...that was it. I almost felt betrayed, hoping for much more fanfare than we even got from Najla's transformation. The one thing that changed then, though, was that I could now clearly read our prophet's spells.

SUPPORT CLASS SPELLS

Name: Sermon, Level: 1
Effect: Bestow all followers of The Old Faith
with a 10 boost to all main stats.
Cooldown: 1 hour, Duration: 24 hours

Name: Godspeed, Level: 1
Effect: Double the duration of all buffs
received from all followers of The Old Faith.
Cooldown: 1 hour, Duration: 24 hours

Name: The Old Faith, Level: 1
Effect: Doubles gained experience points by all

followers of The Old Faith up to level 30.
Cooldown: 1 hour, Duration: 24 hours

Name: The New Faith, Level: 1
Effect: Doubles gained experience points by all
followers of The Old Faith up to level 30.
Cooldown: 1 hour, Duration: 24 hours

NOTE: The buffs can only be cast once
the prophet has been bound to a temple
of worship and while inside.

Alright, the last part wasn't that hard to do either. That meant if any one of these fine new people wanted to get the buffs, they would have to visit the temple every day. That in itself wasn't very problematic considering there was only a one-hour cooldown on her buffs.

"Is this everything?" I asked. "No healing spells or—"

"She has the same basic healing spells as I do: single heal, AOE heal, and debuff cure. Other than that, she doesn't have anything. It might be worth investing in patrons. Double the temple as—"

"No need. The village is already connected to the patrons we worship," Sonya said, interrupting Emma. "Anyone who visits the temple will be able to interact with their patron. Once they've chosen one, anyway."

"Alright, that's good. Hold on." I thought for a long moment and then decided to dump the task on the three beasts by contacting them through the leadership room. *"Benny, Legs, Danara, do you feel like staying here for a day at least? We need to finish some stuff up at New Greystone. We also need to take Najla there and set up the temple and rest a bit."*

"Yeah, sure, but have someone bring us a lot of food. Or just place it in the guild storage, and I'll take it from there," Benny said and I could almost feel his enthusiasm.

"Thank you, Benny. And you two as well, of course. So, why don't we—"

"Boss, there's one thing, though. I think you might want to come see this for yourself."

I was about to demand he tell me what was going on but thought the better of it. If he needed me outside, I would go outside. Besides, the sun was still high in the zenith, so it wasn't like I had anything better to do than bake in the sun after a battle and no sleep for the last 20 hours or so.

"Let's check on Benny, see what's going on," I said, heading straight for the door. The girls followed me, all six of them now. It was getting a bit crowded I had to say, but hey, it wasn't like I intended to sleep with Najla... or Elvina before today.

The moment I opened the door, I heard the sound of a trumpet in the distance, and my guts sank into my feet. No, I didn't have it in me to deal with the Duke right now.

Considering the stomping of feet heading toward the northern gate, I was sure the man had finally come to see what we were all about. It would be interesting to see his face when he found out that one of the arbiters was dead, and that the other had joined our side. Sure, three of them remained, and even though they were all stronger than what I'd faced so far, I was pretty sure of my battle capabilities.

"Boss? There are a lot of them. I figure at least a thousand," Benny said as I made my way onto the palisade. I only glanced at the small army before my gaze wandered back to the village.

We'd been using our downtime to gather all the armor sets that the animus and beles dropped during our battle the night before, so we could easily outfit a few hundred people if needed, but even if you gave someone a sword and a shield, that didn't mean they would know how to use it. More often than not, they'd end up stabbing themselves. Still, my mind began to calculate on its own.

"What the hell does he want now? It's really not a good time," I growled as the trumpet resounded yet again.

I took a moment to study his small army, and it didn't

look all that impressive. They all wore yellow overcoats with black stripes, and their armor looked dented and dull. It was a far cry from what a proper army should look like. However, aside from the ordinary soldiers, I couldn't help but notice the three War Beasts that walked off to the sides along with their handlers. One of them looked like a flaming gryphon, and it had a leash around its neck. The second beast looked like an oversized rat bear with four arms and two heads. The last was a bone snake about fifteen feet long and three wide. It was a chunky boy, well, if you could imagine all the missing meat and muscle.

The last thing I noticed was the colorful, oversized carriage rolling amidst the procession. It was either made from gold or gold-plated as it shimmered under the sun, making it uncomfortable to look at. Selene and Elvina joined me on top of the wall with the others staying down at the gate.

"Do you think it's that peacock again?" Selene asked. "What was his name again? Grilo? Rizzo? Lizzo?"

"Ventilo," I said with a chuckle. She wasn't that far off with the funny names, though. That peacock jester cousin of the duke had really pushed it and he should consider gathering a vast amount of sympathy if he wanted to live through another meeting with me.

The carriage stopped at the head of the small army and out strode peacock commander Ventilo. Great. Just what I needed. However, a moment later, a short, thick man almost fell out of the carriage but narrowly caught himself on the jester's neck, pushing him down into the mud. At that moment, even I felt embarrassed just looking at the scene.

"Is that supposed to be the duke?"

I hadn't noticed Najla climbing up the stairs as I was too busy watching the two Volarna making fools out of themselves. She spoke.

"Yes, he is. The bastard. He's no better than the Order, taxing us just as much as they do." Najla sighed. "They say they offer protection, but all their soldiers do is eat our food and play cards. Remember the boar? If it wasn't for you..." She shook her head..."

"Speaking of which, I can see Samel over there," I said, nodding toward the left of the carriage. Our eyes met, and he gave me a curt nod. "Can you open up a link? Elvina?"

"I'll try. It's that guy who is staring at you, right?" she asked without pointing in his direction. We didn't want to cause him any premature trouble.

"Yeah, him."

It took her a few seconds, but I could feel a connection being established between us, so I jumped right on it.

"Hello, Captain Samel. I'm talking directly into your mind, so don't be alarmed. If you can respond, do so by imagining talking to me with your mind."

It only took him several seconds, which was a surprise in itself.

"Greetings, sir. It's good to see you again, but I wish it was under better circumstances."

"How so?"

"We came here to join Pelis in subduing you."

I snorted, then started laughing so loud that the soldiers closest to the gate could all hear me. So did the duke and his cousin...

"Sir?"

"Samel, Pelis and all his animus are dead, but Danara has become a supporter of mine. All the duke can do is get killed, but let's see this play out. Don't tell anyone anything. Let's see how this unfolds."

"If you say so, sir, but you need to know that there are 83 of us who wish to join you and...wait, did you just say that Pelis and all his animus are dead?"

"Yes, that's just what I said. Oh, hold on, he's doing something dramatic. I'll take you all in once we're done here."

CHAPTER 23 – ANGRY BIRDS

"You! Who dares to laugh at me? And where is Pelis? Send him out!"

I pulled the arbiter's dark armor from the guild storage, which was absolutely filled to the brim, and held it out next to me. It was still stained with blood and would need to be cleaned, fixed, and then identified to see if any of us could use it. Maybe Merek?

"I had to rip him to pieces. He just didn't want to get out of the armor, you see," I said, raising my voice loud enough for most of the soldiers to hear me. The duke definitely did.

His shoulder-long hair was slick with sweat and even glistened in the sunlight. A bright yellow robe with black stitching hugged his body and the fool didn't even wear any boots but some kind of sandals that looked pretty uncomfortable.

"So you are him, then?" the duke yelled, pointing right at me.

I stashed the armor away and faded out to close the distance between us. He stepped back and bumped into the carriage as I appeared closer to him than he probably thought possible. That was another one of those things they weren't used to: seeing someone use real power aside from the Order.

"Hello, Duke Volarna. It's very kind of you to visit us. I am Cade of the Blood Moon and The Old Faith." The duke looked me over grimacing in what I could only imagine was disgust. Ventilo was peeking over the shoulder of the ruler of Volarna City with a vengeful grin. The peacock really thought he'd get justice today.

"So you do know who I am," the duke said with a hint of anger in his voice. "And yet you didn't bother to show yourself in Volarna City."

He crossed his arms and stared at me, looking devoid of any fear, but probably due to the wrong reason.

"I like your God Beasts," I said, using the same name for the monsters all the people in this place did. "I don't think you would be interested in selling them?"

"Selling—what are you—are you insane? Ventilo, tell him! He is insane!" Ventilo opened his mouth to do as he was told, but I didn't bother waiting for his opinion on my mental state.

"I'll give you a fair offer," I said, knowing full well where this conversation would lead. The duke looked past me to the palisade. I knew he could see the people up there but I doubted he could tell how prepared we were.

His eyes landed back on me.

"Such insolence," he cried and snapped his head around to face his army. "Men, get him!"

Instead of letting the situation escalate and killing off all his soldiers, I took a step back and raised my hands to give him a false sense of security. Not that I needed it, but if any of his soldiers attacked first, I would be forced to defend myself.

I faded back out and landed on the wall, taking in a deep breath so I could address his people.

"Arbiter Pelis is already dead if you haven't figured it out yourself already! His animus and beles are dead as well! All of the zealots, inquisitors, and interrogators are dead too! Danara, the fifth arbiter has joined our side. Now, imagine what I can do to you if I wiped an army much stronger than yours in mere minutes!"

That wasn't technically true, and there was no way I'd make ordinary people suffer by using countless debuffs on them, what I would do was let Benny and Danara rip into them. Or maybe have Elvina use one of her traps. If they already needed to die, then I would like to see them go quickly and without much suffering.

"Go home or die! The only things you will find here is death! Don't let your children grow up without fathers and mothers, don't let—fuck this. Duke, are you a man of honor? Or are you a stupid, zealous follower of the Order? Just tell me that! Are you a man of the people, or a man of the coffers?"

The slick-haired nobleman gasped as if insulted by the mere thought of being questioned by someone underserving. His cousin came to the rescue.

"How dare you speak like that to the duke? Do you think you're the only one with God Beasts? We have three of our own, and now you will—"

"Oh, shut up, jester!"

"Ventilo Volarna, you peasants! Cousin, do not let them talk to us like that! They have no respect for their betters!"

I sighed, unable to watch the show go on any longer and I was about to ask Elvina how much longer she needed when Captain Samel saved them.

"I can not watch this any longer! Listen to me! Most of you know how I feel about the Order and the Duke. You also know that I do not have any other family than those standing to my left and right. What you don't know is that I'd already converted once!"

"Which begs the question, how did you fall out of favor so quickly," I mumbled under my breath. As if anticipating my thought, Samel continued.

"It was the saddest day in my life when I had to return to Volarna City and be separated from the Godveil! But now that I'm here again, I can feel the power coursing through my body! I can feel the presence of the Old Ones! Not just that—"

"What are you blabbering on about, you fool? What conversion? What Godveil?" the duke demanded, staring hard at the captain. I jumped back down from the wall and faded over to stand next to the duke.

"It is not your fault that you are weakminded, Duke

Volarna, but it *is* your fault for choosing to side with darkness. Samel, you and those you trust can enter Garm Village. If there's anyone else who wants to join you and become part of the foundation of The Old Faith, you can do so while this foolish man can't do anything stupid."

I faded back into the field, both the duke and Ventilo took a sudden step back as I appeared before them.

I pulled my daggers free and kicked Ventilo back to the ground. He rolled over on his back and cried out like a little bitch as the duke tried to run. Most of the soldiers drew their weapons and shields, but some seemed confused as Samel strode past me with a sizeable following of his own.

"Every man or woman that joins today will receive an armor set that belonged to one of the destroyed animus and beles! You will receive power that will allow you to fight monsters and even animus with a little practice! But most of all, you will be on the side of good for a change! Not that of darkness and the oppressors!"

I usually didn't like to hold speeches or try and persuade large groups of people, so what I did with the villagers earlier and now the soldiers, was something I would happily hand over to Najla, the girls, and Mortimer.

Unfortunately, only the soldiers that already stepped out from the crowd made their way into the village while the rest looked on in confusion and anger. Benny, being the crazy pangolin from another world that he was, charged the three God Beasts, grabbed the flaming gryphon, and kicked the rat bear over on its back. Using his incredible power, he was back in only a few strides, standing in front of the village palisades just behind my back.

"Benny? Why are you holding the gryphon like that?" I asked, unsure what to make of his action. "It's going to gouge your eyes out."

"No, bro. I can tame War Beasts, don't you remember? I want this little birdy as a friend! It's cute!"

"Benny, Gryphons don't bond that easily," Danara said

from the palisade above him. "And besides, it's weak. All the God Beasts they send this way are...faulty so to say."

His ears drooped then as if he regretted his action, and I was sure he would let the struggling gryphon go, but then he flashed his fangs at me.

"Hey, I want to adopt all the War Beasts we can get our hands on, bro. Think I can do that?"

I wasn't even sure if that was a possibility, but the way he looked at me half-pleadingly, yeah, I couldn't say no to Benny.

"Alright, sure." I finally turned back to the soldiers, who still hadn't made a single step forward, and noticed a corpse that was ripped in two. "Ahh, Benny, you killed his handler! Next time be gentler. Don't need to rip people into pieces when you steal their God Beasts, alright?"

We found ourselves in a very strange stand-off. The duke wasn't willing to commit his soldiers, but he couldn't lose face either. Now, there were several ways things could go, and one of them was a massacre. The second was to save him some face and possibly reap some rewards down the road. Next, I could just let him go and call us even after we took one of his God Beasts, or we could take him out and then force his soldiers into our service.

"Duke Volarna," I said, breaking the deafening silence that had ensued. "Can I invite you for a drink? Or some food? We'll be having some festivities in a few days. I would like for us to stay...neutral at least. My fight is with the Order, not with the ordinary people."

The duke stared at me with vile, poisonous eyes. He wasn't someone who would back down just because I suckered him. If anything, I needed to solve this right now...but I couldn't. Not like this.

"Soldiers! Prepare for battle!" Ventilo cried as he gathered himself back up again. He was fuming and looked even more angry than a hissing cat.

"No! Stop!" the duke yelled, climbing on his carriage. "I

will not sacrifice a thousand people just to prove a point! But you," he said, pointing at me, "Should know that they will come for you, and no one will be able to save you or anyone here! Pelis was just a loudmouth, and if you even think for a moment that Balog will underestimate you as that braindead fool did, then you've got another thing coming!"

I didn't rise to the bait and instead just stood there as Benny held the gryphon tight in his arms. It had stopped squirming, seeing it couldn't get out of his grasp, though its tail did burn with a small flame.

I was surprised by the duke's restraint. He had calculated his odds well and chose the best option for himself and his men. He wasn't as arrogant as Pelis, that much was certain, yet he couldn't help himself with the threats. It was a clumsy show of hand that he and other rulers from this place had in common. They felt their power was unquestioned and when I did question it, they'd retaliate like frustrated children.

I walked back to the village as the gates opened.

"Boss, what do you think if I get the other two beasts as well? They're wasted under that fool. I like that rat bear thing with the two heads. Might be interesting to have him around and stuff, you know? And the bone snake...it's pretty cool too. I think it would fit your aesthetic style and shit, man. The lord of pestilence riding on a bone snake. How cool is that?"

I exchanged looks with him and then the girls that were standing up on the palisade. Jeanette looked amused, and so did Sonya and Emma, but Selene not so much. Elvina looked indifferent, and Najla was shocked.

"Say, how long do you need to tame that birdy?" I asked, patting the gryphon's head.

"I don't know. A minute?"

"Well, then you have a minute to see if you can steal the rat bear as well, but look, Legs will get pissy and I would too if I were him. You're trying to do the same with God Beasts what I did with...well, these beautiful, strong, smart, and elegant ladies that want to rip me a new one right now."

"Hmm, yeah, you might be right. I'll focus on the angry bird here first, we can always go out and steal another one down the line, right?"

"What are you naming it?"

"So, like, there was this game where I'm from, it was called Angry Birds, and there was this red crazy bird that was called, well, Red. So yeah, I'm calling him Red."

"Red," I mumbled. "Go figure. Alright, Red, welcome to the family."

I turned back to the duke and his army outside the walls. They were packing up and leaving, which was the smartest thing they could do. Now, I had no idea if he was being forced to cooperate with the Order, or if he was just afraid, or didn't want to lose his riches, but whatever the case, I didn't think we would get along very well in the long run.

"Speaking of which, where *is* Legs?" Sonya asked, looking around.

"He's hiding in the forest. Went down on his belly so the soldiers wouldn't shit themselves," Benny laughed. "Just imagine seeing another one of me but much taller and dangerous-looking. They would have never approached, right? And I would have to kill a lot of people to get my hands on Red."

"I don't think it's a good idea, Benny," Danara said. "Red has a long way to go before he's of any use."

"No, not true. Grom will make him armor, just like he'd done for me and Legs. Don't you worry. Now, what next, boss?"

I turned back to the gate hearing the rustling of armor and found Samel entering. He walked in front of the 82 soldiers who had joined him. They all looked like grizzled men and women who had gone through many life and death situations and not the soft-handed fools that were now picking themselves up and leaving back for Volarna City. Sure, I couldn't blame anyone but the Duke and the Order for any lack of real fighting prowess and power, but we'd change that given some time.

"Samel, what about your faith? Has it returned?"

The soldier nodded and stuck his hand out for me to shake.

"It has and I couldn't feel any better. Just a word of warning, if you will, but that voice in my mind told me that I would temporarily lose access to the Godveil because I was too far away from the source of power."

He looked toward the large statue of the three gods of old. It made sense then, in a way, that he'd lost his newly gained power. Or not. I wasn't so sure as we'd always been able to go as far away from Greystone as we wished...but then again, belief in the gods had been at an all-time high.

"That's good. You will have to stay here for now, but—wait, when did it come back?"

"My access to the Godveil?" Samel asked. "Just after dawn. Why?"

I smiled, genuinely happy that we'd solved an issue I didn't even know we had. Good, that was very good. Now that there was a prophet, the Godveil's influence stretched much further.

"Nothing. Anyway, Benny, can you stay here for a while? I'm going to add Samel to the guild for now so he can hand out armor and weapons as the other soldiers are converted and get their classes, but I need someone to protect them for now."

Benny put up his hand for me to high-five him, and I knew unless I did so he would just stand there for hours. Just like he'd done last time. It looked a bit awkward, but I figured it was harmless enough.

"That's my bro! Sure thing. I'll do my best with Red while we're here."

"And Legs. Don't make me beat your ass."

"And Legs, yes. I'm not that heartless, bro. Legs was with me since the start. I'll never hurt him!"

I took a moment to gather my thoughts and looked around the village, the palisades, and the surrounding forest. The walls needed to be much sturdier, taller, and we'd need to create enough room to place traps and defensive measures along the ramparts.

"Najla, take care of the people. Get them all situated. Group the soldiers near the two entrances and let them use several of the corner buildings as barracks. Spread out food and start cleaning the rubble, get people to come together as a group, talk to them...anything really. I need a day or two to rest, gather my thoughts, and finish some things in New Greystone. Then I'm going after the other arbiters and the duke. Samel, help her. I really hope that you take this role seriously. Najla is very important to The Old Faith, so do what you can."

I sent them both an invitation to join the guild, and they accepted. Both were assigned Officer ranks so they could add more people if necessary as well as retrieve stuff from the basic guild storage. After explaining everything to them and showing them how to go about doing everything including talking over the guild rooms, I finally breathed a sigh of relief. The first stage was over and we were doing great.

Quest: Spreading The Faith V

Description: Continue to help spread faith in the Gods of Old.

Status: 1,186/2,500 Converted Believers

Reward: Establishment of a Divine Military Cadre

There's no way we would have enough people even if I had killed the duke and forced all his men to convert. No, I didn't play the way they did. I would give people what they needed and wanted, and only then would I take over. I didn't have the necessary capabilities to rule over tens of thousands of people, I couldn't feed or clothe them, all I could do was fight. That would have to do for now.

"Ladies? Are you ready to go home?" I asked. "We can all use a breather."

"I'm staying here in case they come back," Elvina said. "I want to cover all sides with enough death that no one will dare attack. And besides, Benny and Legs can't be everywhere at the same time."

"And Danara. And Red," Benny said, squaring his shoulders. "I would appreciate it if you show some—"

"It's fine," Danara said with a weak smile. "We all know it takes time to build trust. Just give me the chance to prove myself."

"Emma? Sonya? Selene? Jeanette?"

"Hey, you took me in when I needed it the most," Sonya said and grabbed my right arm. Emma hurriedly did so to my left.

"You mean I took you in and patched you up."

Sonya stepped in and quickly placed a kiss on her lips, drawing some gasps and strange glances from people standing nearby. They weren't used to such behavior, and truth be told, I hadn't been either, but now I rarely loved anything more than seeing the girls having fun.

"Sure, why not?" Jeanette added. "As long as she keeps her claws off you."

"Deal!" Danara said, sticking her hand out to Jeanette, but instead grabbed and hugged her. "Oh, this is going to be so amazing! We'll become si—"

"No, don't go that far," Jeanette cut her off. "So, we going? I need a bath. A hot one. And good food."

CHAPTER 24 – DOWNTIME

Back in New Greystone, we were met with an interesting sight. The dwarves were getting ready to head out to Garm Village. So were Grom and his family, as well as Mortimer. They'd been waiting for us to reach the village before setting out.

"Ladies, gentlemen," I said, greeting the large group. "You're heading out to help?"

Grom walked up to me and placed his big hands on my shoulders while giving me a big, toothy smile.

"Of course. Are they not our people now as well?" the big elgar asked.

"Yeah, you're right, they are. And thanks. We really need a day to rest and catch our breaths. I'll tell you all about it over the guild room later. We killed one of the arbiters, and Benny stole the heart of another. She's with us now."

"Yes, yes, I heard," Grom laughed, obviously amused by the prospect. "He told me all about it."

"Good, then I don't have to. You can tell the rest."

Grom mock-scowled but nodded.

"What ye want us to do when we get there?" Nalgid asked. "Anything in particular?"

"Find Najla, she's our prophetess, and the guard captain Samel. They're more or less in charge of the village. I didn't want to push things too hard. Let them settle into their roles and new reality. Benny, Legs, Danara, and Red will stay mostly outside the village, making sure you don't get attacked."

"Red?" Mortimer asked. "Who...or maybe it's a what?"

"Exactly. He literally stole one of the Duke's God Beasts. It's a red war gryphon. Oh, you might want to bring along the portable smithy, Grom. Benny wants his new pet fully geared."

Grom grinned and nodded subtly. If there was one thing the elgar enjoyed, it was trying their skill on something new.

"We already packed two of the portable smithies with us," Ferid said proudly. "Grom anticipated we'll be needing em for hammering."

"Good. And thank you. I know everyone's been working hard on the temple, so—"

"No, no, just shut up, will ye," Nalgid laughed. "Mirna, Durtona, Divila, and our daughters are staying behind te make sure everything looks good inside too. Can't be havin' a wedding in an empty shed, now can ye?"

I smiled, genuinely appreciating all they've been doing.

"Look, I promise to repay—"

"Again ye and ye yappin' mouth. Ye don't owe us anything. It is we that owe ye. Oh, and that wendigo head is in the kitchen, along with the two other heads. Ye'll see," Nalgid said proudly. Now, come, sons! Let's show these elgar what real smiths can do, not some fire-fearing folk from—"

"Hey, hold on!" I said, raising my voice. "I don't want any of that crap out there, alright? You can bicker and fool around as much as you want here, but outside these walls, you represent New Greystone, you represent the guild, and you represent The Old Faith."

"Bah! I'll need that drink after all then," Nalgid groaned. "Alright, elgar. Just this time."

He stared up at the taller Grommasch and then headbutted the giant's chest.

"Hah! That'll do!"

I had no idea what they were doing, but if it meant that we could avoid any possible crap out there, I'd be more than happy.

"Hey, you can take a few barrels from the guild store. Can't work on an empty stomach, right?" I said, shooting the dwarf a wink. He lit up like the sun.

"Why didn't ye say that right away? Come! To Garm!"

Mortimer trudged off after them with a small bag slung from his back.

"Callina has prepared some food. It's all in the kitchen but look for her before you eat. Please?"

We waved them off and headed toward the center of the village. The main road led to all of the other facilities and homes from there. I first needed to see someone in particular before I could even think about gobbling down some food.

"Girls, can you find Callina and see what's up? I need to catch up with Banxi real quick. Then we can draft up a bath and...relax."

"Ohh, I like!" Jeanette said excitedly. She grabbed and kissed me, then rushed off to Mortimer's place. Selene ran after her, while Emma and Sonya weren't in so much of a hurry.

"See you soon," I said, giving the two a wink. Emma slid aside her dress, revealing a long leg, and then the two giggled, picking up their steps.

Evil nymphs. I like it.

I found Banxi at the top of the watch tower. He was busy tinkering with a small contraption that resembled Legs very well. It had six, well, legs, three on each side, and a seat for...why exactly? I had no idea what it was, and I didn't even want to know honestly. At least not right now. I was too tired.

"Yer' back," he said, never looking up as he was screwing some bolts in place. "Don't worry, two of mine are on constant watch. One is outside and one is—hmm, where did that shit goblin go?" he cursed, looking for his son. "Ohh, this won't do. I will flay his skin!"

"Banxi, hey, when did you sleep last time?"

He straightened himself and stood proudly, his small arms crossed over his chest.

"Two days ago? I've been making great progress with

the walker. That thing with the six legs? Yes, it will allow me to fight monsters from relative safety, or just pull large carts along toward the next village over. The walkers will revolutionize this world, I tell you!"

I would have been more enthusiastic if I wasn't as tired, and if both his sons were doing their duties.

He put his hand up and hurried up the ladder, disappearing into the very tip of the tower. His voice resounded from above, a plethora of curses followed, and then two goblins came falling down the open hatch before Banxi jumped on top of them.

"Lazy bastards! If I catch any of you sleeping again, I will feed you to the God Beast!"

"Oh, we have a new one. A red war gryphon. He might be particularly hungry," I said with a smirk. He picked up on it and kicked his sons, one time each.

"Ye—yes, dar! Twon' happen again!" the larger of the two goblins said. He had darker green and browner skin than his younger sibling, who looked unripe if he'd been a fruit...

"Alright, so, I'm heading off to have dinner with the girls and then relax. What I need you two youngsters to do, is make sure no one sneaks up on us from behind. Or anywhere for that matter. Can you do that? I'll give you a nice piece of armor if you do a good job tonight."

"Armor? Dar! I want armor!"

"Oh, shut up, Brek!" Banxi hissed at his older son. "They'll do just fine. Trust me. Oh, and I had an idea. Well, a lot of ideas, but what if we converted the ship into a walker? Or installed great weaponry on that beauty. We could use it to patrol the rivers and the lake, providing support where needed."

"We?"

"Captain Mano and I!" he said proudly. "See, I love me some nice ship or airplane. And considering I don't have any more airplanes or parts to make a new one, the best next thing is a ship!"

I patted his shoulder and squeezed just hard enough to show my appreciation.

"We will talk about it, Banxi. As long as Mano is alright with it, we'll do what we can. I'll also send Legs down there to lure out the bigger monsters so we can slay them."

"Deal! Now get, I need to finish this prototype first!"

I made my way across the village square and up the road leading to our home. Merek stood there in the darkness, looking equal shares serious, and dangerous.

"I will hit level 60 tomorrow. When I do, I plan to ask Najla for her hand. She's nice and I...we talked a lot while you were busy, and I think I like her."

He got me there. His proclamation wasn't something that I'd expected, not at all. Najla was cute, she had a nice body, and she seemed kinky enough to get along well with the girls, but I couldn't get too greedy. Elvina would be the next to join my growing group of...wives? Mirna was cute, too, in a slightly more muscled and tad shorter way than the other girls.

"Yeah, alright. I'm fine with that, but you do understand what that means?"

He shook his head.

"No, I don't. Just be open with me. I think you should know by now that I appreciate that most."

"Very well, then. I want you to make the head of the new cadre once it's established. Also, I want you to swear an oath to me, one that you'll never go against me or our new faith, our guild, or whatever we're working for. Having her as your partner will give you a lot of fame and power. Let it get to your head, and I will end you, Merek. That is what you wanted to hear, is it not?"

He let out a sigh of relief.

"Yeah, I figured as much. As long as it's just that, I'm totally fine. There's just one thing—"

"No, I promised. If she wants to become soulbound, then I won't stop her. What's more, it will raise all her stats so much that even arbiters will have a hard time killing her."

"But how does that even work?" he leaned in and whispered. "Will she want to sleep with you?"

I snorted.

"No, my good man, she won't want to on her own, but what she will feel is a drive to screw your eyes out. She will feel every time the girls are even remotely doing anything...naughty."

"Oh," he mumbled. "Oh! Wait! So we'll know whenever you're—and you will know when we—"

I winked at him and then playfully punched his shoulder.

"No one's forcing you to, Merek, but this place is all about compromises. You have no idea how many I'd have to make just today. Also, I'll have Mortimer inspect the arbiter's armor later. If it's any better than yours, you can have it as a 'welcome to the family' gift. Talk to you tomorrow. Think about it before you even propose, alright?"

I made my way up the small stone path leading up toward Brahma's Rest and felt him slink away. He must have misunderstood how the soulbinding card worked and been on edge. All the tension he'd radiated mere moments ago was gone now and he even had a spring in his step.

"Women, huh?" I whispered. "I can't blame you, my friend. I can't blame you at all."

I pushed the front door open to a murder of crows. Or that's at least what Benny called the girls when they were arguing or just screaming over each other. Now, I knew from the tone that they weren't fighting but rather doing something stupid, naughty, or just fooling around. It was just as I thought when I moved out of the entrance and into the main room. All four were naked as the day they were born, chasing each other, and drinking from tall glasses. I figured they hadn't already dug into the strong stuff, but nothing surprised me anymore.

"Hah! He's back!" Jeanette cried as she placed the glass on

a nearby table and almost charged me. She jumped at the last moment and I caught her, holding her naked ass up with my hands.

"Why are you girls naked already? We haven't even eaten yet. And Elvina will rip you all a new one."

"Don't care!" Jeanette said, kissing me feverishly. Her tongue shot into my mouth and it was all over the place.

"Hey, hold on," I said, pushing away from her. "Let me get cleaned up and we can fuck. I doubt you want my cock in your mouth after it's been stuck in this armor all day and night."

"Who says she'd want it in her mouth? Look at her ass," Sonya said with a smirk. Jeanette bent over, showing me her perfect backside. A crystal plug with a glowing gem faceted inside was stuck in her ass.

"She's finally come out, the slut," Emma said as she finished her glass.

"Slut or not, who cares? Sonya's special, so I like doing it with her," Jeanette said. "She's gentle when it counts, so there's that too."

"Gentle," I chuckled. "Yeah, Sorry, but it doesn't look like that to me. Come, who wants to help me take a bath?"

Selene looked off most among the girls and their fooling around. Not that anyone cared, including me, as they were just a joy to look at. Bouncing breasts, jiggling rears, beautiful faces, and perfect bodies. What was there not to love about being in a relationship with more women at once? Especially if they got along...well enough?

Sonya jumped on my back, intertwining her arms and legs so she didn't fall off as I made my way up the stairs.

"Missed me?" she whispered. Selene heard as she was walking behind us, and slapped Sonya's ass hard. Twice.

"Ohh, I like it," the brown-haired beauty said. Her mana manipulation skills were going to take this experience to a new level. Just bathing alone shouldn't cause our emotions to get out of control and the lust meter to pop, but it did.

Emma and Selene helped me out of my gear and placed it on a chair near the entrance to the bathroom. By the time we waded into the water, Jeanette was laying on the tiles with her legs in the water and ass up as Sonya used the crystal plug on her ass.

"Let me show you something," Emma said as I fully slid into the water. She opened a small gearbox and turned it clockwise, then closed the box gain. The water started bubbling and I could feel the mass of mana being released into the bathtub, heating it up all around us.

"So Banxi did it?" I asked as she pushed into me.

"Yes, he did. That goblin is smart, and those three wives of his are smart too, even likable in a way."

"Just as Emma says," Sonya added as she waded through the water and pushed the golden-haired beauty aside. "Emma, can you take over with Jeanette tonight? I will make it up."

Emma sighed but nodded, throwing herself backward into the water.

"This feels so good," she said as bubbles formed at the surface and Sonya's body pressed against mine. I looked down at her wolfish smile.

"I want to hit level two tonight. Deal?"

"Hold on, let me check real quick," I said, opening the soulbound intimacy stats. She was at 73%, so I figured it was possible if we went all night. It wouldn't be fair to the other girls, but I guessed that was the price we all needed to pay for sharing each other.

Selene slid into the water behind me with two sponges in her hands. She handed one to Sonya and used the other to scrub my back, arms, and legs while the latter took care of my chest and manhood. I didn't need much to get hard as Sonya was trying her best to stimulate me with every movement.

I grabbed her rear and pulled her in close, sucking at her nipple. Sonya cried out in surprise but quickly eased into me, both her hands sliding up and down my arms, chest, and between my legs. She felt how hard I already was for her, and Selene pressing her breasts into my back and tracing her fingers up and down my body didn't help much to slow down my blood flow...

Jeanette screamed as her body spasmed, drawing my eyes to her. She was still leaning over the edge of the bath with her rear up in the sky and her hand sliding inside her wet pussy. Emma giggled and kept sliding the crystal plug in and out of her as Selene slid out from behind me.

Sonya pushed a surge of mana through the water, making the hairs on my body stand upright with pleasure.

"Sit on the edge," she said, pushing me backward.

I eased into the cold stone tiles and pushed myself up on the edge, but the elf pushed me further and onto my back. Sonya slid between my legs and spread them apart, licking the tip of my cock. I was about to reach out for her, but Selene knelt next to me and swung her leg over me, placing her slit right over my face. She leaned in and kissed the side of my length, then traced it with her mouth as Sonya battled her for dominance.

I smiled, knowing just how much they wanted both to please me and gain more intimacy so their share of our stats would go up. It wasn't something that bothered me as I wanted them all to be as strong as possible.

My hands slid up her legs and reached in between her thighs, spreading her lips apart as I leaned in, tracing my tongue along her soft flesh. The battle between the elf and the arcanist went well as they both took a side of me, wrapping their tongues and lips around my shaft.

Selene moaned and pulled her head back as my tongue slid across her clit. Sonya used the moment and pushed the elf's head away, taking my length into her mouth with a single bob of her head.

The elven assassin used that moment and pushed her opponent in love's head down all the way. It was a moment that made me almost finish then and there because of all the mana running through our bodies. Sonya gagged for a second but then continued to move her head back and forth, with the elf holding her hair back.

"You're all equally bad," Selene whispered. "All you want is his semen."

"I don't recall you saying no last time," Emma shot back and slapped Jeanette's ass so hard it resounded in the bathroom like a thunderstrike. The swashbuckler cried out and glared at the priestess, who cast a healing spell on her. "Sorry. Got a bit carried away."

I chuckled, shaking my head slowly. They were fantastic, no otherworldly, marvelous, ethereal, and any other word that came even close.

Sonya's hand slid down to my balls and she squeezed hard as if telling me to come already. More mana trickled into my manhood and I spasmed, coming inside her mouth as Selene pushed her head back down. Oh, someone was going to get the spanking of a lifetime once Sonya was done.

The brunette pulled her head back and stared at Selene.

"Bitch. If you think you're getting rid of me so easily, you've got another thing coming. I can swallow everything he gives me."

The black-haired elf shrugged and then nodded to my throbbing member.

"You still need that?"

CHAPTER 25 –
CEREMONY I

The next morning we awoke to a hissing Elvina, who stood over us at the foot of the bed. She looked tired, annoyed, and betrayed.

"How do you think I was supposed to get all that work done with you four fucking like horny little—"

"Shh, not so early," Emma mumbled. "I got a headache."

"No! Shit!" Elvina hissed. "You are all—"

"We're what?" Sonya asked, stirring beside me. I was still playing possum, wanting to see how they handled the situation. "He's finally asleep after a few very hard days, and yet you come in here and want to wake him up because you wet your panties? Show some respect, Elvina."

Jeanette was snoring, so she wouldn't be getting any support from there, but strangely Selene came to her aide.

"She's lost, so don't blame here. I've been there back in Greystone when Giovanni kicked me out. Just cut her some slack, alright?"

"I agree," I said, finally opening my eyes. "Get cleaned up and join us for breakfast, Elvina. Thank you for all the hard work."

"I'll help her," Sonya said and shot to her feet.

"Me too," Emma added. "I think we need to talk a bit more. Why don't you and Selene go downstairs? Callina said that she'd prepare a full spread by dawn."

I squeezed the swashbuckler's naked ass and slid my fingers down her cleft. She stirred and looked over her shoulder.

"What?"

"Come have breakfast with us. Unless you want to spend the day in bed."

Jeanette stretched with a groan, her large chest sliding down the sides. I pushed one of her breasts back up and she giggled.

"Don't do that! It's unflattering."

"Well, it wouldn't have slid down if you didn't have monster tits," Selene jabbed. "They're not like mine, hanging high like forbidden fruit."

Jeanette groaned again and covered her head with a pillow, leaving the rest of her body naked.

"Do you want to have a quicky?"

The pillow was gone immediately and the swashbuckler sat atop my chest, her mouth already wrapped around my length.

"I thought you'd never ask."

I pressed my thumb down her slit and pushed it inside her slowly. Her back arched like that of an angry cat, and her teeth tightened around me.

"Hey, now, little kitty. Don't even go there?"

"Unless you make me!" she mock growled.

I slapped her ass again and pulled her in so I could eat her. Who said I couldn't have an appetizer before breakfast?

We made our way downstairs after everyone had bathed again and clothed. It had been just as Callina promised. A full spread of finger food, sandwiches, juices, and even small sweets was laid out on the main dining table. Everyone grabbed a seat and started eating as Selene and Jeanette made us drinks. I wanted to start off with a small toast, which ended up being cut short when Jeanette drank hers all up.

"Anyway, to us. To this new life, and to...well, our future," I said, keeping it simple. "And to many more years and...orgies."

"I'll drink to that," Emma chuckled, and so did the other

girls.

I popped a small piece of toasted bread smeared with berries into my mouth and made my way over to the sitting area. Three trophies waited there for me. The biggest of the three was that of the wendigo, and two more, smaller ones, belonged to barely unique monsters that had spawned from the guild dungeons.

I first chose the bigger one and then assigned it a space where it wouldn't be as visible. Then, I checked the other two and added them as well.

```
You have assigned a Cursed Wendigo trophy skull.
        Buff applied: Cursed Wendigo II
        Effect: Raise All Guild Member's
            debuff resistance by 8

You have assigned a Gustar trophy skull.
        Buff applied: Gustar II
        Effect: Raise All Guild Member's
            healing   received by 11

You have assigned a Cerv trophy skull.
        Buff applied: Cerv II
Effect: Raise All Guild Member's Stamina by 7
```

All of the three trophy buffs were pretty good. Debuff resistance was always welcome, extra stamina, and so was better healing. We never knew if that single percent or stat point could be the difference between life and death.

I found a small box of monster cards on the table as well and rummaged through them. There was nothing interesting in there for me, but the girls would probably be able to use some of them. If nothing, there were still Merek, Grom and his family, the dwarves, and even the new soldiers. We'd need a lot of cards before everyone had all their slots equipped, even at their low level.

"Girls? Have you gone through the monster card box?" I asked and carried them over to where they were seated around the table.

"Yes. We've already picked out a few, nothing special," Selene said, giving me a sheepish smile. "Not everyone can sleep like a dead man."

I snorted, shaking my head at her amusing comment.

"I'd like to see you take on four of me and then still have enough energy—wait, that sounded so wrong. What I meant is take me on four times. Yes, that's it."

She full-on grinned and shot me a wink as I took my seat again.

We ate and drank while joking around, throwing playful jabs at each other. It was the first breakfast we had in a while where we all sat together and just enjoyed each other's company. There was a lot we needed to tackle afterward, but that could wait a while longer.

The door burst open just before we were about to finish eating, and Callina came rushing in.

"It's time! You all need to go get ready for the ceremony!"

"Ceremony? What are—hey, hold on," I said, looking around the table.

"No buts and no ifs!" Emma said excitedly, jumping to her feet. "We've already got this all planned out, and besides, it's going to be a small affair. Once we take care of the other arbiters and the duke, we can then have a big wedding!"

I had to admit that they'd caught me off guard. Well, not that much that I wasn't prepared for such an eventuality, but it had come sooner than I originally planned.

"You come with me, Cade. The girls need to get ready."

Behind her stood the three gobla, all holding dresses in their arms. The color was identical, and from what I could see, so was the part of the design that was visible.

I was rushed out of Brahma's Rest and pulled along until we reached Mortimer and Callina's place. There, the burly merchant and his wife led me inside. Mano and Rafika were there as well, and their grins told me everything. This wasn't something just for me and for the girls, it was for everyone living in New Greystone.

"Grom gave me the rings earlier," Mortimer said, pointing to a dresser with five small boxes sitting on top. They all looked identical but for the engraved names on the lids.

"Five, huh? I don't even know if Elvina will agree," I muttered.

"You don't have to worry about that," Rafika chuckled. "We've talked to her, both Callina and I. We've become good friends so to speak."

I eyed the two ladies curiously, but neither showed any hint of dishonesty.

"What's more, we've all become pretty good friends. See, when there's no competition and fear of others stealing your man, women tend to get along pretty well," Callina said.

"Totally," Rafika agreed. I wasn't so sure about that, but I wouldn't call them out on it.

"So...the marriage ceremony. Why today?" I asked. "We could have done that in a week or two, or five. It's not something that was very high on my list of important things. Well, not at the very top at least."

"Exactly!" Mortimer chimed in. "See, we knew that as well, and let's be honest, as soon as one danger is taken care of, another one comes along. What *is* the perfect time?"

"Hmm," I mumbled. "That makes sense, but who's keeping Garm safe?"

"No one. Well, Elvina's traps and a few soldiers who will raise the alarm if something happens. Everyone else is coming to make this something grand."

"So, we will leave you to it," Callina said as she grabbed Rafika's hand and pulled her toward the door. "You have half an hour to get ready, so hurry up. We're going to help the girls. See you in a bit!"

The two rushed out, slamming the door shut behind them. I looked at Mortimer first and then Mano, giving them the 'you guys are traitors' stare, but I couldn't hold it longer than a few seconds and just sighed.

"You could have warned me, gentlemen. This has really —"

"Caught you by surprise? Well, that was the point. We all wanted to do something for you, so we've been preparing food and stashing it in the guild storage. It will be as fresh as the moment we stored it away. Then there's the temple. Is there a better way to open the temple for everyone than by having the strongest man in the land marry his five...wives? Well, I have to say, I'm a bit jealous sometimes," Mortimer said all in one breath. "No, scratch that. I can't handle more than my dearest wife. But don't tell her that, alright? She might think I'm getting old."

"Aren't you?" Mano asked.

"Am I what? Getting old?" Mortimer shot back indignantly. "Young man, I can still beat you if—"

I pushed past the two and headed straight for the clothes stand. It was covered by a white sheet. I pulled it aside and eyed the black suit hanging regally from the rack. Its fabric was a weave of shadow and sophistication. The coat looked tailored to perfection and boasted intricate silver embroidery along the lapels, forming an elegant filigree of symbols I recognized from back in Greystone.

The trousers, matching in darkness, flowed seamlessly, their hems brushing against polished leather boots. Silver-threaded cuffs adorned the sleeves, catching glimmers of light as if stars had been woven into the very fabric.

"I...am speechless," I whispered, unable to find any better words. "Who made these?"

"The three gobla," Mortimer said. "I had some spare fabric I didn't know what to do with, so I let them use it."

"And the dresses?"

"All as white as can be, though they are all the same design. We didn't want any of the girls to feel as if they got a worse-looking dress than the others. And yes, they will adjust around the body. Just like your suit."

He joined me at the clothes rack and put his hand on my

shoulder.

"Look, Cade, we've known each other for a long time, so trust me when I say that this is one of the best days of your life. They love you, you love them, right? This ceremony won't change that, but it will show everyone that you are serious about both them and this place. You're ready to put down your roots, and that matters."

"Exactly. Also, Banxi told me about the ship. I can't wait to be of more use to you guys!" Mano said excitedly. "Oh, I would hug you now if it weren't that awkward."

"Leave the hugs for later, you sea mongrel. All you think about is how to get back out onto the water. Let's help the man into his suit."

About fifteen minutes later, we were headed for the temple. Hundreds of people were standing outside with tables lined to either side of the road. They were full of food and drinks. There was even music playing from lutes, harps, and even small drums. It wasn't nearly loud enough for everyone to hear, but I appreciated that someone took their time to try and liven the mood a bit.

Most of the onlookers weren't dressed in fine clothes, but instead, they opted for whatever black and white they had in their possessions. It gave the whole scene a serene, uniform look.

People raised their glasses and cheered as the three of us made our way into the temple. The towering doors opened with a gentle creak, revealing the cavernous expanse inside. As we stepped into the temple, a soft murmur of hushed conversations and the rustle of fabrics, creaking of wood, and wind blowing past us greeted me. The air carried the familiar scent of polished wood, ancient incense, and the subtle perfume of gathered people.

Sunlight streamed through stained glass windows, casting a mosaic of colors upon the marble floor. The symphony of whispers accompanied our every step down the central aisle where guests had already taken their places on the polished pews.

The flickering candles hanging on the walls and pillars bathed the space in a warm glow despite it being day. There was enough darkness present to make out the warm light.

The pews were adorned with ribbons and flowers of various colors to break up the monotony of white and black. The high ceiling, with its arching buttresses, echoed with every footstep that we took.

The statue of the three Gods of old sat where the altar would ordinarily be, watching over us. I felt a shiver run down my spine, almost as if the three were present. The large statue shouldn't be here, yet I knew Najla must have somehow managed to store it in the guild storage, but I hadn't felt any shift in weight, and the marvelous piece of stone was very heavy. Maybe she had—no, I wasn't going to think about it right now. I'd just ask later.

The grandeur of the temple, with its celestial frescoes and towering columns, provided a backdrop for a moment that would forever be suspended in time. Every detail, from the tapestries on the walls to the intricate carvings, spoke of The Old Faith, depicting the three Gods and their battle with Tan'Malas.

As I moved through the sea of well-wishers, most of their faces reflected genuine joy for the occasion. The atmosphere, already burning with anticipation, awaited the final touch—the arrival of my wives-to-be.

How the hell did I even get here? One thing led to another and things somehow got out of hand. I got together with Emma, Sonya appeared dying on our doorstep, Jeanette lost everything and we took her in. Selene had been in a similar situation as Sonya, left to rot and die. Elvina, well, that had been a different situation altogether. We'd definitely gotten closer since coming to this new land, but I wasn't sure where we stood yet. Then the whole intimacy rivalry between the girls...I loved it.

It was plain and simple. I loved every part of them, even

the bickering over the small things like who had taken whose panties or was wearing which dress. Even if their hair was done or not, the make-up...everything. It made me feel as if I was truly part of a greater whole, of something that would always force me to be the best person I could be.

I stopped in front of the large statue where Najla and Merek stood to one side, with Benny and Danara on the other. He was in his pangolin-badger shape and barely rose to his companion's chest, while the former two looked perfect together.

Merek wore pitch-black armor, the one I looted from Pelis, while a long, red dress hugged our prophetess's body. A cowl covered part of her long, curled hair. A golden bejeweled belt was wrapped around her waist and hung down past her knees. The sleeves covered most of her arms, ending just below the wrists.

Danara was dressed in a similarly red dress that didn't do a great job of hiding her body. There was ample cleavage to be seen and the right leg had a deep slit that ended just above her hip. Benny was, well, naked like usual. His tool was hidden away in the smaller form, which was a blessing for everyone present.

"You nervous, bro?" Benny asked as he stood there with a smug expression.

"Does it show?"

"Not really. I'm just teasing you, bro, but joke aside, you look like a freaking hunk, man. Respect."

"You look good yourself, little brother. Thank you for always being there for me, Benny. Next ceremony is you and Danara."

He flashed me a wide grin and gave me a thumbs-up.

"I'll always be there for you, brother. Always. We both will."

The pangolin took Danara's hand and squeezed. She nodded as well. I couldn't say much about her yet, even more so as she'd been an enemy only days ago, but she seemed really into Benny. And if he stayed loyal, I was pretty sure she would be as well.

The towering wooden doors opened yet again, drawing my attention back to the entrance. Bright light spilled into the temple, framing five goddesses dressed in white.

CHAPTER 26 – CEREMONY II

As the girls stepped into the light, time seemed to freeze for a long moment. Their gowns were a masterpiece of fantastic couture that cascaded like waterfalls of moonlight. The pure white fabric seemed both ethereal and weightless as it trailed behind them.

The bodices were adorned with intricate silver filigree that ran down their chests and front center, gathering just above the navel, embracing their forms like a cascade of frost-kissed vines.

The necklines were modest yet alluring, framing the curves of their collarbones. Each step they took sent ripples through the billowing fabric as if the gowns danced to an otherworldly melody. The only differences between the girls were their ears and the color of their hair. They'd all opted for the same hairstyle as well, which was another thing I loved about them. A thick braid was tied around the back with waves of cascading hair falling down their backs. Elvina's platinum white wings trailed behind her, yet they were almost just as translucent as usual. She must have done something special to make them almost as bright as their dresses.

Bright pink and red blossoms adorned their hair, and shiny jewelry adorned with bright gems hung from their necks and earlobes. Five identical tiaras sat atop their flowing locks. The enchanting melody of wind chimes seemed to accompany each step as my five angels walked toward me with Callina, Rafika, and the three Goblas trailing behind them, holding the backs of their gowns up.

I just stood there, taken aback by what they'd managed to do over the last half an hour. Emma was first with Sonya trailing behind her, then Jeanette, Selene, and finally Elvina. Once they'd stopped in front of the statue, the five helpers left to sit with their families in the first few rows of pews. At the very front were Grom and his family, then the dwarves behind him. On the other side was the Mokra Clan with the rest of our friends.

I met their eyes, one by one, and saw all that I hoped in them: love, hope, safety, even the future. That is all I ever wanted. A safe future with all of them.

"We have gathered here today to celebrate a love so strong many of us will never get to feel it," Najla said, drawing everyone's eyes to her. "We are here to celebrate the love between Cade, Emma, Sonya, Selene, Jeanette, and Elvina. I will be honest and say I've never done this before, so please forgive me if I'm off."

We chuckled and laughed good-naturedly. None of us had wed anyone before, and in all honesty, it was just a formality. What mattered was to give the girls their presents and see if the helfar would agree as well. Her being present and dressed for the occasion boded well in my book.

"It has only been a short while since we met, and yet I feel as if I've known everyone here for a very long time. They are genuinely good people trying to do the right thing and help those around them. That is who they are, that is who they promised to be, and that is what we'll remind them of every single day, for he has not only chosen one spouse, but five!"

The gathered crowd cheered and whistled. It was almost as if we were back in Greystone...almost. Emma blushed, the pink in her cheeks standing out stark against her golden hair. Elvina blushed too, while Sonya, Selene, and Jeanette looked more amused than anything.

"Do you promise to cherish, love, and protect them until the end of time, Cade?" Najla asked, raising her voice. "Do you promise to keep them from any harm and to provide for them?

What do you say?"

"I do!" I said firmly and retrieved one of the five small boxes from my storage and opened it, picking out a shiny ring with a golden-colored gem embedded inside.

I approached her first and took her hand. It was a bit different than how wedding ceremonies went back in Greystone, but Benny had told us how people back in his world did things, so we decided to improvise a bit.

"Will you take this ring as a sign of my vow to love and protect you, Emma?" I asked, holding it up in front of her finger. Tears formed right away in her eyes as she nodded hurriedly.

"I do! Always!" she cried, jumping and kissing me. I'd barely managed to slide the ring on her finger when she kissed me. The crowd gathered laughed and cheered. It was only then that she looked down at the ring sitting around her finger. "What is—Cade!"

"Shh," I whispered, putting my finger to her lips. "Let it be a surprise for them as well." I took her in for another moment and couldn't believe what I was seeing. She was so beautiful, no, all of them were, but Emma still held a special place in my heart as the first woman to melt the ice that was me.

I kissed her again and then moved over to stand in front of Sonya, who was waiting anxiously, and produced a second small box. From inside I retrieved an identical ring but with a purple gem socketed inside. I held her hand and brought it to my lips, kissing it as I slid the ring on. My kinky magician gasped as she saw what the ring had done for her, and she grabbed me hard, kissing me.

Screw the ceremony. All that mattered was that the gods and people alike witnessed our love and our promises to love and take care of one another.

"Thank you!" Sonya whispered in my ear. "I love you so much!"

"Love you too, baby. Oh, and you look fabulous. I'd take

you right here and now if there were no people around."

Sonya bit her lip and mock-glared at me for a second.

"Keep that thought for tonight."

I winked and stepped over to Jeanette. Her brown hair looked much lighter as she stood under a ray of sunshine that made her squint her eyes a little bit.

"Hey you," I said, holding the third box out already. It had a ring inside with a light red gem that shimmered as if it was on fire from the inside.

"Took you long enough," she mumbled. "I was already starting to feel neglected."

"Oh, shush you," I said with a wink and leaned in to kiss her. She smelled so good and her skin was silky smooth. They must have used all kinds of ointments and salves until they got to the desired point.

I slid the ring on her finger and she almost fell to her knees. My arm was around her before she could even stumble.

"Why—what is this? What does this mean?" she wheezed barely audibly.

"I'll tell you girls later. Hold the thought, love."

Jeanette stared at the ring, letting me move on without any more hassle.

Selene was next, my black-haired elf. She was a rare one among her people as they were mostly born with silvery hair. Not her. I pulled the next ring out of the box and slid it on her finger. Her eyes never left mine as we just stood there.

"You're a good man," Selene suddenly said. "I definitely made the right choice, and now you have bound me for life...no, not just life, you've bound me even after death. What is the meaning of this, Cade?"

"I will tell you everything later, my beautiful elven killer. You know how much I love you, right? You know how much I love to be alone with you?"

She nodded weakly, blushing despite trying to stay as stoic as Jeanette and Elvina.

"I do, but tonight...you will tell us everything."

293

"I will, my love," I said, kissing her passionately. She almost melted in my arms.

I let go of her and stopped in front of Elvina next. The helfar was an unknown quantity as we'd never even got so close as to even sleep with each other, well, that was a lie as I'd basically told her that I couldn't, not before she was comfortable with me, but still...

"What do you think, little trapper?" I whispered so only she could hear. "Am I someone who will be able to give you happiness? Will I be able to protect and cherish you? Do you even like the other girls enough to share me with them?"

"I don't know," she replied and I could feel her honesty. "Maybe, maybe not. I know that at least you will try. Sometimes that should be enough, right?"

"Sometimes, but we shouldn't agree because of a 'maybe' or a 'perhaps', but rather a 'make it happen' kind of attitude. If you commit, and I'm not telling you to sleep with us...with me...I will give you everything I can and then some. Even if we don't share a bed, you will have the same rights and privileges. And yes, I know that this is a stupid place and time to be discussing these things, but I felt I had to get them off my chest."

I held my hands out, hoping she would accept it without much drama and then, later on, adjust our 'marriage' so she had her own peace, but the helfar surprised me with a tight hug.

"Just promise that you'll keep being you. I don't need much more than that. Not even the girls' club."

"Girls...club?"

"Yeah, where we all hang out when you're not around. Franja, Callina, and even the goblas come to visit. We sing, drink, eat, and—"

"Have gigolos as Benny calls them?"

"No! But hey, that might be a good idea," she chuckled. I slapped her thigh playfully. She had barely even noticed it.

I pulled the last ring out of the box and held it out in

front of her.

"I assume you want this then?"

Elvina nodded slowly, her ears perking up slightly. They were easily two inches longer than Selene's, which was an easy way to distinguish between the races. I had seen a few thrown in between Garm and especially Balan, but it was only a few families.

"I do," she said softly. "If you are willing to give me the same attention as you give the others."

"You can be sure of that," I smiled and slid the ring on her finger.

Elvina's ears twitched again and her eyebrows rose as she probably read the newly-gained passive the other girls had gotten as well. I'd have to explain it to them later, though I wasn't a hundred percent sure either.

"How did you—"

"A favor from a friend. Anyway, come here," I said, putting my finger under her chin and pulling her closer. Our lips met, and she shuddered.

The moment had lasted a bit too long, and I could see the other girls staring impatiently. Najla picked up, though, saving me.

"Now that Cade has exchanged his vows and gifted all of his brides, I pronounce their marriage valid!"

The crowd erupted in cheers, flower petals rained down on us, and a burst of mana surged from within the statue.

```
Congratulations! Your intimacy with
Emma, Sonya, Jeanette, Selene, and
Elvina has risen by 2 levels!
```

```
Reward: Emma, Soyna, Jeanette, Selene, and Elvina
will receive  10 to all stat points. They will both
share and contribute 10  more from and to all other
pack member's stats.
```

```
Monster Card: Soulbound
```

```
Emma: Level 4, 27
Sonya: Level 4, 03
Jeanette: Level 3, 94
Selene: Level 3, 69
Elvina: Level 3, 07
```

I was surprised by the Old God's generosity. Two levels of intimacy weren't something that was hard to attain, but it was nevertheless a big boon. Getting a flat 10 points to all stats and a bunch of extra stat points across the board from sharing others' stats and adding even more back on top was a nice gift, that was for sure.

"Thank you, Tan'Ruad, Tan'Drak, and Tan'Aria," I said out loud. "Thank you for this gift!"

Sonya and Emma made the signs of Tan'Aria, but the other three just curtsied and gave a little bow to the statue. It was strange bowing or saying thanks to a piece of stone, but we'd already seen that it was the real deal.

I turned back to the crowd and raised my hands as if in victory, grinning from ear to ear.

"Thank you everyone for making this occasion a grand one! I promise you all here and today, that I will do everything I can to make sure we have many more of these days! Now! Eat and drink! Dance! Make love! And praise The Old Faith!"

I knew they needed a lot of time to adjust to believing in something else than Tan'Malas, but from what I gathered by talking to Najla, she'd seen everything since the dawn of time sped up countless times. From the day the Old Gods were born into existence, to the splitting of Tan'malas and his reign over the world, and then the very day she'd converted. It wasn't something that people could understand from one moment to another, but what they could do was be made to believe that the dark one wasn't what he set himself out to be.

Benny rushed me and so did Legs. He was in his small form, and the two almost tackled me to the ground. The former was trying to climb up my body, while the latter was just screeching happily as if he understood everything that was going on. One by one, our friends and new family came to congratulate us on the ceremony, which had been very quick and awkward, but none of us really knew how to go about getting married. It's not like we'd been very popular back in Greystone and had attended many parties and marriage ceremonies.

There was one last thing I needed to do, and that was to place the Totem of the Old Gods inside the temple so we'd be hidden from prying eyes. I pulled the item from the guild storage and it automatically offered to be bound with the temple. I accepted, of course, and then felt a sudden tingle running down my spine.

The dome's appearance was very interesting, to say the least. A blue wave of mana expanded from the totem, which engulfed the entire temple and then grew from there to encase an area that was much larger than that of the village. It was visible to the naked eye, shimmering and crackling in the sunlight.

"Don't be afraid, everyone!" I yelled. "That is a dome that will protect us from Tan'Malas and everyone else's prying eyes!"

"Really?" Sonya asked as she hurried over to me. "I've heard about those things, but I've never seen them with my own two eyes."

"I have now that I think of it," Emma said. "There was a similar thing stuck inside an altar in the priest guild back in Greystone. It wasn't nearly as pretty as this one, though."

The totem resembled the three gods sitting on throne-like chairs, carved into a slab of stone. They were positioned one above the other, with Tan'Ruad sitting at the top, Tan'Aria in the middle, and Tan'Drak below her.

"If only we could ask anyone about it. I'd sleep safer if the dome could protect us from attacks as well," Jeanette added as she pressed into my side. I put an arm around her and kissed her forehead.

"Maybe we will get more interesting protective items from the gods in due time. That's a thing for another day, though. Now, what will people say if they see us just standing around here and doing...holy things? We need to get drunk."

"But not too much," Selene said. "I don't think if anyone sees the four of—" she stopped there for a second and smiled at Elvina, "Five of us carrying you around, will set a good example."

"I'll play taxi, bro!" Benny said from behind as he tried to jump me again. "If you guys are too wasted, I'll just carry you to Brahma's Rest and tuck you in nicely! Well, Danara can carry the ladies. I don't want my hands all over their pretty dresses."

I ruffled his hairy head and lifted the pangolin to give him a proper hug.

"You're a real bro, you know that, Benny?"

"Of course, now put me down, will ya? People will start to get strange ideas."

"Sure, sure. Party it is!"

CHAPTER 27 – MONSTER OF THE DEEP

The first several days went by in making sweet, sweet love with four of my wives. Elvina still held back and said she wanted to keep herself for a more appropriate moment. As if anything would even trump a wedding ceremony... However, she kept us company and would watch, ask questions, and study whatever it was we'd be doing.

Intimacy was going up really slowly at level 4, hell, even at level 3. The girls had become much stronger thanks to the gods' little gift, and they'd last even longer than usual, which would keep us busy all night.

The dwarves and the elgar had built Benny and Danara a home of their own out near Garm Village, where they'd moved out to stay all the time. They visited every day, would stay for a few hours, and would then go back to keep the place safe. Red, the war gryphon, had gotten his gear on the first day. On the second, he'd outgrown it thanks to him leveling up so quickly. Benny had fed him some of the upgrader material and he'd shot to level 10, after which he'd eaten some more and soon hit level 25. After his evolution, he had needed a new set of gear, which Grom and Nalgid happily made him. Red was big enough to easily carry me and two of the girls on his back now.

Mortimer was busy identifying everyone's gear, and once he finished with the soldiers, the old merchant started cranking through the stockpile in the guild storage. A few pieces had been interesting, but nothing came close to my own armor, so I didn't bother laying claim to it. Merek, on the other hand, was now a beast in his own right. The set he wore made him nearly invulnerable to physical attacks, but he had very little magical resistance capabilities. Luckily for us, the animus were mostly physical fighters with a much smaller number of beles, cardes, and deces being able to harm him.

Nalgid, Ferid, and Banxi had worked on building a small shipyard that could handle Mano's ship. The plan was to expand it so that at least forty people could easily fit in the hold, to make room for a better generator, which the two dwarves promised they could upgrade, and to provide platforms on which Elvina would be able to set up portable siege weapons and things like the bolt launchers.

Garm, mostly thanks to the soldiers who'd risen in levels and become much stronger thanks to their newly acquired classes, was rebuilt and reinforced quickly. When the soldiers weren't busy fighting monsters they helped in the rebuilding effort by cutting down lumber, stacking stockpiles, gathering stones and helping out with some of the carpentry work. The palisades were growing in size and height, as well as sturdiness. Thanks to the widened wall, there was enough space to build all kinds of defensive measures. Elvina had been busy most of the days and even evenings trying to fortify the place as much as she possibly could.

The civilians had started farming the surrounding land, planting crops and even the saplings I'd gotten back in the Greystone harbor. The fruits grew very quickly and didn't even need much sun or water. The villagers called it magical weed because it grew back so quickly. To top it all off, they were almost considered a weed in a way as they grew so quickly.

The vast amounts of grains and other food that had previously been stored in Balan Village were now part of Garm Village's stocks. The market was open, people were butchering animals for meat, tanning the hides, baking bread and pastries, mending clothes, and doing everything in between.

"I tell you, economics is going to become an issue very soon," Sonya said, sitting in my lap. We were all seated in the first pew of the temple.

A company of soldiers from Garm walked out of the temple chatting animatedly. Their gear was broken in, holes and tears covered their armor, and blood had dried on their skin. Yet none of them had any open wounds.

Emma and Najla did a great job at healing and buffing groups of soldiers returning from the monster farm. The men saluted us respectfully and then headed north back to their village.

Najla and the recently evolved Merek, sat in the other isle, while my girls had gathered around me and on my lap. They were like leeches vying for my attention, and at moments it was becoming a bit much, but I vowed to endure all the...good stuff as well as the other good things such a union brought. Hell, who was I even kidding?

"That one looked cute," Jeanette said, nodding toward the soldiers leaving and elbowing me.

"Uh-huh," I muttered grinning. Her jabs were harmless but persistent and I learned to not give them much attention.

I turned back to Sonya.

"And how do you want to solve that issue of economics?" I asked as she leaned into me and put an arm around me.

"We need to mint coins or use whatever they already have. People won't want to trade meat for bread or fruit all the time."

"Wait, why don't we let Mortimer take care of that?" Emma asked. "He's got enough knowledge to come up with something good and fair. Right?"

"She's got a point," Sonya responded. "Mortimer and Callina both. They've been running his shop together, so she can be of help as well."

I nodded in agreement. It was something I really didn't want to bother myself with. Only two days separated us from Balog's invasion, or one day if he decided to try and catch us off guard.

"What about you, Najla? Do you want to meddle in economics?" I asked, looking over at the prophetess. She and

Merek seemed to have hit it off very well, though I knew from a reliable source he was being a gentleman and waiting for her to propose the next step.

"No, I'm good. I need to have mass soon again, and honestly, having five or six of them daily is all I can really take for now."

"Agreed. We don't want her to overdo it," Merek said protectively.

"Oh, will you look at that!" Selene laughed. "Brother Merek is acting all protectively. That's so cute."

"Shut it, Selene. Pardon the language, Cade."

I waved it off, knowing very well Merek and Selene had been very close way before we ever met. I learned to look past that a while ago. He had no interest in her, at least not as a man would in a woman. Matter of fact, I appreciated their relationship. Selene didn't have many friends from her former life, and Merek was one hell of a guy to have on your side.

"We'll have to name him something like grand minister of finances," Emma chuckled. "Damn...I'm pretty sure he'd jump into it face-first."

"Totally," I laughed, already imagining him in a suit and a few youngsters carrying his books. "Anyway, Merek, you've hit level 60, right?"

"I have. You already asked once."

"Indeed, but the showdown is inching closer. I would like you to take on one of the arbiters by yourself. Maybe the weakest one? What was her name again? I'm sure it was something like Vestibule? Ventil?"

"Vestila," Sonya said, her face set into a frown. "You need to start remembering things better. She's weaker than Pelis was. Well, according to him and you."

"Yes, right. Vestila. Maybe the girls could provide support? I would take on that Balog guy, while Benny and Danara could hit the other...what was his...it was similar to yours I think?"

"Yeras," Sonya muttered. "He's just a bit weaker than

Balog. And then there's the danger of a sixth arbiter since they already know about Pelis. And the army. You can't focus on beating the big bad guys if you need to fight the small fry as well."

"Alright, yeah, then Merek would definitely need to take care of one by himself. Legs could just trample the animus and go for the higher-ranked soldiers, using his great size to an advantage. Everyone else would man the walls and provide support."

"Even the soldiers?" Merek asked. "The new ones?"

I nodded. They should be level 25 by tomorrow, all of them since they've been fighting monsters in groups, sharing the experience points. Also, the buffs our prophetess provided were insanely powerful for leveling up. Remembering I hadn't checked it for a while, I pulled the dungeon stats up.

- The Minor Guild Dungeon, Level 4 (699/10,000), will keep spawning monsters at a rate of 1 per minute and up to 130 in total.
- The level of summoned monsters ranges anywhere from 25 to 38.
- The rarity of summoned dungeon monsters ranges from common, uncommon, rare, to mini boss.
- The monsters can drop level 1 or 2 monster cards, equipment with 1 or 2 enhancements, upgrade materials, and monster ingredients used for crafting.

- The Major Guild Dungeon, Level 4 (101/5,000), will keep spawning monsters at a rate of 1 per minute and up to 85 in total.
- The level of summoned monsters ranges anywhere from 40 to 58.
- The rarity of summoned dungeon monsters ranges from common, uncommon, rare, mini boss, and mini bounty.

- The monsters can drop level 1, 2, or 3 monster cards, equipment with 1, 2, or 3 enhancements, upgrade materials, monster ingredients used for crafting, and War Beast Eggs.

Not much had changed, but just enough to see the monsters were being farmed every moment of the day. That is exactly what we needed in the long run. Aside from the two exterior guild dungeons, we had three that provided us with random monster ingredients, upgrader items, and favor points. Those were being run constantly, refilling our stocks of upgrader materials and monster parts.

"So, what about us?" Jeanette asked. "I'm not sure if we should fight them near Garm. Things could get out of hand real quickly and the village would suffer."

I smiled and shot her a wink.

"The plan is to intercept them before they arrive," I said confidently. There was something I'd already planned for, and I couldn't wait to see it in action.

"Then...why are you bolstering Garm Village?" Jeanette asked. "It doesn't make sense, right? Wasting resources."

"No, it doesn't," Sonya mused thoughtfully.

"Well, I never planned to let them get to Garm anyway. Banxi and his sons have reported scouts. I want them to think that we're preparing for a siege. Don't worry, everything will be just fine. All I needed from Merek was to hear that he would take on one of the arbiters."

"And he will or I'll kick his ass!" Selene snapped at him. "Rare class—"

"Enough," I said, staring into her eyes. "Merek, what is your class, anyway? I never asked after you evolved."

"A Death Lancer. It's a class very similar to yours. Most of my skills stayed the same, but they now add debuffs like disarming opponents, lowering their speeds and power, and things like that. I can fight against bigger crowds just as well as against a single opponent."

"Death Lancer, huh?" I said with a hint of excitement. "We'd be a perfect duo then."

His mostly stoic expression turned into that of anticipation.

"I wouldn't mind trying it out. Anyway, what does Banxi say?"

"About their movement? They should be here soon."

Sonya slapped my shoulder, and the other girls joined her.

"What? Soon? When did you even plan on telling us?"

"Hey, stop hitting your husband, you wretched little things! Do you want to hurt me?"

"No, we just want to—" Emma started to say when Jeanette hissed.

"Yes, we do! You can't expect a lady to go into battle without doing her hair and make-up!"

"I think he can, Jeanette," Selene said. "But we also reserve the right to pay him back. After things are taken care of. Right?"

I sighed, getting to my feet and pushing them off me.

"We need to take care of the monsters in the lake, or well, the one big monster that could try and destroy the boat. Any takers?"

"Hell no!" Sonya shouted.

"You tell him!" Jeanette added.

"Do you really want everyone to see our wet bodies?" Emma asked. She and Selene seemed more amused than anything.

"Fine, fine. I'll send Legs in there to draw the monster out. Merek? You in? But we'll need to fight it in the forest or the water. I don't want their scouts to see our capabilities. Well, yours. They've already gotten word back about my powers."

Merek nodded thoughtfully.

"Shouldn't the dome hide us from prying eyes?"

"From outside eyes, Merek," Najla said, confirming. "Not

those from inside the dome, and we luckily have an option to extend that to Garm as well, but we'll need to build a small temple there as well. I proposed to turn the manor house into one, so we'll see."

"Whatever the case, I want the ship to support us during battle. Everyone's doing their best to make it ready as soon as it can be, so I have faith," I said, already looking forward to deploying our little Deathstar as Benny called it. I had no idea what it was other than that it had a lot of firepower, which was basically the same thing I had in mind.

Merek stretched and cracked his knuckles.

"Want to do it right now? I've got nothing better to do."

"I want to watch from a distance," Emma said, poking my shoulder with a finger.

"Sonya should fight as well," Jeanette said. "She has lightning spells and she can deflect—"

"Why don't we all fight then?" I mumbled. "The whole point is to keep you—"

"Safe? Yeah, we're past that, love," Sonya laughed. "We've been in so many life and death situations, that I don't think you have any right to decide that for us. Also, we're much stronger than we used to be back in Greystone. Most of us are almost level 60, we got some new cards, gear, spells, and then there's you guys. It's just one monster."

I sighed, annoyed she had bested me again. The whole protecting them thing was getting old, I had to agree. They were much stronger than I gave them credit for, so yes, they should join to make it as easy as possible.

"Benny? Can you send Legs over?" I asked over the leadership room. *"Say have him meet us halfway to New Greystone? I want him to dive and get that monster hiding in the deep out."*

"Oh, oh, oh! I want to see too! And why didn't you ask him yourself over the chat?"

I paused for a moment. Chat? That was a new way of using a word for speaking to someone.

"What do you mean?"

"Back where I'm from, we call it chat. In games and stuff. Leadership room and battle room and stuff are so outdated, bro."

"So...chat? Alright. You heard the guy, he prefers the word chat."

"Hell yeah, man! So, can I come?"

"Elvina? Can you control the defensive weapons from afar?" I asked, shifting the conversation to something more important.

"I can, why? Do you want me to come too?"

"Yes. Maybe you could put up a trap or two before we lure it out? We can have a big party here. Roast some fish once we're done?"

"Oh, oh! Gangbang! That's so awesome!" Benny chimed in again, and he sounded very excited.

"Gangbang?" Emma asked. She wasn't the only one confused by yet another new word.

"That's when you have—oh, wait, that's not...a good word. Never mind. We'll be there soon! At the small outcrop?"

"Yes, the outcrop. And hurry up."

A while later, we met up with Benny, Danara, and Elvina who were all riding on top of Legs' back. The spider screeched happily, even holding one of his front limbs up so Elvina could lean against it.

Merek, the girls, and I were already waiting impatiently. I wanted to see what kind of monster it was as we'd never really gotten a good look. All I knew was that it came close to Legs in size but was double as long.

"We start right away," I said as they dropped off the War Weaver's back. Benny and Danara transformed, and Elvina hurried over to a spot between two large trees where she started setting something up. The rest of the girls joined her after casting buffs on everyone.

I had to admit I was both anxious and excited to get the

monster out so we could focus on more important matters like getting ready for Balog. My situation back in Greystone had been different than it is now. Back then I was a nobody, a mid-level plague revenant who had barely risen above the average adventurer stuck in a war with hundreds of thousands of other soldiers and adventurers, but now? Now *I* was the driving force behind this battle and the main actor. As such, I would do anything I could to make sure they didn't hurt any of the people I'd promised to protect.

"Legs, you can go," I said, patting his long front limbs with both hands. He screeched happily and jumped into the water with a loud splash. The spider floated there for several seconds before it started dropping toward the bottom of the lake.

"Benny, keep in touch with him. I want to know if anything—"

A massive blast of mana struck the surface of the lake, and Legs came flying, hitting the shore. Jets of water appeared in the air, floating and swirling erratically. More and more water rose as Legs tried to get away from whatever he'd disturbed. The odd thing was how I hadn't expected anything to come out almost immediately. Maybe they would fight a bit at the bottom of the lake, but not like this.

Two orange, stalky eyes appeared from the water, blinking and moving from side to side as if taking us all in. A flat head rose next, just as orange as the eyes but with a hint of red blotches spread out. It looked just like the carapace of crustacean and beetle-like monsters.

One of the jets of water flew toward us, dissipating as Merek caught it on his shield. My debuffs activated then, and I could feel a great pull at my mana.

```
You have inflicted the (Corrosion)
    debuff on the Torrent Ancient...

You have inflicted the (Dark Presence)
    debuff on the Torrent Ancient...
```

The debuff and buff list went on for several lines, and since I already knew them by heart, I just pushed it aside. I found it interesting that almost all debuffs took root, and that in turn caused something unexpected to happen. The Torrent Ancient, as the monster was called, dove back under the water. I never got to see what would have come next as Benny launched himself on top of the head, releasing his blood mist and freezing the water around him and the monster almost instantaneously. I knew he would need to recover once the battle was over, and the question was if he'd be able to do that in time to fight the arbiter, but in the worst case, Legs would probably be able to handle it by himself.

"Benny, don't get hurt," I said over the chat, as he'd wanted us to call it. "Finish it quickly or get the hell out! I want to see Merek fight as well!"

"No way, bro! That bastard hurt Legs! I'm killing its ass and—oh, wait, Red! You need to finish it off, man! Wait until it's almost dead!"

I sighed and walked over to a nearby rock, sat down, and stared at the lake. So much for seeing the Death Lancer in action...

CHAPTER 28 – THREE LITTLE KILLERS

Killing the monster wasn't as easy as Benny thought it would be. I could have told him right away that fighting something in its own habitat was foolish at best, but he wouldn't have listened anyway.

The ice holding the torrent trapped cracked with a resounding boom, sending chunks of ice flying in all directions, including ours. Merek charged toward the girls, raising his shield in protection. Several of the chunks hit the kite shield but didn't do any other harm.

"Ahh! It's pulling me under! Help me, bro!"

"Fucking hell, Benny! Merek, do you have any aggression skills?"

He nodded and rushed toward the shore, where Benny was struggling with two tentacle-like extensions. A beam the size of my fist erupted from Merek's shield and hit the crustacean's head. The Blood Beast was forgotten right away as the monster climbed on top of the largest chunk of ice and then hurled itself at the shore.

I shot back to my feet as the thirty-foot-long crab-like monster landed just short of Legs, who didn't even seem as large anymore. The War Weaver let out a deafening screech and jumped toward the Torrent Ancient, landing with his spiked feet right on top of the monster. The carapace cracked, but the crab monster wasn't even showing any signs of slowing down. It used its scissor-like pincers to cut through one of Legs' limbs, but the spider didn't give up on its assault.

Blue and red flames gathered around its body and

covered all the remaining legs. The ancient's carapace head and back started to smelt from the insanely powerful fire Legs had produced. Gelatinous blobs of a web-like substance shot out from his mouth, gluing the crab in place.

Merek joined in on the fighting, opening up with the red beam attack again, just to make sure the enemy was focused on him and not anyone else. Several of the water jets that had remained floating over the lake shot out at us, slicing through a nearby copse of trees and the soil.

A lightning bolt struck the creature and a part of its carapace cracked loudly. The trap Elvina had laid earlier came to life then as well, releasing a massive ballistae-like bolt with a drilled tip that spun at incredible speed. The moment it made contact with the side of the Torrent Ancient, the drill tip started digging deep, not losing momentum for several seconds, after which it exploded, ripping out an approximate five-by-five foot hole.

Merek used the opportunity and slid past the tentacles and scissor-like appendages that were swinging in all directions, trying to get rid of Legs and now Benny who had managed to get back on land. The Death Lancer's weapon glowed for a moment as he pulled it back, and then unleashed a flurry of attacks that were almost too fast for the eyes to see. Every jab ripped out more of the carapace, flesh, and bones.

Legs jumped into the air on its five remaining limbs, angling and gathering them downward, creating a sword tip that sliced into the monster's back. Benny hurled himself at the head where some of the carapace had broken off and started biting and clawing, absorbing blood and using his mist to freeze the insides.

Merek lunged back, evading another claw swipe, and lifted his spear over his shoulder, pulled it back as the weapon glowed again. The spear expanded and grew three or four times the size, I couldn't quite say, and threw it at the hole in the monster's side. By then I knew it was already done. The overwhelming mana pressure dissipated quickly and then the

Torrent Ancient deflated, falling to the ground, dead.

"Yeah, so...it only makes sense that nothing can really stand against us," I said over the chat because they probably couldn't hear me. *"Benny, stop eating the head. I want it as a—wait, can we even make a trophy out of that?"*

"It's tasty, bro! Like really good food and stuff."

The backside of the monster suddenly exploded, but not with power. It was more like a popping wart.

"Gross!" Emma and Sonya cried in unison.

"Oh, oh! What if a million tiny torrents come pouring out of its backside?" Jeanette said, excited by the notion of more fighting. Aside from Sonya and Elvina's drill-bolt, none had gotten a single hit in. Me included.

I faded up onto the creature's back to see what had happened and noticed a small group of eggs sticking from what looked like the monster's lower back. Many were crushed, but a few were still intact.

"Oh, this is good!" I said, using the chat as I dropped to where the eggs were. *"You will all want to see this."*

I checked the dozen or so eggs and only three of them seemed intact and were pulsing with mana. A strange thing happened then as they started absorbing the Torrent Ancient's corpse. Legs loomed high above me, staring down at the eggs and screeching excitedly as if knowing what was going on. Benny dropped next to me then and laughed.

"Hey! I know what those are! War Beast eggs!"

"No shit, smartass," I muttered. "What else would they be?"

"No, you don't get it, bro! I can hatch them! Ohh, let me at them!"

The big, hairy werewolf as he called himself, even though it made all of us rather uncomfortable, pushed past me and lowered his hand on the first egg. All three were red with orange and white hues spread out. More of the Torrent Ancient disappeared as the eggs seemingly absorbed everything but the carapace and the skeleton.

"Break, little one!" Benny said, raising his voice dramatically. It sounded very unnatural and guttural. The girls and Merek joined us just as the shell cracked and a baby Torrent appeared from within. The second and third followed right after. They made strange bubbly and clicking noises. Other than their size, they looked identical to their dead parent.

"This is awkward," I said, looking around the group. "We just killed their mother, and they seem pretty happy."

"I'm their new mommy, bro! Red calls me daddy, but I don't mind either way. I'm very flexible when it comes to my children."

I groaned, shaking my head.

"Well, Daddy, they absorbed all the freaking useful flesh. What now?"

"Now? We grow them! They could become like guardians for us in this lake, bro! Protect the ship, the bridge down southeast, and stuff."

"And stuff. Alright, this is totally not what I'd expected would happen. Now you got three more...kids? Danara will need to play the mother full-time."

"Everything for my dear Benny," she said, trying to put her arm around him. "But don't you think you're moving a bit too fast, dear? There's Legs, Red, and now...what are you going to call these three?"

I stashed the monster skeleton and carapace away in the guild storage, feeling a great weight fall over me. The storage was mostly full, and now with the extra weight and space, I was becoming encumbered by it all.

"Freddy, Michael, and Jason! They're going to be killers, I tell you!"

Everyone stared at him questioningly, even the three crablings. Benny didn't seem to mind, though. He just looked fascinated by it all.

"How are you going to feed them? Fish every day?"

"Fish? What are you talking about, bro? Upgraders."

Now it was my turn to give him the blank look.

"Seriously? You want to use all our upgraders? Just how many did you use on Red?"

"Oh, I don't know," he mumbled, scratching his chin and looking away. "About a hundred so far?"

I sighed and shook my head.

"Alright, whatever. If you weren't my little brother I'd kick your ass, but once we've taken care of our problems, I need you to do some dungeon runs and farm upgraders. We'll need a ton more, and the soldiers just aren't doing a good job because they keep...getting hurt."

"Yeah, yeah, don't worry about it, bro. Danara, can you carry one? I'm afraid I'll crush them all if—Legs? I'm sorry, okay, but this is not the time or place—no! I don't like you less than—Come on, man! What are you even—Legs! No! Don't you dare—Alright! Fine!"

The spider kept making hissing noises at Benny as they argued back and forth but ultimately calmed down.

"Okay, I don't want to be present when you two fight, so we're going back to the village," I said, patting one of Legs's limbs. "Good fight, big guy. Keep an eye on Benny, he's getting enamored with shiny...things."

Legs let out a happy screech, and then nudged the Blood Beast with his front leg. He crouched down so Benny, Danara, Red, and the three newcomers climbed on, and they steadily moved toward Garm Village. Everyone was silent for a long moment, even when they were far enough not to overhear anything. Jeanette, as usual, broke the silence.

"Now that was awkward. They're like a bickering couple."

"He reminds me of you," Emma chuckled. "Always clingy and annoying. But not that Legs is annoying, he's a good boy. It's just you."

Jeanette stuck her tongue out and grabbed my right arm.

"Whatever you say, goldy-locks."

A headache was starting to set in. I needed some rest

from everything and everyone. Maybe a few days out in the mountains just by myself? I'd have to see once we 'pacified' the region.

"Let's head back. I want to see how far they're done with the ship."

Sometime later, Elvina and I checked up on the dwarven, elgar, and goblin undertaking. The ship was much bigger than last time I was on board, easily having gained another ten feet or so in width and over thirty in length. It had also gained a new raised platform, which was encased in a palisade-like wall made of wood and monster bones. Something about having the high ground and stuff...

The dwarves were yelling, the goblins were yelling, and the elgar were yelling. It was definitely heated, but Mano wasn't having any of their crap. From what I gathered the minute we stood there, they were trying to decide on what kind of protection to put on the shield generator. And not just that, they wanted to get rid of the masts entirely and use a mana engine, something Banxi had been working on since he learned about the powers that mana offered. Mano wasn't sure, which brought everyone to the shouting match.

"May I make a suggestion?" I said, raising my voice enough so the dwarves closest to me could hear. "Why don't you take the generator and the shield to the hold? Build an extremely durable room around them with enough room for one or two people to maintain them. That way it can only go down with the ship and won't get knocked out by area-of-effect spells and attacks."

Everyone stopped what they were doing, and so did the arguing. They turned to face me and some glared, while others stared with flat expressions.

"Boss," Nalgid said, clearing his throat. "That's not so simple, you know? It would take us a few days. I thought you wanted it done today."

"Well, yes, but just note it down for once we're done with the arbiters and the duke. I don't want such an important piece of—" I said and stopped for a moment. If I insulted the ship by calling it just an item or something, first Mano would probably get pissed, and then the rest as well. "Let's just say, it's one of the most important things we have. We can't risk an unlucky shot or attack to disable it. That would mean the death of...how many people fit on board now?"

"Over a hundred," Grom said proudly. "With the addition of the engine, we could expand it much more than we originally planned, boss. See?" He asked, pointing at the platform above. "Thirty people just there. It's spacious enough to even sleep on the ground if necessary, and we will do something to help with the elements as well."

Elvina raised her hand and waited for me to address her, which was unusual. She spoke over others, or at least tried to when she thought something was important enough.

"What is it, my dear?" I asked, and she let out a little gasp as if having forgotten we were married now.

"I—wait, umm...the weapons platform on the side over there, could we make it bigger if we make counter ballast on the other side?"

"Let me say that ye are very perceptive, lass," Nalgid said with a grin. "We can, and that's what we planned te do, but we need more time."

"And ballast. It doesn't make sense to put just anything there," Grom said. "We will need to—no, Miss Elvina will need to come up with a weapon that is useful."

"Bomb thrower," Banxi cackled. "Something big, like a catapult! Or maybe even a ballista with a drill that can get through armored targets. Once the projectile punches through, the bomb detonates and blows everything up! Brilliant, yes, quite brilliant if you ask me! We could attack walls and fortified buildings and—"

"Banxi, hold on," I said, raising a hand to stop him. "I'm not going to indiscriminately attack targets and kill civilians."

316

"We can keep it to a minimum, you know, I could tweak the destructive force and—"

"Banxi, not now," I said. "We can talk about that later and—no, wait, will this have any effect on the other arbiters? Can you tell me what their weaknesses are?" I wondered whether Banxi was building a contraption that was designed to counter the Order's officers or whether he was just trying to set as many things on fire as possible.

The goblin Mokra Clan patriarch puffed his chest out proudly and put both hands on his hips.

"He asks if I *can*. Of course I can! But...I have no idea. Those kinds of things are kept a secret," he said dramatically, waving me off. "You know, there's one thing they all have in common. What exactly is that you might ask? Well, let me tell you, my good man! They are almost unkillable!"

I waited for a moment as if he was going to say more, but nothing else came out of his mouth.

"So...that's it?"

"That's it? Of course! What do you think me for? A spymaster? I'm a bomb maker! I'm a tinkerer! I'm an inventor! Not a—"

"Alright, alright. Let's get back to the matter at hand, Banxi. How long do you need to make that thing?"

He looked to Elvina, who shrugged and showed him three fingers.

"Three days!" he said hurriedly. "Wait, no, why three days?" he asked, staring at her.

"Three hours, Banxi. Three hours," she replied with a sigh. She turned to the elgar, "Grom, can you extend that part over there to accommodate a...say...Banxi, how strong does the ballista need to be? I already have something I can improvise with. We would just need to adjust the bomb delivery method and—"

I tuned out and made my way off the ship. There were still a few other things I needed to take care of, like unloading the skeleton and carapace. It would have to wait as everyone was busy with the ship, but that didn't matter. It's not like the skeleton would be a decisive factor in any case.

CHAPTER 29 – ALARM BELL

The sun was already setting when the ship was finally done. The girls and I were sitting on the balcony up in Brahma's Rest, watching as they were adjusting the ballista. It was different and had what Elvina called a magazine. Benny had given her the idea, and what it did was store extra bolts so they could be rapidly deployed and released. The only problem was that any integrated bombs could blow the entire ship up, so they'd designed special springs that wouldn't let the long bolts physically touch each other.

"I'm still a bit skeptical," I said, watching as they were drinking and cleaning the mess on the deck.

"They did a good job," Elvina said. "We tried thirty times and every time the bolts slid into place. Also, we put up magical plating between the siege weapon and the deck so that if the bombs do explode, the blast should be pushed away from the ship."

"With an accent on should," Emma said. "You do know that it won't do much, right?"

"Hey, I wouldn't be so sure," Sonya chimed in. "Listen, there is a shield generator, and I can always cast a deflection spell, right?"

"So you want us to be stationed on the ship?" Emma asked. "I don't really mind, but...how do you want me to support you then?"

"You don't. The four of us take the brunt of their attack. Benny and Legs are immortal, Merek has become very powerful, and I...I can handle myself."

"I will always be by his side, so that's why I think I should hit level 60 next," Selene said, wiggling her eyebrows. The girls started laughing and so did I. It just looked ridiculous.

"You or Jeanette, definitely, but I think you should be the one," I said after a moment of laughter. "But only to shadow me, alright?"

"And suck you off when we're not looking," Jeanette mumbled, pushing the side of her cheek with her tongue and making slurping noises.

"Really?" Sonya smirked. "Then why don't you do it right now? That way no one will be jealous while he's away."

"I...no, I mean yes, but not with all of you watching. It's embarrassing," Jeanette protested.

"Really? And it isn't when you squirt all over the place? Someone always needs to clean your mess. You know that, right?"

"Sonya!"

"Jeanette!"

The two glared at each other, huffing and puffing.

"Okay, no one's going to be sucking...anything. I think that they're really going to do as we asked and show up on the last day. Or the night before," I said with a hint of worry. "That night is tonight. We need to be ready for anything."

"Tonight?" Sonya asked taken aback by my words. I nodded trying to force a smile on my face.

"*Hey, boss, what do you want to do with the ship now that it's done?*" Nalgid asked over chat. "*We can push it out into the water if you want. It won't do much good sitting here.*"

"*You're right, but I'm not sure either. What if—hey, how hard is that thing to operate? The ballista? And the ship?*" I asked as an idea struck me.

"*Pretty easy. There are two levers. One is for loadin' and te other for shootin! Who ye want on there?*"

"*What about having one of yours on the ballista? Or the elgar? I wouldn't mind asking Grom to—*"

"*No! We will do it, don't ye give me that I'll ask the elgar*" *crap! I thought ye had a better opinion of me."*

"Nalgid, don't get all dramatic on me. So you'll have one of your own there?"

"Yes, I will. And I'm not dramatic, I want ye to trust me!"

I sighed inwardly. Their bickering sometimes really got on my nerves, but they got the job done. In the end, that's why I respected them all, not how well they could drink or roar drunkenly.

"We won't have enough people to man the ship yet. The soldiers are far from ready, but that will change over the next weeks. We'll handpick long-ranged attackers and a small group of defenders."

Nalgid remained silent for a moment, but I could see he was speaking to his kin and Ferid.

"Why are you silent? Talking to someone?" Emma asked, putting her hand on mine and squeezing. I turned to her and winked.

"Nalgid. Just give me a minute."

"What does he want now?" Elvina grumbled. "Did he break something? I swear, if he did then—"

"Alright, so, we will take care of the ship. Our wives and daughters all use some form of long-range attacks, and our sons can keep them safe. We can man the ship for you and make sure it doesn't get overrun or destroyed if your ladies are on board."

"Hold on," I replied, wanting to discuss it with the girls first. "Nalgid wants his whole family to be on ship duty. I can't put just them there, or it will look as if I'm trying to give them the most secure of places. If no one's there to protect New Greystone, they could destroy it by the time we're done fighting, but at least everyone will be on the ship...the elgar and goblins included."

"I agree," Sonya said. "There's no safer place than the ship. I don't think they have long-range attacks as we do. Elvina can make sure the weapons are in top condition and working as planned while you and the boys take care of the arbiters."

"Sure, why not," Jeanette said half-absently. Her cheeks and ears were red, so I figured she was thinking about something inappropriate. As always.

"I'm taking the monster spawns for the next few hours. Maybe I get lucky and level up," Selene said, shooting to her feet and hurrying off.

"And then it was just me," Emma chuckled, seeing the elf lunging from the balcony. "Yes, I agree, but this one last time. And yes, I know, we said that many times already, but...I don't want to stay behind anymore and let you take on all the burden."

I cupped her cheek and pulled her in for a kiss, fully able to understand her feelings, but I didn't think she was being reasonable.

"Babe, it all depends on your survivability. If you can take the hits, feel free to go to town on the enemy, but you need to—"

"Get much stronger, yes, I know," she said defeatedly. "Anyway, the ship looks pretty cool, you know? They've made it into a floating fortress."

I nodded, beyond satisfied with the work of craftmanship myself. They had gone all out and used a lot of special materials they'd brought with them from Greystone, as well as a lot of the monster parts we'd appropriated from the Adventurers' Guild. The big bones and the spines and other parts had been merged using techniques I knew nothing about. Why would I? The only hammer I'd ever used in my life was one to smack a nail into the wall.

"So, let's do this the smart way. Now, what if—"

The tower bell rang just one time. It was a thing Banxi had added early in the morning to make sure we had a physical way to hear important announcements. A message through our chat followed next. It was the goblin speaking.

"Mugra said that he spotted enemy movement near Tazul, right across the lake! They've split into two groups with the larger going north toward Znica and the smaller around the lake toward

the bridge."

I felt an immediate headache setting in. What I hadn't expected was for them to separate into two groups. It threw my plan out the window. Still, that wouldn't change the end result, it would only force me to exert greater effort.

I didn't like the whole react to the enemy thing, but it's what we'd set up and it was time to respond accordingly.

"We prepared for this. Stay level-headed and follow commands," I replied over the guild chat so everyone could see. *"Tell me what he sees. How many are going south? What are they? The Duke's army, or the arbiters? How many arbiters? Can he make out?"*

As I waited for them to get back with what they saw, I spoke to the girls.

"I'm taking Merek south. Everyone else gets on that boat and you go to Garm. If they arrive before I return, have Benny and Legs engage them in turns, not both at once. They can die if both are severely wounded at the same time."

"I don't like it," Jeanette said. "Maybe it's a trap to lure you out. They should know about Banxi's tower."

"Knowing about it and what it actually does are two different things. Let me ask him."

"Banxi? Do they know what your tower does? And that you can see so far?"

"Never! I never told them anything! The bastards, they wouldn't let me build any bombs within the city! That's why I never told them anything, and I never will! Just imagine if—oh, wait. So, umm, fool! Tell them directly! Why are you telling me first?"

He was obviously talking to his son, which made it okay, but I preferred to keep the cursing and dressing down of youngster goblins out of the chat.

"You crazy old goblin! Don't you yell at me! You're like a slavedriver! I haven't slept in days and now you even berate me? What gives you the right to—"

"Shut up! I'll rip your ears out, you impudent little—start talking before I climb up there and teach you a lesson!"

"Can you two shut up? Kid, what was your name again?"

"Mugra."

"Mugra, tell me what you see. Come on, time is of the essence. Everyone else, prepare the ship. I want everyone to prepare for battle and take the ship to Garm so you can support Benny's group and the soldiers there."

The kid goblin took a moment before he spoke, sounding much more mature than I knew he was.

"Bossman, I see one heavily armored and big guy. He is almost as big as that hairy God Beast of ours, Benny, but fully clothed in armor."

"Clad in armor, you shit! Clad, not clothed!" Banxi interrupted.

"Banxi, shut up, please," I said, losing patience. *"Grom, can you slap him for me if he interrupts again?"*

The elgar raised his hand with a thumbs up, knowing I would see him. Thanks to the Third's Eye, I could.

"Bossman, that armored-clad guy looks dangerous. He has a big, big hammer, and a big big shield on his back. Also, all the others are those animus everyone is talking about. They are fully armored and armed, but there aren't that many. I reckon only a thousand."

I snorted, almost choking on air.

"A thousand animus isn't a small group, Mugra. How big is the other group?"

"Hmm, give me a moment, boss man. Let me do this and— okay. So, it is about ten times as large. Yes, I think so."

"Are you sure? You don't even know how to count, son," Usvee said.

"Ma! I know what a big army is, I promise!"

Great. We had a goblin that couldn't count telling me the size of an army. Alright, that was good. The more animus there were, the longer it would take for them to reach Garm.

"Thanks, you did good. Keep an eye on both groups, okay? I will reward you once the battles are over."

The girls sighed collectively and muttered things I

324

couldn't hear as I was focused on the chat. I felt the same way they did, but there were only two things we still needed to do. The first was to destroy these armies, and the second was to take Volarna City.

"Okay, boss man. Thank you!"

I could see Banxi was protesting about something to Grom, who just shrugged and pointed at his mouth.

"Banxi, what is it?"

"I'm not leaving my offspring behind! You—oh, wait. That's the safest place to be once the southern group has been killed. Okay, I will busy myself with more important matters like making sure we have enough bombs."

The goblin was definitely an odd one, and I could already imagine a grinning Benny. He was probably happy to be out of Banxi's way.

"Merek, meet me at the southern gate. Everyone else, drop whatever you're doing and get to the ship."

"Get to the choppa!" Benny said, finally breaking his silence. It had been odd having him keep back so long, but maybe he'd just been sleeping. From personal experience, I knew he could sleep through chats popping up in his mind, but this was another level entirely. It had probably been Legs or Danara waking him up. Maybe even Red.

"Choppa?" I asked, unsure if I even wanted to know what it meant. *"Never mind. Benny, prepare for battle. I hope Red and your little babies have eaten their fill. They could be pretty useful at level 25."*

"About that, bro, we're not quite there yet, but I can guarantee that they should be ready within the day."

"I don't doubt it at all, Benny. Good job. What did you do with the three little killer crabs?"

"Nothing. They're splashing in the water, practicing how to control water jets and killing monsters. All three can already use them to cut through trees and rocks. Gifted little beauties."

"So you've been working very hard huh? That's good. What levels are they?"

"Around 23. I think they'll hit 25 within the hour if they keep hunting monsters in the water. Why? What is it? Is it happening?"

I explained the situation to him quickly, and if I was any closer, I'd probably be able to see him straighten up and take his charge seriously. Once I explained what I wanted him to do and the ship's firepower, he became excited, which was something I'd already expected. That's why I kept it for last.

"If your three little sons or daughters, or whatever they are, manage to get to level 25 and evolve before the army attacks, I want them protecting the ship. Can you do that?"

Benny didn't respond right away, but I knew he'd do just as I asked. What bothered me was if he eventually got his hands on even more God Beasts, he could become dangerous or stop following orders or requests. I sincerely doubted it, but power had a way of clouding the mind. The little pangolin from back in Greystone's alley had come a long way, and I just hoped that he wouldn't stray from his path. I genuinely liked him and his antics.

"We will do whatever we can to protect Garm, the ship, and the people, bro. But I want to talk to you about something once we've killed all the bad guys. Can you do that?"

"I can, Benny. Look, I need to go now and intercept that other group. Keep me updated once the army arrives and if the torrents evolve. I'll do my best to be there before they make it, though."

I stretched my arms and legs, cracked my neck, and then kissed each of my ladies. They were torn about not being able to go with me, and so was I as many things could go wrong with the ship, but it would be over one way or another.

"Protect each other, alright? No petty squabbles, no...nothing. Just love and care," I said, embracing all four of them.

"Selene?" Emma asked.

"I'll leave her behind for now. She can get to Garm in fifteen minutes if she tries hard enough. Maybe she even levels up before the enemy arrives."

"Then it's my turn!" Jeanette said, bringing her face close to mine. I kissed her forehead and nodded.

"Whatever you say, love. Okay, I need to go. Take care of each other. I mean it."

The helfar was part of our embrace, but her ears were red and she was looking away. It was cute in a way seeing her embarrassed by a group hug.

"Elvina?"

"Y—yes?"

"You're part of us now, alright? That goes for you too. Protect your friends. And don't get hurt, please. I don't know what I'd do without you."

The girls called me out on my bullshit, but I didn't flinch and just kept my eyes on hers.

"I will. Thank you. Good luck and come back soon."

CHAPTER 30 – TELEPORTATION

Merek already waited for me at the southern gate. He was fully clad for war, even wearing a wicked-looking spear I hadn't seen before. It almost looked like a warped lance with sharp edges all along the length and a long, sharp tip.

His face was locked in a frown of steel. An expression he wore whenever killing was at hand.

"Where you got that beauty from?" I asked curiously. It exuded a lot of power, so I was wondering how he'd gotten his hands on it.

"Mortimer. He has a whole stash of unidentified weapons and armor. I picked the lance, paid, and he identified it, then wanted to haggle some more over the price when he saw how good it was."

I sighed. Mortimer never changed. He was a good man, but whenever he thought an item was more worth than his best guess, his tongue would get very loose.

"And I guess you didn't pay him?"

"Oh, I did. I gave him my previous spear. This works much better for me. I've already tried it out against the monsters out back before Selene came running over."

"Good, good," I said, rolling my shoulders and taking in a deep breath. "Let's go. There isn't much to it. We intercept the group and kill everyone and everything, then we head to Garm. You alright with that?"

Merek bowed a little and smiled.

"Lead the way, fearless leader."

We made our way south toward the guild monster spawns to check in with Selene and see how she was doing. She'd most likely read our conversations on the guild chat so I wouldn't need to explain everything from the start.

My elven beauty was sitting on a felled tree. She was panting hard, visibly tired and annoyed. One of her daggers looked as if it had chipped, but I couldn't quite see well enough as she held it out to the side.

"What happened?" I asked as we walked over to her. "What is it?"

"Hit the skull of a freaking rare monster. Chipped my off-hand dagger and tired me out much more than it should have."

"Trophy monster?"

She shook her head and shot to her feet, the irritation gone from her face.

"You're going out?"

I nodded, pulling her in for a tight hug and a kiss. She was warm, sweaty even. That showed just how hard she'd been at work killing monsters.

"Go back and get a new dagger, or have someone repair it. You can't fight well with just one good weapon, alright?"

"I have a spare. And look, I'm so close. Just a few percent off level 60. I can always catch up with them, okay? Please?"

"Sure. Don't do anything stupid. They need you."

"It's as he said, sis," Merek said with a hint of pride. "You need to take care of yourself and join me in the level 60 club. If only Giovanni could see us now, huh?"

"Bah!" she spurted. "Don't ruin my mood, Merek." Unpertrubed by Selene's words, the Death Lancer continued,

"And if he could only see how many War Beasts are walking around as if it's nothing. Hah, the oily bastard would shit his pants."

"Merek!"

"How did you even get along with this guy? Was he always this annoying?" I joked.

"No, that only happened after he joined you. Somehow I have a feeling you rubbed off on him. Now go. I know you're in a hurry. I'll catch up with the others. Just a few more minutes." She was right though. Merek wasn't one to joke around much back in Greystone. He was all duty and order, but I did like the fact he loosened up a bit.

I leaned in and kissed her again.

"Take care. Don't get hurt, okay? I love you."

"I...love you too, Cade," she whispered. Her cheeks went red almost immediately, and Merek laughed heartily.

"You've broken her, Cade. Congratulations on that."

"Ass! Just go and—"

"Die? If you want me to."

"No, I don't want you to die, I want you to go and break a leg or something after the battle's over so I can beat your ass!"

I put my hand around Selene, squeezing her ass and receiving a yelp for my trouble.

"Cade!"

"We need to go. You can beat him as much as you want when we're done. See you later, okay?"

Selene nodded and sighed.

"Stay safe. Both of you."

"Oh, she's still worried about me. Great. See you later, sis."

I shot her a wink and nodded toward the south of the lake.

"Come on. She can take care of herself."

Merek had problems keeping up with my speed, so I had to dial it down a bit. My agility and dexterity were much higher, which allowed me to jump, step, and land perfectly. The air was crisp and cool. Evening was starting to fall on the lands of Duke Volarna. Before the night was over, it would be drenched in blood, I would see to it.

This was only the second time I was going south of the

lake. The first time was when we repaired the bridge and put up a bunch of traps to make sure no one made it to the other side. Since we hadn't heard any explosions, I figured no one really had tried to make it across.

The trees surrounding the south were all cleared away for a hundred yards to allow for a better view. There was nothing of interest down there aside from a small orchard we planted, but the soil had been full of clay so we left most of the land untended.

There were no animals around, only smaller monsters that weren't harmful even to the weakest of our civilians. Given enough time, they could grow more dangerous, but the mana concentration in the land wasn't as high as it used to be in Greystone and only started to increase with our arrival.

"Hold on!" Merek called after me. "I need a minute!"

I stopped immediately. It wouldn't do if we arrived and he was tired out. Besides, we were moving much faster than any army could, even if they were soulless creatures that couldn't feel pain or get tired.

"What is it? A level 60 is already tired?"

"No, not that. I mean, yes, a little bit, but...I wanted to ask you something."

I put my hands on my hips and waited as he caught up.

"What?"

"Well, do you really love her? I mean, do you love them all?"

Now that was a question I hadn't expected to come from Merek. Maybe not from anyone, and yet it made me pause and think for a moment. Love didn't just come from the heart, it also came from the mind. It came from the small things we did for each other, our continued support and uplifting. I had all that with Emma, Sonya, and Selene. Jeanette was a bit of a wild one, mostly enjoying the sex and the kinky stuff, though I knew she cared for me dearly. Elvina was another story. We were warming up to one another, and I had no idea how well that would go. It remained to be seen.

"That's not an easy answer, Merek, and I'm not sure this is the right time."

"Come on, just give me a yes or no. Do you love them all?"

I sighed and crossed my arms, staring at him.

"Don't tell me you're fancying another lady aside from Najla."

"Well, maybe, but I'm not even sure I fancy Najla. She's a monster early in the morning. Cranky, likes to argue, and she even threw a pot at me."

I snorted, which turned into laughter.

"Alright, yeah, maybe you should stay single then, my good man, but I'll give you the short answer. Yes, I love them all in my own way. I would do anything for any of them, though, so if you're just worried about Selene, don't be. I care deeply for her and I would give my life to protect her in the blink of an eye. So, are we done here?"

He smiled proudly and offered me his hand to shake. I did so, obviously figuring he was happy with the answer.

"I'm happy I decided to come along, Cade. Even if everyone I'd ever known is probably dead, I'm happy to be part of all of this."

"I wouldn't have it any other way. Now come on. We got a battle on our hands."

We reached the bridge shortly, and everything seemed just as when we'd left it the previous time. The traps were still in place, and the bridge was intact. I focused my vision on the other side of the shore, but it was mostly obscured by tall trees and hills. I had no idea what we were about to face other than that there were about a thousand animus if the little goblin was to be trusted.

"What's the deal, boss?" Merek said. "Do you want me to take care of the soldiers?"

"No. I want you to draw the arbiter away so I can kill all the soldiers in one fell swoop. Let him feel fear, but don't get yourself killed."

He grinned, nodding.

"I like it. I really do. Mind if I kill him?"

"If you can, yes."

"Great. That's just...great. Alright. Can we cross the bridge? You mentioned traps?"

"Yeah, just follow after me."

I could see the cones and beams of light that designated the trap areas. They were easy enough to avoid if you knew where to step. They included explosions, filaments that could cut through armor and bone alike, two bolt launchers, and spikes that would rise from the bridge itself.

I navigated the traps easily enough and made sure Merek stepped only where he should. Just one of these traps could kill us both. By the time we were halfway through, I frowned, thinking myself idiotic.

"Give me your hand."

"Huh? Why?"

"Just do it."

Merek did as I said and I used Fade to jump the rest of the bridge, narrowly making it on the other side.

"Why didn't you do this right away?" he asked and I shrugged.

"I forgot that I could. Anyway, they're close by. I can hear them."

The sound of countless boots hitting the ground over and over again resounded in the distance, but was gradually becoming louder. I couldn't even begin to guess how many of them there actually were. The little goblin couldn't count. He casually threw the number a thousand around, and though I was confident I could handle such a force, I couldn't say I wasn't worried what the real number of enemies actually was.

I hurried up the nearest hill and looked out toward the northeast. A large host of animus was marching behind a really tall, bald man. He seemed to be just as large as Grommasch. As for his war host, it was easily twice as large as the duke's army when he showed up at Garm Village.

"We've got about two thousand animus here," I said over

the guild chat. *"And a really big arbiter. It might take a bit longer than I anticipated. Has everyone already gathered on the ship?"*

"Only Selene hasn't," Emma replied. *"She said she'll be here soon. We're waiting for her."*

"Alright. We're about to start our battle. I don't anticipate problems, but you never know. If we don't make it in time, bombard the enemy the moment they arrive. Don't waste time."

"Will do," Sonya replied. *"I will make sure of it. My main goal is to keep everyone from getting hit by spells, but I'm attacking them from afar as well, Cade. You can't take that away from me."*

"Never planned to, love. Good luck. Talk to you in a bit."

It was time. They hadn't noticed us as we were hidden against the backdrop of tall trees and the sun was already setting. I now knew what their plan had been, and I didn't like it at all. If they'd succeeded in catching us by surprise in the middle of the night, things could have gone badly for my friends and my family.

I eyed the approaching group for a bit. They wore similar armor and gear, as well as surcoats, which were light red with black lines. The two colors merged with each other in the fading night making it look like a tide of blood flooding the land.

The big guy was just that, a hulking apparition clad in black heavy armor and a significant mana presence. A massive hammer was swung over his shoulder. It had a broad head with small spikes on the flat side and a single large spike on the other.

"Merek?" I asked over direct chat. *"You ready?"*

"I was born ready, bossman. Or big brother. I like that one better."

"Big brother, huh? Well, little brother, since we received buffs recently, and with Najla's buff duration extender, I'm more than ready."

"Be careful. I can't stress it enough."

We clasped arms, squeezing a bit harder than it was necessary, and then readied ourselves, needing a moment to decide on approach vectors. The best way to hit them was from two sides, and that's what we did.

I rushed down the hill and veered off past the arbiter, while Merek headed straight for him.

"Get in formation! Send out the beacon and cast the spell!" the arbiter roared, swinging the hammer in a downward arc. Merek was really strong so I wasn't worried about him deflecting any blows, what did bother me were the man's words.

A blue pillar of light erupted from the backlines and started spreading as I was still making my way toward the animus. No, there were beles too, a few hundred at least from what I could see.

All my debuffs activated on their own, lowering enemy stats, accuracy, dodge, debuff effectiveness, and various resistances, while also absorbing a mass of stats from all the animus caught in the area of (Sapper) debuff's effect.

I didn't want to give them any time to finish doing whatever they were trying to do and targeted the beles back line with a [Pestilent Storm]. A storm brewed overhead, unnaturally quickly, unleashing green and purple tendrils and bolts of lightning that sent the fully armored soldiers flying in all directions and killing most of them upon first contact.

As one, the animus army turned to face me, spread out in a half-circle and charging with their weapons raised. Now, I wasn't so dumb that I couldn't see the difference between the animus of Pelis and that of this new guy with the red overcoat. These were much stronger, easily level 40 if those of Pelis were around levels 25 or 30.

Merek cried out as steel met steel. I glanced toward him, seeing the hammer retract as his shield went wide, and cursed under my breath. This guy was much stronger than I first expected. Either that or I overestimated Merek. Whatever the case, we'd find out right away.

I faded out toward him, using [Backstab]. The shield on the arbiter's back extended and covered his shoulders, deflecting both of my daggers. He still cried out because of my mana reach. Even a few inches of sharp mana piercing his skin were enough to cause him pain.

Dozens of animus charged me, slashing and stabbing with their swords and spears. I faded out of the way and upward, launching myself as high as I could to see what I'd done to the beles in the back of their formation. I targeted the same group with a [Pestilent Wave] as it had the largest area of effect. It was hard to focus on the attack as the light cones and beams were expanding and moving away from them, only to settle some hundred yards away. My attack hit then, utterly destroying the beles as something hit me in the side. It was hard and heavy with small spikes at the point of impact.

I flew over fifty feet from the arbiter's hammer blow. Merek was eating into the animus, killing them by the dozens, but there were just so many of them. My moment of weightlessness ended when [Fade] came off cooldown, and I threw myself back into the battle, unleashing my third area attack skill, [Dagger Rain] right where the enemy was thickest. Hundreds of mana daggers appeared overhead and stabbed downward, piercing anything they hit.

"Coward! Stop jumping like a monkey and come fight me!" the arbiter roared, visibly annoyed by my antics.

"I don't know about you, freak, but I first want to take care of your animus!" I shot back. "Then we can—oh shit!"

A mana blast erupted from the area where the bright beams touched the sky. Three large portals appeared, swirling with dark energy.

It can't be...

Three more arbiters stepped through each of the portals and first hundreds, but then thousands of soldiers followed. Despite having destroyed the beles, they had managed to get, what I assumed was all of the other group here within minutes.

I landed on top of an animus soldier and lunged backward.

"Merek! Pull back!"

"You don't have to tell me twice! What the hell just happened?"

I had no idea, but I sure would like to know. I'd already witnessed something similar two times before, but I had no idea they could go to this extent and teleport in such great numbers. Danara had some explaining to do.

"Hey, big boss!" Mugra said over the guild chat. *"All those soldiers disappeared! There was a big light and boom! They are gone! I can't find them. What now?"*

"Find them, you little flat-eared—" Banxi started to say but I cut him off.

"Banxi, he doesn't need to. We already found them. Or rather, they found us. This new arbiter had his beles summon the rest of the arbiters and their army. Merek and I are... fucked."

CHAPTER 31 – BATTLE BY THE BRIDGE

Merek and I hurried back toward the bridge where we'd have the best possible chance to keep them back. At least for a while. To my surprise, they didn't push hard to catch up and instead, the arbiters gathered at the front with the thousands of animus and beles marching steadily behind them. Among the sea of twisted creatures rose several large behemoths I hadn't seen before. The Order had brought their heavy weapons, cardes and deces, I realized. How would they hold up in a fight against us? It would suck if they were at the rank of that new arbiter. He sure hit hard.

I stopped at the very entrance to the bridge and checked where the nearest trap was along with what kind it was. The messages appearing in my guild chat were starting to distract me, so I went through them quickly as Merek took up a defensive position in front of me. The enemy was about 300 yards away from us and steadily marching our way so I had to be fast.

"What do you want us to do?" Emma asked.

"Speak to us!" Jeanette yelled.

"Cade, you need to talk to us. What is going on? Where do you want the ship?"

"Bro! I'm not letting you die alone! I'll be there as soon as I can! I've already sent Red over!" Benny said next.

More messages were flooding in, but I just read and pushed them aside.

"Come as close as you can to the bridge," I replied over the guild chat. *"We'll make our stand here. There's nothing else to say.*

Merek and I will last a while, but I have no idea how long. Hurry up if you don't want to see us bullied by the big bad arbiters."

I sounded much more relaxed and confident than I actually was, the whole reason being the new arbiter.

"Did he hurt you?" I asked worriedly. "That big guy hits really hard."

"Yes, he does. I saw you flying. Did he break anything?" Merek asked, glancing over his shoulder.

I shook my head and stretched in all directions, just to make sure.

"No, and then there's that shield of his. It moved on its own even on his back."

"That too. It nullified two of my attacks," he grumbled, wiping sweat off his brow. "What now?"

"Hold on," I said, checking the traps again. The closest one to where we stood were three entangled spike traps and a single bolt launcher. Those would be enough to possibly kill a few hundred, but I had a better idea.

"How many people can you provoke into attacking you?"

"I don't know. A hundred? A thousand? It is area-of-effect based, and the range is pretty large so I could technically make a good number of them attack me, but I can't survive that kind of onslaught."

"And you won't have to. We will do a little bit of cheating. Just sit tight and wait for my signal."

Minutes passed and I had to admit that I was getting anxious. Sure, our friends were on the way, but I doubted they could get here within half an hour. Benny on his lonesome? Maybe 15? And Red? I had no idea. If he was even worth anything from a fighting standpoint.

"Benny?" I said, opening a direct chat to him. "What can you tell me about Red? His fighting power at...what level is he?"

"Red is 42, bro."

I snorted. The little griffin was rising in levels even faster than Legs had back then, and I found it pretty scary. Given some time he would probably outgrow Benny considering all he'd been doing lately was chasing tail.

"And what did level 42 do to him?"

"Hah! You will see it in a bit. He can spew fire like a dragon, bro! And some other things, but we haven't really tested them out. He only evolved a few hours ago, you know?"

The enemy was about 100 yards out by now and I could feel the mass of mana radiating off them. Unlike the duke's soldiers, these were killing machines that reacted at an arbiter's mere thought. That perfect control over the animus and the other tiers was exactly what made their military force so formidable. The commander could order the entire army to move, stop, or attack with a single thought.

Seventy yards out and closing.

"Merek, you will provoke everything you can to attack you and then move into the water. It's deep, but you shouldn't drown. Then—"

The army stopped as one about thirty yards out. It was close enough that I could hit them by throwing a stone or using my debuff attack skills.

"What is it? Why did they stop?" he asked with a hint of panic.

The mixture of yellow and red overcoats was enough for my blood to start boiling. Two distinctive armies, and yet they were here, together. I took notice of the arbiters. There were four of them, including the big hammer-wielding guy. Was he perhaps from Luferson? There was only one way to find out. Beat him up and ask him...

The first out of the three was a woman, which I assumed was Vestila, she looked like she was in her thirties with short green hair and a battle dress instead of full-plate armor. She held a small crossbow in each hand.

Next was a man not older than me wearing dark armor, just like Pelis and the giant, covering most of his body including the head. He wielded dual long swords that glowed with a hint of blue light. From his back hung another weapon, but I couldn't make out what it was from the angle he stood at. I assumed this guy was Yeras, which left the final man standing just ahead of them and in the center, Balog. He was on a different level than either of the other three arbiters. A long halberd protruded from his shoulder, with a wicked sharp blade and counter spike on the opposite end. His armor was white with streaks of orange and red spread across.

"Balog," I said, raising my voice enough so the man a the front of the army could hear me. I couldn't see his face as it was hidden behind a helmet, but he was easily a head taller than both of us, but not quite as large as that giant with the hammer.

"New...strange man. I have been looking forward to seeing you," the arbiter replied, making his way toward us. It didn't look as if he had a single worry in the world. Not even us. "I see you have fallen for my trap. You're not as smart as they led me to believe."

I remained behind Merek, who stood there with his shield and lance out in front of him. Showing a hint of fear might goad the arbiters into making mistakes, and I was all about exploiting them. At least until Benny arrived, then I'd just let him rampage through their armies.

"Maybe, maybe not. Pelis certainly thought me dumb enough to sit down and have a drink with me. It was a very peculiar thing."

"Drink with...the likes of you?" Balog snapped, raising his voice. "He wasn't the brightest among us, but he was loyal!"

"And a chatter mouth. Told me all kinds of things. I even know how strong you arbiters all are."

Balog stopped about ten steps away from us and I could feel his disdain. He still couldn't believe someone like us had bested his arbiter. Sure, I cheated a little, but that wouldn't have changed the outcome, just the time it took for me to kill him.

"He begged for his life, too," Merek added, finding his courage again. "Cade here cut his head off with a single cut."

Balog just stared at us, his hand moving to the halberd

on his back, but he stopped.

"Why are you here on this land? Where did you come from? And most important of all, why are you causing trouble?" he asked, his eyes glowing behind the helmet.

"That won't do, Balog. The game I played with Pelis was called one-for-one. I ask you a question, you answer, then you ask me one, and I answer. However, I'm not sure I need anything else from you other than..." I shifted in place, narrowing my eyes on him, "Well, alright, we can play. Interested?"

I thought I'd give it a try despite Balog's obvious lack of enthusiasm for small talk. At least I'd buy some time, I hoped, but the arbiter seemed less than enthused with the idea.

Balog straightened and his hand grabbed for the shaft of his halberd again. With a deft movement, it was out and in his hands in a flash.

"You will talk one way or another, strangers. I shouldn't have listened to the Order and just wiped you out right away! Heretics should burn, after all."

The arbiter charged alone, swinging the halberd in a wide arc. I was shocked to see him advance like that by himself. After all he had an army of able bodies at his disposal. Once again, the powerful of this land showed their arrogance.

His halberd had an incredibly large range, but he wasn't alone in wielding such a weapon. Merek caught the attack on his shield and jabbed the lance forward, almost catching Balog's left arm. The arbiter twisted and jerked his weapon a tiny bit and seemingly activated a skill as the bladed side erupted with mana, hammering into Merek's shield again. He fell to a knee and almost toppled to the side as the halberd came crashing down again.

"Keep him busy for just a few minutes," I urged over our chat and faded away past the two and well out of Balog's reach.

I appeared behind Vestila, opening up with a [Backstab]. My buffs and debuffs flared up, and she froze for just a brief instant, but that was more than enough for my kris to dig deep into her shoulder.

The female arbiter cried out as a shriek overhead drew everyone's attention. Red, the armored gryffin, soared through the sky, flapping his massive wings. For a moment, I felt as if I were back on Greystone's walls and looking on at the Valtorian army as our War Beasts bombarded them with spells and magical bombs.

My danger senses flared up as something lunged for me. I slashed out with my second dagger on instinct, deflecting a yellow glowing long sword. The second slid just above my forearm but still drew blood.

I kicked out and faded toward the edge of the soldier formation, opening up with a [Pestilent Wave]. Red, at the same time, flashed overhead again, his mouth glowing red for a moment before a torrent of flames streaked at a downward angle. The magical attack bathed the enemy animus in fiery death and killed whatever was inside the armors.

A hammer blow narrowly passed by me as I unleashed a second area-of-effect attack, [Pestilent Storm], aiming it at even more soldiers. The attack only needed several short seconds to activate, and once it did, a storm unleashed on the soldiers below. They had been awfully motionless for the first ten seconds or so, but once the second attack hit, their arbiters must have ordered them to spread out and fight back.

Red streaked overhead yet again and unleashed a second flaming breath attack, and despite catching dozens in his blast along with my two attacks, we hadn't even scratched the surface. There were easily 10,000 animus present, just like the info from before had told me. With just us three fighting here, there was no way we'd last.

I took a chance as I coasted through the air and checked on Merek. Sparks erupted as Balog's halberd met Merek's shield. He was holding his own, but for how much longer? I glanced over to the lake next and still couldn't see anything. There was no way they'd make it in time.

I faded out toward the wounded arbiter and pulled two

small vials from my storage, throwing one at Vestila. The hammer-wielding arbiter pulled his shield free and protected her. Most of the acid fell away to the ground where it ate into the soil and into Vestila's boot. She cried anew and jumped out of the away as I threw another vial. Hammer caught it on his shield yet again, and it just exploded harmlessly against it.

Yeras came up from behind, darting in with both his long blades. I countered with a [Backstab] that took me toward Vestila. She was the weakest link, so I needed to get rid of her first. Hammer seemed to anticipate the move and had several of his soldiers attack at the same time, hitting my shoulder and back armor. Their attacks bounced off as my armor was way too strong for ordinary attacks to pierce it, but it prevented me from executing the arbiter. For the second time.

I used [Fade] to get out of the soldiers' midst but something pulled me out of the skill midway. A piercing pain came from my left leg as I landed on the ground. Yeras was standing over me, one blade stuck into my leg, and the other coming straight at my face.

I had to agree then that I was done fooling around. They were stronger than I had anticipated, well, some of them were, and if I kept pushing it, Merek or I might even get hurt for real. I stabbed out with my bird of prey dagger, catching Yeras in the side. Getting a foot up between him and myself, I kicked out hard and sent him stumbling off me. With a hard yank, his blade came free.

"Fucking weaklings," I cursed, activating [Dark Presence], [Plague Domain], and [Pestilence Aura]. Everyone's dodge rate and accuracy stats dropped, and the boost to my stats only rose even further.

I shot to my feet and lunged at Yeras. The hammer arbiter stepped in my way, but I was ready for him, launching an [Assault] on him. His shield came up to defend against my attack, but my daggers' reach extended beyond the several inches of magical steel his shield was made of. The attack went through the shield and pierced his forearm.

I slid around him and pulled two more vials free, lobbing them at his side and back. The shield shifted again and encased his back, defending against one vial, but the other exploded against the hammer arbiter's hip, eating through the armor and into his leg. I followed up with a [Blade Storm], hitting both him, Yeras, and the soldiers behind with a storm of mana cuts.

My offensive debuff, [Apex Predator], finally bypassed their defenses, and lowered everyone's stats by 15% in a 50-foot radius, adding more debuff stacks and allowing my [Stolen Power] passive to increase my stats even further. I was much stronger now than I'd ever been as I was drawing on hundreds of extra stat points. It was almost intoxicating.

The animus surged forward then as one, throwing themselves at me. I was quickly overwhelmed and no matter how weak their attacks were, I couldn't go on using strong attack skills as all the mana in my body would be used up and I'd be left defenseless. It was time to retreat after all.

I faded back out and toward the bridge, checking on how Merek was doing. Balog was pushing him back with a slightly longer reach and an overall better weapon, but they were definitely close to one another in level and skill.

"Merek! Pull back!"

He didn't reply and just used his skill to provoke an aggressive stampede from the animus that were already flooding over us and hurried into the river. I did the same from the other side, forgetting about the previous idea. Unfortunately, things weren't going to work out that way, but we could still—

"No! Do not follow them!" Balog roared. "Pull the animus and beles back. That bridge is trapped! I can see it!"

Okay, that wasn't something I'd expected. Not at all.

"Red! Pull back to the other side of the bridge and wait there! Merek, hold on."

I faded toward him and grabbed the man. He was barely staying afloat in his much heavier armor. A sudden barrage of tiny bolt-like needles flew toward us. Merek brought his shield up, but it was much harder to do while swimming, and several grazed his hand and my cheek.

```
You have resisted a debuff.
You have resisted a debuff.
```

"Merek! Debuffs?"

He shook his head, grinning.

"I resisted two it says."

I looked over at the shore and found Vestila, the only female arbiter, standing there and pointing two small crossbows at us. She pressed two levers, and more needles flew our way. This time I helped Merek put up his shield and they all deflected harmlessly. I turned toward the other shore and faded us across, narrowly escaping a possible clusterfuck.

CHAPTER 32 – BITCHSLAPPER

Red landed on my shoulders, digging his fucking talons into my meat. He was extremely heavy and just as deadly as Benny had told us. Those two things were usually a good thing, but not when you had a gryphon pretending to be a parrot and trying to perch on your shoulders.

"Hey, Red, you're a bit too heavy for me, big guy. Maybe you could use Grommasch to perch on. Or Benny."

The big red War Beast let out a deafening screech and flapped his wings two times, then got off my shoulders and landed next to me. His head was at the same height as mine, which made him a big, bad boy.

"You'll need to let the girls ride you later, Red. I think they'd be pretty excited. And I'll feed you some super rare things so you can become an even bigger, redder, bad boy."

I ignored the enemy on the other side of the shore, who just stood there motionless. Even the four arbiters were just staring as if waiting for us to make the first move.

"Red, you pretty little angry bird," I whispered, patting his head. "Why don't we get you to level 60 as soon as possible, huh? I'd like to see what you will turn into."

The gryphon squawked and rubbed his head against me affectionately, but then pulled away and stared at me questioningly.

"Hey! Are you trying to steal my son away?" Benny asked over our direct chat.

"Red is not your son, fool. And I'm not—well, I am. I just tried bribing him. Guess it failed."

"Well, yeah! He's in my stable of War Beasts, but look, if you promise me...okay, whatever, Red. You little traitor," he muttered and I could feel him sigh from wherever he was. *"He just said that he wants to be your mount. He liked how you patted him and the smell of death around you. It's beyond me what he sees in you over me, but whatever, bro. I'll take one for the team."*

"And I'll make it up to you, or something. By the way, when do you plan to get your ass here?" I asked, rubbing Red's cheek, and then looked back over to the arbiters. "And you, my little angry bird, why don't we get some more upgraders into you? Or do you want to kill some more of those bastards and get to level 45 that way?"

Red screeched and flapped his wings, taking to the air. Vestila used that moment and released two barrages of glowing needles, but Merek, sensing the attack coming, intercepted them with his shield.

"Go! We'll keep them distracted, my pretty little bird!"

I faded toward the center of the bridge, choosing a spot where to land safely as if to show them that it wasn't trapped after all. Putting one foot in front of the other, I steadily made my way across in a straight line as if to accentuate the matter.

"Come! Let this bridge be our last stand!" I yelled, staring straight at Balog. He didn't seem bothered by my provocation nor by the torrent of flames my gryphon Red was scorching the back lines of animus with.

Even when I reached the end of the bridge, none of them moved aside from Vestila, who released another two barrages of needles my way. I faded out again, appearing a single step away from the halberd-wielder, and opened up with a [Plague Storm]. A mass of plague daggers formed around me like a swarm of oversized, glowing locusts, and shot toward the arbiters and the animus standing at attention behind them. Dozens of the daggers struck the four, none dealing great damage, but the list of debuffs washing over them was long.

My own buffs and debuffs procced as well then, and the familiar rush of power flooding my body was almost ecstatic.

I stabbed out with both daggers, not even using any follow-up skills, and one passed by Balog's defenses, cutting across his chest. He snapped his halberd around, hitting me in the side with the shaft. If I was any weaker, I was sure he'd break a rib or two.

I felt a massive but familiar mana signature close in fast. A bloodcurdling howl cut the air and Benny came crashing down, stomping Vestila flat and killing her outright. He was on top of Yeras in a heartbeat, ripping into the arbiter with his claws. It only took him two hits to get the better of the dual sword wielder, but I stopped him.

"No, not yet! Benny! The reason why I haven't tried harder is so Red can kill the animus and feed on their experience!"

"Oh! Okay, bro! Can my three little killers join in?"

"Have at them!"

Out of nowhere, three high-pressure water jets cut into the enemies closest to the lake. None of the soldiers died right away but after the jets came together, they cut through animus within a single heartbeat.

The arbiters seemed to be so taken aback by Benny's appearance and sheer power that they froze in place. It was the same way I'd felt when Zekan caught us by surprise, and here I was in the same situation. The dark mage had used us as a farm, livestock to increase in power and we were doing the same to this army. It felt wrong. Not because I cared for the well-being of the animus, those soulless creatures were less than cattle, but because I didn't want to turn into something I not only despised, but also ...And it was hard to admit, something I feared.

It felt wrong...even more so that the moment we'd retreated to the other riverbank, all fighting had ceased. He was afraid to move across the bridge and...no, maybe there was more to it. The arbiters had thousands of soldiers to spare, yet they didn't move across the water...or the bridge.

"Benny! I need the remaining three arbiters alive so don't

you dare kill them! Not yet!"

"Alright, bro! I want to fight this big guy! He looks strong!"

"He's different, so don't let your guard down, just in case!" I yelled to be heard over the magical mayhem Red and the other three newly hatched War Beasts were causing. It was almost as if they were competing against one another to see who could kill more of the animus.

I lunged through the throng of dark spawns and past Balog, grabbed Yeras, and faded out as far as I could just as Benny lunged past me and slammed into the hammer-wielding arbiter. He hadn't spoken so far, but that didn't mean he was mute, maybe he was also under someone's influence, someone like Balog. That also begged further study.

"Merek! Grab him!" I yelled as I appeared as far overhead as I could and threw Yeras across the river. There was no way I could throw him as far, but Merek was on it, tagging him with the provoking skill. The arbiter fell into the water...and disappeared below the surface.

Red grabbed me before I could fall into the water too, his talons digging into my shoulder pads and my skin. It hurt, but I didn't mind. I felt a surge of pleasure as the wind buffeted my face and we streaked up into the air, then glided over the enemy army, that was something indescribable.

"You can let go," I said, tapping his talon as we passed over what I thought was a small group of beles and cardes. They all belonged to the group wearing yellow overcoats. I dashed in between them, opting not to use any skills. I needed to know how powerful they were, but only found myself disappointed when they all died just as easily. One of the cardes used some kind of attack skill on me in tandem with one of the beles, but the attacks were so weak I parried them with my daggers.

My sense of danger screamed at me and I threw myself to the side and the ground. Balog's halberd passed right overhead, glowing a bright red. It missed me by several inches. If the attack had hit me, I knew it wouldn't have ended well, despite me holding back and just testing them. Just because I had hundreds of stat points, it didn't mean that I was invulnerable.

I caught myself and pushed off with both feet, jumping right at the one remaining arbiter. Not wanting to kill him, I activated [Quick Attack] and aimed at his legs. The daggers missed him by a literal pace as he sidestepped using a skill, blurring out of the way and bringing his halberd down in a counterattack. It struck my back but was absorbed by the armor and me twisting out of the way. Where a deep gash could have been there was now only a thin cut. It pissed me off, but I kept my cool and followed up with [Assault] to lower his speed. The attack connected and ripped into his belly.

Balog cried out and jumped back into the mass of animus. Dozens surged forward, attacking me with ordinary physical attacks. Even if it was the head arbiter's army, they were unable to do anything to me. Just what had happened for the soldiers of Tan'Malas to devolve so much? And as soon as the thought sprung to mind, I had the answer. The dark one used to reanimate the believers of Tan'Ruad, Tan'Drak, and Tan'Aria, as well as monsters that used to be part of the Godveil, but what happens when there's no more Godveil? What happens when all you can reanimate is an ordinary man? Sure, he becomes more powerful than the ordinary soldier and the perfect mind-linked slave, but his abilities are basic.

I let out a deep sigh of relief as that was the moment I realized something very important. The only real dangers I had to worry about were the pillars, the original sinners who had committed unspeakable atrocities on their own people to gain immortality through Tan'Malas. Everything else was just...crap.

A massive explosion shook the ground then, sending animus flying in all directions. Pieces of armor and weapons peppered the other soldiers around them as more explosions struck the army formation. Now, the problem for the arbiters was that they had nowhere to go, no one to summon them out, and no way to fight us despite the numbers. And now with the arrival of our battleship, all I had to do was sit and watch as my girls and the War Beasts grew in level.

"Benny! Rip his arms and legs off or immobilize him! I don't want the hammer guy to be able to hurt anyone when we interrogate him! I'm going after Balog!"

I faded after him into the midst of the animus that had formed up to protect his retreat and activated a [Pestilent Wave]. It had become my favorite as it had a really large area of effect, and it knocked anything it hit down, both giving me a better view and allowing me to see ahead.

The wave ripped through the reanimated soldiers and disintegrated them upon contact, only their armor remaining behind. Balog defended himself using the halberd and some kind of skill, but his left arm was rotting away as he stood there on shaky legs.

"Give up and I'll grant you an easy death, Balog! Or I might even adopt you!"

"Never! I would rather kill myself before—"

I lunged after him again, slashing away both his arms. They fell next to him on the ground, blood spurting from the stumps. I grabbed him and faded out toward the shore.

"*Bring the ship in closer,*" I said over the guild chat. "*I need you to heal this arbiter. I don't know if the animus will die too if he's gone. Can't have that before you kill them all.*"

"*Seems you had it all under control, boss man,*" Nalgid said.

I could see him on the prow of the ship with a shield in hand. Ferid and Grom stood around him, all wearing shields of their own. They must have figured that the three of them made a fine wall if any kind of long-range attacks came their way. Good thinking.

"*We had. I just didn't want to risk it and, you know, give the kids some free experience. Are the soldiers with you?*"

"*We are, Master Cade,*" Samel replied over the chat. "*And we want in on the experience. Do you think you could provide us some help just until we establish a foothold?"*

I grinned, proud of his proposal.

"That's the spirit, Samel. Sure thing, I—no, we'll do something even better. These animus are really weak. I've picked out most of the beles, cardes, and deces, so all they have going for them are numbers. I want everyone out, all the dwarves, elgar, goblins, soldiers...everyone who wants some free leveling experience, to come out and get your hands dirty. Emma and Najla will provide healing support, while Jeanette, Sonya, Selene, Elvina, and I will try and keep everyone safe. Deal?"

A loud cheer rang out from the ship and two more bombs landed nearby, rocking the ground. Balog was speechless and just frantically looking around as if we had lost our minds. I would probably feel the same way if it had been the other way around, so I couldn't blame him. What I did blame him for was all the crap that he's probably done to the civilians of the dukedom. Not that the Duke is any better...

"You are so fucked, Balog. Maybe you think you have an idea, but you truly don't," I said with a grin. "Both you and that hammer guy."

Balog grinned back through a bloody smile.

"It is you who is fucked," he said stone-cold as if he didn't feel the pain of two lost limbs. "The moment Lomar is dead, his brother will feel it. And do you have any idea who that is?"

I shook my head, but I already had a suspicion. The funny thing was that Balog just revealed a very important piece of information, all willingly, without even realizing that he'd done so.

"The pillar?"

"Yes! The pillar! We're like squabbling children before him! He's one of the ancient ones from before our time, stranger. He was there when Tan'Malas reawakened and—"

"So was I," I said coldly. "I was there too, Balog. I was there when the three Old Ones beat him like a little bitch. The only reason why he won is the darkness reanimation ability he has. It is a very unfortunate thing for us people that we used to be great warmongers and hunters. He used that against us, swarming the cities with vast armies that dwarfed our own. But now? Yeah, there's a new big bad guy in town, and that's me. And do you know why?"

"Because you think you're strong?" he snorted and spat at me, but missed. I slapped him like a little bitch but kept him from falling over onto the ground.

"No, it's not that, though I did enjoy bitchslapping you," I chuckled and slapped him again for good measure. He grunted and glared at me but I ignored it. "I might even call myself the bitchslapper. Yes, I like that, but now I'm getting carried away. See, I didn't even try that hard. All you had going for yourself were the animus? You? Weak. Hammer-guy? Lomar was it? Yeah, weak. See, the one thing you guys had going for yourself was that I didn't know just how weak and pathetic of a lot you were. Now that you decided to heed my invitation and showed just how shitty of an army you have, I am pretty sure I can take your pillar in two minutes at most."

"Two minutes at—you! You are a blasphemer! You are a rodent, a roach! He will step down on you with divine anger and crush your bones to—"

I slapped him again, this time knocking loose a tooth.

"Shut up. I want you to tell me a few things, and if you're honest, I will grant you an easy death."

Balog glared at me as if I was the vilest creature in the world.

"What?"

"Why did you go south when the animus can't pass over water?"

He literally froze and didn't move, breathe, or speak for a long moment as animus died all around us. His mouth finally moved after I counted to 27 seconds.

"Because I knew you would want to protect your village. I feigned a slow march north around the lake, knowing you would spot Lomar and with some luck kill him. That would awaken the pillar and bring down his wrath on you if we failed."

"Instead, he teleported you and your army in. Neat. How does it work? How far can you teleport? How many at once?"

Balog frowned as if offended by my flurry of questions.

"How many questions?"

"A few more."

"And the healing part?"

I shrugged.

"You screwed yourself when you said that Lomar needs to stay alive. He's now worth more to me than you are."

Once I stopped speaking, I realized I'd made the same mistake he just had.

"I see. Then have him tell you everything. Oh, right, he can't. The pillar ripped his tongue out."

To me, it seemed as if Balog wasn't willing to bite the dust just yet. Alright, I had different ways to make them talk. If threats didn't work, I could always try bribes and maybe even heal and restore his arms.

No, there was an even better way.

"Emma?" I shot over my shoulder. "Can you reach him from the ship?"

"Let me try!" she yelled back and a moment later, a golden healing wave fell over him. His arms didn't regrow, of course, but the stumps closed and he let out a gasp of relief.

I grinned and shot the arbiter a wink.

"See, I think we're about to become great friends, Balog. Great indeed."

EPILOGUE

It took us several hours until all the animus were taken care of. A vast scorched field littered with broken weapons and incinerated pieces of armor and equipment slowly steamed away in the wake of battle.

The loot was incredible, though a large number of armor and weapons had been damaged beyond repair by lobbing bombs and Red's flaming attacks. The fire just melted everything together.

No one got hurt, aside from the two arbiters. A few of our soldiers had lost their lives when they dropped their guards. Not everyone was able to handle the power the Godveil gave them. They grew arrogant and suffered for it. Wars bring death to all, no matter how much one side dominated the other.

Red had evolved again at level 45, which was unexpected. He still remained a gryphon, but where the soft feathers used to cover his chest and belly, now sat red dragon-like scales. Bony growths intermixed with more scales now covered his entire neck and head, providing even more armor. He'd grown roughly double the size and was now truly a sight to behold, especially with the two new extra wings that he'd sprouted from his back. They were red with dark and white wingtips.

Benny's three little killers had undergone their second evolution at level 25 and were now large enough that they could envelop the entire ship with their bodies and tentacles. My Blood Beast little brother was two levels short of 60, while Legs had arrived pretty late and had now fallen behind. Everyone else from Danara to the soldiers that opted for our new religion, had grown as well and most reached their first evolutions, with some even getting close to their second.

The dwarves, goblins, and elgar proved to be very capable as well, killing hundreds of animus by themselves and not getting into trouble a single time. Merek was disappointed for having to watch over Balog and Lomar. The latter had his limbs broken, but not cut off as we didn't want to risk his brother waking up even from minor damage.

Several days passed and everything returned to normal. Mortimer was busy identifying gear, and strangely, both of Yeras' long blades turned out very interesting and were perfect for what I'd become. They were identical aside from color and some of the effects as they were randomly assigned by the Godveil as Mortimer identified them.

Several other pieces of armor and accessories were also more suitable than what I already had, so it was with great joy that I accepted them all.

NAME: Obsidian Reaper Blade

DESCRIPTION: The Obsidian Reaper Blade is a short sword made by sacrificing the souls of 1,000 animus, which is also where the name comes from. There is no other known process of creating this kind of Reaper type weapon.

EFFECT 1: Adds 16 Dexterity, and 16 Agility

EFFECT 2: Increase Defense Penetration by 21

EFFECT 3: Increase Attack Reach by 31

EFFECT 4: Increase All Debuff related stats by 15

NAME: Scarlet Reaper Blade

DESCRIPTION: The Scarlet Reaper Blade is a short sword made by sacrificing the bodies of 1,000 animus, which is also where the name comes from. There is no other known process of creating this kind of Reaper type weapon.

EFFECT 1: Adds 16 Dexterity, and 16 Agility

EFFECT 2: Increase Critical Hit Chance by 32

EFFECT 3: Increase Critical Damage by 56

EFFECT 4: Increase All Debuff related stats by 15

SPECIAL EFFECT: Increase all Skill,
Spell, and Ability levels by 2 when
both Reaper Blades are equipped.

The two blades were incredibly powerful and with both blades adding all debuff related stats, they brought me back pretty close to what the two daggers provided. Both blades were longer than the daggers, so I'd have to practice a bit, but the raw power they provided against a single target was much greater. I wondered what they'd look like when Grom upgraded them to +9 or whatever he could manage. It made me almost drool...

NAME: Plaguebearer Orichal Pants

DESCRIPTION: The Plaguebearer Orichal Pants are made by mixing dark Orichal skin with ground Purple Locust essence. The pants are very durable and the perfect choice for plague based classes.

EFFECT 1: Adds 13 Stamina, and 11 Strength

EFFECT 2: Increase Physical and
Magical Resistance by 32

EFFECT 3: Increase Debuff Resistance
and Effectiveness by 46

Considering my previous armored pants were very basic, getting this kind of gear was like winning in the arena. Getting great physical and magical resistances along with debuff stats was just perfect.

The last item I got was another ring, and since I had two hands, I could use two rings. It was nothing special compared to the Ring of Life, but I was more than happy with it.

NAME: Ring of the Stalker

DESCRIPTION: The Ring of the Stalker is a rare type of jewelry that is made using the paril bone protecting the Aznakuda's heart. It bestows great stats upon the wearer.

EFFECT 1: Increase All Speed by 10

EFFECT 2: Increase Accuracy and Attack Reach by 14

EFFECT 3: Mark a target and gain the ability to track them for 24 hours.

The piece of jewelry was interesting and also tailored toward my original class, though I didn't really have much use of things like marking a target. If I'd had it back in Greystone, oh boy, that would have been a different story, but now? The attack reach and the increased speed helped a lot, though. Speed was a universal stat that everyone benefited of.

One thing that worried me was that my experience level was still stuck at level 60 and we hadn't found a way to get past that bottleneck. Maybe if I killed the pillar I'd get lucky, but that wouldn't solve our problem. I needed that information so everyone could get past level 60, not just me.

The dwarves and elgar had built a smaller temple just outside Garm Village with a separate building adjacent to it where we had the basic patron statues placed on pedestals so people could get more intimate within their classes. A steady influx of people from the surrounding villages saw the number of converted rise, but it was far from enough to get to the next level.

Quest: Spreading The Faith V

Description: Continue to help spread
faith in the Gods of Old.

Status: 1,493/2,500 Converted Believers

Reward: Establishment of a Divine Military Cadre

Nothing had changed when it came to the quest description or reward, but then again, we hadn't sacrificed any more of the arbiters. Vestila and Yeras had died in freak accidents, if you could call Benny's rampage that, and Danara was now a part of us.

We were sitting on the balcony of Brahma's Rest where the girls were doing each other's hair, or rather Selene, Sonya, Emma, and Elvina were, while Jeanette was busy trying to reach level 60. She was so close and didn't want to give up. They all were, but since she was a front-line fighter, I promised her that she could go next.

I looked out onto the lake where Red was circling overhead and dodging attacks of the three little killers. Well, they weren't as little anymore. Each was as large as the ship, and I figured the lake was going to become too small for them once they all hit level 60. That was still a ways off, but it was a matter we would have to consider down the line. For now, though, I had the perfect use for them: digging a new river that would surround the entirety of Volarna City.

Everyone had settled back into a daily routine aside from Banxi, who was so overwhelmed that he had no idea what he wanted to work on and just moped around in his workshop. I'd have an interesting task for him soon enough, but first, we needed to take care of a little problem.

"I think it's time," I said and all four of my beautiful wives turned to look at me.

"What is?" Sonya asked before the others could.

"That we got rid of the duke. My ass hurts from sitting around, and things aren't going to solve themselves. Balog and Lomar are both powerless, but the fool could somehow kill himself and awaken his brother. I want to be ready."

"Are you going alone?"

I shook my head slowly.

"No, the six of us are. Jeanette just finished I think," I said, feeling a small surge of power coming from the south of New Greystone. "Get ready. Red can carry us all."

As if reading my mind, the armored gryphon let out a loud squawk and spewed flames into the air as if he were a dragon and not a, well, I had no idea what he was. He obeyed me and we worked well together, but I couldn't access any of his stats, only Benny could, but the pangolin told me that he'd released the gryphon from his menagerie. It was just another one of those things on a long list of to-do's.

Lost in thought and stuck making plans for what to do with Volarna once I'd liberated its people from the Duke, the flight over to the castle passed quickly. The girls were busy chatting and pointing at the two villages we hadn't yet the pleasure of visiting, Znica to the northwest, and Tazul to the northeast.

The former was built into the side of a cliff and looked as if its main purpose was to provide the castle with stone and ore. The village had a tall, sturdy wall and scores of guards placed on top. Tazul, on the other hand, was farmland as far as the eyes could see. People were working in the fields, harvesting what looked like wheat, mostly, but also fruits and vegetables. Numerous carts were being shipped north toward the castle and they were escorted by soldiers who hurried the civilians.

"What do you think?" I said, pointing down at the small caravan of carts. "Is he trying to turtle up?"

"Most likely, but I don't see what good it will do him," Sonya replied as she peeked over Red's wing.

"Whatever the thought, I don't think we should leave any Volarna alive today, even if they're children. His bloodline needs to go," Selene said coldly. "Unless we want possible trouble down the line."

Emma slapped the elf's shoulder and shot her a mock scowl.

"What are you on about? Kids? Selene!"

"Hey! Don't hit me! I'm just saying what needs to be done!"

I sighed, equally unimpressed by her proclamation. Maybe we'd be lucky and wouldn't have to kill that many people...

Red let out a deafening screech as we approached the city walls. They were decently tall and wide enough for several soldiers to rush past each other. Large, yellow-black banners hung off the walls with the Duke's sigil, a black tower in a circle of thorns at the center. Towers were spread about fifty yards apart and there were five of them, all crammed up in between the narrow pass. Beyond that was a sea of colorful roofs and large tents spread out in the city square. I figured that was the market. It wasn't nearly as large or spectacular as Greystone, but the city had its charm.

Two buildings stood out against the backdrop of the city. The first was the castle with tall walls of its own, towers, a gate, and even an inner bailey. It was nestled against a cliff in the western part of the city and the facilities inside the premises looked as if they could house a thousand people on their own. One of the buildings I recognized as a barracks, and I already had a plan for it. The others were probably for the staff and their families.

The second building I took notice of was just a keep sitting across the city near the eastern cliff. It had no wall and almost looked like a dilapidated prison.

Thousands of people were rushing about with purpose, and barely anyone gave me even a secondary glance. God Beasts were rare, but not so rare that people had never seen one. In fact, I noticed about ten or so spread throughout the city, walking among the people or in chains. That would make a nice project for Benny and his menagerie could grow exponentially if he wanted to adopt all of them.

Hundreds of soldiers were manning the castle's walls, but not a single one of them so much as shot an arrow or a bolt our way. They seemed hesitant to fight but didn't want to be perceived as weak either. Before anyone could get a stupid idea, I urged Red toward a massive balcony overlooking the city just below the inner keep's roof. It was tall enough to provide a view over the inner walls.

There were only two people seated there, eating and drinking merrily, while a small army of servants attended to their needs. They didn't notice us at first as no one had sounded an alarm, which was yet another strangeness, but I honestly figured they all just wanted to get rid of the Duke and weren't interfering. Once our shadow loomed over their table and the steady sound of flapping wings resounded above them, the Duke and his cousin, Ventilo, finally looked up.

I patted Red's neck and pointed down to the balcony. Even with the magnificent Gryphon's size, there was still enough room for two more of his kind along with the tables and sitting area. It was truly large.

"Fancy seeing you here, Duke," I said as Red finally stopped flapping his wings and jumped off his back. I helped the girls down and we made our way over to the table where they were seated. Both he and Ventilo were silent, their eyes darting from the gryphon to me and then the girls.

"Screw this! I've had enough of your shit, cousin!" Ventilo cried and shot to his feet. He backed his chair up and tried to run around the table but somehow managed to stumble over one of the chairs surrounding the table, slipped, hit the balcony railing, and fell over the side.

"Ohh, that's going to hurt," Jeanette winced.

"You think?" Sonya snorted as the former peacock's cry was cut short and followed by the audible thud of his body hitting the courtyard below.

Screams rang out from people who'd been going about their business when Ventilo's body splattered against the stone floor of the courtyard below. We all stared at each other in shock as the realization passed of what just happened.

"That guy has the worst of luck," Selene mumbled. "I wouldn't want to be in his shoes."

"Or the Duke's," Emma sighed. "Everyone, who is the head maid or the head servant around here?"

A woman in her early forties raised her hand, then lowered it hurriedly and sobbed.

"I—I am the—"

"Hush. Come here," Emma said, offering the woman her hand. "No one's going to do anything to you, that's a promise. Also, the Duke is already dead, but he just doesn't know yet."

"W—what are—I—"

The Duke finally seemed to process what was going on and started sputtering nonsense, then grabbed for what little hair there was on his scalp and screamed.

"Hold on now, Duke, my good man. You can't go crazy just yet," I said, grabbing his collar and slapping him across the face. I stopped then and thought for a moment. It was immensely satisfying to slap people around like I'd done with Balog as well. Maybe I'd have to make a habit of it. It seemed to have a great effect on people.

"Y—you! Listen, khm...I know you defeated Balog's army, I was...Uhm...I was awaiting your visit. See I think we can come to an agreement that can benefit the both of us. Volarna is a big, rich city, I can raise the taxes, cut you in on—"

I slapped him again, this time bruising his cheek and drawing blood.

"Calm down, you fool. I'm keeping Lomar and Balog alive in my dungeon."

His expression soured even further and he turned his nose up to me.

"Screw you, mongrel! You smell of peasants and dung! Go ahead, take it! Take it all! They will avenge me! I have always been a loyal—"

I smacked him again, and this time he fell on his back, screaming bloody murder and calling for help. I sighed and turned toward the head servant.

"Is there anyone that could take his place in leading this land? Someone who will be good to the people?"

The woman nodded furiously, opening her mouth to speak but the Duke shot to his feet with a speed I hadn't expected. Still, all it took for me was just a single movement of the hand and he was down again, spitting two of his teeth out.

"You, stay," I said, berating the duke as I waggled my finger. "You, lady, take me to them."

"No, don't you dare! He's a traitor, I tell you! Do not take them to—"

"Red, eat him."

The gryphon didn't even bother waiting for a second command. He snapped his giant beak at the Duke and bit him in half, gulped him down, and then ate the rest. More of the servants screamed and two even fainted, but not the head servant.

Several minutes later, we stood in front of a cell of the castle dungeon. A man with a long white beard was chained to the wall with a single arm as the other was missing just below the elbow. He was filthy and had obviously seen better days.

"You have guests, my lord," the woman said with a curt bow. "This man has just...killed...your brother. I mean, his God Beast ate the—"

The bearded man chuckled and shook his head as if in disbelief. He took a seat on his bed and the chuckling quickly turned to laughter.

"So, my brother has finally gotten what he deserves. How poetic," the man said with a crooked smile. "After all this time...yes, now I can die in peace as well."

"Die? How come?" I asked, pulling the grates from their hinges. "There's so much to do."

"Do?" he asked, still laughing. "What is there to do? If you have a God Beast that can defeat all the soldiers, the Order, and my brother, then—wait. You're not here to conquer this land, are you?"

He sat upright, the smile disappearing from his face.

"No, I'm not. I'm here to do much more than that. Now how, about you and I have a chat, Canoras? See, this lady here told me that you genuinely love the people of this city."

The man called Canoras stood and straightened the dirty rags hanging off his malnourished body and bowed deep.

"That is why I'm here, good sir. Now, can we cut to the matter at hand? Why are you here?"

I grinned and shot the man a wink.

"Get him cleaned up, fed, healed, and then bring him to my new office. We have a lot to talk about, starting with how to defend ourselves from Luferson Castle. Then we can talk about the Old Gods. I'm pretty sure he's going to appreciate what I have to offer. Hell, maybe we can even help you regrow that arm."

THE END OF THE FIRST ARC

Made in the USA
Columbia, SC
03 January 2024

29804423R00204